Liz –

ARCHAIC DECEPTION

THE GUARDIAN OF EMBLEMS

May this fantastical adventure
ignite your imagination + sense
of exploration!

JOE DAYVIE

Printed in the United States of America

ISBN-13: 978-0-578-35298-5

A Mother's Love Never Dies

Thank you Mom for showing me unconditional love, patience and the strength to follow my creative passion. You may have passed too soon but your love will forever stay strong within.

This novel is dedicated to my husband, Anthony. His unwavering support and love allowed this story to blossom into what it became.

Deep within the dark, forested region of Tillerack, perched on a thick branch amidst the cool air, two friends hid behind large leaves as footsteps rapidly approached. Though they were both afraid, Smolar found his courage and took control of the situation. He knew his friend, Promit, was terrified and that they couldn't flee quick enough, so climbing up was their best option. They felt secure, due to the elevation and the privacy provided by the foliage, and sat silently as the footsteps slowed directly beneath them. The sound of crinkling detritus shook Promit to his core. The friends glanced at each other, wondering who the men below were. Peering through a slit in the foliage, they were able to vaguely see their pursuers.

"Where did they go!?" one man asked. He was tall, thin-framed, and wore dark clothing, his face forgettable and unrecognizable. A second man stepped into view. He was smaller, yet exuded a strong presence. His authority and confidence were palpable. He wore a thick coat, with a large fur hood over his head, hiding his face. He appeared to have a stick or club in his hand.

"They must be nearby. They couldn't have gotten too far," the shorter man said, his voice unusually deep. The men slowly walked the grounds, in search of Smolar and Promit.

Smolar looked at his friend and noticed the stone-cold fear in his eyes. He grabbed Promit's arm and gave a confident, consoling nod. As Smolar looked for an escape route, his friend grabbed his arm and pointed to the men below. Suddenly, the hooded man exposed his glistening, wavy snow-white hair. As he looked at his partner, the white-haired man grinned so wide it exacerbated the long, horizontal scar across his left cheek. He raised the object in his hand, closed his eyes, and murmured to himself. Instantly, a bright light shone as panels slowly began to open from the top, then down the sides. What initially appeared as a club revealed itself as an illuminated wand.

"The Novalis Rod," the slender man whispered in disbelief. "You had it this whole time?"

"Was just waiting for the right moment to use it." The white-haired man looked at the rod as he held it higher, his grin now a full smile of joy, confident he had found what they were seeking.

Smolar instinctively turned away, his eyes too sensitive to the light. Glancing at Promit, he was stunned to see him staring directly at the object. Smolar was about to pull Promit toward him when the unbelievable happened. His kind-hearted friend vanished. All he could see were small, blue granules in the silhouette of his body. Moments later, the remains followed the direction of the rod, as if being vacuumed. Their hiding spot had been revealed and Smolar knew he needed to escape.

"We got him," the shorter man hissed.

"Wow." His partner stared at the rod. "Should we head to—"

"Shh…" The white-haired man held his hand up and pointed above. His partner gazed up, unsure what he expected to see. The Novalis Rod highlighted the entire forest, which Smolar used as an opportunity to escape. Far behind him was an opening to a dark cave. He was unsure if it was the same way they had come, but knew it may be his best chance for survival. Smolar glanced at both assailants. Time stood still for a moment. The light from the rod dissipated and the three of them evaluated the situation in stark darkness.

"Come down willingly and we won't have to use—" The two men looked at one another, stunned, as the creature vanished before their eyes. Terrified of his next move, Smolar jumped down and raced for his life. "You little shit," the white-haired man grunted. "Let's move!"

As the pursuit began, Smolar realized the entrance to the cave was further than he'd anticipated. He appreciated his running start, because the two men were catching up. As he jumped over rocks and debris, Smolar heard a howling sound amplify until a small explosion on his right catapulted him against a tree. What was once a large boulder was now a dozen small rocks. Smolar had no idea what device had been used against his friend, but their current weapon was one of mass destruction. He staggered up and scrambled toward the cave entrance. Smolar's legs were on fire, ready to give out. He continued to push himself harder than ever, hoping there was still a chance for Promit's survival. As Smolar approached the entrance, he heard another howling sound and threw his body against the ground, diving into the abyss.

The two men halted at the entrance and looked down into the gaping hole.

"You going down there, Vanilor?" the slim man asked, exhaling heavily.

"Fuck no," he gasped for air. "We were asked for one, and we caught one."

"Right, so why bother with that one?"

"If we brought *him* back two, our reward would be greater," the white-haired man proclaimed, and the slim man rolled his eyes. "Besides, those creatures were presumed extinct ages ago. If we've seen two, then you can bet your ass there are thousands more."

Wielding the deactivated Novalis Rod, Vanilor sat against a rock and secured the weapon in a satchel across his chest. The slim man followed, resting a moment.

"I can't believe we really saw one," he admitted.

"No shit."

"They're smaller than I'd expected."

"The hell you mean by that, Morty?" Vanilor exclaimed, standing up to display his four-foot-eleven height.

"Oh calm down." Mortimer laughed. "Didn't mean shit by it."

"Your judgements will be the death of you."

Ignoring his partner's words, Mortimer glanced down the colorless void. "I wonder what's down there," he pondered.

"The fucker probably jumped to his death." Vanilor chuckled as Mortimer's mind began to wonder. Ignoring the thoughts, he knew the mission was completed and they needed to move.

"We should head back. It'll take a while to return home from here."

"Always the responsible one, Morty," Vanilor said with a chuckle.

In Sartica, a twenty-third birthday was commonly celebrated with food and alcohol, and for Jacob Emmerson it was no different. Though his eyes were shut, nursing a hangover, he tried his best to fall back asleep. Regardless of his position in bed, it was a losing battle. Eventually, he succumbed to defeat and cracked open his eyes, welcoming the warm sun that shined through the window.

"I still have some time before the heat arrives," Jacob told himself. As he sat up in bed, the headache traveled down from the top of his head. He glanced at his nightstand and recognized two of the four pain pills from the night before. Jacob carefully pooled some water inside his mouth, dropped the pills in and swallowed. *Twenty-three years old and I still make a swimming pool in my mouth for pills – thanks Mom.* Being a morning person, Jacob forced himself up with a hesitant grunt.

As he headed toward the bathroom, he observed personal belongings on a bookshelf. A few books written a hundred years ago, an unlit candle, birthday cards from loved ones, a stone carving of their regional symbol, and a fifteen-year-old cracked mug with a faded picture of Jacob smiling with his mother. The books had never been read, even though he'd owned them for years. The candle was given to him by his mother and once belonged to his great grandmother. He cherished the mug most for sentiment; however, it currently held writing utensils.

The stone carving, gifted by his parents, represented Sartica, but it was also a historical reminder of what had happened during the War of Kings. Having reigned supreme over the others, the Divinity King defended his territory and its civilians, most notably against a vicious King Klai and the ravenous quorian race. Surviving their deceitful attack, the Divinity King and his mercenaries were the reason Sartica and the other regions existed. Jacob had the history engrained in his upbringing as his parents often thanked Divinity in their daily lives. Numerous Sartician symbols were located throughout their home, in honor of their sacred King.

Without warning, Jacob shuddered and closed his eyes as a strange vision appeared in his head. A memory – a *dream*. It was a man, brown hair, prominent chin. He couldn't recall anything outside of his face, which alone was already quite vague. Opening his eyes, gazing back toward his bookshelf, he lost concentration, knowing he wouldn't recall anything more. Jacob wished he could've remembered the context of the dream, but he knew the harder he tried to, the less successful he'd be. He pushed it aside, hoping more would reveal itself in time, and went downstairs for coffee and a morning hello.

"Jacob, my son. How're you feeling? Have fun last night?" his mother, Anna Emmerson, asked him. Her brown eyes were filled with judgement, concerned whenever her children indulged in alcohol.

"Not too bad. Could use some more sleep, but otherwise okay. You?"

"You came home late last night," she slyly accused, disregarding Jacob's response. Anna was unable to sleep until she knew her son was home safe. She did the same when her daughter, Catherine, had lived at home.

"Yes, but still earlier than I expected," Jacob responded in an energetic tone. "It really was a wonderful evening. Even Catherine stopped by."

"That's great! Then I imagine you're going into work today?"

"Hell no," Jacob replied. "I already took the day off, so I plan to enjoy it."

He didn't have the courage to tell his family he was unemployed. The veterinary office he worked for was in financial ruin for too long and shut their doors a couple days ago. Jacob knew word would soon spread and needed to come clean before they were informed elsewhere.

"Just don't ruin anything with your job, son. They've been very good to you."

Jacob nodded and poured himself a cup of coffee. It was a habit he wanted to quit, but not during a hangover. Caffeine was something to avoid when suffering from constant anxiety. He had indulged in coffee for years, resulting in sweats, jitters and a couple panic attacks. Fortunately, he switched to decaf a few years ago, allowing him to still enjoy the warm taste in the morning without any harsh side effects. His family was aware of his anxiety, inherited from his father, Ben.

Sitting on the counter were two coffee pots: decaf and regular. Jacob appreciated the gesture, being the only decaf drinker.

"What're your plans today, Mom?" Jacob asked, stirring creamer into his coffee.

"Straighten up around here, then help your father with a couple things. You're more than welcome to join us if you'd like."

"Not today, thanks."

She looked disappointed. Ben and Anna Emmerson always dreamt their children would show interest in their business. Emmerson's Minerals was created thirty years ago, early in their marriage. The desert heat of Sartica created the perfect foundation for mineral formation and concentration. Copper, iron and silver were some of what the region offered. Jacob and Catherine spent their childhood going on excursions with their parents for the business. It was entertaining as children, but as they matured, the trips became less appealing. The family only traveled the inner perimeter of Sartica, but it was enough to startle Jacob. He showed clear signs of anxiety and discomfort. Anna quickly noticed and his parents agreed to shift his efforts elsewhere within the business. Ever since those early times of exploration, Jacob grew a sense of comfort and serenity for his homeland. His sister had a polar opposite experience. While her interest in the business dwindled, her curiosity for the world of Diveria grew.

When she was seventeen, Catherine traveled to Tillerack and remained there for five years to study ecology. The region was covered with forests, containing obscure species of plants and animals. She was given the opportunity to study under biologists, scientists and engineers to further broaden her education. It was a long distance from Sartica, but it allowed her to pursue her strong passion for the environment. It was not a decision Anna and Ben initially accepted, but they ultimately gave their blessing. The experience was life-changing, something Anna Emmerson deeply understood since she was born and raised outside of Sartica. Catherine returned home a different person, adjusting her lifestyle to improve her footprint in Sartica, and ultimately Diveria.

"Morning, Jacob." Ben startled him from behind.

"Hey, Dad. What's up?"

"Alright. Didn't sleep great, but that's nothing new. Went for my walk this morning before it got too hot. Having cereal now, jump in the pool, then shower. It's going to be a beautiful day, around a-hundred-and-five Fahrenheit, so it would…"

Jacob's mind began to wander. Though he loved his father, Ben had a habit of rambling so much it tested Jacob's patience. Sometimes Ben's face would turn red if he forgot to breathe.

"…so if there was anything you need, let me know before I go," Ben kindly informed his son.

"Will do, Dad." Jacob zoned out, clueless of the conversation. Ben slurped the last of his cereal, tossed the bowl into the sink and waved goodbye to go swimming.

"I'm surprised the bowls never break," Jacob hissed. He never understood why his father consistently made a loud mess. He didn't understand much of his father's actions.

8

"Not yet." Anna was clearly irritated too, but was accustomed to it. "What are your plans today?"

"Not sure. Possibly meet Catherine for a bite to eat, take a small drive around the city. It's a beautiful morning."

"Sounds nice. Just remember, we have dinner tonight with her and Andrew at five o'clock."

"That's right. I'll make sure to be home early and help out." He stood for a moment, contemplating what he could recall from his dream. Not only were mother and son close to one another, they shared a unique relationship with dreams.

Ever since she was a child, Anna had vivid experiences while asleep. At first, she never thought much of them, but she eventually learned her dreams typically had hidden meanings. There was usually something to learn or interpret – whether it was being shown an event that hadn't happened yet or interacting with someone who had already passed. Anna's experiences continued well into her adulthood. Much to her surprise, as Jacob grew up, he too had begun to experience vivid dreams. This allowed mother and son to form an even deeper bond, sharing their strong interest and belief in their visions. Jacob often informed his mother of his dreams, curious to know what deeper meaning they may have.

Standing quietly beside her, Jacob decided to hold off revealing his latest dream. He hadn't remembered much, so he found discussing it pointless.

"Everything okay, son?" she asked as he placed his empty coffee mug in the sink.

"Of course." Jacob smiled. "I'm going to head out. I'll see you in a bit, Mom."

"Be safe," she said sternly. Anna shook her head and chuckled to herself. As she looked down at the freshly empty mug, she whispered, "Like father, like son."

Sartica was broken into four territories in the north, south, east and west. The Emmersons lived in West Sartica, while Catherine and her husband lived in the south. West Sartica was affluent, with large homes and a particular, comfortable lifestyle. Jacob knew he'd have to relocate to the north or south if he lived alone. East Sartica was mostly for industrial and commercial space. It housed a majority of warehouses, storage units and business-related properties. Technically, a fifth territory existed in the center of town, but it was reserved for the leader of Sartica.

The Ersatzian Field was a large, triangular, fenced-in garden, with every plant, tree and flower known to exist within Sartica. Located directly in the center of the region, its vibrant colors and fragrant smells were admired by all. It was a botanist's dream. Though beautiful, the Ersatzian Field served a secondary purpose. It provided the external decor for the monstrosity that existed below – the Subterranean Domain.

It was the home for Sir Kalvin Troveria, the leader of Sartica, and his entire royal family. Little was known of the internal design since a formal invitation was required for access. Even though their residence seemed daunting, the royal family had a lovely demeanor and good reputation within the region. Sir Kalvin was often seen walking the streets of Sartica. It was generally accepted that he loved the warm weather and occasionally escaped the confines of his domain.

Due to their extreme heat and little rain, Sartica was often in an excessive drought. Throughout the entire region, there were only two bodies of water. The larger, more populated location was Larkspur Lake. The smaller, more intimate destination was Lotus Lake. They differed vastly in appearance. Larkspur Lake, in North Sartica, had glowing, golden sand on the shoreline that allowed for a stunning view, particularly during a sunset. Lotus Lake, in West Sartica, had pure white sand, a beautiful contrast against the water. As someone who avoided large crowds, Jacob frequented Lotus Lake for serenity and peace.

The landscape of Sartica was mostly flat with only a few tall structures. The entire region was open, surrounded by mountainous sand dunes, and a color palette of tan, brown and orange. Such colors limited the heat within all buildings. Some residents added color to their properties using artificial grass, colored sand or painting unique rocks found throughout the region.

Sarticians understood it wasn't safe to explore too far, especially due to the extreme, unbearable conditions. For the seldom few with a curious mind, there were unspoken whispers and rumors that Sir Kalvin could facilitate transportation safely to and from another region, as in the case of Catherine Emmerson.

Whether aimlessly wandering or with a destination in mind, Jacob enjoyed driving around his hometown. It was a way for him to decompress and ease his anxiety. While his unemployment loomed over him, he was reminded how nice it felt to be free. He knew getting accustomed to such a lifestyle was dangerous, but he wanted to enjoy the remaining four weeks of his severance. Battling a hangover, he didn't commit himself to much. After running a few errands, Jacob was excited to meet his sister for lunch. Though the two were personally different, they were bonded together.

As Jacob stepped out of his car, he shuddered and shut his eyes as another vision came to mind – a grand hallway leading into eternal darkness. The only detail he remembered was the bright marble floor which flowed into the blackened pit. As someone who had a fear of the unknown, Jacob was left with an ominous feeling. Similar to before, he wasn't able to recall any other details. *A man's face and a darkened hallway,* Jacob thought to himself as he walked into the restaurant.

Meeting at Butte Bar, a local establishment in West Sartica, Catherine and Jacob hugged as she wished him a happy birthday once more. He ordered bubbling root, which consisted of sparkling wine and fruit juice, topped with a thickened cactus root to stir. She ordered ginger water to aid in her ailments from the night before.

The conversation flowed effortlessly, the two confiding in one another about most things – there were few secrets.

"Have you told Mom and Dad about work yet?"

"No. I know I need to but…"

"It's time. They'll eventually find out and—"

"I know, I know. You're right." Jacob sighed.

"You know how Mom gets." The two laughed, understanding their mother's disposition. "At least you could always work for them if—"

"I couldn't spend the rest of my life working for them."

"Even if it's just temporary. It's work…"

Jacob shrugged, unamused by her suggestion, regardless of how rational it sounded. "You know, I had a strange dream last night…" he said, hoping to shift topics.

"About what?" she asked, aware of his history.

"I don't exactly know, but it was strange." Jacob closed his eyes, trying to visualize more, but it was no use. "I don't remember much of it. Just the face of a man and a dark hallway." He paused, feeling unsettled. "It was creepy… I felt as though someone was lurking in the darkness…"

"Sounds more like a nightmare to me," Catherine remarked. "You tell Mom yet?"

"No, I don't remember much, so there's nothing to explain." He chuckled. "Memories from the dream keep popping into my head, so if I can recall more, then I'll mention it. It was just… eerie. It's bugging me."

"You'll remember it when you least expect it, and feel much better. I'm always aggravated when I can't remember something I should."

"You're probably right," he conceded.

The two continued to converse as time passed. They shared a few drinks, but Jacob made sure to not get intoxicated. He knew he had dinner with the family that evening and didn't want to appear sloppy. Eventually, they wrapped up and Catherine demanded to pay the bill due to Jacob's unemployment. They hugged, parting ways until they'd reconvene at their parents' house.

On his way home, Jacob thought about his unemployment discussion with his sister. He knew tonight would be a convenient time to tell everyone, so he didn't have to repeat himself, but he was concerned about telling his parents. Anna continuously reminded him how fortunate he was for his work. His father, Ben, excessively worried about his finances. He knew there were only days left before they found out elsewhere.

"Sooner the better…" Jacob whispered aloud, as he pulled into the driveway. He decided if the moment felt right and he could muster up the courage, he'd inform the family.

Pulling up to the house, he saw his mother and father in the backyard through the fence. He smiled. Since the property's perimeter was surrounded and secure, everything within the yard was open. Just through the gated entrance was a large, paved area for all their cars, which was where Jacob parked. There was a little yard on the left side of the driveway, in front of the house, comprised of colored sand and two large boulders from the open desert. Just right of the driveway was a larger space with a variety of desert plants. Anna's initial gardening concept was great, but it quickly became overcrowded. It took the talent of a landscaper to re-organize the layout. There was a white fence, three-feet tall, extending out from the front of the house, mostly to secure their dog, Chicken, in the backyard. The family found it dangerous for her to wander through some of the shrubs and cacti.

Following the pavers through the garden, Jacob passed the gate and entered the backyard. Anna was starting up the grill.

"Hello, son. Hope you had a great day," Anna said in a warm-hearted tone, always happy to see her son.

"Yeah, Mom, it was lovely. I thought it'd be hotter, but it's been nice." Jacob looked toward the table as Ben brought out some dinnerware. "Need some help?"

"Yes, please go help your father. He doesn't know what he's doing." Jacob wandered toward Ben to greet him and take over. His father returned inside to finish getting ready. While setting the table, Jacob observed the bushes in the distance. He heard rustling but couldn't see anything.

"Hey, Mom, you want a glass of wine?" he shouted across the yard.

"Jacob, stop shouting!" she instinctively shouted back. "Yes, please, that sounds wonderful." Jacob smiled and walked closer.

"Red or white?"

"You choose."

Jacob thought for a moment and remembered it was not as hot as he expected. "Red?"

"Add an ice cube for me."

"Of course." As he walked onto the back porch, Jacob heard the rustling again, but this time noticed a slight movement of leaves. "Chicken, are you in there?" He laughed to himself, opening the door to go inside.

Jacob and Anna enjoyed most wine; rarely did either one toss a glass. He knew what he enjoyed, and Anna wasn't picky. He pulled an unfamiliar bottle with a silver horse head on the label. The pour revealed its translucent red color, indicative of a lighter-flavored wine. Jacob took a small sip, gave a nod of approval and poured them both a glass, with an ice cube for his mother.

"Ah!" Jacob shouted, almost knocking over a glass. "Hey, baby girl, there you are." Chicken wanted love from Jacob. Although she admired Anna over anyone else in the house, her adoration for him was clear. He knelt to pet her. After a minute, Jacob grabbed the wine and returned to his mother, with Chicken trailing behind.

"Cheers!" Anna and Jacob said, clinking glasses.

"When do you expect Catherine and Andrew to arrive?"

"Around four-thirty... so another fifteen minutes? I should go inside and grab the meat. Time to get things going."

"Anything I can do to help?"

"I'm good." She smiled. "Thank you for the wine."

Jacob walked toward the unkempt fire-pit and sat down with his glass of red. He used the time to think about his parents, particularly Anna, and her desire to have him work for their company. He had no genuine interest working for

Emmerson's Minerals. However, he knew there would be perks working for his parents. Jacob was comfortable with the flow of his life. It was confined to West Sartica, near loved ones – it was his home. He had no curiosity or desire to leave, like Catherine. He didn't consider himself an explorer. Jacob wondered if his complacency aided in his inability to recall the location of his recent dream.

Suddenly, the front gate opened, disrupting Jacob's concentration.

"They're here!" he shouted loud enough for his parents to hear.

"Stop yelling!" Anna turned the corner with a plate of raw meat for the barbecue. Jacob waved towards his sister and brother-in-law as they entered the backyard. Anna greeted them both, Jacob following shortly after. Ben heard their arrival and came outside a few minutes later. Jacob offered to grab drinks – Andrew asked for a beer and Catherine a glass of water.

"Want ice?" he asked.

"… With a straw." The siblings chuckled. Jacob had received this special request from Catherine since he could walk.

The family conversed until dinner was ready. As they made their way to the table, Jacob noticed they were low on wine and grabbed a fresh bottle from inside.

"Never hurts to have extra," he justified.

"Wow, no hangover from last night, eh?" Andrew was impressed as Jacob placed the wine on the table.

"Actually, not too bad." He chuckled.

"Go easy on the wine, son," Anna suggested.

"Would *you* like some more?" Jacob asked, ignoring the snide remark from his mother.

"Yes, thank you," she replied. Though he always recognized the double standard his mother had with wine, it never bothered him.

When Anna cooked a meal, everyone knew there would be leftovers. In her home region of Prateria, Anna's family always opened their door to friends and family.

15

Her parents never knew who may surprise them for dinner, so they always made sure to cook extra – a tradition she continued.

Everyone filled their plates, moaning in anticipation for the delicious food. The aroma was a mixture of tender, grilled chicken with chili powder, half a dozen thin steaks with lightly crusted herbs, a vegetable medley, buttery long-grain rice, savory lizard tails, a lemon zest salad and hot baked rolls.

Looking around at one another, each of them wondered who would take the lead to speak before the meal. Such tradition wasn't maintained by everyone in Sartica. The Emmersons, particularly Anna and Ben, were devoted to honoring and thanking the one who sacrificed himself for the good of others.

"Ben, would you like to?" Anna suggested. Ben nodded, lowering his head; the rest of the family followed.

"We'd like to thank the Divinity King for all he's provided and done. We sit here this evening honoring him with this glorious food and each other. May his memory and light always live on, bringing happiness to us all." Ben raised his head with a smile.

"Thank you," Anna said. "Now please eat before it gets cold." She observed her family helping themselves to the meal she'd prepared – it brought her great pride. Once she knew everyone was content, Anna allowed herself to enjoy, too.

Silence fell upon the group as everyone focused on their overflowing plates. Fortunately, the table was in the shade and there was a light breeze. It made for the perfect environment to be eating such a hot meal.

After a few minutes, Catherine and Andrew glanced at one another. He took a sip from his beer and not a moment later, she grabbed the attention of everyone with two words.

"We're pregnant." Everyone at the table, including Andrew, was stunned by the words. Anna's silverware fell from her hands. "I'm sorry, I expected to say a few words before blurting that out." It was one of the few times Catherine felt nervous. Andrew held her hand.

"Congratulations!" Jacob said, as he held up his wine glass. "That's amazing! How'd you not say anything when we met earlier?"

"I wanted it to be a surprise for you all, together." She smiled.

"What!? I can't believe this!" Ben immediately stood up and hugged them both.

"Thank you!" Catherine gleamed, yet awaiting her mother's response. "We just found out yesterday and—"

"You're only telling us now!?" Ben yelled with excitement and laughter.

"We would've told you sooner, but we wanted twenty-four hours for us to relish in the moment. You're the first three to know. We're meeting with Andrew's parents tomorrow to share the announcement with them."

"Aww, I could not be happier for the two of you." Jacob was elated for them, though he had no desire to have his own.

"Wow, that's amazing. I'm happy for you both. Shocked, but happy." Anna's words expressed excitement, but her tone did not.

"What's wrong?" Catherine immediately asked. Her body language shifted.

"Nothing, I'm fine."

"Something's up."

Though their relationship was filled with love, Anna and Catherine didn't always agree.

Anna took a breath to speak, but stopped herself to contemplate her words. "You're young, you both are. Why rush into something like having a child?" Anna looked directly at Catherine, making strong eye contact.

Catherine composed her thoughts. "We're prepared to have children. We've been married for five years, been together even longer. We both work, enjoy what we do and are financially able to provide for a family." Her words were confident.

"Hmph," Anna nudged her head forward in acknowledgment. "The fact that you *think* you're prepared proves you aren't."

Jacob poured a little more wine for his mother and water for his sister. She expressed a sharp look of aggravation, so he sat back down. Confrontation was not something Jacob handled well. The argument upset him as his heart rate increased.

"Does anyone else need a drink?" Ben offered. Andrew held his beer up, suggesting he was ready for another. The table fell quiet between the four of them. When Ben returned with two beers, Jacob knew he was stressed. His father rarely consumed alcohol.

"No matter what, there will always be concern, Catherine. We are your parents, but of course we're ecstatic to welcome an adorable baby into our family." He looked over at his wife, attempting to change her energy. "Cheers!" The three men held their drinks up, while Catherine and Anna knew the discussion was far from over. Ben had no intention of choosing between his wife and daughter.

"Obviously I'm happy for you two. It's just difficult for me to understand why you'd want to start a family now. You need time to grow, know what you want out of life. Explore what options you'd—"

"Options like working for the company?" Catherine interjected.

"Those are your words, Catherine, not mine."

"We all know you want me or Jacob to take over the business, and it aggravates you that neither one of us have any interest in doing so."

As each interaction passed, Jacob allowed the red wine to meet his lips. While it brought temporary relief, it didn't ease his fluttering heartbeat, steadily rising.

"Is that such a bad thing?" Anna asked.

"It's bad when your greed blinds your perception of happiness," Catherine replied.

"And what about you, Jacob? Do *you* have anything to say about this?" Anna shifted the interrogation toward her son. Jacob instantly felt a rush of panic. Though it was just family, it was a uniquely heated discussion. He preferred to walk away, but knew that wasn't an option.

"I-I'm... I'm not sure. Part of me wasn't interested but recently, just today in fact, I was toying with the idea of working with you both." Jacob tried to please everyone, which was easier to do separately than in a group setting.

"Liar," Catherine blurted out. "Not once did you mention it at lunch. We both know you have absolutely no desire to work in the business, and never will. Though right now…"

"What!?" Jacob asked, angry that she'd hint at his unemployment.

"Never mind."

He felt the anxiety coursing through his veins. While Anna could be daunting, Jacob was typically intimidated by his sister. He attributed it to her intellect and eloquent speech. Catherine was a tough competitor to go up against.

"Hey… this isn't my fight." Jacob tried to stand up for himself. "How'd I get dragged into this?" The second he spoke, he knew how foolish he sounded. His anxiety was showing, and it was getting worse. Jacob struggled with speech when he was younger. Fortunately, the issues resolved themselves with age; however, they returned when faced with worry or stress.

"No, this isn't *your* fight. This is *our* fight that you've been avoiding for years." As Catherine's frustration increased, so did Jacob's anxiety.

"So this has been a discussion behind my back for a while now." Anna felt betrayed by both her children.

"How'd we go from a beautiful baby announcement to a family argument?" This was all Jacob could muster to deescalate the situation. Beads of sweat poured down his forehead, glistening in the sun, as his legs violently shook.

"I cannot believe you're quietly sitting there when we've discussed our dismal interest in the company."

"I've honestly… considered how it… would—" Jacob said slowly.

"Stop lying!" Catherine shouted at her brother. Though aware of his anxiety, she was too disappointed in her mother to notice.

"I'm not lying!" Jacob shouted back. Uncomfortable, he grabbed his glass of red for a sip. Though subtle, his right hand vibrated enough for the wine to sway. Jacob wasn't sure how he mustered the energy to shout. He felt proud to defend himself, but embarrassed by how he must look to them.

"Children, please stop," Ben said. It was quiet for a moment.

"It's true that I've had little interest in the company but lately—" Jacob tried to explain.

"You just told me today you couldn't spend the rest of your life doing it," Catherine interrupted.

"You've got to stop interrupting me. I'm going to lose my mind."

"Then speak the truth," she quickly rebutted without eye contact. Jacob was certain his family could see his heartbeat through his neck. The rise in his anxiety hindered his ability to filter his thoughts.

"I'm telling the truth. I've considered it lately. Even though there are differences from my last job, I think there would—"

"Wait," Ben interrupted, forcing Jacob to feel his words weren't being heard. "What'd you just say?"

"What now?" Jacob asked.

"From your *last* job? What are you saying, Jacob, were you fired?" Realizing he had admitted defeat, Jacob became more annoyed with his sister. She had forced him into the discussion, causing him to speak under pressure.

"Are you unemployed?" Anna asked. Jacob's legs shook even more, and he was relieved no one could see the movement under the table.

"Yes…" he replied, "but I wasn't fired. They filed for bankruptcy and closed last week." Everyone was stunned, including Catherine, who pretended not to know. "I was given a severance package, so I have some time before it's gone."

"And you plan to sit on your ass until then?" Ben hissed. One of the biggest lessons they tried to instill in their children was a strong work ethic. "Every day not working is a missed opportunity for prosperity."

"Jeez, I get it. I'm not doing nothing. I took a week to mentally decompress before jumping back in. It was needed. It's not that big a deal. It happens. I'll be back at work soon enough."

Jacob was stunned at the turn of the conversation. *How did this become about me?* Anna and Ben were hurt. Catherine was quiet and didn't seem to move except to take a drink from her water.

"Well, we can discuss that another day. Nothing we can do about that now." Ben noticed the anxiety on his son's face and decided to halt the conversation, for now. The table fell silent. Neither side was going to concede, so nothing could be done.

"Are you finished?" Anna stood up, turning to Andrew. He had been long done, as his utensils were on his plate and beer nearly empty.

"Yes, thank you," he replied. As Anna grabbed a couple more items from the table, her husband lifted his glass up.

"Cheers to our new baby girl or boy in the family!" Ben exclaimed, in one final attempt to change the tone of the dinner. Anna and Ben exchanged glances as she walked toward the house with various plates. This signaled everyone else to do the same and bring everything inside to clean. Both Jacob and Andrew offered to wash dishes, but Anna politely declined. Cleaning, on her terms, was therapeutic.

Within minutes, everyone dispersed. Ben went upstairs to the bathroom, Catherine sat in the kitchen and Anna continued cleaning. Jacob walked outside to pour more wine. He finished the bottle, ignoring his mother's empty glass. Though he could still feel the adrenaline coursing through his veins, Jacob felt slightly relieved. He didn't know if it was admitting the truth of his unemployment, the ending of their horrendous dinner, or both.

As he turned around, he noticed Andrew walking outside with a full beer.

"I'm sure that was not the announcement you two had in mind," Jacob tried to joke.

"No, not at all." Andrew sipped his beer. "Your sister was so excited to tell everyone. We had a long discussion about how and when to tell our families. She insisted on telling you all tonight. We would've told both our parents tonight but mine weren't available. Now I'm happy they weren't," he jokingly replied.

"Can't say I blame you there." Jacob sipped his wine. Andrew sympathized about his unemployment, which Jacob appreciated, then he picked up a few more plates and brought them inside. Jacob grabbed two bowls in one hand and his wine glass in the other. Once more, when he least expected it, another vision from the dream he'd had appeared in his mind. It was an unfamiliar, colorless symbol etched in stone. He had no idea what it meant or why he remembered it, but he sensed there was more to it.

Unlike his previous visions that day, this one came with a sense of urgency – a sense of importance. Momentarily distracted, Jacob lost his balance, causing one bowl to crash to the ground, shattering into small pieces. The sound refocused his attention to his surrounding reality.

Anna, Catherine and Andrew rushed outside to check on him. While his sister and mother expressed judgement, Andrew was kind and smiled. Jacob placed everything on the counter and grabbed the broom to clean up the mess. Just as he scooped up the last bit, Chicken ran over with her tail wagging. It immediately brightened Jacob's mood. Even though the evening had gone to a dark place, there was some good that occurred. His family knew about his unemployment, they were aware of his interest in the family business, and most importantly, there would be a new baby in the family.

After a little additional conversation, Catherine and Andrew eventually left, Ben went to his office to focus on work and Anna went to sleep early. The exhaustion of the evening, plus the wine, caused Jacob to go to bed earlier than normal too. Lying there, he reimagined the three visions that appeared to him.

The man's face.

The blackened hallway.

The cryptic symbol.

He couldn't understand why his mind recalled those moments of his dream. Since the details were unique, he decided it'd be worth talking to his mother to see if she'd recognize anything. He knew that was second conversation they would have, after discussing the events that unraveled at dinner. He cleared his mind before the arguments could replay, and went into a deep slumber, shockingly easy due to his wine consumption.

3

When he fell into the cavern, correctly identifying the path home, Smolar felt instantaneous relief, knowing he'd escaped his attackers. Though there were five paths to choose from, he stayed right. It was the same path he and Promit took on their arrival. It was impossible for the human eye to see through the darkness, but Smolar didn't have to worry about that; a quorian's vision was heightened.

As the sense of fear dwindled, Smolar began to worry. Guilt and shame quickly surfaced for Promit's safety. His good friend had been captured, for which he accepted responsibility. Smolar had persuaded Promit to travel to the outside world of Diveria again. Since their first attempt over a month ago was successful, he wanted to try a second time. Promit was initially hesitant because he felt they were lucky, but Smolar convinced him. What was supposed to be a short trip turned into a life-changing, unforgivable nightmare.

Smolar collapsed to the ground, placed his head in his hands and sobbed. It had been years since the last time he felt this sad, fifteen years to be exact. He vividly remembered the day of his parents' death and recognized the raw emotion that consumed him. Smolar was thrown back to that dark mental state, as he tried to unravel what he had just experienced.

"Promit... he just disappeared. How is this even possible?" He paused for a moment, held back some tears and looked down at his arms. Smolar's beautiful royal blue pigment was transformed into a blotchy mess with mud and dead leaves. He tried to clean himself off but his focus remained on Promit. Had he been killed or captured? Smolar told himself Promit was captured and pushed any other options out from his mind.

"That rod, what was the name? I know he said it." Smolar tried to recall the weapon the white-haired man had used, but he was unsuccessful. He sat on the ground, defeated, uncertain how he could show his face back home. Remaining in the path of darkness outside the city seemed more appealing to him. He wasn't certain how to get rid of the ugly feeling within.

Smolar shifted his focus off himself and onto Promit. This put the situation into perspective. If he fled, he'd be solidifying the death of his friend. No one else knew what had happened, and even though he didn't have much information to go off of, Smolar was his best bet at survival. As uncomfortable as it would be, he knew he needed to reveal their failed adventure.

There were quorians in the city better equipped to handle the unusual circumstances. Though Smolar didn't know who they were, he knew who to contact to get the ball rolling.

BOOM!

Smolar shook from the loud noise far away. Promit was in danger and prolonging the inevitable only put his friend at greater risk. With a deep inhale, Smolar mustered up the courage and continued forward.

The cavern was dark with a pungent odor. A couple small flames flickered along the walls, but most areas were encapsulated in darkness. Ooze seeping through some cracks made for a messy journey, but it was expected from such an ancient space. The path eventually led to what seemed like a dead end. Smolar stood in front a large rock wall that spanned the entire width and height of the cavern. Without a quorian's heightened vision, there was nothing to be seen. Even the majority of quorians couldn't identify what was in front of Smolar unless they were well-read in history and legends.

According to folklore, many years after the attempted genocide during the War of Kings, a Quorian Ruler named Sir Horlix executed one of his strange and peculiar ideas. After numerous secretive expeditions into the Outer World, his creation of the Enchanted Gate had become known amongst his inner circle, and eventually throughout the city. It wasn't until his disappearance and presumed death that his son Raynor, who succeeded him, sealed the gate, forbidding any quorian to leave the city.

Smolar was not a heavy reader, but he was made aware of the minor details from his good friend, Fravia Deallius. She frequently visited the quorian library and was a wealth of information. Unbeknownst to her, she provided him with the information needed to explore Diveria.

As Smolar stood in front of the Enchanted Gate, he knew what needed to be done. The gate was an enormous stone wall with thousands of engravings and carvings. Illegible even for a quorian, the detail was too advanced for Smolar to understand. These inscriptions could be seen by anyone who wandered down into the cave. Interestingly, to a human eye, the massive wall had dozens of darkened spots, concealing the finger-sized holes within the wall. Since quorians have their heightened vision, they're granted access through the darkest areas. Out of countless possibilities within the wall, there was only one correct gap to identify. Unfortunately, the contents of the holes continuously changed, so if a quorian took too long, it would reset while they remained in front of the gate. Most of the gaps were empty, with a small light at the end. Its seemingly safe appearance could lead to a deadly outcome, so it was crucial to spot the correct gap.

Walking along the length of the gate, Smolar glanced at every space and pocket along the stone. Eventually, his eyes found the gaping hole he'd been looking for. Inside the correct, non-illuminated gap was a large, sharp spike. To ensure the configuration wouldn't change on him, Smolar inserted his index finger and firmly pressed it against the sharp point. With one extended exhale, he pressed forward and shrieked as the spike punctured his finger. The sensation wasn't terrible, but Smolar didn't enjoy inflicting pain onto himself.

As his ivory blood dripped out of his finger and into the path beneath it, Smolar reached into his pocket and pulled out an untraditional stone key in the shape of an orb. The complex engravings on the wall coincided with the markings on the key. With his finger still in the wall, Smolar placed the key in his left hand and raised it up.

When the spear receded, he pulled his hand out, noticed the small prick in his finger, and watched the hidden mechanics reveal itself to him. Suddenly, segments that appeared engraved into the wall protruded outward. Piece by piece, it revealed itself in a circular, counter-clockwise motion until an octagonal-shaped box appeared. As it opened from the inside out, Smolar quickly raised his hand and inserted the key into the open slot. The space was only big enough to contain the orb. Once it felt the weight, the doors shut and Smolar stepped back in anticipation. Though he'd done this a few times, it still made him anxious.

A small hole appeared from the center of the Enchanted Gate and crystalized water seeped out. Instead of dripping down to the floor, it flowed straight into the air, defying gravity. Smolar approached the pooling water as it formed its own crystalized orb midair. With the hand of his injured finger, he grabbed the orb. Smolar instantly felt himself transcend his physical presence before reappearing on the opposite side of the wall. Though it only lasted seconds, the process was physically draining. Smolar bent over, gasping for breath, allowing himself a moment's rest.

Once he realized where he was, the adrenaline kicked in and pushed him to persevere. Smolar turned around, grabbed the stone key from the wall's containment and placed it in his pocket. He stepped away as the Enchanted Gate reclined its protrusions back into the wall. The engravings shifted to ensure the key's location remained hidden.

I'm home, he thought.

When Smolar turned around, he was reminded of the old debris left in front of the gate to conceal it. Some knew of the gate's location, but it was generally understood to be unusable since traveling was forbidden. Ironically, it allowed privacy for Smolar to use the gate. He peeked his head around the rubble to see his beautiful home of The Quo. When no one was looking, he jumped out and scurried along, blending in with the ground.

The Quo was a large, booming city where only quorians resided. Since traveling was banned, their entire race existed in one location. It was encapsulated in a large cavern with metamorphic rock walls that extended beyond what could be seen from the bottom level. Although the walls were shades of gray and black, many areas exuded various shades of blue from what was housed on the ground level.

The city was where King Klai had been slain during the War of Kings. The ground floor housed the Enchanted Reservoir, which was considered their most sacred and holy ground. It contained a beautiful pool of crystalline water, identical to the liquid from the Enchanted Gate. This blue hue resonated brightly throughout the cavern, resulting in a whimsical color palate throughout the city. While it was forbidden to consume or touch, it was strategically bottled, to maintain its purity, for quorian disbursement. It was considered disrespectful to King Klai to speak while visiting the Enchanted Reservoir.

Above the ground level were thirty floors that encompassed the entire height of the cavernous city. Shooting up out of the Enchanted Reservoir stood giant, thick stalks which connected a complex, reticulation of pathways for quorians to walk along. The stalks gleamed a light green hue that majestically blended with the blues, glistening throughout the city.

The fifth floor, known as Restaurant Alley, happened to house the Enchanted Gate Smolar had transported through. Certain areas were reserved for farming and wine making, while others were used for dining. There were popular restaurants like Draka's Diner and Raw You Can Eat, serving delicious meals for various palates. Something all of the eateries offered was the traditional quorian alcoholic beverage – aliquo. Tart with a sweet, zesty aftertaste, it was a favorite amongst the community.

None of the other floors within the city had an appearance quite like Restaurant Alley, though there were certain levels Smolar would often visit. The twenty-fourth floor was where he lived. The twenty-seventh floor, also known as the Belvase, was mostly used for larger gatherings and social events. The highest floors were reserved for the Quorian Ruler. Technically, anyone was able to visit the thirtieth floor as it housed Lady Vixa, their current ruler. Private and accessible only from within her home, there was a secluded thirty-first floor where Lady Vixa would sometimes reside.

As the floors continued above Smolar's four-foot-tall body, he was reminded of his disdain for the lower floors. While The Quo had always been home for him, he never felt a visceral connection with it. Unfortunately, Smolar never experienced what other jovial and exuberant quorians had. He stopped questioning his different viewpoint years ago, assuming it had to do with his family history. It wasn't until he left the city and entered Diveria that he'd resonated with a place.

Along the side of the cavernous walls were elevators at every ninety degrees. Powered by The Enchanted Reservoir, it was an example of how the site of their fallen king centralized their city. On the southern end of the fifth floor, Smolar entered the elevator and pressed '30'. As the car ascended, he attempted to verbalize what he'd experienced. Uncertain how to explain their escape, Promit's capture and his betrayal to Lady Vixa, he sensed an upcoming shift, especially given his complex relationship with the Quorian Ruler.

DING.

He'd arrived – the thirtieth floor. It wasn't typical for quorians to visit the top floor, but Smolar's situation was unique. He wasn't just knocking on the door of their ruler, he was knocking on the door of his former residence.

As Smolar walked towards his destination, he admired the view above. Known as The Great Barrier, quorians admired the only view they had outside the city. The eternal twinkling stars and phases of the moon had always brought him, and many others, peace. Having lived with the Quorian Ruler, Smolar learned it wasn't an accurate depiction of the outside world. Regardless, it aided in his imagination and welcomed the distraction.

As he stood at her door, eager and anxious, Smolar knew he needed Lady Vixa to help him save Promit. Unfortunately, he knew there'd be a price.

Knock, knock.

With no response, he tried again.

Knock, knock, knock.

Smolar knocked harder, yet only received more silence. As he raised his hand to knock a third time, the door opened, exposing Lady Vixa's home. Smolar pushed the door ajar.

"Hello?" he murmured. As Smolar stepped inside, he felt her presence beside him.

"Smolar." Lady Vixa spoke in a gentle, carefree tone, standing in the corner of her room with a book in hand.

"Hi, Lady Vixa. Sorry to bother you but I need to speak with you." Having once lived there for years, it was strange, yet comfortable, returning to his former home.

She paused, sensing his concern, and placed the tome down. As she walked towards Smolar, he was reminded of her intimidating presence. Standing six-feet tall, she towered over everyone in the city. Everything about her figure was slender and elongated. Her face was delicate, timeless, with her silver eyes, button nose and quaint smile. The light blue complexion was a shade rarely seen on quorians. Around her neck was the Amulet of Eymus – a beautiful, bright-red jewel which she never removed. Smolar never knew the origin of the amulet, but he knew she had an arrangement of jewelry. Her stark white hair was nearly the length of her body, with a widow's peak hairline and kept in a high ponytail.

"What's the problem?" Lady Vixa asked, motioning for Smolar to sit as she did. Her eggplant robe exposed her strong, elongated legs.

"Something happened, and I need your help... but I'll need to explain some things first."

"Alright." Lady Vixa was a woman of few words.

Smolar was nervous and he knew she could tell, but he was confident she would help. He knew of her abilities and majestic ways. The quicker he vocalized the problem, the sooner it'd be rectified. As Smolar spoke, Lady Vixa remained calm. Though she seemed disinterested, he knew it was her demeanor. With some nerve and confidence, he dealt the first blow and told his story.

"That's when Promit and I transported through the Enchanted Gate," he paused, expecting a reaction. She stared at Smolar, waiting for him to continue, so he did. He explained their first excursion to the Outer World. He described the cold, dark and wet environment, the sound of the debris beneath them and the swirling air around them.

"So you came here to tell me you broke a cardinal rule?" She leaned forward.

"Partially... but there's more."

Lady Vixa sat back in her chair. "Alright. What else?"

Smolar told her about their second escape, the one that happened a few hours ago. His heart raced. He was approaching the climax of the story but was afraid to voice it. Saying it out loud made it real.

"While we were up in this plant, two men appeared."

Lady Vixa became suddenly interested. "Two... men? From the Outer World?"

"Yes." Smolar hoped for Lady Vixa to speak again but she waited to hear more. "They were looking for something." Smolar paused and took a deep breath, in a poor attempt to cover his nerves. "They whispered, scurried around... they were on the hunt. We tried our best to stay out of their way. We didn't mean to get—" His mind spun.

"And?"

It was the moment of truth. Smolar's life was about to change. "They took him." It was done – Smolar had said it. Lady Vixa stayed in her chair, leaning back with her legs still crossed. "Please say something."

"What do you want me to say?"

"I don't know," Smolar sulked, his heart racing. Lady Vixa observed his sorrow and pain.

"So after Promit was taken, you ran to safety, returned to the city, and came straight to me?"

"Yes."

"Were you followed?"

"No."

"How can you be certain?"

"They followed me until the cave but that was all. I heard them walk away." Silence fell upon the room. Smolar was too ashamed to speak, unless requested. Lady Vixa eventually stood up, walked over to her corner desk and grabbed a bracelet from her drawer. She smirked and returned to Smolar, handing him the jewelry.

"What's this?"

"Confirm I correctly understand," she said, gathering her thoughts. "You stole my key to the Enchanted Gate, escaped to the Outer World, *twice*, put yourself, another quorian, and our entire city at risk, to end up having your own friend, Promit, captured." Smolar sulked more. He felt useless, worthless, and insignificant – like when he'd learned of his parent's deaths.

"Yes," he admitted.

"And which region did you travel to?"

"I'm not sure. There were numerous symbols, but I kept it on what was already selected."

"And you haven't touched it since?"

"No."

"Alright. Please give me back my key. You still have it on you, yes?"

Smolar reached into his pocket and returned the stone orb to the Quorian Ruler.

"Thank you. Now please place this bracelet on. It'll help the situation."

Smolar was intrigued. "I'm not sure how this will help but..." He placed the bracelet on. It immediately morphed, tightening around his wrist. "Wha—"

"That is my Bracelet of Fury. It'll ensure you never leave The Quo so long as you're wearing it." Smolar was stunned as he looked down. The band comprised of silver metallic vines that constricted against his royal blue pigment. In the center of it was a hardened crystal, the same color as the Enchanted Reservoir.

"You said this—"

"Even though you'll never have your hands on my key again, this is added protection. I cannot have you leaving, it's too dangerous. You put yourself and everyone here at risk."

"I know... I'm sorry. I don't—"

"It's too late for apologies, which is why you'll wear that bracelet."

Smolar knew he was wrong. He felt minuscule as frustration bubbled within. "What about Promit?"

"You've done enough, Smolar. Go, let me ponder," she hissed. Though stern, Smolar was surprised by her underwhelming reaction. Considering the severity of the situation, he expected a more dramatic response.

"Can't I—"

"Please leave." Lady Vixa stood up and opened her door to escort him out. Turning around on her front step, he gazed up at her delicate face as she looked down upon him. He felt the disappointment exude through her eyes until she looked above him and closed the door.

With a heavy heart and a sense of defeat, Smolar walked toward the cavernous wall to take the elevator home. All he wanted to do was save his friend. He looked down at the new accessory on his left wrist. Smolar felt trapped and the punishment inappropriate. *Surely I could be of some help. I went through the Enchanted Gate, I know the terrain, I've seen the men…*

DING

He entered the empty shaft along the north wall, pressed '24' and descended upon the floor he called home. Mostly residential, the only business on the twenty-fourth level was Draka's Corner, a bar near the elevator entrance. Despite not often drinking, Smolar stopped for a glass of aliquo to aid in the possibility of sleep.

"Hey, Jarvie…" Smolar exhaled, sitting down. Jarvie Jruk was the bartender and owner of the establishment. Though Smolar wasn't a frequent patron, the two often saw one another in passing.

"Hey, Smolar, how's it going?"

"It's been a day."

"No good, pal, sorry to hear. Anything you wanna talk about?"

Smolar yearned to unload his worries and concerns, but thought it best not to. The whole city didn't need to know what had happened – not yet.

"Not really, thanks. Just stopping by for one aliquo before heading home."

"Coming right up," Jarvie replied. "Sometimes it's best to let things settle and sleep."

"Exactly." He mustered a polite smile as Jarvie made his drink. Looking around, Smolar noticed a framed receipt on the wall. "You still have it up."

"What?" Jarvie followed Smolar's gaze. "Of course." He chuckled. "You were my first sale when I opened this joint. I'll keep it up for as long as I remain open." The kind owner handed Smolar his drink and he took a sip.

"Mm, perfect."

"Thanks, pal." The owner smiled. Jarvie Jruk was a simple quorian who kept to himself. With no co-workers, Smolar didn't see Jarvie have an active social life outside of the bar, but he seemed content with his life choices. Smolar both sympathized with and envied him.

"Looks like we'll have a full moon soon." Jarvie pointed up.

"Yeah, couple more days," Smolar responded without looking, lost in his thoughts.

Proficient at his job, Jarvie could always read a quorian, and he knew Smolar was lost in his thoughts. He decided to give his customer some space. Eventually, Smolar finished his drink, thanked Jarvie again, and wished him a good evening.

Walking toward his home, he recognized a familiar residence in the distance, just five stories below. It was a small, one-level home with two front-sided windows and a fake plant outside the door. Smolar's heart fluttered the longer he gazed. His concern for Promit's safe return caused him to seek out his childhood home. It reminded Smolar of when his life was simpler, happier. He recalled his father's laughter, his mother's hugs and all the joy that once was. Then he remembered the familiar voice from the night that forever changed his life, just days after his eighteenth birthday.

"I'm so sorry," Lady Vixa had said. "You're going to live with me now." Her voice had been empathetic and nurturing. It was one of the only times Smolar had ever heard her speak in such a manner.

4

Uncertain of his sudden location, Jacob Emmerson stood on a cobblestone path, fog in the distance, with a large manor on his right, and eternal darkness to his left.

Hello, he mouthed, but no sound was heard. In a slight panic, Jacob tried to shout louder. *Hello!*

Nothing. Unwilling to enter the blackened void, he turned right and headed for the building.

After a couple steps, Jacob realized he was unable to hear his own footsteps. His concern grew; however, he became infatuated by what stood in front of him. A presumably ancient, three-story manor built entirely of large brick loomed over Jacob. With numerous pointed tips and windows, he noticed it was as deep as it was wide.

Is it... alive? Jacob wondered, due to its intimidating presence. His heart fluttered.

Hesitantly, he continued down the cobblestone path, uncertain if it was safe to gaze upon the structure. Jacob immediately noticed the elongated windows on each of the three floors, alluding to the enormous height of each story. The lighter windowpanes were squared-off with a large cross in the center and a small stone awning above. He recognized and admired the peculiar dimensions of the front of the building. Along each end stood a spiraling tower ascending higher than the rest of the building. At the center of the second and third floors were two large balconies.

Gazing upon the shadows of the stone, Jacob had a realization. *Why is there no color?*

He feverishly spun around to see anything else in his view, but the fog was too thick. All he could see was the manor in front of him, and eternal darkness beyond that. Jacob felt his blood coursing through his veins as his anxiety increased. Without any options, he continued down the path.

Beside the cobblestone, there was nothing to see – no flowers or landscaping. The land was barren with an ashy grey hue. With no intention of stepping off the path, he arrived at the entrance and counted nine steps to the door. Checking his surroundings once more, Jacob noticed the cobblestone path behind him had vanished. Only fog and eternal darkness remained. The air thinned out, each breath more difficult than the last, and Jacob sweated nervously.

Glancing back at the main entrance, he admired the enormous door, nearly quadruple his height. As intimidated and unwelcome as he felt, Jacob had no choice but to go forward. The closer he got to the door, his anxiety increased. He tried to steady his breathing, unsuccessfully. His nerves escalated with each step he counted.

Five. Six. Seven.

Jacob's right eye began to twitch, which occasionally happened when extremely stressed. His mouth went dry and his hands, though sweaty, were ice cold.

Eight. Nine.

He'd made it. He approached the front door, with its two large, luxurious glistening doorknobs. The greyscale appearance maintained, and he knew if there was color, they'd have a metallic finish. Unsure what had happened behind him,

Jacob struggled with the decision to turn around. He knew a panic attack was on the horizon, but his curiosity won. With a slight turn, Jacob's question was answered. His eyes met a wall of darkness, all nine steps consumed.

His heartbeat in his throat and, gasping for air, Jacob's instincts stepped in. With no control of his body, his hand rushed for the massive doorknob, icy like his palms, and swung the single door open. He lunged inside and slammed the door behind him, immediately feeling a violent vibration as the eternal darkness won the battle outside. Silence still remained.

As he stood inside the mysterious structure, bearing his weight against the stronghold door, Jacob had a peculiar sensation. Something was different. His sudden need to gasp for air had dissipated and the beating of his heart in his throat had vanished. His mind and body were no longer riddled with the anxiety and stress. The weight from his shoulders had lifted and he could stand taller. Jacob had gone from the start of a panic attack to blissful ease, allowing him to examine his surroundings.

Much larger than the exterior claimed it to be, the inside of the manor was a gargantuan open space. Colossal columns, gleaming floors and traditional-style furniture filled the area. The various shades of gray proved there should be an assortment of colors. Staircases were on both sides of the hall with numerous walkways overhead, one almost above him in the entryway. Directly ahead of Jacob were a variety of desks, most of them empty.

As he took a few steps forward, a tall, husky man in a suit walked toward him. Jacob froze. Unsure of what to do, he attempted eye contact, but the stranger walked by, as if he weren't there. Confused, Jacob continued on, receiving no acknowledgement from passing individuals.

After the desks, Jacob passed a plethora of unique objects, paintings and artwork on display. Though tempted to rest in one of the numerous plush couches, he pressed on toward the end of the enormous space.

His attention was immediately drawn to the back wall where a stone mural resided. Similar to the rest of the manor, its size towered so high he couldn't clearly view the top. Jacob wondered if it was the largest piece in the entire building. He found it impressive, memorable.

My vision, he thought to himself. Jacob wondered if he was reliving the dream he'd had the night of his twenty-third birthday. In that moment, he realized he'd never been cognizant of dreaming while in a dream. It was a peculiar sensation. With an internal chuckle and a better sense of comprehension, Jacob looked to the left.

On both sides were two grand, luxurious hallways with massive chandeliers and more stone columns. The left was entirely illuminated, down to where it veered at the end. The right, though similar, was shortened by a blackened void. The consuming darkness would normally revive his anxiety, but Jacob remembered the strange euphoria he'd felt since entering the manor. He'd remained calm, stress-free.

He recalled another memory – the darkened hallway. His current view and his vision were an identical match with one stark difference: the white floor. He knelt down to touch it, as smooth as it appeared to him before. This confirmed he was correct in thinking he'd returned to his dream. He knew it was imperative to discuss this with his mother.

Regardless of its familiarity, he still had no desire to enter the questionable pit. Instead, he turned left into the welcoming environment. Before he could reach the hallway, a woman walked nearby.

Excuse me, he mouthed, yet silence remained. The woman continued on, without any recognition of his presence. Walking past elaborate, wide doors along the hall, Jacob slowly observed every detail. Something grasped his attention on his left. The doorknob. *It's jiggling.* Jacob cautiously walked toward the door as he watched the movement of the doorknob slow down. When he finally approached it, the motion stopped.

What was that? Is someone there? He looked up and saw an inscription above the door.

What language is that? There were letters and words but nothing Jacob could possibly speak. He tried to open the door, but it was locked. Unable to seek answers to his questions, Jacob took a step away and looked right, down the grand hallway.

What... Who is that? Off in the distance, a man was staring at him. He was slightly taller, dressed in a tuxedo, with brown hair, prominent chin, tan complexion and a regular build. The stranger's gaze was strong and possessive, triggering Jacob's final vision.

That's who I saw! Just as he prepared to introduce himself, he heard a voice in his head.

"So you remember," the stranger's voice entered Jacob's mind.

"Vaguely. My name is Jaco—"

"I know who you are, Jacob Emmerson."

"How are we—"

"Where are you?" the stranger interrupted.

"I don't know."

"Where do you come from?"

"I just entered this place and I—"

"What are you seeking?"

"I was wondering what was behind the door," Jacob said. The strange man down the hall never once broke his gaze. His eyes focused and consumed Jacob's presence. He couldn't understand why no one else acknowledged him but this man couldn't look away. Jacob waited to hear a response but there was none.

"Nothing to say?"

Instantly, Jacob began moving backwards, away from the stranger, away from the jiggling doorknob. His feet hovered above the glistening floor. He feverishly looked around for a way to stop as he had many questions and wasn't ready to leave.

Now in the main corridor, Jacob moved slowly by the individuals walking through the space, still confused why no one acknowledged him. He reached out to grab a column to halt his movement but his hand changed transparency and passed through the stone, as if he were a ghost. Jacob was glad of his ability to remain calm while inside these walls.

As he approached the front door, it slowly opened for his departure. Uncertain if the path had reappeared, Jacob gazed outside and was pleased to see the cobblestones once more. Hovering over the threshold of the manor, anxiety and fear flooded his body. The rush was more debilitating than he'd expected, causing him to hyperventilate.

Jacob, alone and clueless of his location, was on the edge of a panic attack, concerned for his safety. He was being levitated down the stairs and along the cobblestone path, and he began to thrash his body around. His mouth screamed for help, but no sound could be heard.

When his feet touched the ground, he collapsed, curling up into the fetal position. With only a view of eternal darkness on the horizon, he slammed his eyes shut and began to chant, rocking back and forth, pleading with whomever could listen.

Bring me home. Bring me home. Bring me home.

His whole body shuddered as the panic attack took control. He didn't know what to do and his crippling fear of the dark didn't allow him to open his eyes.

After what seemed like an eternity of agony, Jacob heard the faintest sound in the distance.

"*Jacob,*" a voice whispered. He tried to overcome the panic, but it wouldn't let him.

"*Come on, Jacob!*" the voice said, louder, forcing him to gasp for breath and widen his eyes.

"Wha—"

"Jacob, are you alright?"

His body ricocheted up from the bed, drenched in sweat, his heart racing. "I'm home!?" He gasped for air.

"Where else would you be?" his mother asked. "Calm down, calm down. You're alright. Bad dream?"

"Ye-yeah, I-I guess so," Jacob stuttered, catching his breath.

"Must've been some nightmare," she insisted. There was a silence between the two as Jacob allowed his body to relax and his lungs to regain oxygen.

"Actually it wasn't scary," Jacob corrected. "It just felt so real." As he gathered his thoughts and returned to reality, he was reminded of the last time he spoke with his mother. His anxiety subsided as his guilt awoke.

"I'm sorry for dinner last night. It was not—"

"It's alright, son. I'm sorry for my behavior. I shouldn't have—" She hesitated. "I shouldn't have been so angry."

Jacob and Anna shared a smile and she left his room to return to bed. He felt foolish having his mother run into his room like he was a child, but it was comforting. There was nothing unexpected or stressful here. It was familiar, easy.

He threw his head against his pillow as he remembered the dream. "The darkness, nine steps, the manor..." he whispered to himself. "No sound. No color." He closed his eyes, easily envisioning it all. "The people ignoring me, the mural in the back wall... the man. The strange man who wore a tuxedo." He opened his eyes again. "My visions..."

Jacob didn't understand why he remembered everything the second time. Though experienced with dreams, he sensed something unusual with it. Instead of his subconscious mind wreaking havoc, it seemed as though he'd left his home and physically traveled to the manor. His perception of reality was much stronger than it normally was in dreams.

As he lay there, trying to process everything, he had another startling thought. Ever since Jacob's twentieth birthday, the legal age to consume alcohol in Sartica, he'd realized that drinking hindered his ability to dream, or at least remember them. Acquiring a restful, sober night's sleep didn't guarantee a dream, but going to sleep drunk guaranteed no recollection of them. The last two nights Jacob had the unique experiences, he'd consumed numerous glasses of wine and went to sleep tipsy or drunk.

"Why would that change now?" he thought to himself. He felt the pressure of countless unanswered questions. He desperately wanted to return to where he'd gone, but he knew it was impossible. Before he forgot any details, he wrote everything he could recall in the leather-bound book beside his bed, filling three pages.

When he closed the book, Jacob recalled the personal moment of the experience – the disappearance of his anxiety. Trying to manage it had always been an issue for him. The constant battle between body and mind. Suffering from anxiety his entire adult life, Jacob didn't know any better. He knew it wasn't ideal, but he'd begun to avoid certain situations, shifting his life to avoid triggering it. Until his time in the manor, he hadn't realized how incredible it felt to be alive. He vividly remembered the euphoric rush when the panic and worry expunged from his mind and body.

What was so special about that building?

Upon his immediate departure from it, the stress had ignited itself, but stronger. He'd felt as though he was having a heart attack. He'd never been so frightened for what could happen due to his mental state. His current awareness of his anxiety only exacerbated it. Jacob closed his eyes and breathed slowly, resulting in a concerning realization.

"The message was simple," he whispered. "I need to ease my mind."

Considering the heightened emotions over the family dinner and the whirlwind of thoughts running through his mind, Jacob waited a few days until he spoke with his mother. It allowed for their emotions to settle between one another and for him to gather his thoughts. He wanted to process what he could on his own instead of running to her in desperation. With a new outlook on his anxiety, Jacob tried to avoid alcohol for a few days. He knew his dependency on wine was heavier during stressful events, so he also avoided such situations for the time being.

"Any luck on the job hunt?" Ben asked, coming in the house from work.

"Nothing yet," he responded. Jacob had barely thought about his lack of employment the last few days.

Jacob and Ben had briefly spoken about the family dinner, mostly to discuss their excitement for the child. He confided in his father about his lack of desire to get involved in the company. Ben understood, but he didn't share the expectation Anna did for his children. He respected their decision, but wished the message had been delivered differently.

"Is it raining yet?" Jacob asked with anticipation.

"Thankfully no, it's remained dry," Ben replied. "Let's hope it stays that way."

Living in a desert climate, the weather was typically sunny and warm, which meant water conservation was an important part of their routine. Though no one wanted to be in a drought, Ben loathed the rain, preferring warm, sunny days. Jacob, similar to his mother, welcomed the rain. It brought him a sense of serenity, easing his anxiety. The crisp smell, with the droplets' musical tune, aided in the whimsical visualization of watching the rain fall. Jacob would lose himself in his environment and effortlessly balance his mind. Like dreams, he and Anna would often express their hopefulness and excitement for such weather.

"Jacob, you're home!"

Jacob jumped, startled by his mother. "Hey, Mom. Yeah, just been upstairs."

"You've been so quiet; I had no idea."

Though he'd just come in from work, Ben left the two in the kitchen and wandered into his office. He spent most of his time in there getting work done, which no one complained about. Anna examined the inside of the refrigerator, deciding on what to make for dinner.

"How do chicken cutlets sound?" she asked.

"Sounds great," he said with a lingering thought. With just the two of them in the kitchen, Jacob decided he was ready to discuss his dream as she removed chicken breasts from the freezer to defrost.

"You remember when you woke me from that nightmare a few nights ago?" Jacob blurted out.

"Oh! Yes, you know, I meant to ask you about it the other day, but it slipped my mind." Anna sat beside him at the kitchen table. "Do you remember anything?"

"Every. Single. Detail." Jacob paused as he tried to find the words to express his emotions. "It was more than a dream... it was an experience. I remember everything so vividly."

"Tell me," Anna said, intrigued.

Jacob recounted his experience, explaining every detail he could recall. When they discussed the mysterious man, he confirmed having not recognized him as the questioning ensued, until he was forcibly removed from the building.

"I was barely above the ground. My feet dangled as I moved backwards. Curiously enough, I still had no anxiety being there. It was peculiar." Jacob was eager to hear her opinion.

"Seems like you may have incorrectly answered his questions," Anna suggested.

"Hm, possibly," Jacob pondered. "That's actually a very good thought."

"Is that when you screamed?" she asked.

"No, once I was removed from the manor, a startling amount of fear overwhelmed me. I was alone, surrounded by darkness and fog. It terrified me, but then I woke up."

"That really is a peculiar dream, I—"

"That's not even the whole thing," Jacob interrupted. "The night before that, on my birthday, I think I had the same dream."

She sighed. "You think?"

"Yes, because that next day… you know, when we were all together last,"—Jacob rolled his eyes mentioning their unfortunate family dinner—"I had visions of this experience. I saw the dark hallway, the man's face and a symbol from the wall. Nothing more or less, and the visions were foggy. I didn't understand what they were from until the next night, when I had the vision dream."

"That… is quite remarkable," Anna responded.

"It felt so real…" Jacob paused. "Normally when I dream, there are moments of clarity and mystery. It's almost like putting a puzzle together… but this… was different. It was as though I traveled to this other place. I don't know how to explain it."

Anna expressed a look of comfort. "I've had a similar experience once," she admitted, "many years ago. It was different than what you've explained but there are similarities. The emotional relief, the colorless appearance, the man…"

"What!? How come we've never discussed this?"

"It never came up. Ultimately, nothing came from my dream." Anna stood up. "My advice would be to follow your emotions. Hold onto the relief you felt and work toward making that a reality." She walked out of the kitchen, ending the conversation.

"Wait! Mom, I would love to hear—"

"I'm going to check on your father. We can talk more about this another time."

"But—"

"Another time," she insisted.

5

Exiting the Northern Forest of Tillerack proved to be a challenging task. After a few days of circling the woods, Mortimer and Vanilor finally arrived back in town. They were elated to complete the hardest part of their mission; they'd successfully caught a quorian. Though its friend had escaped, they had only been instructed to catch one. Vanilor Dipythian, the smaller framed, white-haired man, secured the Novalis Rod in his possession, which he was privately given by their regional leader. Neither he nor his partner, Mortimer Hullington, the taller, slender man, knew of its origin; they just accepted it was a tool to aid in their mission's success.

"We're finally out of the fucking forest!" Mortimer said. "I know we need to head back but how about a quick drink? We've been in the forest for too long and we deserve it."

Vanilor was eager to return home for their reward, but found it difficult to turn down a stiff drink. "Shit. Alright. One quick drink, then we head back. *He*'s expecting us."

They entered their temporary car and drove towards the center of Tillerack. Due to Vanilor's height and wielding the Novalis Rod, Mortimer drove the car.

"Where should we stop?" Mortimer asked.

"Let's just stop at the first, good looking bar we see. We can have a beer or two, grab a quick bite and then get the fuck out of this region."

Mortimer chuckled at how one quick beverage turned into drinks and food. It was around 4:00pm when they approached an establishment called 'THE Bar.' It was an underwhelming, one-story building made of brick – exactly what they'd hoped for. They parked one block away along the street.

"I assume we're taking that with us inside?" Mortimer nodded at the rod.

"Open the trunk. There's a bag I brought in case we needed to stash the rod away." Mortimer released the valve and Vanilor walked toward the back of the car. Inside was a black leather satchel. He placed the Novalis Rod into the bottom and tossed it around his chest, where he felt it safest.

"Now let's go have that fucking drink!"

THE Bar was crowded with loud folk during happy hour. Walking through the men and women conversing about life, work and various topics, the two men noticed an open table in the back left corner and sat down.

A waiter quickly approached them. "What can I getcha?"

"Two wheat beers at your recommendation please!" Vanilor shouted.

"Can you believe this shit's over?" Mortimer asked as the waiter walked away.

"Fuck yeah, man. We just became rich." Being a spy for their leader, Vanilor never expected to be offered the mission. It made him feel empowered, alive. Not only did he idolize Brugōr, the leader of The Barren Land, for his wealth, he yearned to one day harness his power. Completing the mission guaranteed Vanilor and Mortimer financial security. With a wife and two children at home, Vanilor considered it a unique opportunity to secure each of their future endeavors.

The waiter dropped off the two beers and placed their food order.

"What do you think'll happen when we get home?" Mortimer wondered.

"What else is there to say at this point?" Vanilor sipped his beer and paused. "All we need to do is hand it in and we're set. Rich beyond our wildest dreams."

Mortimer heard the excitement in his partners' voice but couldn't match it. "What do you think they'll do with him?"

"The hell should I know?" Vanilor considered the creature for a second, but with such a hefty reward, any shame he felt quickly left his mind. He whispered, "Not my problem. Our job was to capture one of them things and bring it back. Nothing more, unless he's offering more."

Mortimer knew his partner was right. Though he'd agreed to the terms, he couldn't shake an unsettling feeling. He tried his best to suppress it.

As they enjoyed their beers, the waiter dropped off their food orders. Both were vegetable-based since the region took great care to protect their wildlife. Vastly different than The Barren Land, which heavily relied on meat for their main source of food. Displeased, they consumed what they could until they were content. Neither one found it delicious, but it satisfied their hunger. Normally Vanilor would've demanded better, but they needed to remain unnoticed. They ordered another round of beer to help chase the taste away.

"It's been great to have you on this mission, Morty," Vanilor admitted.

"Of course," he responded in a stern voice. "Same here." They raised their mugs and clinked.

As they continued to drink, the crowd grew in size and volume. Conversations could be heard from neighboring tables without effort.

"My boss is even worse than yours! He humiliated me today," a random patron yelled.

The two men glanced at the drunken group. Laughing at the fools around them, Vanilor and Mortimer decided it was time to depart. They didn't want to overstay their welcome in a strange region, especially since the mission wasn't complete until they met with Brugōr. The two paid their check and exited THE Bar. It was 6:00pm as they walked one block toward their car and noticed something awry.

"The fuck is this?" Vanilor shouted, feverishly looking around for the culprit. Mortimer reminded him to calm down and not draw attention to them. Though swearing was common in The Barren Land, they knew other regions were not as crass.

"Shit… seems we pissed someone off," Mortimer suggested, examining the two intentional gashes in both right tires. Darkness was imminent and both men were uncertain of what to do. The damaged car had been stolen after they safely hid their own vehicle outside the Southern Forest to ensure they blended in.

"We should've never fuckin' stopped here," Vanilor hissed. "Now what're we gunna do. We need to get to the Southern Forest soon."

"Let's just call a car to bring us to the outskirts of town."

"You fuckin' dumb?" Vanilor hissed. "Might as well hand the rod away. Discreet, Morty. We must be discreet."

Mortimer looked around, as an idea came to fruition. He considered it, but knew it would build upon his existing shame from the mission. Regardless, Mortimer understood their urgency to return home.

"What is it?" Vanilor asked. "There's something brewin' in your mind."

"Well…" Mortimer hesitated.

"Spit it out, man, we need to get moving."

"There were many drunks still at the bar," Mortimer reminded him. "We could find the drunkest group of mongrels there, bullshit a bit and get them drunker. Eventually, we offer to drive one of them home, take their car and leave." He instantly sensed guilt in the shameful suggestion. "Once we drop them off, we would just borrow it to the forest edge and leave it. It would be reported missing and easily found the next day," Mortimer added, hoping to alleviate some of the shame.

"That should fuckin' work," Vanilor said with a smile. "Love that brain o' yours. Let's go."

As they evaluated the crowd with judgement, the two men realized their choices were limited.

In the back corner was one man taking shots alone, on his cell phone, seemingly annoyed with the recipient. The two men decided someone alone was trickier to persuade. A few tables over at a bar-top counter were a man and woman having drinks. Considering it could be a first date or a couple, it would be tricky to obtain a vehicle. Their actions could be misconstrued and lead to a bigger, violent scene. Continuing to survey the room, Vanilor noticed a community table toward the left side of the bar where three men, each with different drinks, sat on one end. Between them was an empty basket with crumbs, implying they'd been there a while. Vanilor considered it a great opportunity to interject their conversation. After some contemplation, he looked at Mortimer and motioned for him to follow.

"Anyone sittin' here?" Vanilor asked.

"No, buddy, enjoy," the man said. He toasted his wine to Vanilor, smiled at Mortimer and returned to his friends. They sat down beside the group and ordered another round of beer. It was their safest option to avoid being drunk. While they waited for their drinks, Vanilor and Mortimer discussed Tillerack, the weather. All neutral topics, in case one of the three men overheard them.

After ten minutes, Mortimer heard the man with wine mention the haunting within Southern Forest of Tillerack.

"Excuse me," Mortimer said. "Sorry to interrupt but I couldn't help but overhear your discussion about the Southern Forest."

"Oh yeah," the man joyfully answered in a slightly drunk tone. "It can be very scary to explore, especially in the dark. You've heard about it?" Vanilor glanced at Mortimer, knowing they'd successfully joined the discussion. He smiled.

"No." Mortimer and Vanilor both shook their heads.

"Really? Seems to be what everyone's talking about these days."

"Well—"

"We don't typically keep up with local news," Vanilor interrupted. "Especially ghost stories."

"I get that, but I'd still be careful if you travel in the northern or southern woods. Some have claimed strange sightings and peculiar activities in the last month or so. One child claimed to have seen a small monster with silver eyes."

"Oh." Mortimer and Vanilor darted looks at each other, curious if the fables were actually quorian sightings. "Thank you for the warning…"

"Michael," the man replied. "The name's Michael Grinshaw."

"Nice to meet you, Michael, I'm Mortimer." He grinned as the two shook hands. "Friends call me Morty." Vanilor darted him a look, aggravated to disclose his real name. "This is my friend, Thomas." Vanilor nodded politely.

"Pleasure. This is Lionel and Bo." His two friends waved and smiles were exchanged. The group of men joined together and discussed various topics. While Mortimer genuinely enjoyed himself, Vanilor subtly reminded him they needed to move along.

Mortimer shouted, "Let's have a toast!" Everyone grabbed their glasses when Mortimer changed his mind. "Actually, let's do this right. We need to order a fresh round of shots." He stood up, went over to the bar and ordered three double shots with two shots of water. As he walked back to the table, their new friends were adamant they could not drink more.

"That's one shot!?" Lionel asked.

"Yeah, I asked for one but the barkeep was generous," Mortimer said as he carefully passed them around, ensuring he and Vanilor received the water. Once everyone had shots in hand, Mortimer stood at the head of the table to toast.

"To strange encounters, meeting new people…"—Mortimer looked at Michael—"…and having a fucking blast!" The five of them roared and tossed back their shots. Three men squirmed with the strong liquor while Mortimer and Vanilor acted displeased by their water.

Twenty minutes later, Mortimer was having a good time, speaking mostly with Michael. As he began to lose track of time, Vanilor shot his partner looks to remind him of the reason they'd returned to THE Bar.

Mortimer pushed his right shoulder into Michael. "Doing alright?"

"Yeah, Morty, thanks." He chuckled. "Shots aren't my thing. I think the last one hit me hard." Mortimer laughed as Michael's torso weaved.

Acknowledging the time, Lionel announced he needed to head home. Bo and Michael agreed. It was getting late and they all had work tomorrow. When Michael stood up, he realized how hard the liquor had hit him. He supported himself on the table, preventing a fall.

"Whoa, you alright there, buddy?" Mortimer asked.

"Ye-yeah, just need a minute," Michael stuttered.

"Guess you were right about that last shot." Mortimer gave him a pat on the back.

"Told ya." Michael laughed. He walked a few steps and stopped. Mortimer followed.

"You alright to drive home?" Mortimer asked, genuinely concerned.

"Honestly, no. It's probably best if I—"

"You know," Mortimer interrupted, "I could drive you home in your car."

"Very kind of you, but I can't let you do that. Don't worry about it, I can just call a taxi."

"That'll take an hour for them to arrive and cost you. I'll do it for free." Mortimer smiled. "How far away do you live?"

"Uh, well…" Michael stared at Mortimer. "Just northwest of here, about ten minutes."

"Perfect! Where are your keys? I'll drive you home tonight. Let's go *Thomas*," Mortimer said in a sarcastic tone.

Whether it was the alcohol, the persistence or that Mortimer had made an impression on Michael, he gave up and accepted the friendly help. Michael waved goodbye to his two buddies, then the three men gathered their belongings and stepped outside.

"Where did you park?"

Michael pointed right. "Just two blocks this way."

"Okay, let's go. Thomas, grab the car and follow us." Mortimer motioned, acting as if they had a second car to follow with. As they neared Michael's car, he started to sway. Mortimer swiftly grabbed his shoulders and stood him upright, surprised by his solid stature.

"Thanks," Michael said with his eyes nearly closed.

"You're welc—" Mortimer was interrupted by the sound of Michael vomiting on the corner of the sidewalk. Mortimer gave him space, ensuring he didn't get sick too. Once he was finished, the two walked on until Michael pointed out the car.

"There it is." Mortimer was impressed by it: an opulent, two-door car, slate gray exterior with white and black interior.

"Nice car."

"Thank you."

As they entered, Michael rested his head against the door and Mortimer jiggled the keys into the ignition. Glancing in the mirror, Mortimer noticed Vanilor enter their car a few blocks back. Knowing he was unable to follow, Mortimer felt a sense of freedom. The mission was a bigger burden than he'd anticipated. Having twenty minutes away was rejuvenating, even with Michael in the car.

They arrived at Michael's home ten minutes later. Mortimer looked over and realized he was fast asleep.

"Hey." He nudged Michael. "It's time to wake up. You're home." Michael's eyes slowly opened as he fought the weight of his eyelids.

"I like the sound of that." Michael chuckled. He looked around at the familiar surroundings and smiled. "Thanks again, man. It's very kind and more than you needed to do."

"Not a problem, Mike. It was a great night and I'm glad to have been there to help." The two men got out.

"Where's Thomas?" Michael asked, standing behind the car.

"He stopped to fill up the tank and should be here in a few minutes." Silence fell as Michael stared at Mortimer. "You should go inside, get some rest." Mortimer laughed nervously. "It was great meeting you and I hope work isn't too challenging tomorrow."

Mortimer held out the keys and placed them in Michael's hand. As he grabbed them, he pulled Mortimer forward and the two shared a small kiss on the lips. It lasted only a few seconds, until Michael pulled back with a nervous chuckle. Mortimer's mind raced. He'd never kissed a man. He didn't know if he was more shocked that a man had kissed him or that he'd kissed someone ten minutes after they threw up.

"Take care," Michael said with a smirk. "Maybe I'll see you again soon." He shuffled the keys in his hands, opened the front door and waved goodbye to Mortimer as he shut the door behind him.

Mortimer turned around, flabbergasted. He walked down the street, passing a few homes, until he pulled out the key to Michael's car. Mortimer stood in the street contemplating his actions. Already suppressing the guilt from the mission, he struggled with having taken advantage of an innocent, kind man. One that left Mortimer with more questions than anticipated. His mind raced with guilt, shame and curiosity until he quickly remembered why he was standing in the middle of the road. *Vanilor.*

Mortimer evaluated the quiet house. With no trace of Michael, he entered the vehicle, switched into neutral, and pushed it into the street. Once the car was off the property, he jumped in, started the ignition and quickly drove away. He hoped to not wake Michael, but the thought of seeing him again excited Mortimer.

"What am I thinking?" he whispered to himself. Consumed with questions and doubt, there was only one thing Mortimer was certain of. "No fucking way am I mentioning this to Vanilor."

6

Perched up above her city, Lady Vixa observed the quiet pathways below. She glanced toward the wide and open platform of the Belvase on the twenty-seventh floor. *They're starting to clear it out*, she thought. In preparation for a party, her party. One-hundred years ago, she succeeded as their Quorian Ruler when her father, Lord Erko, died.

Lady Vixa's mother died when she was younger, so it was just her and her father. Lady Vixa idolized her father and he did anything necessary to ensure her happiness. Lord Erko was also well-respected and admired throughout The Quo. He managed the community, led by example, and ensured everyone's safety. Not one accident occurred under his ruling.

With a heavy heart, Lord Erko knew his position would eventually go to his daughter. While he loved her, his traditional views were that only male quorians should rule. There were only two cases in quorian history that a female came into power. They each found a male counterpart and held a Proclamation ceremony to express their devotion and loyalty. Once married, the male quorian became the new ruler. This concept was widely accepted throughout history; however, Lady Vixa diverted from the social expectancy, refusing to let history repeat itself. While some didn't welcome the break in tradition, many were excited for the possibility of revolutionary change within the community.

Unfortunately, the excitement was short lived. With Lord Erko's stance on her expected course of action, his daughter was never properly prepared for ruling. All he instilled was that her future husband would take control and her role would be to support him. After his death, a lonesome and vulnerable Vixa, with the given title of Lady, trusted her intuition. She followed her father's suggestion of maintaining a low profile, delegating jobs and accomplishing minor tasks, but it stopped there. There was nothing more she fulfilled of her father's wishes.

Lady Vixa knew she'd never marry a male, so going against her father proved difficult. It was an unexpected burden that strongly affected her leadership. Her complacency disappointed much of the city, especially within the female community. Lady Vixa felt the lack of support compared to her father, which only furthered her apparent laziness. Regardless of their opinion, quorians accepted her as their ruler and maintained respect, no matter the circumstance.

As her one-hundred-year anniversary approached, the Blue Diamond Jubilee, Lady Vixa couldn't believe how quickly time had passed. She never asked to become ruler and certainly never wished for a ceremony.

"I did what I felt was right, yet also expected of me. I did my best, and it wasn't good enough. Why celebrate it?" she whispered to herself. She turned around, unamused by the preparations below, and went inside her home.

Lady Vixa considered the concerning news Smolar had brought to her. Well versed in quorian history, she compared the situation to what had happened to Sir Horlix many years ago. She knew he was the first, and last, to explore outside their city walls, until now. Unfortunately, that scenario didn't provide her with insight, but she had an idea of who she could summon to help resolve the problem, and ultimately save Promit.

Everyone within The Quo vehemently believed their history and story of origin. During the Age of Kings, their dedicated and loyal King Klai maintained freedom and prosperity within their territory. Life for the quorian race was enjoyable – they were free to roam the terrain and explore the unknown.

When the War of Kings started, the gargantuan rulers began to vanish one at a time – King Azur, King Iaga and King Depthus. Some of their deaths were confirmed, while others disappeared without a trace. Eventually, the only two left were King Klai and the Divinity King, the latter being the stronger of the two. They met multiple times, though it was unknown what for, until the Divinity King returned with ten of his men.

The two had a disagreement and moved away from quorian territory, leaving the ten men with the rest of the quorians. Though the community were curious about their presence, they cautiously continued their routines. In the meantime, King Klai and Divinity's meeting heated to unfathomable proportions. A deafening blow was heard, causing an insurmountable amount of smoke and debris. The event triggered Divinity's men to brutally kill every quorian in the area.

As a peaceful group, the quorians weren't prepared for such violence. Parents attempting to defend their families were met with a painful demise. The men were ruthless, showing no sympathy for even the youngest of children. Few quorians were fortunate to see their loved ones before they were murdered. Many parents watched their children scream out in agony only to be slain moments later.

It was a massacre.

Though there were only ten men, they were coordinated and well prepared to brutally murder the non-violent community. As they burned down homes, they had an assortment of weapons for mass destruction. Their agility and brute strength made them nearly invincible with their spears, knives and explosives.

Clinging to survive the unexpected attack, King Klai noticed the attempted genocide of his race and conjured up powerful spells that even surprised the Divinity King. Although they were nearly a fair match, it came to a brutal end when King Klai generated a crimson wall of fire, fifty-feet high across their battleground. The distressed and distracted quorians became an easier target for the brutal murders, as the men showed no mercy.

The Divinity King soared into the air, picked up King Klai, and slammed him down with all his might for his final blow, causing them to plummet well below the earth's surface. After they both collapsed into the newly-formed cavern, both kings remained silent, no movement ensued. The lucky quorians still alive feared the worst for their deity, and they were right to do so.

Divinity's men used this time to exterminate the rest of the race. If a body twitched after death, they'd impale their spears twice more. Their goal was obvious, their orders clear.

Extinction.

Quorian blood covered the terrain, leaving behind an ivory river in a desolate land. Once the men felt secure in their mission, they congregated and rested as they awaited their king.

Half a mile below the surface, the Divinity King opened his eyes, his body atop the other. Blood rushed out of King Klai's head, confirming Divinity's win. He attempted to escape, but it proved difficult. He didn't have the stamina for incantations, so he relied on brute strength. He tried multiple times to climb the walls but continuously fell, destroying the surrounding walls and widening the space.

Eventually the Divinity King found solid footing, reached the top of the tomb and walked away, presumably towards his murderous counterparts. That was when the twenty small heads rose out from King Klai's blood. *Survivors.* Most of them were children, with a few being slightly older. No one expected to survive the massacre, but they listened to their parent's instruction. The children were to hide under King Klai if he perished, but no one expected them to climb into a tomb and hide in his blood.

Follow Klai, Go Awry.

The only factual proof that existed were the final twenty quorians of their race

– the reason they existed in secret. With precise documentation, the survivors, known to quorians as *the Saviors*, resided within King Klai's tomb. As time progressed and their population grew, they built out the cavern into what became The Quo. Eventually, the original saviors died, but their legacy and memory lived on, considered to be as sacred as King Klai himself.

Lady Vixa was not only well aware of the history, but she was in possession of it. The Klai Chronicles was their collection of everything sacred to them. Bestowed upon the Quorian Rulers, it included ancient enchantments and documents of their history, including the original writings of the Saviors. Everyone learned of the twenty saviors, but only Lady Vixa knew of their unique capabilities, and that death simply ignited their inner spirits.

Returning to her sleeping quarters, she approached the mirror. Staring at her own reflection, swaying her head to allow her hair to flow, Lady Vixa smirked. Reaching her right hand outward, it effortlessly penetrated the glass, rippling the reflection. Her hand instantly landed on what she'd hoped for and pulled it out. Holding it with both hands, she looked back at her reflection as the rippling eased. She smiled.

"It's been a long time since I've taken you out, my distant friend."

The Klai Chronicles.

"It's time we seek assistance," she whispered to herself. Lady Vixa didn't have the answer to the problem at hand, but she was confident one of the Saviors would.

She'd forgotten the weight of the tome, needing both hands to carry it downstairs until she placed it on a center pedestal, beside the moonfeather tree. The foliage towered over most quorians, but matched Lady Vixa's stature. Residing in a dull, brass pot, it was lusciously green with dozens of pure white, fully-bloomed feathered flowers. They were as white as bone, and yet, at certain angles, the flowers glistened in the light, sparkling from the illuminated chandelier above.

"Hmm…" Lady Vixa stood in front of the tree, contemplating the flowers. "I'll take this one…" She paused. "And this one. Perfect," she said examining the two flowers. Moonfeather trees were once commonly seen throughout the cavernous walls of The Quo. Unfortunately, they were not properly tended to and faced extinction. Only a couple, personally owned, remained in existence. Lady Vixa's tree, however, was different than the rest. Hers was nurtured using only water from the Enchanted Reservoir, due to its enlightened properties. Lady Vixa placed the Quorian Blade beside the tome, a weapon she hadn't used in years.

Passed down through the generations with the Klai Chronicles, the Horlix Blade was forged deep within Mount Marlock, the hottest place across Diveria. Its name was unusual since there was nothing sharp about it. The bolster was the shape of a dragon's body – the top its head, the bottom its claw – and the handle was the dragon's elongated tale. The body of a serpent was where the blade should be. Between the heads of the dragon and serpent flowed a glistening blue hue, presumed to be the blood of King Klai. It's the only object the Quorian Ruler possesses harnessing the most powerful substance of the quorian race.

"Let's hope this works," she whispered, hoping she could recall one of the cardinal enchantments she learned at an early age.

With a vial and crystal bowl from her desk, she added all the objects to the center table. She tore the two moonfeathers into tiny pieces, gently placing them into the bowl. Next was the vial, which Lady Vixa opened and slowly poured into the bowl. The feathers swirled around as the purified water from the reservoir began circling in a counterclockwise motion. She stared at the movement, hovering over the bowl. The feathers eventually disappeared and the mixture appeared a dark purple. Finally, the movement halted. Lady Vixa grabbed the Horlix Blade and placed the pointed tip of the serpent's tail into the mixture.

Poof!

A small plume of smoke appeared over the bowl and lingered, barely visible. Lady Vixa released her grip on the Horlix Blade as it remained upright. She closed her eyes and focused until she sensed universal clarity. Instantly, a gust of wind entered the room, swirling her ponytail upwards. Widening her eyes, Lady Vixa opened the Klai Chronicles and feverishly turned the pages until she located ten blank pages, both front and back. With uncertainty, she chose one page at random, grabbed the Horlix Blade, and stabbed the center of the page with the dull end. The Klai Chronicles ricocheted from the force and Lady Vixa released her grip. Once more, the blade remained in position as it released a blue fog onto the page. Taking a step back, she carefully examined the page, noticing illegible scribblings and symbols.

For the first time in years, Lady Vixa unclasped the Amulet of Eymus from around her neck and placed it into the bowl. The mixture bubbled, aggravated by the placement of jewelry. The contents of the bowl grew and the smoke plume extended beyond Lady Vixa's height. It bubbled so violently, the crystal bowl clanged atop the table and fluid splashed onto the ground. The cloud hovered over the floor.

A captivated Lady Vixa stepped back as the plume lowered and grew. Glancing at the Klai Chronicles, she saw the once cryptic and archaic symbols had transformed into a legible language. The page had been filled and though she wanted to peruse them, there was only one word she needed to say aloud.

Neetri.

The plume continued to grow, the bowl continued to rattle, and the Horlix Blade remained in position.

"Neetri!" Lady Vixa shouted. The bowl dangerously approached the edge of the table as the cloud grew. The noise reverberated off the walls – the swirling fluid, the clanging of the crystal, the constant bubbling and the hum of the smoke plume. She patiently waited, aware timing was crucial, but then it happened.

Lady Vixa watched the crystal bowl tip over the edge of the table. She wanted to leap for it but knew it'd be a wasted effort. She hoped for the best and repeated herself one more time, quickly.

"Neetri!" she yelled in a furious panic. The crystal bowl met the floor and shattered, causing the contents to spill. The Horlix Blade fell and rolled off the table onto the floor. The plume of smoke dissipated. What was once noisy enough to vibrate her home had vanished and Lady Vixa was surrounded by silence. She picked up the blade and saw the dark purple fluid at her feet. Slowly walking around the table, Lady Vixa noticed the shards of crystal along the floor. She sighed, as it had been a gift from her father.

Taking a few more steps to examine what had become of the smoke plume, Lady Vixa froze in place, utterly shocked by what lay across her floor.

"Wh… are…" Vixa had never summoned one of the Saviors, but it appeared her attempt had been successful. Before her sat a pale figure, nearly ivory in color, but with a hint of blue. Though its head was lowered, Lady Vixa immediately noticed two protruding, crooked horns through the icy, shoulder-length hair. The rest of the body was covered in a blue and purple robe with intricate gold edges and symbols.

Suddenly, its head rose and locked its silver eyes with Lady Vixa's.

"Neetri?" Lady Vixa mustered. "Are you Neetri?" She noticed the Savior was female and smiled at her kind face, though she showed no emotion. Her button nose and pursed lips remained still longer than the Quorian Ruler expected.

"Yes, Lady Vixa, it is I. Your call was heard and accepted. How can I assist you?"

"We have an urgent matter involving one of our own and the Outer World," Lady Vixa informed the enchanted being.

"Horlix was wrong to build those gates…" Neetri revealed. She levitated herself and stood up beside the Quorian Ruler. Strangely enough, they were equal in height. "What has occurred?"

"Two younger quorians unknowingly escaped, but only one returned. Promit Grundimmer, the other one, was captured by two men."

"And what have you done so far?"

"That's why I summoned you." Lady Vixa admired Neetri's appearance, impressed by her height, presence and beauty.

"You've done *nothing*?" Neetri's soft voice was filled with disappointment. "Your father was right; you should have just married."

Lady Vixa shuddered as her words seemed more painful than Lord Erko's death. "I requested your assistance to help execute my plan," she rebutted, trying to hide her pain. "I cannot leave the city without jeopardizing our community. There hasn't been a quorian outside our city in fifteen-hundred years, the last being—"

"Sir Horlix," Neetri interrupted. "And you've bore no children?"

"No," Lady Vixa admitted, "and I don't plan to." There was an unspoken understanding between the two.

"So there is no successor in case…"

"I have an idea, but it's still too early," Lady Vixa replied. "If something were to happen to me, it would be chaotic. A quorian captured and their ruler dead…"

"Yes," Neetri agreed, looking back at Lady Vixa. "It would be troublesome." There was a short pause. Intimidation wasn't something Lady Vixa often felt, but Neetri's presence was so strong. Consuming. "So what's your plan?"

"As one of the Saviors, I know what your appearance is capable of," Lady Vixa admitted. "It would allow you to safely traverse the region, find the men who captured Promit and bring him home." Lady Vixa walked over to her corner desk. "I have a few—"

"You summoned me for something a simple enchantment could do? Ever create a metamorphic potion?" Neetri sneered, stopping a confident Quorian Ruler in her tracks.

"That'll alter an appearance once and remain the same for everyone. You know that's different than what you, a Savior, can do. With unlimited capabilities, you'll naturally appear as a familiar face to anyone who looks at you. Never the stranger, always trusted." As Quorian Ruler, Lady Vixa saw the Savior in her true form. "I need someone who can adapt into numerous environments and civilizations.

Better to prepare for the unexpected."

"I?" Neetri hissed, unamused by Lady Vixa's casual, yet arrogant, demeanor.

"We," she corrected. "We need your assistance in bringing Promit home safely. Not just for me, but for his family, his mother who has passed, and the entire city."

"What if something goes wrong? How do you plan to communicate? How do you plan to bring Promit home? What about gaining knowledge from my exploration?" The two stood there momentarily in silence. "There is far more than just me going out there to grab him. This is a serious matter, one I fear you haven't fully considered." Neetri walked around the room, acknowledging the mess Lady Vixa had made from the enchantment.

"First, next time you summon one of us, use less substance from the reservoir, it'll make for an easier cleanup." With the wave of her hand, Neetri cleared up the mess, leaving only The Horlix Blade, the Klai Chronicles, and her Amulet of Eymus on the table, which Lady Vixa quickly placed back around her neck. "Secondly, where do you keep the ancient relics? We'll need some assistance."

"In the corner desk over there." Lady Vixa pointed, following the Savior.

"That's not a very secure place for them."

"My home is secure, and it's a convenient spot."

Choosing not to respond, Neetri sensed the ancient relics in the bottom right drawer and pulled them out.

"Let's see." She observed them all. "Ah, this is perfect. I'll take the Klai's Eye," Neetri said, looking at Lady Vixa's uncertain face. Though smaller in size, the necklace replicated the appearance of King Klai's golden eye. With its scaly blue pigment, the outer ring was gold with veins approaching the eye. It was one of the oldest relics the Quorian Ruler had in her possession.

"It'll allow you to hear what I hear, see what I see. You'll be able to gain knowledge from my locations, see the regions, hopefully see the culprits, and eventually Promit," Neetri explained. By the look on Lady Vixa's face, she assumed the ruler had no idea of its ability. "Now I'll just create a quick metamorphic potion for Promit and I'll be on my way."

The two worked together, gathering the materials and ingredients necessary for the enchantment. They both knew the process and with Lady Vixa's abundance of Enchanted Reservoir water at her disposal, it didn't take long.

"Not to rush, but the sooner—"

"No need to explain." Neetri stopped her. "I think I remember my way down to the gate – fifth floor?" Lady Vixa nodded. "Perfect. In which region did the altercation happen? Where am I traveling to?"

"Tillerack," Lady Vixa recalled, having visited the gate to check the last known destination. "The Enchanted Gate should place you in the middle of the forest. Smolar, the quorian who escaped, told me all he could. There were two men, one slender and tall, the other more distinguishable. He stood around four-feet tall, crisp white hair and a scar on his face. He wielded the weapon they used to capture Promit."

Neetri paced around the room as she analyzed the information from Lady Vixa. "Perfect. This recently occurred, correct?"

"A couple days ago," Lady Vixa said.

"Then I should go. I shall leave at once and will keep you updated." Neetri had all she needed. Her mission was clear. She was about to walk out the door when Lady Vixa interjected.

"Wait, aren't you forgetting this?" Neetri turned and saw Lady Vixa with the key to the Enchanted Gate.

Neetri chuckled. "My dear, I've been around since well before those portals were created. I'll always have my personal access to traverse as I please." Lady Vixa lowered the key, placing it back on her table. "My knowledge of recent history is limited to the few times I was summoned, the last being from your father, Lord Erko." Lady Vixa's eyes curiously widened. "I know there were expectations and he's clearly left an impression on you. As a female ruler, I know it is a different role to upend compared to most. You have the passion, desire and intellect of your father. Ignite it. Follow the will of our king, and not the shame of your father." Neetri smiled and walked out the front door.

Stunned by the Savior's words, Lady Vixa froze in place. Now that a plan was set in motion, she knew it was time to address an overdue conversation – Promit's family. Lady Vixa didn't want rumors to spread throughout the city; however, she also couldn't admit the truth. She needed to ensure a sense of security for the family, yet portray an accurate depiction of when they could expect him home.

Smolar couldn't sleep much as he lay in bed, fiddling with the Bracelet of Fury. There were many questions he still had for Lady Vixa. *Who were those men? Why did they attack us? Where did they come from? How did she plan to save Promit?*

Riddled with insomnia, he threw on some clothes and raced toward the thirtieth floor. When he reached her home, he immediately stopped, noticing the front door open. Smolar followed his instincts and jumped behind one of the stalks, listening.

Peering around the corner, he saw a female quorian exit Lady Vixa's home and glide toward the elevator. Smolar questioned his sense of reality as he contemplated the possibility of seeing a ghost. His mind told him one thing, but he couldn't ignore what he had seen. Though it had been fifteen years since seeing her face, he would never forget what his mother looked like.

Nothing could stop him from rushing toward the elevator to reunite with his presumed-perished mother.

7

"Hello? Anyone home?" Catherine Emmerson-Cromwell opened the front door of her family's home. She hadn't seen anyone since the family meltdown days ago. Riddled with guilt, she'd been unable to sleep well the last few nights. Though justified in her opinion, she hated upsetting those she loved.

"Hello!?" she tried again, hearing a noise from the staircase.

"Hey, sister," Jacob responded from atop the stairs.

"Little brother." Catherine's tone softened. "How're you doing?"

"I'm alright. It's been an interesting few days." Jacob hesitated, sensing the awkwardness in the air. "How're you?"

She nodded as they both exchanged smiles. "I've been better." Catherine sighed. She deeply cared for her younger sibling. Being mindful of his anxiety, she decided to not unravel the events of dinner with him. "Do you know where Mom is?"

"I believe she's out in the garden," Jacob said. Each knew the other was saddened and apologetic for their behavior days prior, but Jacob sensed something more.

Shame. *Regret.*

Though she hadn't revealed anything, he felt it was related to how she treated her mother, considering she was becoming one herself.

Catherine walked through the pristine dining room and into the kitchen. Through the window, she noticed her mother working in the garden. Anna seemed at peace. While she rubbed her belly, Catherine took a deep breath and walked outside.

"Hey, Mom."

"Hello," Anna responded, without turning around. "How's it going?"

"Honestly, I haven't slept much."

"That makes two of us," Anna quickly rebutted, sticking her trowel in the soil. She stood up, turned around, and made eye contact with her daughter. The silence was deafening.

"My announcement didn't exactly go as I'd planned," Catherine said.

"No, I imagine not. I'm very happy for you two, I was just surprised."

"It was shocking to everyone. That's why we made the announcement."

"You never had a strong desire to have children, to be a mother. I was surprised to see you go down this path so early in life."

"I'm twenty-eight. I'm not a child."

"Yes, but if you never had a strong desire, then why start now?"

"Andrew and I have been together for years, have gotten married and are ready to have children."

"Are you ready, or is he?"

"How can you—"

"It's a fair question to ask, Catherine. You've never showed signs of wanting children or motherhood."

"I never said I didn't want children." She stopped herself from revealing her true fear of repeating and developing the same critical, tough love as her own mother. "I just wanted to experience life first." Catherine minimized her disappointment in her mother. She didn't want the conversation to escalate. "Once Andrew and I discussed the reality of children, we decided it was time. I didn't expect this to cause such turmoil."

Anna sensed her daughter felt overwhelmed. Uncertain if it was their discussion or her pregnancy, she sympathized. "Catherine, I apologize for any heartache I've caused." The two embraced for a quick moment. "I just want to make sure you agreed upon this momentous occasion for yourself and no one else."

"Of course, Mom." Even as she said the words, Catherine wondered if she had just lied to her mother.

"Just so much work to be done around here," Anna said in a jovial tone, returning to her garden. Catherine sighed, aware of her mother's discontent to continue the conversation.

"Would you like some help?"

"There's no need, thank you," she replied as her daughter gazed at her watch. "Everything okay? Do you have to go?"

"Actually, yes. Sorry." Catherine paused. "We're meeting a couple of friends for our reveal."

"How nice. Well, you don't want to be late."

"I love you, Mom."

"Love you too, Catherine."

Catherine made her way back toward the house, comforting her slight baby bump. Though relieved to converse with her mother, Catherine sensed it was a facade, and now her mother had inserted self-doubt into her mind. She pondered whether she and Andrew were foolish to take the leap.

"Leaving so soon?" Jacob asked, as Catherine neared the front door.

"Oh—" She paused, returning to reality. "Yes, sorry. We're meeting some friends to tell them the exciting news."

"I hope they handle it better than we did," he said with a chuckle. With a heavy heart, Catherine smiled and walked out of her family's home.

As the hot, dry sun beat down on her, Anna Emmerson gathered her belongings. She paused when she heard someone approaching from behind.

"Oof, it's hot! I'm shocked you're still here," Jacob said.

Anna chuckled. "I'm calling it a day. Much too hot." She turned and smiled at him. "Tomorrow, I'll pick up where I left off. This yard is in desperate need of color."

"It's beautiful."

"What're you up to?"

"Well, if you're done out here, any chance you'd want to pick up our conversation from earlier?"

"Which one?"

"Your experience. I want to know what it was about." Anna nodded, though hesitant to reveal her past if her assumptions were correct. She mentioned his father wouldn't be home for a couple hours, so they went inside to discuss.

Their living room was elegantly decorated with a candlelit fireplace, fresh flowers from the garden, a monstrous, yet stylish, piece of art from Anna's hometown of Prateria, and a black fireclay table with intricately-carved obsidian lion heads on the edges. The luxurious decor was overshadowed by the inordinate amount of family portraits, heirlooms, candles and miscellaneous trinkets, resulting in a warm and nurturing environment.

"So," Anna started from the corner of their elongated, white couch, "what would you like to know?"

"Well…" Jacob hesitated, sitting across from her. "Everything. I want to know anything you're willing to share."

"Okay, but be patient. It's been a while," she said. "Your father doesn't know any of this either. Only my mother knew, and now you."

"Oh. How come?"

"You know your father." She raised her eyebrows. "He doesn't follow this kind of stuff."

"You're right. Still…"

"You learn to save your energy after being married thirty years." They both chuckled.

"So," Jacob started, eager to learn his mother's story, "how old were you?"

"Twenty-one. Not too long after my birthday."

"You were still back home, weren't you?"

"Yes." Anna thought about that time. "My life completely changed after this vision."

Jacob felt his anxiety rise. "Sounds like this story would pair well with wine. Interested?" He stood up to pour a glass. Having restricted his alcohol consumption for nearly a week, he felt justified.

Anna chuckled. "Sure, red. Throw in a few ice cubes, please." He graciously poured them each a glass and returned to the living room. They clinked their glasses and took a sip.

"What do you remember?"

"Fire," Anna responded. "It's the first thing I see when I look back. In the beginning, I was on a concrete path that led to an open field. As I walked down, surrounded by light fog, I noticed low waves all around me, maybe a foot high, emanating from the ground. I instinctually knew it was fire, yet in that same moment realized there was no color."

"You too!" Jacob shouted. "But wait, how did you know it was fire without the color? The heat?"

"No, it was strange. There was no heat, but I knew. The motion of the waves with embers dissipating above, it was eerie." Anna took a sip from her glass, as she unraveled the details in her mind. "I walked to the end of the path, and stopped when I met the fire. Without heat, there was no physical warning to stop. I knelt down and placed my hand over the flame. There was no pain, no angst, no sensation.

"Examining the land up ahead, I realized there were numerous planter boxes, maybe a dozen or so. Varying in shapes and sizes, each contained a mixture of unfamiliar flowers and plants. They were beautiful. Though there was no color, I recognized the intricacies of the petals and flowers. I desperately wished to see their vibrant hues. The horticulture would've been mesmerizing." Anna broke eye contact with her son, envisioning her experience.

"That sounds incredible. It's a shame you couldn't see everything in its full glory."

"Yes, but I feel blessed to have seen what I did." Anna smiled.

Jacob took a swig from his glass and brought his legs up onto the chair, like his mother. "So, what did you do?"

"I looked at the nearest planter box and noticed an inscription along the top. Unfortunately, I was too far away to read it. All the boxes had symbols on them but none of them could be read from my location. Considering the fire had no effect on me, I decided to take a step forward."

"Into the flames?"

"Yes. It seemed strange, but my mind was curious. I had to make an attempt." There was a pause. "So I did. I placed one foot forward and felt no pain. Slowly, I placed my entire body into the flames. My body and clothing were a repellant… it was peculiar. Even more strange was when I turned around and the cement path I took had disappeared."

"Just… gone?"

"Yes. I had no choice but to place one foot in front of the other to see what would happen. When my entire body passed the threshold, I had a momentous realization." She paused for some wine. "Similar to how you described it, my own struggles and worries lifted off my shoulders. Instead of anxiety, I carried anger and resentment."

Though he knew his mother could be tough, Jacob was shocked to hear she struggled with anger.

"It was freeing, exciting. Similar to what you said, it was a euphoric feeling."

She paused, yearning for the sensation once more. "Before that moment, I hadn't realized I suppressed such feelings. I'd carried it around long enough that I had become accustomed to it."

"Isn't it a surreal feeling?" Jacob added. "Letting go of burdens you didn't know existed…" He paused, struggling to discuss raw, real emotions with his mother.

"It was a teachable moment…" Anna lingered with resentment. "A moment I wish I'd appreciated at the time. Unfortunately, that wasn't the case." She took a deep breath and moved past her emotional admission. "Having a sense of safety within the flames, I went to the nearest planter box and examined the flowers. The inscription was in an unfamiliar language. I assumed it was to identify the various vegetation. I examined what was inside the box and recognized a flower.

"It was like a Calla Lily; however, it had two rounded petals, wrapped around one another. The inner looked smooth and silky, unsurprisingly, but the outer seemed rigid, rough. I grabbed the flower by the stem to examine it closer. Unfortunately, I hadn't noticed the small, unsuspecting thorns along it. As prickly as a rose. I pulled back as the sharp thorn stabbed my index finger." Anna rubbed her thumb and finger together, blankly staring at them. She could still feel the sting.

"Did it hurt?" Jacob asked.

"Yes, but there was no emotional connection with the pain. I never felt frustrated or angry. I watched the colorless blood drop from my finger." Anna allowed herself a moment to reminisce before she progressed.

"There were two rows of planter boxes along each side of me. It was apparent someone took great care of the plants, especially with how unique they appeared. One box held a tree, very tall and slender with only wilted leaves at the top. To my left was a container for a thick vine or twisted trunk of sorts. I want to say it was a tree, but I couldn't be certain. It grew straight up, in a spiral fashion, and came to a point, which didn't seem too sharp. Another had dozens of small flowers that must have been an arrangement of colors." Anna sighed. "I really wish they'd been in color…"

"Did you ever have the chance to go back?" Jacob blurted out. Subconsciously, he wanted to return to his own experience and hoped his mother would provide some insight.

"Unfortunately, no. It was the only time I traveled there."

"Oh."

"Remember, I was young. I didn't have a strong desire to do so."

"Why not? Seems like a paradise of flowers for you."

"You're right, but there's more to the story."

"Of course." Jacob chuckled and sipped again.

"Once I reached the end of the fiery field, my attention was drawn to what was ahead. Seemingly out of nowhere, a massive building was off in the distance. The way you described the structure in your experience reminded me of this one. Unfortunately, there was a large wall of flames that blocked the entryway. Unlike the ones I stood in, they roared well above my height. It was intimidating even without the color or heat." Anna paused. "I stood in the field for a moment, examining the sight, when I noticed a man beside the home. I don't remember any details due to the distance, but I knew he was looking at me. *I could feel it,*" Anna hissed to her son.

"Did he say anything?" Jacob wondered if it was the same figure in his vision.

"Nope, not one word. He was surrounded by flames, somewhere between the field and the building. Curious, I walked in his direction. Eventually, I returned to a new cobblestone path and immediately felt heavier with each step. Realizing the emotional burden had returned, I became aggravated with the man in the distance."

"What did he do?"

"Nothing, but I felt as though he was playing games. I walked toward him to inquire more, but halfway there, the flames around the stranger grew extremely high. They roared for a moment until they crashed down, revealing an empty ring of fire. Somehow, he'd disappeared. When I turned toward the open field with bustling plants, they were gone. No planter boxes, no trees, no flowers. All that remained was the open, fiery field. I approached it, wondering if I could see anything, but this time I felt the heat. The flames were roaring and I couldn't go back." Anna waited, envisioning the memory. "It was scary."

"I could only imagine…" Jacob empathized. Mother and son simultaneously sipped their wine, though Jacob nearly finished his glass. "So what else?" he asked.

"That's really it." She shrugged. "Between the heat from the various fires, I was sweating. I wanted out."

"So you left?"

"Well, yes. It was as if I was looking down on the experience, able to leave when I wanted. Once I became uncomfortable, it was time to go. "

Jacob sat for a moment, observing his empty wine glass. "Aside from our departures from this place, our experiences were too similar to be a coincidence." He felt validated in his thoughts. "What're the chances?"

Anna shrugged in acknowledgement. "I'm glad we had this chat. It's been many years since I thought about it. Even more since I've discussed it."

"When was the last time you told someone the story?"

"My grandmother, your great grandmother. We vaguely discussed it because she, too, had an experience of her own."

"What!?" Jacob was flabbergasted. Now three members had shared similar experiences. "Okay, how is this not discussed in our family?" Anna remained quiet. "Did she tell you about hers?"

"She shared details but it was many years ago, I honestly couldn't recall the story." Anna thought for a moment, brushing her brown hair with her fingers, as if to help her brain recall. "It may have involved the ocean? Maybe?" She tilted her head. "I don't know, sorry, son."

"How about your mother? Did she—"

"No, she never mentioned anything," Anna said abruptly.

"Okay…"

While he could've spoken on the subject for hours, Anna closed the conversation, which he respectfully obliged. The discussion far surpassed his expectations. While he accepted his great grandmother's story may forever be lost, he reminded himself of the wisdom he'd learned about his mother's experience and their apparent family tradition.

8

It had been over a century since Neetri had walked through The Quo. She wasn't sure she'd ever get the chance to meet Lady Vixa, or if she ever wanted to. Though fond of her father, Lord Erko, Neetri was disheartened by his stance on female rulers. She never supported the idea only males could claim the title, so she feared what it would mean for Lady Vixa's reign. Though the power she harnessed was different than the Quorian Ruler, she, a female Savior, felt she was a good example of how a female could explore her power gracefully. Neetri knew it wasn't appropriate to voice her opinion, but she felt a responsibility to remind Lady Vixa of her inner strength.

Silencing her subconscious, she focused on the rescue mission – travel to the region of Tillerack, find the two men and rescue Promit. Just as the elevator doors were about to close, a stranger squeezed through into the carriage.

"Floor… one… please…" he said, breathing heavily.

Neetri glanced quickly and pressed the button. She stepped aside as they began their descent.

Smolar looked up at the quorian, startled to see his mother looking down on him. He was trembling in confusion. All he wanted to do was shout and hug her, but he needed to understand the situation.

"Sorry," he said, catching his breath. "Thank you." Neetri nodded with a disinterested expression. "What's your name?"

"Erva." Neetri hesitated, not expecting to speak with anyone.

"Nice to meet you, Erva." Smolar said her name with an inquisitive tone. It wasn't his mother's name, so he tried another tactic. "I'm Smolar." He carefully watched her face for a reaction, but there was nothing. Neetri nodded and the two stood at opposite ends of the carriage.

Smolar remained in the back corner, perplexed. Her appearance, stance and demeanor were identical to his mother, but her tone and name were different. In conversation, there was nothing that triggered him to assume it was her and she seemed unfazed by his name, which he knew wasn't very common. He remained silent, glancing to see her destination was the fifth floor.

19... 18... 17...

DING.

The shaft stopped and multiple quorians entered, giving Neetri and Smolar further separation. He avoided the other quorians, keeping his focus on her. The doors shut and they descended again.

16... 15... 14...

"Smolar!" a familiar voice shouted. He noticed Erva didn't react. "How's it going?" A sweet, bubbly quorian tugged on his right arm and spoke in a high-pitched tone.

"H-hey, Fravia," he mustered, distractedly. Erva was looking ahead, with her head down.

"H-h-h-h-hey there? That's all I get?" she imitated, causing him to grin.

"Hi, Fravia," Smolar bashfully corrected himself, pulling her close to him. "Sorry, I'm on a mission," he whispered.

"Ooh, what're we doing?"

7... 6... 5...

DING.

The door opened and Erva shuffled to exit. Smolar glanced at his friend and back toward the quorian resembling his mother.

"We'll catch up later," he suggested, exiting the car.

"You're up to something, Smolar. Don't think I'm leaving you to handle this on your own," she replied. Fravia Deallius was slightly shorter than him, a powder-blue pigment, silver eyes and flowing white hair that almost covered the left side of her face. Glancing at the quorian Smolar was focused on, a puzzled Fravia darted her eyes between the two, noting the resemblance.

Knowing she wouldn't let up, Smolar sighed. The two squeezed through the crowd and scurried along the pathway, remaining hidden.

Being the location of Restaurant Alley, the fifth floor typically had heavy traffic. Children played amidst crowds of hungry quorians and intoxicating aromas. The smell of sweet fruits and savory juices distracted Fravia from their target. Fortunately, Smolar remained focused. Knowing she'd be disappointed to be separated, he grabbed Fravia's hand and steadily moved forward.

"Why are you following that—"

"I'll explain after," Smolar interrupted. In their five years as friends, Fravia hadn't seen him so entranced.

"There seems to be a resemblance between—"

"I know. I'm still trying to figure it out myself," he interrupted again. "It's just someone I saw Lady Vixa speaking with."

Suddenly, Smolar noticed Erva stop at the end of a pathway near a familiar pile of rubble. The two jolted behind a supporting stalk, secretly observing their target.

"That pile…" he whispered to her. "That's where—"

"—the gate is located," Fravia interjected, surprising Smolar. "Oh come now," she said with a smile. "Did you really think *I* wasn't aware of the Enchanted Gate? It was created by Horlix, you know." A cerebral visitor to the quorian library, Fravia proudly showcased her vast knowledge of quorian history.

Smolar laughed.

The stranger looked around and casually walked behind the debris. Smolar followed, with Fravia behind. He moved with a purpose, yet slow enough to not cause a commotion. Once they approached the rubble, he checked his surroundings, ensuring no one was watching them, and moved swiftly to the other side with Fravia.

The space between the gate and the rubble was small. There was nowhere to hide.

"Where did…?"

"She's gone," Smolar interrupted. "She left."

"She?" Fravia asked in a perplexed tone.

"Yes," he said, examining the walls.

Unlike the city's entrance, the inner gate wasn't as convoluted. Though still plastered with scribblings, illegible for Fravia and Smolar, there weren't dozens of questionable holes for them to place their hands into.

"But didn't you notice how—"

"Hmph."

Noticeably ignored, Fravia didn't finish her sentence. Smolar looked toward the center of the gate and put his hand over the small, circular indentation. He scowled, realizing the key hadn't been recently activated.

"What? Did you find something?" Fravia wondered, slightly agitated by his disinterest in her.

"No, I was just feeling around," he murmured, having never been a good liar.

With a heavy sigh, Fravia smirked. "Looking for the *key*?" Smolar widened his eyes in surprise, partially disappointed. "Hehe… you forgot how much I know."

Defeated and outsmarted, Smolar confessed. "Fine, I was. I—"

"Hah! I knew it!" Fravia exclaimed, jumping in place. "I knew it was true."

"I-I thought you already knew?"

"I had a hunch, but you confirmed it." She smiled and pointed. "Wait! That means you've seen it?" Fravia entered Smolar's personal bubble. "What does it look like? Oh, I bet it is as beautiful as this gate. No, probably better!" She admired the gate, wondering of the key's appearance.

"You played me, well done." He sighed as a jolt of confidence overcame him. "Although…"

"What?"

Smolar turned to her with a witty smile. "Now *I* have knowledge about something *you* don't." As he entered her personal space, she welcomed it, yearning for his presence. "I know what the key looks like. I've seen it with my own eyes and felt it with my own hands." Fravia gasped. Suddenly, Smolar understood the addiction, the power. Wielding important information placed him in a persuasive position, and Fravia was exactly the ally he needed.

"Then let me help you," she insisted. "I'll help you find out who *that* was, and in return, you can show me the key, deal?" She gleamed at him with an intoxicating smile he couldn't refuse. Smolar glanced down at his Bracelet of Fury, uncertain he'd ever be able to access the key from Lady Vixa's home again. He looked back up at her gentle eyes and decided he'd find a way. Smolar needed to know why there was a doppelgänger of his mother roaming the city.

"Done," he said with a wink. "Now how do you suggest we learn anything?"

"Where else but the Quorian Library, of course," Fravia joyfully explained. "Filled with knowledge beyond your wildest imagination. All our answers are there… we just need to find them."

"But of course." Smolar chuckled. "It'll be like finding a needle in a haystack… blind."

"You'd be surprised what can be revealed when surrounded by a wealth of knowledge."

As Lady Vixa left the Grundimmer residence to return home, she remained confident in her plan. Unfortunately, it was accompanied by sadness and concern. The conversation with Promit's father went well, but there was an unexpected shift. Lady Vixa made sure to keep an open mind, aware Promit's family could react in a multitude of ways, yet was ill prepared for what had happened.

Upon her arrival, Promit's father and little sister answered the door. She sensed his curiosity and the little one's excitement, but he graciously welcomed her inside. Their home was warm, small, and comfortable. It wasn't filled with extravagant items or excessive decor, yet had all the necessities needed in a home. As Lady Vixa walked toward the couch to discuss, she noticed a framed photo of three quorians. First was his father, who appeared younger and happy. Beside him stood a young Promit, embracing his father tightly. The third individual was a pregnant female, closer in age to his father.

She remembered Promit's mother died giving birth to his younger sister. Lady Vixa felt sympathy for the family – those who were present and captured. She sensed the happiness and love from the photo, and it saddened her to see such a drastic shift amongst the family dynamic. In her mind, she understood their pain as she longed for more time with her father.

When the two quorians and their ruler sat in the living room, the inquisition began. Promit's father asked a barrage of questions, many of which any would ask if given the opportunity with the Quorian Ruler. Unusually, few of them involved his son's disappearance.

There was a shift when Lady Vixa brought up Promit, and the *mission* she had recruited him for. His curiosity dwindled. The questions slowed. She felt the need to purge the information from her mind to ensure he understood the story she wished to portray. Though he asked if Promit was safe and would return home soon, he didn't ask any follow-up questions. Lady Vixa was tempted to admit the truth, simply for a reaction, but knew that wasn't wise.

Ultimately, she kept the details vague and suggested that Promit and Smolar were both working on a secret, yet secure, mission. She informed Promit's father that his son should be back home *soon*, but only after they successfully completed the task. He accepted the information without hesitation or question.

As she approached the front door of her house, Lady Vixa felt a deeper sense of responsibility to ensure Promit's safe return. It had nothing to do with her being the ruler. She couldn't fathom that his only remaining parent cared less about his safety than she did – a complete stranger. If she was able to recognize it, she sensed Promit felt the lack of affection too.

Smolar found himself inside the Quorian Library – a place he seldom visited. Having lived with Lady Vixa and missing his own parents, he never felt a deep connection to indulge in the history of the quorian race.

Located on the fourteenth floor, the hallways were well lit with thousands of delicate books. A suitable size for a quorian structure, it was nearly impossible to get lost in the library. The rows were categorized by genre, and with how often Fravia had visited, she knew exactly where they needed to go.

The two had been friends for nearly five years and had vastly different minds.. Smolar had an excitement for exploration and the world outside the city. Fravia, though curious about the outside world too, had a passion for her quorian community, made apparent as she gleamed walking through the tall hallways. She considered knowledge a compelling weapon.

"If we plan to find out anything, we should consider what we know so far," Fravia suggested, beside an elongated table in the history section.

"Right," Smolar replied, pondering for a moment. "There's a connection with Lady Vixa. She had the knowledge and means to access the Enchanted Gate…" Fravia removed a book titled *Hidden Away* from the shelf and placed it onto the table. "Then the obvious, more startling concern for me, is her appearance."

"Finally, yes. We need to discuss why you're referring to—"

"She's nearly identical to my mother," he interrupted.

"Wait… what?" She turned around. "Your mother!?"

"Yes, I know you didn't know her but—"

"That quorian was the spitting image of *you*, Smolar. Not your mother."

"What!?" he shouted, momentarily forgetting his environment.

"Hey," a voice loudly whispered from around the corner. "You have got to be qu—" He stopped as his eyes gazed upon Fravia. "Oh! Ms. Deallius, it's you." He grinned.

"Gemery," Fravia replied, her voice increasing an octave. "Always a pleasure to see you. I apologize for my friend's ignorance." She turned to Smolar, chuckled and winked. "Sometimes I can't take him anywhere. I'll make sure he's more respectful toward the storytellers around us."

"Thank you." He nodded, staring at Smolar just long enough to express his disapproval of his presence. "Is there anything I can help you find?"

"Not today. I'm just helping a friend become educated with some unfamiliar quorian history." She smiled coyly. Smolar was impressed by how quickly she adjusted the narrative. Gemery's face slightly sulked at losing the chance to help her, so she left him with hope. "If something comes up though, you know I'll come to you."

"Alright, sounds great." Gemery's smile returned as he left them alone. Fravia looked back at Smolar to resume their conversation in a quieter tone.

"Seems like you have an admirer," Smolar suggested.

"Oh please." Fravia disregarded the comment. "Back to our disagreement, are you certain of who you saw?"

"If you're asking me if I'd forgotten what my mother—"

"No." Fravia halted his implication. "I just… I know what I saw and you know what you saw. How could they be so starkly different?"

"I don't know…" Smolar wondered. "For the record, I know it wasn't her. Not only because she died many years ago, but when she spoke, her voice was different."

"You spoke to her?"

"Yes, before you met me in the elevator. She said her name was Erva."

"Erva? What a unique name… but that's the type of information we should gather for our research. Is there *anything* else you can recall that could be helpful?" Fravia asked, eyeing another book from across the table.

The Greatest Loss.

Smolar knew there was one more piece of information worth sharing – that the stranger hadn't used the key to access the gate. After he and Promit experimented, they noticed the keyhole presented a subtle glow for a short while. But revealing this information meant admitting blame for Promit's captivity. Smolar contemplated how important it could be.

"Smolar?" Fravia asked, noticing his daze. "Everything okay?"

"Well..." he stuttered. Though difficult to confess, Smolar refused to keep making bad choices, possibly further harming Promit. Terrified how she may react, he needed to do all he could to right his shameful wrong.

"What is it? Did you remember something?"

"There is one more thing, but it's kind of a long story. You should take a seat."

Both quorians sat down at the table with the couple books she had already removed. With a deep breath, Smolar disclosed everything that had happened. The initial exploration, the second adventure, Promit's unknown condition and the discussion with Lady Vixa, displaying the Bracelet of Fury she'd given him as a punishment. She was astonished at what had happened, uncertain of what to say.

"I wondered where that piece of jewelry came from," she said, looking at Smolar with shameful eyes. Fravia sensed his pain and decided against reprimanding him. "Do you think this stranger is linked to the situation with Promit or no?"

"I suppose it's possible, but I don't know. There's no reason to think so. This is only happening because her appearance was identical to my mother." He sighed. "For all we know, this stranger could be devious, with Lady Vixa unaware of the danger." The possibility that danger had entered their sacred city startled them both.

"Thank you for being honest with me, Smolar." She held his hand across the table. "You know I'm always here for you." The two shared a touching moment that Fravia was excited to finally have and Smolar didn't realize he needed.

"I appreciate it," he said defeatedly. "I appreciate you, Fravia."

"Well then," Fravia broke the silence that had briefly settled, hoping to lift Smolar's spirits and confidence. "Let's get moving and get to the bottom of this."

"Yes."

"So to recap what we know,"—she stood—"this... stranger, who called itself Erva, could be male or female with an unconfirmed appearance, knew Lady Vixa and had access to the Enchanted Gate without means of a key. Is that everything?"

Smolar reviewed the details, confirming he had nothing else to add.

"Alright, well it's something. I'm not sure Erva is its actual name, but I don't recall it within the historical section. Regardless, we should keep an eye out for it. Lady Vixa probably has the answers we're searching for, but I'd imagine that's not a route you're looking to go?"

"Ideally not. She's not too happy with me right now." He shook his wrist, jingling the bracelet.

"Then we have two questions to answer. Who has access to the gate without a key, and who can appear differently amongst quorians? If we can answer these questions while remembering the possibility of the name Erva, we should be able to get a better idea who, or what, we saw."

"Where should we start?" Smolar asked, sounding hopeful with Fravia's positive attitude.

"I've pulled a couple books already involving quorian history. Start browsing through them for anything that could relate while I gather a few more options."

As he cracked open *The Greatest Loss*, which heavily discussed the events between King Klai and the Divinity King, Fravia scanned the shelves with purpose.

"That must've been a sight to see," he said.

"What, exactly?" she asked. "Watching the death of our innocent King or having everyone you ever knew and loved murdered in an attempted genocide?"

"You know what I mean," he objected, remembering the War of Kings was a sensitive subject for her.

"I know," she said, lightening up. "I just can't imagine how those survivors – Saviors – felt. They were children. Running for their lives, leaving their loved ones to be murdered. In a single, catastrophic event, they gave up their freedom and entered a period of suppression, one that we still live in." Fravia halted and grabbed another book from the shelf, placing it on the table.

Leaders Long Gone.

"Interesting title," Smolar said, changing the subject. "What made you grab that one?"

"It has an insurmountable amount of information, as you can tell from the size. To learn more about the Enchanted Gate, why not read about the quorian who created it?" Fravia shrugged.

"You clever little…" He chuckled. "Goodbye King Klai, Divinity and the pure bloods. Hello Sir Horlix." He closed *The Greatest Loss* to inspect the tome she'd laid before him.

"Well, well… look who knows his history."

"Some of the stuff you tell me sticks," he said, then snickered.

The two quorians remained silent for a moment as each of them skimmed their respective sections – Smolar for Horlix and Fravia for any relevant book titles. There was an abundance of resources, but they didn't have time to browse them all. As she rounded the corner to another row of historical knowledge, Smolar located the right section.

"It's unfortunate for his son that Sir Horlix was never found," Smolar whispered, but when he looked up, he realized Fravia had wandered off for more books.

As he continued to read, Fravia stood alone in the hall scanning for relevant books. With a discouraged sigh, she was uncertain which would be worth spending their efforts on. Pulling a book off the shelf, she felt a hand on her shoulder

"Hey." Though the voice was familiar, she was easily startled.

"Gemery." She giggled. "Hello."

"I'm so sorry, Ms. Deallius. I didn't mean to frighten you."

"Me? Never." She laughed. "And as I always tell you, please call me Fravia."

"Of course, Fravia." He bowed slightly. "Still seeking answers, I presume?"

"Yeah… unfortunately it may take some time."

"Maybe I can help," he suggested. Though he welcomed the idea of Fravia in the library for extended periods of time, he wanted to help her.

"I don't think so." She paused, reviewing all the details and explanations it would take in her mind. "There's too much to explain and yet the topic is still too vague."

"I may not be able to provide the answers you seek, but I know who would." His reassuring smile intrigued Fravia, as it wasn't a look she'd seen before.

"Oh?"

"Yes. Please follow me," Gemery said, excited to be in a position to privately help Fravia.

He led the way down the corridor, passing other halls of books, one of them being where Smolar sat. Without saying a word, Fravia waved her hands to get his attention. When he looked up, she placed her finger to her lips to ensure his silence and instructed him to follow.

The devoted librarian looked back and smiled at Fravia, which she returned, before turning around. Smolar appeared behind her shortly after.

Gemery had worked at the Quorian Library for as long as Fravia could remember. Tall and skinny with a kind face and gentle touch, she considered him quite handsome. Had her heart not already been smitten by the longing love she had for the quorian behind her, she may have been able to envision herself with him. Fravia found intellect and knowledge very appealing.

He entered the non-fiction section in search of one title in particular. "It should be right... around... here." He stopped to gaze at the book. "This is it." Smiling at Fravia, he noticed the two were no longer alone and scowled.

"The questions we're seeking involve him," Fravia said, batting her eyes. Though clearly displeased, Gemery continued to assist the two on their quest for answers. He removed the book from the shelf and opened it to page forty-seven.

"*Legacies and Legends,*" she whispered. "I haven't heard of that before. Sounds more like fiction?"

"It's exactly where it's meant to be." He smiled. "Now hold hands," he instructed, linking with Fravia's right hand as her left clutched Smolar's.

After Gemery mumbled a few words, *Legacies and Legends* slammed to the floor as the group of three turned from a solid state of matter into gas and were sent into the book, slamming it shut behind them. With no one present around, the book levitated off the ground and returned to its place on the upper shelf of the non-fiction section.

They'd been transported into a narrow, dark blue corridor with gold illuminating from the other end. Rusted candlesticks lined the walls with small flames, providing just enough light to brighten their path.

"Follow me," Gemery instructed as he traversed down the staircase. Fravia and Smolar made sure to walk behind the slender librarian.

"How did we—"

"I'm not sure," she interrupted.

"Where are we—"

"I don't know."

"Did you know about this?"

"No, I never knew this existed." Fravia directed her attention to Gemery. "Where are you taking us?" Unfortunately, he didn't respond, though he heard the entire conversation behind him.

After their short descent, they arrived in a tall, but small, chamber.

"Welcome to the Hall of Antiquity," Gemery announced. "Home to some of the most archaic and timeworn records in the quorian community and beyond."

The towering, candlelit space was narrow, yet illuminated the books below. Two rows of thickly-bound books upon glistening golden shelves were split between the side walls. Fravia and Smolar looked at one another, stunned.

"There must be a hundred books in here," Smolar said.

"Eighty-four to be exact. Forty-two on each side," Gemery informed his guests. Fravia took only a step forward when he put his arm out. "You may each only choose one, so be wise."

"How do you—"

"*One.* That is all." Fravia had never seen Gemery be demanding before. She found it refreshing. "Nothing leaves this room. Read their titles, consider your options and choose your weapon. Instead of searching within the book for an answer, allow the book to search within you for the question."

Fravia stared at Gemery, wondering where this other personality had been hiding. Smolar walked toward the right while Fravia veered left. They began reading the first few titles aloud.

"*King Klai's Death,*" Fravia said, instinctually reaching out to grab it.

"You may only choose one, Fravia," Gemery gently reminded her. "You may want to read the other titles before making a decision." She listened and realized how difficult the choice would be.

"*Female Quorian Rulers,*" Smolar read aloud, thinking of Lady Vixa.

"*Locating The Telepathy Stone?*" Fravia wondered. "I don't even know that that is…"

"*Infiltrating The Great Barrier,*" Smolar said. "These books cover a variety of topics."

"I thought the answer to our questions would be here?" Fravia asked Gemery. "How do you know we will find what we're—"

"Keep looking, both of you. You will know when you see it." Gemery retreated into the hallway, giving them their privacy. They continued walking down the hall, reading the titles of their books. Both were uncertain why the librarian had brought them there until Smolar read a peculiar title.

"*Divinity's Return.*" The implication caused both quorians to shudder. "He came back?" Smolar wondered, intrigued at the thought.

"Yes." Fravia turned to respond. "Many years ago. After hiding from his murderous rampage, there were whispers that he'd returned to the land he once ruled." The two fell silent for a moment. "Now that you mention it, I remember reading something a while ago…"

"What?" Smolar turned to her.

"It was questioned whether Divinity's return was the reason Sir Horlix even created the gates."

"Wasn't it to expand the city, or research or something?"

"It's generally accepted Sir Horlix wanted to gain more knowledge about the Outer World for the sake of quorian survival, but apparently, he was a very quiet ruler. He did what he wanted, when he wanted, and often without explanation. This style of leadership fans the flames for rumors and whispers to spread."

Standing in the darkened corner, Gemery turned his body to hide his smile from Fravia's impressive wealth of knowledge.

"Was there ever proof Divinity did return?" Smolar asked.

"I… I'm not sure."

With both of their mind's curious about Divinity's return, their conversation fell silent as they returned to each of the titles to browse through.

"*Unlocking the Enchanted Gate,*" Fravia whispered to Smolar. "This may be the answer."

"You heard what he said," Smolar reminded her. "Go through them all first." He leaned toward her, making sure to whisper. "Technically we don't need to unlock it. We need to know how one can pass through without the key." Fravia nodded, thankful for Smolar's level-headed mind. Her passion for books and knowledge brought temptation with each title she read.

"*Where Are The Purists Today?*" Smolar read. "The purists... as in the traditional pure bloods? The Saviors? Where are they *today*? I'd imagine they're long dead."

"*The Original Enchanted Gate of Pritus*," Fravia read.

She couldn't shake the feeling that was the book she was meant to choose, even though she'd never heard of the name before, but Fravia continued reading, as instructed twice already.

Both quorians noticed a shift in the titles. Instead of discussing quorian folklore and history, the names were more unique – personalized.

"*Your Passion of Knowledge*," Fravia read aloud in an inquisitive tone.

"*A Caretaker's Mission.*"

They both decided to stop reading the remaining titles aloud, as they were obviously meant for their eyes only. Each of them looked over their shoulder a couple times, ensuring their privacy, unaware the other was just as captivated by their own titles.

Your Parent's True Passion. A Quorian's Role. A Heart-y Love.

Fravia understood the power behind the Hall of Antiquity as she was compelled to pick up each title, particularly the last one she saw – *Fravia's Legacy*. She found it unsettling to see her name embedded in a book. As much as it pained her, she knew it wasn't time to read its contents.

Smolar stood quietly, nearly frightened by the titles he'd seen before him.

Your Admirer. A Haunting Message. Lady Vixa's Dark Secret. Promit's Fate.

Each of the names implied answers to many questions he yearned to know but wasn't courageous enough to find out. His masochistic curiosities forced him to continue reading until he arrived at the end and gasped.

What Really Happened to Your Parents.

Smolar instinctively reached out and placed his hand on the spine of the final title.

"Smolar!" Fravia said, halting him. "We should discuss the title you're choosing if you wish to find resolution."

"The one in my hand will provide me with more resolution than anything else here." He'd rarely spoken of his parents, though he thought about them daily. Lady Vixa had privately revealed to him the truth about that night. Smolar trusted her explanation, but being faced with the question awoke something within him he didn't know existed.

"Please." She grabbed his arm. With a sigh, Smolar released the book. Fravia glanced at the spine of the novel he had nearly selected – it was blank. "I can't read the titles meant for you. They're all blank."

"Oh?" Smolar was surprised, but relieved. He wasn't looking to discuss the matter of his parents and that night.

"What was it?" she asked.

"Nothing, you were right. We have to evaluate them all and decide which one has the answer we seek." Smolar moved away from the personal titles and into the historical ones, which Fravia was able to read. As they scanned the titles, Smolar found himself distracted by the book he nearly chose. His mind roamed with endless possibilities and he knew he'd have to confront the Quorian Ruler at some point.

"This one…" Fravia pointed towards a familiar title.

"*Where Are The Purists Today?*" Smolar read. "What makes you say that?" Fravia returned to her side of the room and scanned the names. She asked Gemery what to do when they'd decided.

"Pick it up and read what's inside," he said, smiling. Without consulting Smolar, she picked *The Original Enchanted Gate of Pritus* and opened it. To her surprise, the book didn't have a large amount of history. There weren't pages of information to scan through or an index to search. There was just one sentence for her to read. Her eyes widened.

"Fravia... what is it?" Smolar asked. She looked up at Gemery and then back to Smolar.

"*Where Are The Purists Today?*" she said. "Choose that. Open it and read its inscription." He followed her instruction.

"One to twenty to be summoned by the ruler, their appearance they adjust to protect and maneuver."

Both Fravia and Smolar stood on each side of the room, wielding their chosen titles to solve the identity of the stranger who vanished. Aware of both inscriptions, Fravia knew they'd found their answer, as unbelievable as it was.

"What does yours say?" Smolar asked. She looked down and repeated what had already been engraved in her memory.

"Though an anagram may mask, the purist don't have to ask."

9

Rubbing his eyes from the morning sun, Mortimer knew the events from the night prior weren't a dream. There'd been moments he wanted to analyze and others he wished to forget. He initially felt the responsibility to leave, but with Vanilor fast asleep, he turned to relive the night.

Mortimer brought his left hand to his lips. The kiss excited him, distracting him from the Novalis Rod or the quorian within. It had been a couple years since he'd shared that with a woman, but never with a man. He had no attraction toward Vanilor, or any man for that matter, *so why Michael?* Uncertain of what to do, Mortimer rubbed his right temple as a headache began to slither its way from the back of his head to the front. He grunted.

Mortimer didn't expect to return with Michael's stolen car and find Vanilor inside THE Bar. He knew they should have gotten on the road, but his heavily intoxicated partner suggested drinking, to which he agreed. The one glass quieted Mortimer's inner voice. After an unknown amount of time and endless amount of wine, Vanilor and Mortimer found themselves outside the bar with nowhere to go.

"We can't drive," Mortimer said.

"Ahh, fuck it. You… you…" Vanilor staggered. "You drive."

"Fuck off," Mortimer whined, holding himself up against the wall. They agreed it wasn't worth destroying their only means of returning home, so they found a hotel and stayed the night. The two men shared one room with two beds and decided to leave at sunrise.

Mortimer hissed as a sharp pain ran along the right side of his head. He conceded and rolled out of bed to grab some medication from the bathroom. The noise startled Vanilor.

"What the fuck!?" Vanilor shouted, as he strained to look at Mortimer. "What're you doin'?"

"Grabbing some meds. Too much shitty alcohol," Mortimer responded. Vanilor heard the rattling of pills.

"Damn," Vanilor murmured, noticing the time. "Grab me a few, won't ya? We gotta get on the road."

"Sure." He shook a couple extra pills into his hand as he stared out the bathroom window. Their room was on the second floor, overlooking the street below. The Northern Forest was off in the distance. Though beautiful, he was relieved they'd be leaving soon. Just as he lowered his gaze, Mortimer noticed someone standing alone on the street. The familiar face had black hair, a dark complexion and was clean shaven. He wore a red-and-black checkered shirt with brown pants.

Mortimer panicked. "How the…?"

The figure looked like Michael. As he pressed against the window for a closer look, Vanilor shouted from the other room.

"You get lost in there? The fuck are you?" Mortimer jumped. He hastily returned to Vanilor and handed him the medicine.

"Here ya go, you son of a bitch." Returning the medication to the bathroom, Mortimer surveyed the surroundings, but the stranger had vanished. Though it looked like Michael, he couldn't imagine it feasible. He swallowed the pills, along with his concern, and began to pack his belongings.

When Vanilor went to shower the celebratory stench off his body, Mortimer gazed upon the satchel housing the Novalis Rod. He wondered about the creature within, sympathizing for what it must be feeling. Presumably in pain and terrified. Mortimer cocked his head as a small wave of guilt entered his mind. Not only had they taken him from a friend, but the creature had no idea where he was or what had happened. Looking out the window at Tillerack, Mortimer sighed.

"The fuck you looking at?" Vanilor hissed.

"Just this town and what we've done." Mortimer struggled to hide the guilt.

"Think of the riches, man. We're set for life," his power-hungry partner said. Mortimer grunted in response, displeased with his outlook on the situation. Noticing Mortimer's tone, Vanilor returned to the bathroom to get ready. He was too excited to let anyone hinder his happiness. Bare chested and hair still wet, he looked at himself in the mirror and smiled.

"You rich fuck," Vanilor said to his reflection. Considering wealth a necessity in life, all he wanted to do was rush home and present their success to Brugōr.

He slipped his arms through his brown buttoned shirt, maintaining his gaze in the mirror. While placing his pants on, Vanilor became unsteady and slammed his right shoulder against the wall. After pulling them up, he glanced outside the window. Two stories below stood a familiarly large man with garments similar to those worn in The Barren Land.

At first, the stranger was looking directly ahead, but then he raised his gaze and immediately locked eyes with Vanilor. Brugōr.

Vanilor opened the window. "Sir? What're you doing here!?" He shouted, but there was no response.

"What?" Mortimer asked from the other room. "Who are you talking to?"

"You won't believe who's here." Vanilor turned to look at Mortimer. "I wonder if word got back to him because it seems Br—" He stopped.

"What happened? Why'd you—"

"The fuck. Where'd he go!?" Vanilor hurled his body forward, out the window, to survey the ground below. The man he believed to be Brugōr had vanished without a trace.

"Did you see Michael too!?" Mortimer asked, approaching the bathroom.

"Michael? Fuck no. I saw Brugōr!"

"Brugōr? Why in the world would *he* be here?" After questioning his encounter with Michael and his partner experiencing a strange sighting of their leader, Mortimer sensed they needed to leave. The two stood silent as they glanced out the window looking for any familiar faces.

"Let's gather our things and head out. The sooner we finish this mission, the better," Mortimer said.

"Sounds good, man."

The two men exited the hotel and approached the stolen car in an empty parking lot. Mortimer jumped in the driver's seat while Vanilor entered the passenger's side, gripping the satchel with the Novalis Rod around his chest. He reached to put his seatbelt on and noticed a familiar figure in the distance. Vanilor froze.

"Look! There he is," he said to Mortimer, letting go of his seatbelt.

Mortimer looked and saw Michael staring back at them.

"How the fuck did Brugōr get here? Did he not trust us to return—"

"Brugōr?" Mortimer interrupted. "What're you talking about? That's Michael."

"Have you lost your Vin damn mind, boy?" Vanilor raised his eyebrow. "I know we're hungover, but that's our fuckin' leader. I don't see that dipshit Michael anywhere."

"What are you talking about?" Mortimer rebutted. "Maybe you were too drunk to remember, but that's Michael. The same Michael whose car we stole."

The two men looked at one another, perplexed at how they could confuse such opposing appearances. With Vanilor's back to the man in question, he didn't notice as he marched toward them.

"We may disagree on who we see, but you can't argue that he's heading straight for us…" Mortimer's eyes widened as Vanilor turned around. The man walked with long strides and a quick pace, a stern look on his face. Vanilor tried to open his door, but his partner instinctively locked it.

"What are you—"

"*He* doesn't seem happy." Mortimer made sure to exclude names. "He's coming at us... fast." As they looked at the angry man approaching them, Vanilor and Mortimer suddenly realized they were both wrong.

"That... isn't Brugōr."

"And it's not Michael."

Vanilor shot his partner a look, wondering how he knew anything about the man from the bar.

"We gotta go!" Mortimer shouted, fumbling the key with a nervous shake into the ignition.

"Drive!" Vanilor said, clutching his satchel.

With a false sense of confidence, Vanilor opened his window. "We don't know who the fuck you are, but you have no idea who the fuck you're messing with, you son of a bitch!"

The stranger revealed a small vial of clear liquid from inside his left palm and grinned proudly.

"Damnit," Vanilor whispered, attempting to close his window. The assailant uncorked the vial and hurled its contents at them. Most of it splattered on the car, eroding the glass and paint. Vanilor screamed in pain as a small amount hit his face.

"FUCK! My Vin damn face!"

"Shit!" Mortimer finally shifted gears and sped off. His arms shook in fear of their dangerous stalker. "What the fuck was that!? Are you alright?"

"Does it look like I'm fuckin' alright!? Get us the fuck out of here! Shiiiit," Vanilor shouted. He lowered the sunshade to look in the mirror, cringing when he saw numerous bubbled up spots eroding the outer layer of his skin. "What the fuck was that about!?"

"Someone knows what we've done…"

"Bullshit. There's no way anyone could've found out." Vanilor ripped the visor off the hinge and threw it into the back seat. "I don't know who the fuck that was, but we need to get out of here and back home."

"Fuckin' A." Mortimer's adrenaline was racing as he wondered why he'd ever agreed to such a mission.

Within the confines of her home, Lady Vixa experienced the events in real time from Neetri's point of view. When the assailants fled, the disguised Savior stared down the car as it drove away. The Quorian Ruler wondered why she hadn't acted until she noticed something in the distance. As the car drove further away, a blue plume of smoke trailed behind, revealing their path.

"Another enchantment…" Lady Vixa said, aware she couldn't be heard.

Neetri quickly observed her surroundings to locate a vehicle. She noticed a woman nearby with her door open while she checked the trunk. Neetri seized the opportunity, though uncertain how to maneuver the device.

Entering the vehicle undetected, she examined the mirrors and noticed the woman was still in the back. Neetri remembered the assailant yelled drive and recognized it near a lever. She finagled the gear into drive and began to move forward.

"Hey! Get out of there!" the woman yelled from behind. Pressing and kicking what she could, Neetri eventually learned the purpose of both pedals and firmly pressed against the gas. The vehicle roared forward, furthering the distance between her and the vehicle owner.

"Neetri! Be careful! Slow down!" Lady Vixa shouted.

The initial motions were sharp, but Neetri eventually gained control. She held the monstrosity of a machine tightly and directed it toward the blue smoke, following the assailants.

"There you go, Neetri. Ease into it."

She followed the smoke through the town of Tillerack and toward the Southern Forest. While focused on their trail, Neetri was mesmerized by the lusciously green world around her, yet also noticed the consuming tall structures, roaring cars, and streets packed with people.

"There are so many humans..." Lady Vixa whispered, fright filling her tone.

The blue trail eventually entered a wall of trees, forcing Neetri to slam on her brakes. Returning the gear back to what it was, she ensured her discretion as she located the assailants' vehicle. Upon closer observation, she realized it had been abandoned.

"Why did they get out? Did the machine break?" Lady Vixa wondered, rubbing the Amulet of Eymus around her neck to ease the stress.

Neetri investigated, but nothing remained – no rod or satchel. Staring into the forest, she noticed a path suitable for their vehicle.

"Maybe it couldn't run anymore," she said, observing her surroundings. "I can vaguely see their path. I'm going to follow them using that machine again. Wish me luck," Neetri said.

The journey through the Southern Forest of Tillerack was uneventful but beautiful. Lady Vixa couldn't bring herself to disconnect from Neetri's sight. Experiencing another region without having to leave The Quo was mesmerizing. She suddenly felt grateful for Neetri. Had she not agreed, the entire rescue mission wouldn't be possible.

Neetri carefully maneuvered the vehicle while appreciating the world around her. She found the scent of damp leaves and blossoming flowers intoxicating. The bright sun she had felt moments ago partially vanished behind the towering trees. The darker atmosphere allowed the vibrant greens, pinks, yellows and blues to stand out. Neither quorian had ever experienced such an environment, and had the situation not been so dire, she would've explored further. It had been the first time Lady Vixa understood the yearning for exploration outside their city.

"This is beautiful," Neetri said. "I've never seen or felt life thrive as much as I do here. It's an honor to have been called for this concerning mission, so thank you, Lady Vixa."

Touched by her appreciation, the Quorian Ruler smiled as she found herself forming a bond with the Savior. Though she expressed much disapproval and disappointment in her, Lady Vixa knew Neetri wanted her to be the best quorian she could be, which was something her father lacked.

Due to their adoration for the Southern Forest, they were surprised when they finally exited into Diveria, or as quorians referred to it, the Outer World. The opposite from the environment they had just experienced, the Outer World was endless and exposed to the elements. The sun glared across a perfectly blue sky as Neetri drove through an emerald field of grass. Though she couldn't see far, she noticed a colossal mountain to her left, just beyond a body of water, and shuddered. Looking in the mirror beside her, she saw a faint object, nearly impossible to identify, high in the sky.

"I can barely recall what the open world looked like eons ago, but I can tell it has significantly changed since then," Neetri said, reminding herself to learn more about the Outer World upon her return to the city.

The journey was uneventful as she passed a smaller region on her left, surrounded by a barbed-wire fence and a wooden wall. Unfamiliar to either quorian, Neetri continued to drive as the emerald fields transitioned into a patchy, tan mess. What was once luscious and vibrant became barren and limp. Though protected by the vehicle, Neetri sensed the heat escalate as the sun continued its path to the horizon. Peering through the waves of heat resonating from the ground, she saw a large object in the distance.

"The hue is headed straight for whatever that is. It must be where they're taking him," Neetri said, roaring her engine onward. The questionable sight before them slowly revealed itself, towering far beyond what their eyes allowed them to see.

"*What in Klai's name is that?*" Lady Vixa was stunned.

"I don't ever remember seeing this," Neetri said in astonishment.

Glistening shades of gold and tawny, the sphere was so large Neetri couldn't tell exactly where the rounded edges were. Oscillating in place as a contained sandstorm, they watched as boulders, dead plants and debris floated within it. The vision triggered Lady Vixa to recall hearing about a region encapsulated by a gargantuan sandstorm for protection.

"It must be a barrier for this desolate area," Neetri suggested.

Lady Vixa suddenly remembered the name. *"The Barren Land."* She panicked. *"No...Neetri, turn around!"*

Neetri continued driving with increased speed. Following the blue smoke, she stared at the base, recognizing the assailants and their vehicle. It was metallic silver with unusually sharp edges and boulders in the center of all four wheels.

"There they are," Neetri said.

Like a car crash waiting to happen, Lady Vixa couldn't look away, terrified. She had confidence in the Savior's ability, but the uncertainty of the men beside the large sphere worried her.

Approaching the base, Neetri slowed down as the two men stood outside their vehicle. Neither one held the satchel across their body. She brought her car to a stop and got out.

"Hey, you!" Vanilor shouted, darting a look at Mortimer. "Tell me something. Are you from Tillerack or The Barren Land?" Still uncertain if it was Michael from THE Bar or Brugōr, the leader of The Barren Land, Vanilor hoped to resolve the uncertainty, but Neetri remained silent.

"Michael?" Mortimer added. "Is that you?"

"They know," Lady Vixa whispered. *"They suspect something is up."*

Still silent, Neetri slowly walked toward the men and the cylindrical wall behind them.

"Whoever you are, w*hatever* you are, your journey ends here. The Barren Land is no place for the likes of you," Vanilor shouted.

Neetri hissed, startling both men.

"It would be wise of you to leave," Mortimer shouted. "We have no business with one another."

"You have someone that doesn't belong with you." Neetri sneered, ready to charge.

The men glanced at each other with shock. They were certain the voice didn't belong to Michael or Brugōr. It was monotone – androgynous.

"Fuck off, you wretched beast." Vanilor retreated to their car and demanded Mortimer do the same. He refused to let anyone ruin his chances of financial freedom when they'd come so close.

"For your own sake and survival, leave. Please," Mortimer begged. He entered the car and roared the engine into drive.

"What the fuck was that about?" Vanilor argued. "You looking to be friends with that thing? It tried to kill us, and you're being nice?"

"We're not completely innocent, Vani." Mortimer stared at the satchel on his partner's lap. "It knows what's inside the rod."

"Maybe, but shit. It's not our Vin damn problem. We were called for a mission and we executed it. It's time to claim our prize. Let's go."

Mortimer grunted. "Home... finally," he whispered to himself accelerating the car into the sphere surrounding The Barren Land.

Behind them, Neetri returned to her car and followed them in.

"If those simple-minded humans can penetrate the barrier, then I'll be fine," she said, slamming the pedal down. "If those murderous humans mess with one of us, they mess with all of us. Prepare to face the wrath of what a true quorian can do."

"*Neetri...*" Lady Vixa whispered, worried for the Savior's safety. "*Almighty King Klai, please protect the honorable Neetri. If it were just the two men, I wouldn't be concerned, but we have no idea what this sphere can do. Please watch over her.*" It was the first time Lady Vixa had prayed to their majestic king in years.

When Neetri drove into the sphere, she entered the heart of the sandstorm surrounded by debris. Unexpectedly, it seemed as though time slowed down. As she eased up on the gas, she noticed the large boulders and trees slowly passing by. While it caused little damage to her car, the sound was deafening. It proved difficult to drive straight when everything around her spun. Fortunately, the assailants' lights were visible so she maintained her steady speed.

As the debris floated by her windshield, Neetri noticed the bones and fossils of small animals, creatures and bugs. The number of objects slamming into her car increased, but she remained focused on the lights up ahead. Slowly increasing her speed, Neetri ignored her surroundings. She focused on her mission, the two men, and the poor, lonely quorian in captivity. It wasn't until the remnants of a skeleton slammed into the driver's side window that she lost focus.

"*No!*" Lady Vixa shouted.

Turning to her left, she was face to face with the upper half of human remains – the skull, both arms and half its torso. Though she'd been through more terrifying experiences, like the death of King Klai so many years ago, she hadn't expected such a horrific sight. Neetri surveyed the scene ahead for the vehicle's lights. With a glimmer to her right, she cut the steering wheel and shifted direction. Just then, another skeleton slammed against the back end of her vehicle. As she ignored the horrific sights outside her car, she wondered how thick the sandstorm was.

In that moment, Neetri's tires spun loudly while her speed steadily declined. Pressing down hard on the pedal, she heard the engine roar as the assailants' lights disappeared. She and Lady Vixa watched everything around them plummet as the vehicle levitated up into the sphere. Neetri released her foot from the pedal and reached into her pocket. Ignoring the metamorphic potion reserved for Promit, she grasped the slimmer vial of water from the Enchanted Reservoir.

"I knew this would prove useful." With a grin, Neetri popped the cork off. She closed her eyes and began to chant in a language foreign to Lady Vixa. Boulders, gravel, human remains and animals continued to pummel the vehicle, but it didn't deter Neetri. She remained focused, for Promit's sake, knowing she needed to safely remove herself from the sphere and locate the two men.

Once she completed her chant, Neetri opened her eyes and smiled. Looking directly into the rearview mirror, she confidently spoke to Lady Vixa.

"And this, my dear, is why it's critical to understand the king's dialect." She winked. Eerily, there was a small pause in the collisions against the vehicle. Neetri tossed her head back and raised the vial to empty its contents into her mouth. She could already sense her enchantment activating a protective barrier around the vehicle for her safety.

Before a single drop could reach her mouth, a force slammed into the car. As she lost her grip on the vial, it hit the window and shattered, the liquid splattering across the interior, leaving an insufficient amount to consume for her enchantment. It was only thanks to the security of the seatbelt and her own strength that Neetri didn't fly through the window.

"*No!*" Lady Vixa shouted.

Neetri quietly shifted her smile into a concerned frown of defeat. The Quorian Ruler panicked. Not only had an innocent, young quorian been captured, she feared one of the Saviors could meet their demise. Regardless of the outcome, Lady Vixa knew it was her fault they were in this predicament.

"Lady Vixa," Neetri spoke calmly, darting her eyes in anticipation, "if you can hear me…" Neetri continued looking left and right. "I'm sorry." Her hands left the steering wheel and she looked at herself in the mirror, touching her ivory-blue face. "Number thirteen," she whispered. "You've come a long way."

"*Don't speak in such a tone, Neetri. Get out of there!*"

After a moment of silence, Neetri closed her eyes and spoke, bringing upon the most terrifying moment of the Quorian Ruler's existence. "I know it's you, Divinity. Show yourself."

"*Divinity!? What in Klai's name are you—*"

"Did you think you'd enter this domain without my knowledge, you foolish creature?" a deep, menacing voice slowly exclaimed.

Neetri grunted, refusing to dignify the presence with a response. Suddenly, a gargantuan, mechanical face appeared in front of the vehicle – a floating head.

"Hello, again." His voice billowed through the car, causing an internal vibration to the bone's core.

"Divinity," Neetri responded.

"Divinity... as in the Divinity King!?" Aware of his inconceivable power and brutality throughout quorian history, Lady Vixa hadn't expected to ever see his presence in her lifetime.

Without warning, everything went dark. No sight, no sound. There was nothing left. The Quorian Ruler feverishly darted her eyes around, but there were no signs of life. Their connection had vanished. Lady Vixa opened her eyes, disappointed at the sight of her home.

"What did I witness!? Where did she go? Neetri! Please come back!" she yelled, fighting back tears. "I can't do this without you…" She closed her eyes numerous times to reconnect, but it was useless.

With the little hope that remained, Lady Vixa hurried toward her desk and wrote down her final visions.

"Divinity King. Large floating head. Wide, purple brim hat. Five-speared crown. Mechanical in appearance." She closed her eyes, trying to recall any other details. "Deep voice, unfamiliar. Spoke slowly." Raising her eyebrows, she added a final note. "Neetri knew? She expected him?" The Quorian Ruler glanced over her words, reconfirming it was all she remembered.

As her adrenaline subsided and reality returned, Lady Vixa sensed a terrorizing fear. Unlike anything she'd ever experienced. The attempt to save Promit had failed and her mission with Neetri had resulted in a frightening reunion with the most powerful king to have existed. The same one that ordered the genocide of their race.

As she turned to wallow in sorrow, Lady Vixa noticed she wasn't alone.

"H-He-Hello, Lady Vixa."

"Smolar... how long have you been there?" she asked.

"Long enough to have questions."

As Jacob lay in bed, he recalled his vision from a week ago, comparing it with his mother's. With the exception of a euphoric feeling and the mysterious man, their experiences were considerably different. He closed his eyes and envisioned the peculiar man in a tuxedo, wondering why he appeared to them both. *What was the connection?*

Jacob remembered his great grandmother had an experience, though Anna couldn't remember the details. He wondered of the possibilities. *Where was she? Was it emotionally driven? Did the same man appear? Did she tell anyone?* His heart fluttered, though he knew his questions would never be answered. He wished his mother remembered more, or asked more questions, but there was nothing he could do. Time had tarnished the knowledge.

Widening his focus, Jacob's curiosity expanded.

Has this been a pattern in our family for years? Did it start with my great grandmother or someone before her? Has it always been women?

Why me?

There were too many unanswerable questions and Anna didn't have much to share.

To silence his mind, Jacob shut his eyes. Unexpectedly, he envisioned his sister,

Catherine, pregnant with his niece or nephew. He smiled. Though he had no interest in having his own children, the thought of being an uncle delighted him.

With good thoughts on his mind and his physical body melting into the high thread count sheets, Jacob eventually entered a peaceful state perfect for sleep… and his second experience.

Jacob was surrounded by a luscious green field with red, pink and white flowers along both sides of the cobblestone path. *Color.* Beyond that, he observed the familiar fog with the darkness behind it. He looked up at the twinkling stars in the night sky with a half-crescent moon, though its appearance seemed bigger than he was used to. The air was chill, but not cold. He knelt down and placed his hands over the grass.

It's wet, Jacob thought. The landscape was healthy and taken care of.

Turning around, his heart rate escalated and his palms began to sweat. He took slow, deep breaths as he identified the structure.

The manor. I'm back.

He whispered 'hello' to himself, to check for sound, but he was met with silence.

With trepidation, Jacob slowly walked down the familiar path he'd traveled a week ago. The ability to see color brought a certain warmth. The manor was made of old, weathered stone, large and gray. The double-door entryway was blackened iron with glistening silver doorknobs.

Jacob looked down and noticed the same nine steps in front of him as before. He wondered what made him return to this peculiar place.

What happened? Why now?

Though he wasn't scared, Jacob's curiosity and nerves awoke. He walked up the familiar stairs and gazed behind him with each step. During his initial visit, the darkness consumed everything behind him, but not this time. Though surrounded by darkness in the distance, it didn't move closer. He was able to retrace his steps.

Standing in front of the familiar door and the silver doorknobs, Jacob acknowledged his breathing patterns, trying to maintain a steady, healthy pace. He was excited to see what was inside, and how it would appear with color. As his mind raced, he anticipated the emotional change that the building caused. Keen to be stripped of his anxiety and worry again. Jacob yearned for such control outside of his dreams.

Placing his hand on the silver doorknob, he noticed minor carvings within the metal. He hadn't seen them before, but his hand felt them as he gently turned it to open. Looking down at the glistening white marble floor, Jacob stepped forward and instantly felt the euphoria he'd hoped for. It left him speechless.

Though he felt a sense of familiarity, seeing everything in color presented him with a new experience. He closed the door behind him as he admired the intricacies of the marble floor. He realized the brown shoes on his feet made no sound as he walked. The columns were glittery gold, walls lined deep crimson. The central room remained open through the upper floors. Everything was organized and meticulously placed, with various individuals walking about. He could see movement on the two floors above but he lowered his head, focusing on what was in front of him. Since Jacob had no idea where he was, he decided it was best to take the same path as before.

He walked forward, toward the desks, but this time they were both occupied. They were made of a shiny, black material – Jacob assumed it to be obsidian. The two seated figures looked nearly identical in their formal suits, with no ties. Short brown hair, similar features, skin smooth like the marble floors, and their gender not apparent. Jacob tilted his head, confused at what they were doing with empty desks. Despite no paperwork or information to read, the figures acted as though they were working. Silently, Jacob smiled at them both without acknowledgement and walked on.

As he traveled toward the back of the room, he observed everyone in passing and had a sudden realization: others noticed his presence. Some of them looked at him, even making eye contact. Jacob was startled, but not afraid. Had his anxiety not been stripped, he knew the experience would've been different. He wasn't sure he would have made it this far inside.

A figure approached him, nearly identical in appearance as the two seated at the desks. As he walked, the stranger looked past Jacob, who remained still, but he made eye contact and nodded in acknowledgment with a grin. Jacob returned the gesture as he breezed by, grazing shoulders.

He continued toward the back of the grand hall, where he gazed upon the mural. He only glanced at it momentarily during his initial visit, but his second viewing mesmerized him. The addition of color brought an unexpected depth to the piece. Standing back, Jacob noticed a total of nine symbols, in three rows of three, with the center being larger than the rest. Each of the symbols had a glowing orb associated with it – each a different color and fog moving within. The black veins of the marble gave the appearance it was cracked in multiple places. Upon closer inspection, Jacob recognized the bottom left symbol, which represented his home of Sartica. Displayed throughout the city on certain buildings and within the royal family, he even had a sculpture of it in his room.

Why would something from my home be included on something here?

Uncertain of the answer, Jacob walked toward the end of the room where he gazed upon the same two hallways. The illuminated white marble was more appealing than the darkness to the right.

There were various white doors on both sides, with inscriptions above them. Between the door frame and the unusual writing was a colored orb, like the mural in the previous room.

Was that there before?

He looked back at the mural and smiled, realizing the colors matched.

There must be a connection between the symbols, orbs and doors.

Jacob knew it was easy to recognize, but he felt proud to understand something in the strange location. He closed his eyes, trying to recall which doorknob moved last time. *Third from the left.*

He walked to the third door and looked up at the inscription. Though he still couldn't read it, he noticed the miniature orb underneath was a dark brown. Jacob placed his hand on the doorknob and turned it clockwise but it barely moved. When he tried counterclockwise, the doorknob froze. His curiosity peaked, knowing he wasn't entering through the door.

Who could have been on the other side? Were they trying to enter or exit?

Jacob turned right to look toward the double doors, curious as to what was behind them. He moved in that direction, but noticed a familiar figure when he turned around.

"*It's him,*" Jacob thought, remembering their method of communication. "*Hello again.*"

"*You remember me,*" the sharply-dressed man replied. His words echoed in Jacob's mind, though his tone was deeper than Jacob could imitate.

"*This place… this manor.*" Jacob struggled to find the words. "*It's consumed my mind this last week.*" He stood deathly still as the mysterious figure focused on him. Its presence was palpable and intimidating.

"*Manor?*" The figure squinted his eyes.

"*It's what I call this place.*" Jacob looked around the grand hall. "*Unless there's some other name I should use?*"

"*The manor will do, for now.*" The figure brought himself closer while maintaining a stern look.

"*Who are you?*" Jacob blurted out.

"*My name is Giddeom.*" The two men stood in front of one another, barely ten feet apart. "*You look just like…*"

"*Like who? I look like who?*" Jacob asked.

"*No one. Your mind is racing. Go ahead. Two more questions.*"

Jacob wanted to choose wisely, uncertain if he'd get another chance to ask.

"Where are we?"

"We are in his home," the voice said.

Disappointed in the first answer, Jacob hoped he'd elaborate. *"Okay..."* he stalled. Unfortunately, he was met with silence. He decided to ask a different question. *"Why am I here?"*

Giddeom pondered the question. Though the two communicated telepathically, Jacob only heard what was chosen for his ears. They stood without exchange for a few moments longer. Finally, Giddeom walked toward Jacob and stood directly in front of him.

"You were called by me. Preparation for the new era is nearly complete." With those words, Giddeom reached out and grabbed his right elbow with his left hand. Jacob shut his eyes as excruciating pain cascaded through his body, radiating from his elbow. He felt a continuous jolt from his head to his feet. Giddeom's grip quickly released as Jacob's knees gave out and he collapsed to the ground. He yelled louder than he'd ever remembered doing before, and he finally heard it. *Sound.*

After a short moment of agonizing pain, it began to fade. Jacob's eyes were tightly shut as he gripped his right elbow. He took deep breaths, massaging the area until the hurt dissipated. When Jacob finally opened his eyes, he was stunned, disappointed by his surroundings.

"I'm... home." Jacob lay in bed, sweating, partially covered by his bedding. The house was silent, no one disturbed by his scream. He climbed out of bed to examine his elbow. Though he rubbed it and bent it in many directions, there was nothing to be seen. There was no sign of injury, not even a scratch. Jacob looked around the room, unsure what he was looking for. A door, a gateway, or a clue.

Giddeom watched Jacob vanish before his eyes, knowing he'd returned home while his pain subsided. He slowly traversed outside the grand hallway, passing the large marble mural in the entryway, and walked into the hall of eternal darkness. It was only accessible by Giddeom due to his ability to see through the facade. What initially seemed like a grand space shrunk down into a narrow corridor.

With his enlightened sight, the walls, floor and ceilings appeared a stark white. At the end of the corridor was a set of double doors. The luxurious handles glistened gold, matching the esthetic of the rest of the space. The door opened widely, as he entered a glamorous, yet empty, throne room – impossible for anyone but Giddeom to access.

The throne, which stood on a ten-foot slab of marble, was shaped for a king, massive in size and weight. While its appearance was breathtaking, it was a facade. As Giddeom approached the throne, he placed his hand through the gargantuan seat. It was nothing more than a hologram. What was real, however, was the marble slab the hologram rested upon. He walked around the back and entered a small, hidden passageway located within the marble.

The hallway was dark and narrow, but short in length. After a few seconds, Giddeom arrived at the Imbroglio. He hadn't frequented the contorted room often, but he knew how to traverse through to reach his destination.

Defying gravity, the Imbroglio was a puzzling space made to break the strongest minds due to its unfathomable passages. The labyrinth of staircases led to various dead ends and locked doors with every path having a unique destination. Without the ability to retrace his footsteps, Giddeom knew it was impossible to escape the room without proper precautions and knowledge. Those who sought out a linear path met their demise due to the continuous loops intentionally implemented for protection. Though *his* masterpiece was extremely safe and secluded, *he* took no chances.

Giddeom entered the Imbroglio, maintaining the correct path to not waste time. After ascending two staircases and descending seven, he crossed a few bridges and finally entered an underpass, directly above the main entrance. The remainder of his path was linear. He continued until he reached the marble door, sensing the presence on the other side. He exhaled and opened it.

Inside was an intimate room with a small, dimly-lit center and a monumental silver throne with intricate purple carvings. It was the largest object Giddeom had ever seen, but he knew it was appropriately sized for who it belonged to.

"Hello, Giddeom," a ghastly voice echoed in a soft, ambiguous tone. Atop the throne was a gargantuan, five-pronged crown firmly planted on a purple-brim sorcerer's hat.

Giddeom bowed his head as a sign of respect. "Your Majesty."

"How did the second meeting go?" the voice asked. The crown levitated and a figure appeared beneath it, now wearing it atop its head. Though aware of his identity, Giddeom always shuddered any time he was in his presence.

The Divinity King.

His skin displayed shades of purple and black with a leathery appearance. His entire body comprised of large, silver tattered armor with expansive golden pieces around his waist. Every piece of his armor was large enough to pull off and be used as a deathly weapon. Most notably the two scythes that pointed upwards from his chest to the brim of the crown and the dozen golden thunderbolts embedded with blue gems around his waist.

Divinity's head was shaped in black leather. His facial features comprising sharp and crude silver that remained still. When the Divinity King spoke, he didn't lower his gaze.

"I think he'll do." Giddeom paused, pondering. "He may not be my first choice, but I'm confident we'll see a different result this time." Giddeom looked up in silence, as Divinity turned his head left.

"So long as he's better than she was," the Divinity King said and Giddeom nodded. "Make haste. The safety of the artifact is the primary concern. The Barren Land will need assistance."

"Of course." He nodded again. "I guarantee history won't repeat itself."

"You better be right," Divinity threatened. "The acquisition of knowledge prompts prestigious strength. Reveal only what's required for him to complete the task."

"Of cour—" Giddeom didn't respond quick enough. The Divinity King had vanished and the crown levitated back down onto the throne. There was nothing more to be said. Giddeom turned and exited the throne room, closing the marble slab door behind him.

Gazing upon the Imbroglio, Giddeom sighed. He traveled back to the main structure in preparation for Jacob's memorable third return. He knew it would require an abundance of work and effort, but he hoped the attempt would be a success.

It was morning, and thirteen-year-old Rexhia disobeyed her mother's instructions to stay nearby. She was told it would be fifteen minutes until breakfast was ready, yet managed to scurry her way into the Bazaar. Just down the road from their home, the Bazaar was a large, interconnected community within The Barren Land. Consisting of larger streets and narrow pathways, it confused even the most well-versed navigators.

Rexhia kicked her small, red ball as she roamed the outskirts of the Bazaar. Swiftly moving between strangers, her two large, braided buns and few cords beside her face swayed gracefully in the air. Those around her smiled, admiring her perfectly innocent smile, almond complexion and crisp brown eyes.

Though surrounded by tall buildings, the heat from the sun was strong in the region, warming up the land by early morning. Everyone stood outside to promote their goods. The outer limits were occupied by merchants selling products and services. Rexhia knew to avoid the depths of the Bazaar, though she was curious to one day explore it.

"Come here for your spices!" a shop owner yelled.

"Furs and robes at a discount! Today only!" an older saleswoman shouted. Rexhia noticed her kiosk had an abundance of supplies. She held her ball and admired the patterns on the fabric.

"Hey, little girl," the woman said kindly. "Like what you see?" Rexhia stared at a blanket for a few seconds, then raised her charming eyes up at the woman, smiling.

"They're beautiful," she replied. The merchant was smitten.

"Tell ya what, little one…" The saleswoman looked around and pulled a few towels out from behind her kiosk. "Pick one. One you think your parents will like." She smiled. "Just tell them Daphne's Design gave you one and they can come back anytime for more."

"Okay!" Rexhia giggled. She considered her options and picked the fluffiest, most colorful towel. "This one."

"Excellent choice, my dear. It's one of my favorites as well." Daphne smiled. She carefully wrapped the towel up and placed it in a bag for the girl. "Here you go, sweetheart."

"Thank you!" Rexhia jumped with excitement.

"And remember! Tell your parents – Daphne's Design!" she shouted as Rexhia walked away, kicking her ball along the path.

Rexhia turned left and went down another alley, remembering the path she took to return home. Distracted by the contents within the bag, Rexhia kicked the ball too hard and it rolled into a distant vendor's kiosk. She tiptoed toward the stand to reclaim her ball and heard the vendor speaking with a man, hissing every word.

"And the locator will identify the location?" the vendor asked.

"Yes. You see the flashing red light?" the stranger said.

Rexhia quietly eavesdropped until their conversation ended, which was when the vendor noticed her.

"What're you doing, kid!?" he yelled, looking at Rexhia and her ball.

"Sorry, mister. I didn't mean to—"

The shopkeeper chuckled. "That's alright, girly. Just having some fun, I take it?" The silver-haired man towered over Rexhia, only shifting his eyes down to acknowledge her.

"Yes." There was a pause. "My mom is cooking breakfast and said I could explore until I was ready."

"All alone?" he asked. "What mother would allow their child into the Bazaar alone?"

Rexhia hesitated. "Yes?" There was a moment of silence, but then she found some confidence. "We live nearby and I'm here enough to know the area."

The shopkeeper didn't believe her. He stared down at her and Rexhia froze, uncertain if she should leave. There was an aura of intimidation from the man. "Well, since you're waiting, would you like to try some berries? Just picked them fresh this morning." The shopkeeper revealed a small, sealed container of berries she hadn't previously noticed.

"I'm not sure I should—"

"Looks like you already have something from another vendor, why not enjoy these too? Just make sure to share them with your mother as well." He smiled. "Maybe she'll have you come back for more."

Rexhia was hesitant, but never passed up free offerings. "Gee, thank you, sir." He placed a handful of the berries in a bag and handed them to her.

"These are called glimboberries – glimbos for short. Have you heard of them before?"

"No."

"You can eat them raw or cooked. Tell your mother they're full of nutrients."

"Okay, mister, thank you."

The man nodded as his gaze returned upward, surveying the street. "You should probably head home, child. By the looks of it, you've been out here longer than fifteen minutes. You've been with me nearly that long." Rexhia realized he was right. "Go on," he said. She nodded, thanked the man, and jogged back the same direction she'd come, kicking her ball along the way.

As she weaved through the crowd, Rexhia exited the Bazaar. Her eyes adjusted to the bright sun. The terrain was a dry, open desert, split into two sections. The higher mesa was the terrain where individuals entered The Barren Land via The Lost Sphere. It was uninhabited. The lower, main level, known as the valley, was where the community resided. Surrounding the perimeter of the valley were cliffs a mile high. There was a single path that connected the two on the south end of the region. Though it was a desert, there was one water source in the middle of The Barren Land known as Karg River. It flowed north to south, with both ends leading into the mesa cliffs.

Upon Rexhia's arrival home, her mother shouted. "Rexi, where ya been!? Breakfast has been ready for nearly ten minutes now."

"I was only gone fifteen, Mom." Rexhia kicked her red ball into her room and approached her mother.

"What have ya got there?" she asked, putting down her fork.

"Merchants offered me some of their goods, so long as I told you about them." Rexhia was proud of her gatherings, but Osvita Dimmerk felt differently.

"The luxury of being free is not meant to be," Osvita exclaimed.

"I know, Mom…" Rexhia sighed, having heard it before.

"Clearly you don't." Osvita picked up the towel and the bag of glimboberries and placed them on the counter. "Where'd you get these berries?"

"One of the merchants. He called them glimboberries."

"Glimbo…berries?" she asked. "I've never heard of them. Are you sure you heard him correctly?"

"Yeah. He said they're sometimes referred to as glimbos?" Rexhia was shocked to hear her mother hadn't known of them either, considering her profession.

Osvita Dimmerk was a renowned chef within The Barren Land with a passion for food since before the birth of her daughter. Her success happened over time, mostly through word of mouth. As she accepted new clients, her popularity increased, and her demand soared. Unable to manage her success alone, she hired an associate chef, Nigel Hatherton. They'd made hundreds of dishes and catered events for most of their community.

"You really need to stop taking things from strangers." Osvita tossed the bag on the counter. "Now eat some breakfast. It's getting cold." Rexhia gladly sat down to eat. Her mother always made elaborate meals with extras to be had. Though Osvita knew breakfast was only for the two of them, she prepared enough food for six. There were a few vegetable omelets, waffles with fresh marmalade and butter, a bowl of fresh fruit and three parfaits. The extra crispy bacon provided a delectable aroma throughout the house. Rexhia's mouth watered as she made her plate, halting when someone knocked on the door. Osvita insisted she continue while she attended the visitor.

Following her mother's suggestion, she finished preparing her plate before devouring some bacon – it was her favorite. Rexhia couldn't hear the whispers outside, but she felt the visitor was kind. Her mouth was filled with a piece of omelet when the door closed.

"Who was that?" Rexhia asked.

"Finish chewing and ask again," Osvita ordered. When her daughter did, she answered. "A catering request from the castle."

"Really? Can I come!? There are all sorts of—"

"Absolutely not," Osvita insisted. "You're never stepping foot inside those castle walls. It's no place for a child." Rexhia tried to challenge her mother, insisting she wasn't a child, but it failed. She continued eating, though the food had lost its sweetness. "Besides, I don't even know if I plan to accept. Having to feed…"—she glanced down for a party size on the note she'd taken—"…one-hundred people in six weeks? Seven courses? I'm not sure I can make it happen."

"Isn't it frowned upon to say no to *him*?" Rexhia asked.

Osvita knew she was right. The demand was cleverly disguised as a request. Brugōr, the leader of The Barren Land, always got what he wanted. Though she was right, Osvita didn't like hearing her daughter become submissive towards him, or anyone – especially a man.

"A question asked is a demand in disguise," Osvita whispered to herself.

"What?"

"Nothing, dear. Just remember, you'll never get in trouble for saying no. It's your right to say no. There's always a choice."

Osvita walked over to the sink and began cleaning dishes, distracted by her recent job request.

"So?" Rexhia asked, putting her dishes in the sink.

"So, what?"

"Are you going to accept the job?"

Osvita looked at her daughter, choosing her words carefully. "It's a tough choice, dear. Unlike your father, I've never worked for Brugōr or within the castle walls. I could politely decline and handle the situation, or accept it and encourage my business to thrive from it. Anything worthwhile comes with its struggles." Osvita tried to use the opportunity as a teachable moment, but it fell short. Rexhia didn't entirely believe her. She felt her mother ultimately had no choice and tried to remain positive.

"Well, I guess that means we will see a lot more of Nigel!" Rexhia exclaimed. Osvita grinned and shook her head.

"Yes, it does, my dear." She smiled, more than she should have. "I'll call him shortly."

"I really like him. He doesn't ignore me because of my age, like some others do."

Osvita fumbled with the correct words to say as conflicting thoughts entered her mind. She was about to change topics by inquiring about the towel her daughter had brought home when a loud noise roared through the valley. They both froze and stared at one another.

"Stay put," she demanded, though Rexhia followed behind. Osvita opened the door, walked outside, and joined the rest of her neighbors as they observed from a distance.

On the opposite side of the valley, a large vehicle roared down the only passage from the upper level with a faint plume of smoke trailing behind. Too far away to visualize the drivers, Osvita assumed it involved Brugōr and his regime. The vehicle was metallic silver with sharp, rigid edges and unusual boulders where hubcaps would be. She realized her assumption was correct. She had seen that vehicle at the castle before.

"What do you think that's about?" her neighbor, Crogin, asked.

"I'm not sure. I would have to guess some business at the castle." She looked at him sympathetically. "How's Suzmina today?"

"Good." He paused. "Well, fine. She was heavily sleeping until those idiots stormed in." The sound of coughing was heard in the distance. "Coming, darling!" he shouted inside the house. "I must go, but keep me updated if you learn anything."

"Oh, Crogin, before you go, I'm going to make her some of my finest sweet potato, vegetable soup. I even have a few brand-new berries to add to the mixture," she said. Though neighbors for nearly a decade, he hadn't shared exactly what his wife suffered from the last few years. Osvita genuinely sympathized for them both and wished there was more she could do.

"Oh, thank you, Osvita. Suzmina will be delighted." They exchanged smiles and returned to their homes.

"What was that all about?" Rexhia stood in the doorway, but didn't understand what had happened.

"I'm going to make Suzmina and Crogin some fresh soup, and I'll even use those new berries you brought today." Osvita felt a wave of excitement, uncertain of the last time she cooked with a new ingredient.

"What about that noise?"

"Oh, it was just someone entering the valley." Osvita thought it best to change the topic. She felt Rexhia didn't need to focus on the matters of the castle. "Would you like to help me prepare the soup?"

"Sure…" Rexhia hesitated.

"What is it, dear?"

"It's strange. You've been invited to work at the castle, and now strangers arrived, possibly linked to the castle? Do you think it's connected?" Rexhia grabbed a potato and the peeler from her mother's hand.

"You have such an imagination, little one." Osvita smiled. Rexhia knew her mother was lying. *Little one* was a term her mother only used when she was hiding something.

What are you hiding, Mom? She kept her curiosities within and smiled as she worked beside her mother to prepare the delicious soup for their ill neighbor.

With an expansive valley, The Barren Land was divided into different sections: Karg City, the Outer Limits, the Bazaar, the castle grounds, etc. Running throughout the land, Karg River was the only source of water. With shades of pearl white and aqua, the winding river flowed north to south at a rapid pace. At fifty-feet wide and forty-feet deep, it was too treacherous to swim across. There was only one path for civilians to cross and that was over the bridge near the southern end. It was narrow but wide enough for two cars.

Equidistant between the two ends was an area of workers that focused on maintaining the river. They helped ensure its safety and cleanliness. Among those individuals was Whark Dimmerk, husband of Osvita and father of Rexhia. He'd worked on Karg River since moving to The Barren Land, and he and his companion, Grum Lagom, had worked together every day.

Though Grum had worked at the river longer, Whark was his boss. He was responsible for the filtration and purification procedures, handling emergency events and ensuring proper protocols and tests were correctly executed. The position required him to maintain order, delegate tasks, and continuously resolve unexpected issues. Whark tactfully performed the tasks, whereas Grum had no interest. He sought out a stress-free life and the chance to enjoy the small pleasures bestowed upon him. Whark and Grum worked well together, which allowed their friendship to blossom.

It was a typical hot day with the sun shining upon them. Grum was submerged in the water, obtaining samples along the river wall ten-feet below the surface. Whark wanted to check the sediment was stable and water containment was maximized. With the river being their only water source, it was crucial to secure as much as they could. It was at that moment they heard a loud roar echo throughout the valley.

Whark turned around but didn't see anything. He gazed down at Grum, whose head just appeared out from the water.

"Do you hear that?" Whark asked.

"I felt it," Grum replied. Both heard a rumbling gradually get louder.

"Get out for a moment," Whark said.

Grum sighed. He wasn't annoyed – just lazy. He found it soothing to lose himself in the water and wanted to return to it. Since Whark was his boss, he respectfully obliged and climbed out.

"You hear that humming? It sounds like its coming from over there." Whark pointed toward the south end of The Barren Land. Grum squinted as he noticed something.

"I hear it," Grum said, rubbing the water off his bald head. "And I see it. There's someone coming into the valley. There's a vehicle speeding down the ramp."

Whark hadn't noticed anything there, though his eyes weren't what they used to be. He saw the trail of dust coming down the ramp with the vehicle just ahead of it.

"Who do you think it is?" Whark wondered.

"I don't know…"

They stood in silence as the vehicle reached the bottom of the valley floor and continued speeding along toward them.

"Uhh…I sure don't know, boss, but it looks like they're coming straight at us."

Whark agreed, though he had no idea why they'd have visitors. Just then, the vehicle sharply turned left and drove parallel along the Karg River.

"They're not coming here – they're heading toward the castle grounds. Seems like Brugōr has visitors." They both sighed in relief.

"Hopefully he's expecting them." Grum chuckled. "If not, they're in for a rude awakening." He laughed harder. Whark couldn't resist smiling – Grum had that effect on others.

Just as the two returned to work, Whark noticed something trailing behind the vehicle, but when he turned around to ask Grum, he'd already got back into the water. Looking back at the vehicle, he was unable to identify or visualize the passengers.

"You don't drive like that unless you possess life-changing knowledge or precious cargo," Whark whispered to himself. His mind raced as he glanced over at the sight of the castle. "Which one is it?"

12

Smolar had always been impressed by Fravia's memory and wealth of knowledge, but he was speechless when she deduced who they'd seen. Once she read the contents of her book, she knew the answer.

Though an anagram may mask, the purist don't have to ask.

Fravia recognized Pritus, the original name of the Enchanted Gate, an anagram for purist. Short for pure bloods, they eventually became known as Saviors. Embarrassed by its simplicity, she knew it was the reason it'd been overlooked. It wasn't until they left the quorian library that Fravia revealed to him the stranger was one of the twenty original quorians who survived the War of Kings and the death of King Klai. Though they had no evidence, they both agreed Lady Vixa had summoned it for assistance in rescuing Promit.

As surprised as Smolar had been, he was relieved to know someone as powerful as a Savior had been summoned. Aware he'd suffer from lingering guilt, he looked forward to having Promit home and putting the situation behind them. Smolar's mind suddenly switched to his family.

His parents.

After his revolting experience reading the titles, Smolar decided to meet with Lady Vixa to privately discuss his parents and what had occurred that fateful night.

He hadn't expected to walk in on the Quorian Ruler in the middle of a mental breakdown.

Since separating from Fravia, and before intruding on Lady Vixa, Smolar had thought about his parents, and the family he once had. He envisioned Erva and her identical appearance to his mother.

Why look like her?

He thought about the last time he spoke with his father and wished him a good night's sleep. He recalled the last time he saw his mother's smile and felt her embrace, walking into his bedroom for a seemingly uneventful night.

He was only eighteen.

Smolar had been in bed when he felt a stranger gently wake him up. As he opened his eyes, he was startled to see Lady Vixa. Having never interacted with her before, it was the last quorian he'd ever expected to see. Before he could speak, she insisted he follow her. Impressionable and confused, Smolar respected the Quorian Ruler enough not to question her judgement. He assumed his entire family would follow, but as he gathered his belongings, he realized his parents weren't around. When he inquired about their whereabouts, she reassured him they'd discuss it when they arrived at her home.

With whispers and wandering eyes from passing quorians, the two ascended to the thirtieth floor and safely entered Lady Vixa's residence. Though unfamiliar with a child in her home, the Quorian Ruler graciously welcomed Smolar and showed him where to place his belongings before sitting down for a pivotal conversation.

"So…where are my parents?" he politely asked.

"Smolar," she started, struggling to find the words, "I'm terribly sorry, but your parents passed away last night, unexpectedly." Her tone was unusually comforting and gentle.

"There must be a mistake. I just spoke with them last night. We said goodnight, everything was normal," he said in disbelief. "We had plans to meet at Restaurant

Alley this morning."

"This is where it gets complicated. I'll be honest with you, because they're your parents." Smolar began to realize the severity of the situation and the reality of her words. "What I'm about to say must remain private, to ensure the safety of you and our community. There was an intruder last night. They somehow managed to breach our city and—"

Smolar lowered his head as a few tears rolled down his face. She heard him weep, but felt uncomfortable consoling him. "I know, dear, I know. This is terrible. I can't imagine how you must feel, but I must ask you to focus. These next few moments are important. I want only the best for you and your parents."

Smolar looked up with watery eyes. "Y-yes?" he sniffled.

"Unfortunately, your parents were caught in the crossfire. An evil force had been trying to gain access to our city for a while now, and finally succeeded. Regardless, it had been taken care of and the situation deescalated."

Smolar was stunned. "How did someone enter our city?" he asked. "Why us? Why my parents?" His tone grew louder.

"I don't know why. All I know is it won't happen again." Lady Vixa approached Smolar and held his hand. "He entered our city through the Enchanted Gate – an ancient device, thought to be deactivated and once used to transport between regions." Silence fell between the two and before Smolar could speak, Lady Vixa interjected. "Listen, my dear Smolar, I'm in no position to ask a favor, especially at such a devastating time for you. This situation may define you now, but I know you can overcome it. You'll grow well beyond what you could imagine. This is why I ask you to please keep this information private. No one can know about the intruder or the workings of the Enchanted Gate."

"But…shouldn't we warn others? Let them know how to protect themselves?"

"The intruder has been vanquished, the gate permanently sealed. It's impossible to happen again. Ignorance can be the strongest defense." Lady Vixa smiled at Smolar to console him.

He knew she was correct about one thing – the moment did define him. He was never the same again. Smolar upheld his word to her ever since that ghastly day. Whenever he was asked about his parents, he explained their deaths were caused by an unusual home accident and immediately changed subjects.

For fifteen years, Smolar had respectfully accepted Lady Vixa's tale. She was the Quorian Ruler. Excluding King Klai, she was the most trustworthy and sacred individual he'd known. He was agitated to have had a strange book, in a secluded chamber, deep within the quorian library, cast doubt on that.

Smolar knew a conversation needed to be had with Lady Vixa. Not only did he want to confirm certain details, but he knew it'd be cathartic to freely speak about their passing after so many years.

Arriving at the door of what he once called home, he gave a few gentle knocks, hoping to not disturb her. Shockingly, the front door creaked open on the final knock and Smolar entered. He feared for her safety, an emotion he'd never felt for her before. He immediately noticed Lady Vixa standing beside her desk, writing. He froze, regretting his decision to enter her home. Smolar slowly walked backwards, trying not to pry.

"Large floating head. Wide, purple brim hat. Five-speared crown. Mechanical in appearance," Lady Vixa said. Smolar froze, analyzing her words. Though disinterested in quorian history, everyone vaguely knew what the murderous Divinity King once looked like, particularly his purple brim hat and five-speared crown.

It could only be one individual, Smolar thought. She turned around to sit and was startled by his presence. Smolar's eyes widened.

He'd been caught.

"H-He-Hello, Lady Vixa," Smolar hesitated.

"Smolar," she hissed. "How long have you been there?" Her gaze pierced his soul. He felt the frustration billowing within her.

"Long enough to have questions," he sharply responded. Smolar knew better than to question her actions. He'd never committed such an act. Though guilty and embarrassed, his mind only raced more. The key. The Enchanted Gate. A Savior. The Divinity King.

"What brings you here now?" she asked.

"We need to talk."

"Another time. It isn't the—"

"It's an urgent matter," Smolar insisted. It startled her to see him be so assertive, disregarding his manners.

"It can wait until morning." Lady Vixa was emotionally drained from everything she'd witnessed, most tragically the disappearance, or possible death, of a Savior at her expense.

"With all due respect, Lady Vixa, I heard what you just said. If I assume correctly, and you're referring to the Divinity King, then it cannot wait until morning. It may already be too late."

"You're not coming here to tell me another quorian has been captured, have you?" Lady Vixa wasn't amused by Smolar's visit, but knew he wasn't leaving. He sighed and shook his head, choosing his words carefully.

"I didn't mean to interrupt you, but your door was open, and I wanted to make sure everything was okay."

"I appreciate your concern, but obviously you came here for a reason." She didn't have much patience. Her mind was focused on the vision of Neetri and what could've happened. The last thing she wanted to do was have a mindless discussion.

"I recently stumbled upon the Hall of Antiquity." Smolar's head was down, shameful of his words.

"How do you *stumble* across such a room?" Lady Vixa's eyes squinted as Smolar's head shot up.

"So you know of it!?"

"Of course I know of it. How do *you*?" As she anticipated his response,

Smolar's excitement caused him to stumble over his words.

"The librarian there offered to help and—"

"Gemery…of course." She sighed. "I'll need a word with him."

"Well," Smolar continued, ignoring her comment, "we were in the quorian library and—"

"We?"

"It's kind of a long story, but her name is Fravia. Fravia Deallius."

Suddenly, Lady Vixa felt the need to spend a bit more time with Smolar and welcomed the longer version. "Please, enlighten me." She sat back on her couch, anticipating a long discussion.

Smolar inhaled and embraced the truth. He mentioned how it started with seeing someone who looked like his mother leaving her home, going into every event afterwards. He described how Fravia came into the situation – their conversations and assumptions. As he told her everything, he noticed her body language. Normally the Quorian Ruler's movements expressed judgement and arrogance, sometimes even complacency. He found it interesting to see her intrigued by his story, considering the actions he'd taken.

"How did it look like my mother?" Smolar asked. Lady Vixa paused, contemplating her words as Smolar correctly identified the situation.

"It's part of her ability," she confessed. "She appears as someone who resonates within your heart."

"So that's why you summoned her? You hoped her ability would allow her to rescue Promit?"

"That…was the plan," she admitted with a heavy heart.

Silence fell upon the room as he evaluated the situation, unaware of her saddened response. Smolar thought about his parents and what he'd seen in the Hall of Antiquity.

"Was there something else, Smolar? You seem hesitant."

He hadn't realized it was obvious. "Well…one thing. At the end of the Hall of

Antiquity was a book with an unusual title," he said quietly.

"Yes, some of those titles are…curiously named for its reader. It's a most unusual place."

"Well…the final book startled me." He paused. "It read, '*What Really Happened To Your Parents?*'" Smolar blurted it out, nervous the words wouldn't be uttered otherwise. He blankly stared at Lady Vixa, uncertain of what to expect from her.

"Ah." She nodded slowly. "Well…that's a lot to process, Smolar." He found her tone surprisingly soft, her eyes welcoming. It was unfamiliar to him. There was so much he wanted to say, yet he also wanted to hear from Lady Vixa.

The silence continued. As she turned away, he noticed something on her face. *It can't be. I must be wrong*, he thought.

She stood up and stepped away, her head lowered into her hands. He heard a noise from her he couldn't quite place. Her shoulders shuddered as Smolar heard her exhale.

"Lady…Lady Vixa…are you…?" He wanted to say crying, but didn't want to make her uncomfortable. "Are you okay?" he asked.

"Father…guide me. Help me through this," she whispered. "Show me the path of resolution. Forgive me for these deaths and absolve my soul." Her volume increased on the last few words.

"Deaths!?" Smolar exclaimed. Lady Vixa turned around, exposing her true emotions. Rolling down her gentle face, out from her silver eyes, were tears. It was the first time Smolar had ever seen the Quorian Ruler cry. She cradled her face in her palms, sobbing harder.

"Lady Vixa…" he spoke gently, uncertain how to manage the awkward situation. "What's going on?" Smolar approached her but stopped when she spoke.

"There's just so much…too much…I can't fix this." Tears continued to roll down her face. Some landed in her palms, while others rolled down her elongated neck and onto the Amulet of Eymus. Smolar was startled when he noticed the amulet absorbed any tears that touched it.

"Please…what can I do to help?"

"I'm…I don't know," Lady Vixa exclaimed, returning to her seat. Smolar admired her in their awkward moment. There was no instruction manual on how to handle someone's emotional state. He remembered what he partially heard her say, unsure who she was talking to. He figured that was a good place to start.

"Who…who were you just speaking to? You seemed to be asking for help." Smolar's expression was kind, concerned, though she wasn't yet making eye contact.

"I—" She hesitated, unsure if she wished to be truthful. "I was speaking to my father."

"L-Lord Erko?" Smolar was almost certain that was his name. She nodded.

"He always knew what to do. He always had the answers," she said, locking eye contact. Smolar felt her pain as he looked into her glistening, silver eyes. She rubbed the amulet around her neck. "You see, Smolar, Lord Erko always handled situations with respect and decency. He taught me a great deal, allowed me inside his mind…" She hesitated, wiping the tears from her eyes. There was a relief in discussing her emotions, something she was not used to.

"It's okay. Take your time," Smolar reassured. Lady Vixa nodded, appreciating his kindness and understanding. She'd rarely allowed herself to be in a vulnerable state, especially in front of others.

"My father provided me with enough knowledge to reign until I eventually passed the role onto my husband. Knowing that wouldn't happen, I found myself stuck somewhere between the two, trying to make my father proud and being the Quorian Ruler this city needs me to be, as best I know how." The tears subsided as she shared her pain with Smolar.

"If you knew you weren't going to have a male partner, why not focus on being ruler of our city?" Smolar wondered, shocked to hear her internal struggle.

"It's difficult to perform a task which brings disappointment or shame to a parent." The two unknowingly shared an identical thought – Smolar's parents. He never had the opportunity to ensure pride or disappointment. Smolar sighed, thinking about his own situation, trying to hide his internal struggle.

Lady Vixa acknowledged his emotion, so she continued to talk, changing subjects. "I've been able to perform most tasks as Quorian Ruler, but when Promit went missing, there was a shift. The Quorian Ruler should be able to manage the scenario safely, but I didn't know how. That was when I called upon the help of a Savior, Neetri."

"Neetri?"

"Yes, that is…*was* her name." She sighed.

"She told me her name was Erva," Smolar admitted.

"A Savior does what's needed to ensure safety. Their appearance, name, voice – everything."

"Probably best to look like someone who's alive," Smolar suggested. "Had she looked like anyone else, I wouldn't have followed her and we wouldn't be discussing it."

"Hm. Everything may have its purpose," she admitted.

"Wait…did you say Neetri *was* her name? What do you mean?"

"Y-yes…" Lady Vixa's mood shifted to sadness again. She explained what had happened since Smolar last left her home. She mentioned her thoughts, summoning Neetri, following her travels, The Barren Land, and ultimately her disappearance with the Divinity King. Unfortunately, her plan had imploded just when he walked in.

Smolar didn't know it was possible to feel more overwhelmed than he already had.

"I'm now responsible for a missing quorian and the presumed death of a Savior. It's irresponsible and unacceptable." Lady Vixa felt sorry for herself. Smolar was too overwhelmed to console her, but he tried once more.

"It seems like you're pushing away the role of Quorian Ruler. You can't run from it. You need to embrace your title and take action. You're powerful. You're capable of greatness. If an issue arises, re-evaluate and re-assess." Lady Vixa jolted her head back and gave Smolar a jarring look. He was embarrassed to address her in such a manner, but he was too overwhelmed to filter his tone or words. "I'm sorry. I don't mean to be rude. It's just very…" Suddenly, Smolar broke out into tears. He tossed his head into his hands. She stared at him, shocked at his reaction.

"My dear…" she said in a quiet tone. Lady Vixa moved to sit beside Smolar. "For what you have gone through, you have no need to apologize. I am the one who should apologize." She raised Smolar's head to make eye contact and smiled. "Thank you for being direct and honest. You're right." Smolar sniffled, cracking a smile. "You are incredible and, if anything, I owe you more apologies than you can even begin to understand."

"There is no need for—"

"No," she interrupted. "I'm deeply sorry for everything." Smolar didn't understand what she could possibly apologize for. "I should have been more present when you came here. It was such a challenging time for you, and I wasn't much help. Too often I avoid emotions and I should have been there for you. To talk to, to cry with, to help. I did none of those things…and for that, I am sorry."

Smolar felt her genuine emotion. For the first time, he sensed her love. "I-I don't know what to say." Smolar battled a whirlwind of emotions. Happiness. Resentment. Love. Relief. Sadness.

"You don't have to say anything," Lady Vixa said with conviction as she stood up. "What did you say was the name of that final book in the Hall of Antiquity?"

"*What Really Happened To Your Parents?*"

"You know, Smolar…we should probably have a discussion," she said. "But first, I think we should take that bracelet off you."

Her suggestion brought a smirk to his face as he nodded in agreement. With an effortless wave of her fingers, the Bracelet of Fury unlatched and fell into Smolar's lap. He rubbed his wrist like an itch he hadn't been able to scratch. Lady Vixa grabbed the bracelet and smiled. Just as she prepared for a long-overdue conversation, there was a knock at the door.

"Hello?" Lady Vixa called out. Opening the door, she was bewildered at the strangely-familiar quorian in front of her house.

"Fravia!?" Smolar exclaimed, peering through the doorway.

"Smolar! I knew you'd be here," Fravia replied, relieved to see him. She looked up at the Quorian Ruler. "Lady Vixa." Fravia bowed, waiting to be invited in. Lady Vixa recognized the name from Smolar's story. With the identical knowledge between the two, she invited her guest inside.

"Please come in." She smiled and Fravia entered, approaching Smolar and thanking Lady Vixa along the way. The group reconvened in the living room.

"Something told me I'd find you here. I wish I'd known, I would have joined you." Fravia glanced at Lady Vixa and smiled.

"It's best we were private," he said. "Lady Vixa and I were almost done. Think we could meet in Restaurant Alley in fifteen minutes?" Smolar asked.

"Of course, my apologies, Lady Vixa. I didn't mean to barge in. It's not typical of me. I was raised better."

Suddenly, Lady Vixa recalled why Fravia looked familiar.

"That's why I know your face," she said. "Your parents…Lucemia and Reagor Deallius, correct?" The Quorian Ruler had worked with her parents numerous times due to their medicinal knowledge and research.

"Yes." She chuckled. "That's them."

"Brilliant. Please, I must ask you not to speak a word of any of this to them, or anyone else."

"Of course! You can trust me." Fravia rambled when she was nervous. "Did you tell her about…?" She looked at Smolar, then turned to Lady Vixa. "Did he tell you about…?"

"Yes, we've informed each other about all we know," Lady Vixa said. With the Quorian Ruler's blessing, Smolar revealed their conversation about her plan and confirmation of Neetri's identity.

"Who did she appear as for you again? I forgot," Smolar wondered.

"What? Oh, just some family member, but that's not important." She disregarded Smolar's question and turned to Lady Vixa. "So you claimed Neetri perished?"

"Possibly. I'm hoping I end up able to see her again."

"If Neetri perished, wouldn't The Klai Chronicles confirm that?"

"What?" Lady Vixa stood up, stunned by Fravia's knowledge. "How do you know—"

"She's a wealth of knowledge," Smolar said, shrugging.

"I read it in the quorian library. While the demise of a Savior is rare, it can happen. If events make it so, the Klai Chronicles will shine brightly and the page from which you summoned her will burn, disappearing forever."

"That's remarkable!" Lady Vixa paused. "I really need to speak with Gemery regarding his access to the Hall of Antiquity."

13

Catherine and Andrew Cromwell were elated to expand their family, though it was unexpected. Having children was a discussion the couple had had before sharing their vows. Andrew had always wanted to be a father, while Catherine was open to the idea. She'd always adored children, but didn't yearn for motherhood. It had grown with the love of her partner.

With both their families and friends aware of the exciting news, Catherine and Andrew gathered those who could at their home to host an intimate gathering. The two-story house located in southern Sartica was recently renovated with the help of Andrew's knowledge and Catherine's design.

Why pay for someone else's upgrades when you can build it to your liking? Catherine often said to family. It kept them busy for numerous years, but they had something to show for it.

"I'm so glad you were able to make it down here," Catherine exclaimed to Andrew's parents, both of whom lived in the most eastern part of Sartica. Their commute was just shy of ninety minutes, so they didn't travel to their home often. His mother gave a kind response, happy to spend time with everyone. His father made a sarcastic yet funny remark, thanking the kids for the invitation and free beer.

There were around twenty-five family and friends at their home, three of whom were the Emmersons. Though thick and muscular, their dog Moose was an incredibly sweet and gentle dog, greeting everyone as they passed by.

Moose stood by the white, double doors, whimpering.

"Aw. Catherine, he wants to go outside," Anna said, nodding to Moose. She and Ben sat at one end of the dining room table. Anna had a special spot in her heart for dogs, sometimes showing them more compassion than people.

"No, that dope just wants some food," Ben responded to his wife. Anna jabbed him with her right elbow. He jumped. "Ow!" he said, rubbing his elbow in an exaggerated manner. "You see the abuse your mother gives me?" Ben smiled. Anna rolled her eyes, slapping his arm again with a smirk while Ben repeated his humor. Catherine opened the door, allowing their dog outside on the back patio.

Anna and Ben whispered to one another, then he jolted in his seat.

"Oh, honey bunny." It was his nickname for his beloved daughter. "Just a small gift to say congratulations." He handed Catherine a sealed envelope, a tradition of Ben's to give a greeting card for every occasion.

"You two didn't have to do anything," Catherine said, opening the envelope. She pulled out the card and read it aloud. "Hello Baby,"—she opened it, revealing the joke—"Goodbye Sleep." The parents-to-be chuckled. Taped to the inside of the blank side was a check. Catherine turned the card to examine the amount, immediately reacting.

"We cannot take this. It's too much," Catherine whispered to them.

"You absolutely can, and you absolutely will," Anna demanded. Catherine tried to return it, but her mother refused. It was a losing battle. "Don't do this, Catherine. You're going to get me upset, please." Anna's tone always changed when she said this phrase. Catherine smiled and hugged both her parents, graciously accepting the gift.

"Thank you, guys," Andrew shook hands with Ben and hugged Anna.

The four of them were so deep in conversation that none of them noticed Moose outside the door, waiting patiently to be let back inside. Jacob, who was being social in the living room, noticed from afar and walked toward his family.

"Poor baby wants to come in," he said, opening the door to welcome Moose in. "Oh, it's actually quite beautiful outside." He refilled his glass of wine, then walked out onto the patio.

"That breeze does feel nice," Anna said. Though Sartica was filled with desert heat, the evenings sometimes provided its residents with a cool breeze.

"It's freezing outside!" Ben shouted. Anna and Catherine both scolded him for being so loud as a few of their guests looked in his direction. Anna followed her son outside to enjoy the cool air while Catherine walked off to socialize with her other guests. This left Andrew alone with Ben, though he was too kind to walk away.

"You want a beer, Ben?" Andrew asked, knowing he rarely drank.

"Have no fear, I'll pass on the beer," Ben exclaimed.

Jacob curled up on the outdoor sofa chair. Though there was a slight chill, his second glass of red wine kept him warm. With the eternal silence around him, his mind reverted to his most recent, second experience. His mind had raced ever since he awoke that morning. Though he initially wanted to talk to his mother, he waited a few days. He wanted to organize his thoughts before unloading more information. Knowing he had more experience than his mother concerned and excited him. He wanted to process and absorb it organically without outside influences. There were a couple moments that startled Jacob; however, the most memorable was his time with the stranger, whose name he now knew.

"*Giddeom.*" As Jacob whispered his name into the empty sky, he spotted a shooting star in the center of his view. It was so bright and prominent that he nearly spilt some wine. He jolted forward, astonished.

Just then, Jacob heard the door open behind him.

"Hey, son." Jacob didn't have to turn around to know who it was. It was one of the gifts a mother bestows upon their children.

"Hi, Mom, how're you doing?" he asked. Anna sat beside him, a small glass of red wine with two ice cubes in hand.

"Not bad. Your father was making a fool of himself, again," Anna smirked while Jacob chuckled.

"Of course he was." They took sips of their wine in unison. "You know, just before you walked out here, a shooting star soared across the sky," Jacob said with awe.

"Did you make a wish?" Anna asked, believing in superstitions.

"Darn…" Jacob sighed. "No, I was too focused on other things, I didn't even think about making a wish." Though he wasn't as superstitious as his mother, Jacob picked up a few habits. Wishing upon a shooting star was one of them.

Anna looked at her son curiously. "What's on your mind?"

"Oh…" Jacob considered whether he wanted to bring up the second experience now or wait for another time.

"Is everything okay? What's wrong?" Anna had panic in her voice. She was a strong-minded individual, but consistently worried if her children were okay. She sat forward, staring at Jacob who just realized her sense of concern.

"Oh, yes, everything is fine, Mom."

"Well, what is it?"

Jacob knew she wouldn't rest until he provided a sufficient answer. "Well…I was just thinking about the experience I had."

"What about it?"

He took a sip of wine. "Not the one we walked about. I actually had a second experience the other night."

"What?" Anna stared at her son.

"I returned to the same place, same feeling, same building." The excitement showed in his voice.

"And you're sure you didn't just envision it for a second time?"

"Absolutely. The exterior of that manor was different. There were flowers. There was *color*." Jacob's mind began to race in excitement. "Everything looked different. There were things I hadn't seen before." He closed his eyes. "It was beautiful. White, pure, clean." He gazed upon his mother once more. "The strange man appeared again."

Anna's face suddenly changed in anticipation, remaining silent.

"Still no sound, but we spoke telepathically. Instead of questioning me, he welcomed me to ask him three questions, though it only brought upon more questions." Jacob sipped his wine, as he felt a chill down his spine, uncertain if it was from the weather or his memory.

"Go ahead," Anna insisted. They grabbed blankets from the chest between them for warmth.

"He said his name was Giddeom and—"

"Gid-Giddeom? Did you say, Giddeom?" Anna confirmed.

"Yes, such a strange name." Jacob chuckled. "That isn't even the strangest part." Anna gazed out upon Catherine and Andrew's yard. She took a hefty sip of wine, the ice cubes chilling her lips. "He said that we were in *his* home. I have no idea who *he* was." Anna remained silent. "I wanted to ask a follow-up question, but knew there was a chance he'd remain vague. I decided my final question was to ask him why. Why was I brought there? You know what he said?" Jacob asked, gaining the focus of his mother.

"What?"

"'You were called by me. Preparation for the new era is nearly complete.'"

"Giddeom," Anna repeated, still mesmerized by the name.

"What is it? You seem…distracted. Is it the name?"

"I just…"

Jacob sat forward and sipped some wine. "There *is* something."

"Well, the thing is…" Anna hesitated. She had the words in her mind, but contemplated whether she should say them aloud, aware how profound they'd be.

It intimidated her. "I've heard that name before."

"Giddeom!?" Jacob was taken back. "Where? It's such a peculiar name." After a few seconds of silence, he continued. "Maybe there's a connection?"

"Interestingly enough…there is."

"Wha—"

"Back when I had my first *experience*, I had a conversation with my mother." Jacob nodded, remembering the story. "At that time, my mother and I had a discussion about our family history. Informing me. Warning me. These visions are not unusual in our family. She told me about her mother, my grandmother, Edith. She had these experiences as well, countless times. It became a regular occurrence. Eventually, they became a part of her life and she was consumed by them. Edith was rarely present in the lives of her loved ones, including her own daughter. She was forbidden to discuss any details about what she did or where she'd go.

"My mother told me Edith unexpectedly disappeared for weeks at a time, without notice. This caused great tension and animosity amongst the family, particularly for my mother." Silence fell between the two. Noticing everyone inside enjoying their time, she continued. "As time progressed, all of Edith's relationships crumbled. She wasn't present enough to sustain them. Her husband and both children learned to live without her. When her son, my uncle, died, it solidified the emotions within the family. Edith was blamed for his death, though it was a heart attack. My mother and grandfather opposed her lifestyle so much they never saw her again."

Jacob couldn't believe what his mother was saying.

"When her husband died, Edith never visited. They questioned if she'd already died from the loss of her son. I imagine when my mother died, Edith wasn't present either. She would've been over one-hundred years old."

Anna took a sip of wine, so Jacob took that moment to speak.

"I can't believe all this. Everything you're saying is shocking…" He paused.

"But it still doesn't answer where the knowledge of Giddeom comes from." Anna smiled.

"It was passed down through the generations. At a young age, my mother was told by Edith to follow any visions from a man named Giddeom. Eventually, she learned Giddeom was responsible for taking her mother away. This caused my mother to *loathe* the man. In her eyes, he was a murderer." Jacob understood the change in dynamics. "So when I told my mother about my vision…"

"It enraged her."

"Exactly. She told me to avoid him at all costs. No matter how persistent or tempting it may be. Continuous propaganda from a young age could lead to a dangerous existence. Ultimately, I listened to her and after his first visit, I never met with him again," Anna said in disappointment. "At the time, I trusted her opinion. As I matured, my thoughts shifted. I realized my mother was emotionally driven to hate this man and everything her mother did, even though no one knew the context of the situation." Anna caressed her son's hand with a smile.

"I know this is a lot to hear. I didn't want to unload everything unless I knew for certain your vision, experience, or whatever you like to call it, was the same. You confirmed it with the name Giddeom. It's too unusual of a name to be a coincidence," Anna said as he nodded.

"I understand why you didn't say anything before. I would've probably done the same." He looked over the backyard, pondering.

"What're you thinking?"

"Well…I'm thinking about Edith. I'm thinking about how she willingly distanced herself from the family and how the family exiled her. It's just sad." He thought for a moment before blurting out, "I don't want that to happen to me."

"Oh, Jacob." Anna comforted him. "That wouldn't happen to you."

"I have no idea why this man visited me multiple times. There must be a reason and I need to pursue it."

"I think you should," she responded.

"Really?"

"I'm not saying blindly agree and disappear. I'm suggesting you learn more. It isn't wise to make assumptions off someone else's experience. I know my mother would be disappointed, but see what he has to say." Anna felt a weight lift from her shoulders. It wasn't a conversation she'd expected, especially outside her daughter's home.

Jacob had more questions, but he decided to let the information settle. He was happy, relieved. Not only had he learned some history, but he knew he hadn't been alone. He wasn't crazy, and he had his mother's support.

"Well, now I hope Giddeom calls me again soon." Jacob chuckled.

"You know…there may be something we can do."

"Something *we* can do?"

"My mother told me if Giddeom becomes too persistent, contact the leader. Maybe if we go to the Subterranean Domain and speak with the leader of Sartica, he could help," Anna suggested.

"You want to just walk up to Sir Kalvin Troveria and request help?" Jacob smirked at the idea. "It's the royal family."

"Seems crazy, but it's worth a try." Suddenly, the doors behind them opened.

"Are you two okay out here? You've been here a while now. A few of my friends are heading out," Catherine remarked.

"Sorry, my dear. We lost track of time," Anna replied.

Catherine closed the door as Jacob and Anna made their way inside.

"There's just one more question I wanted to ask," Jacob said, empty wine glass in hand. "Am I wrong to think these experiences always happened to women in our family?"

"No, you are correct. Though we share a similar perception with our dreams, I expected Catherine to have one or two of these visions. Not you."

Jacob thought about her response, but they were interrupted once more and he knew the conversation was over.

14

I'm on my way to meet the leader of Sartica, Jacob thought as his mother drove them to the Subterranean Domain. It was only twelve hours earlier that Anna had revealed their family history and familiarity with Giddeom. Aware his mother didn't have the answers, he'd hoped Sir Kalvin Troveria of Sartica would. It brought him comfort to know he hadn't been alone. Jacob wished he could've had the chance to talk with his great grandmother, Edith, and gather some insight.

The sun hadn't yet risen, but the sky had a beautiful, celestial hue. With the region still dark, Jacob couldn't visualize Lotus Lake to his left, reminding himself to visit the peaceful place soon. With twenty minutes remaining until they reached the Subterranean Domain, Jacob asked a few questions.

"Hey, Mom, did any of your other siblings have these experiences?"

"Not to my knowledge. I suppose they could have at some point, but it's unlikely. Sounds like only one woman – person – per generation. Giddeom visited me only once and you now twice."

"I guess so." Jacob thought about how it must have been for her with the family. "How about your father? What did he think?"

"I don't think he ever knew," Anna replied.

"What!? How did he not know?"

"My mother didn't want to bring attention to it. She only confessed to me because of my vision," Anna explained. Jacob understood her point, but disagreed with the choice, so he moved on.

"And you still have no idea why I'm the exception to the tradition of women?"

"No. Maybe there were men chosen years ago and in recent years it's been women?" Anna guessed, but she had no inclination as to why. "I'm sorry I don't have more information. Perhaps Sir Kalvin will know. The royal family keeps many secrets within their walls – this topic may be one of them." Jacob knew his mother was probably right. "I certainly expected your sister to be chosen."

"Chosen…" Jacob pondered. Suddenly, he sat up straight. "I got it!" he shouted. "You're *chosen*. It's a choice."

Anna remained perplexed – it wasn't a revelation. Previous family members either chose that life, went against it, or were simply not given the option. "Yes…we already discussed that."

"It appears Giddeom chose me for…whatever it's about. If he wants me to accept, then I have demands. I need answers."

"Are you sure you want to be abrasive towards this guy?"

"You said it yourself, you expected Catherine to be the one with these experiences, but she's not. I am. There must've been a reason to change the pattern." Jacob felt confident in his opinion, while Anna remained uncertain.

"You make a good point. There must be a reason, but…"

"But?"

"But you also know nothing about him. This man, Giddeom. He's communicating with you telepathically in, well…essentially your dreams. If he can do that, who knows what else he's capable of. You mustn't get yourself into trouble."

"I know, Mom. I won't be so harsh, but I think I have leverage to ask a few in-depth questions," Jacob replied.

"Just be careful."

And with those words, Anna and Jacob arrived at the center of Sartica – the Subterranean Domain. The two parked a few blocks away and walked toward the home of the royal family.

"How do you expect to speak with Sir Kalvin?" Jacob wondered.

"Trust me, he will be outside," Anna said with confidence. She'd always followed the royal family closely – fascinated by their lives. When Lord Arthur died just over ten years ago, Anna Emmerson was glued to the television. His death and funeral were consistently covered, not missing a single broadcast. It consumed her.

After the morbid hype of his death, his son vanished, relinquishing the title. As such, Lord Arthur's succession passed to his late brother's son, Kalvin. Anna's fascination with the royal family continued as she learned his leadership style, love interests and hobbies. One consistency in his routine was to walk the Ersatzian Field early each morning for peace and meditation.

The Ersatzian Field was filled with luscious, voluptuous plants and flowers, most of which were never seen within the region. It was a botanist's dream. Unfortunately, it was a beautiful illusion since most of the plants were fake. Some were real, but even Sir Kalvin had difficulty differentiating between them. Most civilians of Sartica knew the Ersatzian Field was fake; however, they still appreciated it. The royal family valued the environment but wanted to use their resources wisely.

The three-sided pseudo-garden formed a triangle surrounded by a black wrought-iron fence for protection and privacy. The east and west walls maintained a consistent barrier, while the southern wall housed the main entrance into The Ersatzian Field. Though it was admired for miles, it was merely a distraction from the main attraction.

Directly underneath the Ersatzian Field resided the home of the royal family – the Subterranean Domain. The 25,000 square-foot structure was protected from the surrounding elements. It housed the entire Troveria family – Sir Kalvin, his mother, one sister, two brothers, an aunt, one uncle, one grandmother, and two cousins. Little was known of the domain since outsiders were rarely granted access. When non-royals entered for an event or meeting, they were only allowed to view certain rooms. With the secrecy surrounding the Subterranean Domain, many Sarticians whispered rumors of its contents.

The sun was barely approaching the horizon as Jacob and Anna arrived at the western wall of the Ersatzian Field. She felt far more confident in their mission than he did. Jacob felt it was too easy. Glancing inside the garden, they noticed it was empty.

"I don't see anyone," Jacob said quietly. Anna didn't either but suggested they walk around the perimeter of the field. "It's early. I'm sure he's yet to come."

After parking, they walked along, inhaling beautiful, fragrant smells. He stared off into the garden, enchanted by floral scents. He hadn't sensed it before. Jacob wasn't one to stop and smell the roses.

"It smells incredible. I thought most of the plants and flowers inside were fake."

"Most are," Anna replied. "Some are real though and give off a beautiful scent in the center of town during certain times of the day." Jacob chuckled at his mother's passion for the royal family.

They turned left and began walking along the southern wall of the perimeter. The streets were empty in the early hours, with an occasional runner or cyclist.

Someone walked by with a steaming cup of coffee, causing Jacob and Anna to lift their noses. Its scent, with the crisp air and fragrant flowers, was hypnotizing. Jacob craved the taste of coffee, acknowledging his exhaustion, only awake from the adrenaline.

Passing the main entrance, there was still no sign of Sir Kalvin. They continued along the perimeter when Jacob noticed the whimsical look on his mother's face, enthralled by the Ersatzian Field. He didn't want to say anything to ruin the moment for her. It warmed his heart to see her so genuinely happy. It wasn't a look he'd often seen.

They rounded the corner from the southern wall to the eastern wall. He reluctantly looked through the fence.

"Still no one," he whispered.

"Patience, my son."

Jacob nodded, though his patience was fleeting. He was disinterested in waiting for someone he didn't expect to show.

Suddenly, Anna tossed her arm out in front of her son, halting his movement. Jacob peered through the wrought-iron fence and squinted. He saw a few bushes, two large trees and a beautiful red-and-pink flower bed. Though he couldn't distinguish between the real and fake flowers, he knew the movement beyond them was real. *Is that him?* Jacob thought. He took a few steps forward, along with Anna. Both locked their vision onto the figure.

Admiring a flourishing tree beside him, Sir Kalvin Troveria stood six-foot-two-inches tall with short jet-black hair and an olive complexion. Dressed in his shimmering silver morning robe, he was oblivious to the outside world.

"Is that *him?*" Jacob asked. Speechless, Anna nodded. She'd only seen him a couple times, but she knew this was different. They were going to communicate with a royal for the first time. Jacob fixated on Sir Kalvin as his anxiety awakened.

As he walked off in the field, Anna nudged her son, suggesting he speak up. With fear and trepidation, Jacob shouted the one word that brought them there. "Giddeom!"

Jacob clamped his hands over his mouth, startled by what he'd just done. Stunned, Anna looked around, relieved that strangers weren't nearby to hear. They both gazed upon their leader who stood as still as stone. His head turned, his dark eyes piercing Anna and Jacob. His defined chin and clean-shaven face were in plain sight as he walked toward them.

Anna's heart fluttered in excitement. She tried her best to focus and maintain composure. Enduring the opposite end of the emotional spectrum, Jacob was riddled with anxiety. His hands were sweaty and his face red. A single bead of sweat dropped from the left side of his forehead. He was worried how Sir Kalvin would judge his anxiety and his mind spiraled.

Sir Kalvin approached the fence.

"Hello." He smiled and nodded. "Who might you two be?" He was charming with a soft tone. Anna looked at her son, hoping he'd speak.

"My name is Jacob. Jacob Emmerson. This is my mother, Anna," he mustered, trembling. "Sorry for shouting, I shouldn't have been so blunt. It just blurted out and—"

"Thank you for coming over to us," Anna interjected. She gave her son a warm smile as if to say *everything will be okay*. He yearned for his mother's assistance. Sir Kalvin smiled sincerely at Jacob, acknowledging his nerves.

"It seems as though someone shouted a peculiar name..." Sir Kalvin raised an eyebrow.

"Yes. I did. It was to catch your attention."

"It worked." He chuckled. The leader had impeccable posture while awaiting an explanation.

"Well, as I mentioned, I've been visited by Giddeom and—"

"Ah, so I *did* hear you correctly," he contemplated. "I'm going to open the gate along the southern wall for you to enter the Ersatzian Field." Anna nearly fell over while Jacob was relieved to know he hadn't upset the leader of Sartica.

"Of course," Jacob remarked. Anna nodded. There was suddenly a shift in emotions. Anna, who was once exuberant, felt nervous. She was entering the grounds of the royal family and wanted to maintain a respectful composure. While Jacob's nerves hadn't vanished, he felt justified to be in his presence.

The two returned to the southern gate and met Sir Kalvin at the entryway.

"Hello, and welcome to the Ersatzian Field," Sir Kalvin said. "Please, come in." Jacob and Anna walked past the threshold of public domain and into their private property. They were mesmerized by their surroundings.

The Ersatzian Field was more intimidating than Anna or Jacob had expected. Though they'd seen and smelled it from the streets, it didn't compare to the sensation when surrounded by it. It consumed them. There were tall and short trees, some with needles. Certain species had green leaves while others bore bare branches. Their trunks ranged from skinny and smooth, to thick with chunks of weak, peeling bark. There were an abundance of bushes and shrubs in a variety of shapes and sizes. Some were aesthetically trimmed, some were perfectly shaped for privacy and others were randomly placed to be admired. The field had an abundance of green from the foliage; however, that only represented half of the color.

Regardless of where the two looked, Anna and Jacob always had a few dozen flowers in their line of view. They seemed to grow out of anything possible. They sprouted from under rocks, on the side of trees and even wrapped around most of the gated perimeter. All the flowers ranged in color, size and petal shape.

The aroma from the abundance of life in the Ersatzian Field was arousing. Jacob expected it to be overwhelming, but the clean, fresh smell blended well together. There was a hint of fresh cut grass, with lavender, hyacinth, and jasmine. Though Jacob didn't know many flowers, he could identify a couple of them.

"This is incredible. It's stunning. Beautiful," Jacob said, Anna nodded.

"It seems as though there's a conversation to be had." Sir Kalvin spoke in a stern, yet kind voice. A patient man, he composed himself as his curious mind wondered about the mention of Giddeom.

"Yes, of course," Anna replied, glancing at Jacob.

"Right." Jacob didn't know if he should explain the situation or jump into his experiences. The silence lingered for just a moment too long, causing it to be awkward.

"I heard you correctly, no? You mentioned Giddeom? How do you know of this name?" Sir Kalvin asked.

"Yes. He's visited me twice now," Jacob replied.

"So you've been chosen?"

"That's where I'm confused." Jacob turned to his mother for comfort. "We know our family has a history of meeting with this man."

"To our knowledge, Sir Kalvin, my grandmother was the last one we assumed to have worked with him. There was always mystery surrounding her though. Everything was secretive," Anna explained.

"Edith," Sir Kalvin replied, shocking them both. It was impossible for him to have been around during her time.

"How did you…?"

Sir Kalvin laughed. "I didn't know her. She passed before I was born. I know of her through our family."

"*Your* family?" Jacob wondered.

"Why would Grandma Edith be connected to…" Anna stopped, aware of how awkward her implication would be.

"In a way, our families have been connected for a long time," Sir Kalvin admitted.

"So that's why everything she did was so secretive. She was working alongside the royal family." Jacob felt relieved to have answered one of his many questions.

"It's more…involved than that," he rebutted. "I don't think it's quite what you think."

Jacob's momentary relief dissipated as he was left without an answer once more. "You mentioned being chosen? Chosen for what?"

"That's an answer *he* must reveal. I shouldn't get involved with that."

Jacob was perplexed. He didn't know how the highest-ranking individual of Sartica couldn't discuss it. Did Giddeom have more authority than their leader?

"Okay…"

Sir Kalvin sensed Jacobs' discontent, but was cunning. He recognized how unique the situation was and couldn't let it go to waste. "How about this: why don't you and I discuss matters further in the privacy of my home? As you both know, privacy is of the utmost importance. Your great grandmother respected and fulfilled this duty."

Jacob glanced at his mother with guilt. He knew how badly she'd want to enter, and she had made the meeting happen.

"In the meantime, Anna, you are more than welcome to roam around our luscious garden. The Ersatzian Field is home to a variety of species – some you may not see anywhere else in Sartica. I can have my assistant check on you. Make sure there isn't anything you need while you wait."

"That's very kind, thank you." Anna nodded. Without words, mother and son confirmed with one another that each of them would be okay. Jacob smiled as Sir Kalvin led the way for him to follow.

Anna was fulfilled. Though she couldn't find the words, she knew her son was where he needed to be. She turned around and focused her gaze upon the beautiful foliage and intoxicating aroma. Uncertain of where to begin, she walked to her left and started from the corner gate to walk the perimeter.

She found herself back in a similar situation as the one experience she had – surrounded by unknown plants, trees and flowers. Though there was no large building in the distance, she was standing atop the largest structure in the region – the Subterranean Domain. Anna suddenly had a poetic realization that she, like her son, was where she needed to be.

"Thank you for understanding the need for privacy. Our conversation shouldn't be too long," Sir Kalvin expressed.

"Of course. So long as my mother is fine. She's the reason I'm here, after all." Jacob chuckled, trying to lighten the mood. Sir Kalvin smiled.

The two men walked toward a small hill, covered in dark green moss. It was small enough to climb, but large enough to not see past it. He knew they were going into the Subterranean Domain, but Jacob had no knowledge of the structure, except that it housed the royal family. The thought of entering their home flared his anxiety, but he tried to ignore it.

The two men walked along the right side of the small hill. As they rounded the corner, Sir Kalvin turned around to face it. Jacob followed and was surprised to see it had completely vanished. There was no green moss.

"Here we are," Sir Kalvin said. In front of them stood a gleaming, golden door, as if it were just polished.

"Where did this…? I didn't see this from outside, and we walked the entire perimeter." Jacob was confident such a bright door wouldn't have gone unnoticed.

"You aren't able to see this from outside. It's one of our added protections." Sir Kalvin smiled. "A sense of security is fundamental for a home."

15

Located at the north end of Karg River and surrounded by a ten-foot obsidian wall, the grounds of Brugōr's castle could be seen from nearly anywhere in the valley. While the castle grounds consisted of numerous towers and structures, none of them compared to Kurhal Tower – the largest structure in the valley. Soaring over half a mile high, the Kurhal's metallic iron walls glistened in the sun. The purpose of its design allowed the leader access to the entire valley while intimidating those who approached it. It was a constant reminder for all civilians that they were being watched and to act appropriately.

Whark visited Brugōr's castle enough times that he no longer feared its towering appearance. He perceived the Kurhal as the weakest point in the valley, surprised it hadn't crumbled to the ground yet.

He had traveled to the castle grounds to investigate the sudden arrival of questionable guests. Their trail from the vehicle had led him to a smaller, cylindrical tower on the eastern side. It coincidently abutted the obsidian wall beside the Karg River, which provided Whark with an excuse for his visit. Though he'd never visited the shorter building, he knew a simple lie should suffice.

He approached the entrance with one guard, who asked to see his access pass.

"I'm here to check the perimeter of the interior walls to ensure there's no seepage into Karg River. We've found higher than normal contaminant levels along the riverbed opposite the wall."

"Why not check the wall then?" the guard asked.

"We have, and it's not eroded. Besides, the contaminants are not obsidian, so it couldn't be from the wall." Whark was impressed by his own sporadic justification.

"Fine. Just stay quiet and be quick."

Whark nodded and entered the tower. There was a circular staircase wrapped alongside the stone walls with rooms jutting outwards. From the ground level, he visualized four accessible doors to investigate.

Feeling the guard's eyes on him, he feigned interest in the lower edges of the wall, pulling out a small beaker to place a few pebble samples inside. Whark made eye contact with the guard, realizing his face was that of confusion.

"With just a couple of these, I'll run a test for any remaining particles. See if it's a match," Whark explained, wearing his black leather gauntlets.

"Great, you're done. Let's go," the guard insisted, as he looked up at the third doorway from the bottom. Whark noticed and stated his rebuttal.

"Unfortunately, I must check the entire perimeter due to—"

"Little shit. Fine, but be quick." The guard looked up again. "Keep your head down and your mouth closed." Whark nodded as the guard turned around, disinterested.

After a couple minutes, Whark made his way to the front of the staircase, watching the guard carefully. As he prepared to make his daring ascent, a visitor approached the entrance. Fortunately, it was a chatty guard who came by to discuss work politics.

"Can you believe they're getting divorced?" the newcomer asked.

The guard glanced at Whark on the floor wrapped in tattered beige clothes held by a brown leather belt and snakeskin boots, exposing his toes. Riddled with judgement, the guard rolled his eyes and returned to his counterpart. "No. It's fucking awful. That bitch better have it coming."

Whark used the opportunity to quietly bolt up the staircase. He checked the first door, but it was locked. As he carefully approached the second doorway up the short and narrow steps, he noticed it was open, impossible to pass without being seen. He pressed his back against the cold stone and turned his head around to peer inside. Voices were barely audible, but no one was in sight. Whark felt confident the people were further away, so with a deep inhale, he scampered past.

After a pause, Whark reached the third door, which was also open. He knew the two men speeding across the desert had entered this tower, but he wasn't sure this was the correct room. He hoped his hunch from the guard was correct. He brought his ear to the end of the doorframe, listening to the conversation.

"I'll notify him you've returned. He'll want to meet with you both and hear of your success," a woman said in a rugged tone.

"Perfect. We're excited to see him. He mentioned a dinner in our honor?" an unusually deep male voice said.

"Vanilor," a third voice pleaded. "Is that really necessary? We've completed the mission. It's over."

"Bullshit!" he rebutted. "He mentioned it, Morty."

Vanilor and Morty. What unusual names, Whark thought.

The woman grimaced. "I believe he plans to host a gathering for the success of the mission."

"Fuckin' A. See, buddy? Ask and you shall receive."

"I suppose." Mortimer sighed.

Whark was ready to put faces to the voices and carefully twisted his neck to look.

"Should we wait here?" The man with the deep voice was short, yet strong. *Vanilor.*

"There's no need. Just hand me the Novalis Rod and you're free to roam until he's ready." The woman was tall with long, flowing blonde hair. Without seeing her face, Whark knew of her beauty.

"If you don't mind, Shrenka, I'll hand it to him myself." Vanilor gripped his bag. Whark sensed the contents were important.

"Actually, I do mind." Shrenka tried to grab the bag but failed. "The rod is property of the castle and must be returned, immediately," she hissed.

"Well it's here, on the castle grounds. It's home. Brugōr can have it when we see him."

Whark watched as an unamused Mortimer and a proud Vanilor exchanged glances. In his momentary distraction, Shrenka's right arm extended out and grabbed the satchel around Vanilor's body, tearing the strap. Whark gasped, covering his mouth for silence.

"How dare you defy me and threaten to keep what is ours." Shrenka's voice was sinister, dark. It echoed within the walls of the room. Whark found himself unexpectedly frightened. Mortimer stepped away and Vanilor lunged forward, but she was too quick.

"Nice try." She chuckled and even her laugh was sinister. She pulled the contents of the bag out and held up the inactive Novalis Rod. Whark was shocked to see such a disappointing object. She threw the bag at Vanilor's face and flailed her right arm down toward the floor with the rod in hand. Panels opened and lowered from the tip of the rod, and a bright, golden light illuminated from within. Whark retreated behind the wall, blinded by the light.

"Shit!" Shrenka yelled. "Is that thing alive?" Whark positioned himself low and turned his head, not expecting to see what was on the other side. He gasped, though no one noticed

A quorian.

Its wrists and ankles were shackled to one another, eyes closed and body unmoving.

"What happened to him?" Mortimer asked.

"He's been inside that thing. What'd you expect him to look like?" Vanilor smirked.

Whark immediately knew what he was staring at. His vision went blurry as the room began to spin until he toppled over – landing directly in front of the doorway.

"Who the fuck is that!?" Vanilor shouted.

"What're you doing here? Who the hell are you?" Shrenka asked. Mortimer, rubbing a peculiar pendant around his neck, was too mesmerized by the quorian to acknowledge him sprawled on the floor.

Whark saw three sets of eyes looking back at him: Shrenka, Vanilor and the quorian on the ground. Feeling the pain and sorrow from its eyes, he was happy to see the quorian alive. Then, the panic rushed as he began to question his fate. There was a moment of pause and then everything happened.

"Get him! Brugōr will have your head if he gets away!" Shrenka shouted. Vanilor lunged forward, however Whark pushed himself off the ground and stumbled back down the stairs. Vanilor's body slammed against the floor, his jaw taking most of the blow.

"Motherfucker!" Vanilor shouted. Though Shrenka glared at Mortimer, he didn't move.

As Whark made his descent, the guard ran up, sword in hand. With little experience in combat or self-defense, Whark sensed trouble. He looked down to the ground floor, but he was too high to jump. He'd survive the fall, but feared breaking his legs. He turned around and glanced at an enraged Shrenka when a piercing shriek echoed throughout the tower. Knowing it was the captured quorian, Whark's heart sank. He shivered, imagining the torture they were inflicting. He desperately wanted to save the victim, but he needed to save himself first.

The guard was moments away from killing Whark and he decided to use the only defense he knew, already apologetic for the damage it'd cause. He dug into his pocket and pulled out a small, black vial. Osvita consistently reminded him to protect himself around the castle grounds, as she never trusted their leader.

Though he felt differently, he obliged her wishes. The objects for protection typically varied, depending on what Whark did that day. One time he carried a small knife from river buildup. Another time, he brought cyanide powder for a water treatment. Most recently, he carried a large shard of glass that Grum found beside the river.

With the guard just steps away from him, Whark flung open the tightly bound seal and tossed its contents at his attacker's face. *Sulfuric acid.*

"I'm sorry," Whark said, though the guard didn't hear it over his wailing. Whark looked back, making eye contact with Shrenka.

"You will not get away!" she shouted. "We'll have your head soon enough!"

Whark exited the tower, adrenaline coursing through his veins. He wanted to head toward the main entrance and flee, but he could hear guards approaching. He knew once they entered the tower, it would only take seconds to have Shrenka give orders for his capture.

Whark needed to act quickly. He turned left and squeezed between the obsidian wall and the tower, heading north within the castle grounds. Flattening his body against the tower, he remained still, catching his breath. He needed to escape, but didn't know how. He looked toward the obsidian wall, but knew he couldn't climb. It was crafted to be jagged and sharp so no one could enter, or escape.

Whark heard what sounded like an army enter the tower – feet stomping, weapons and armor clanging. With a deep exhale, he pushed away from the tower and ran north, staying as close to the obsidian wall as possible.

Though the grounds were big, there wasn't a lot of space to hide. Whark carefully advanced, darting behind objects and structures for cover. Fortunately, the commotion at the east tower captivated the attention of many. He knew he had a window to escape, but it was quickly closing. He'd soon be the mouse in a pit of ravenous snakes.

Whark stopped and darted behind a massive, decorative pillar, stunned. There was a small, thin opening in the obsidian wall. Apparently it was not as indestructible as he'd thought.

When it was clear, Whark brought himself closer to the apparent exit. After careful examination, he realized it was more of a crack than an opening, but it was probably his only means of escape. He peered through to see a guard defending the weakened spot. He was larger than the one he'd faced earlier – his muscles screaming to be freed from the confines of his armor. His axe was beautifully crafted and heavy, though Whark sensed the guard could swing it with the greatest of ease.

"Officer Kincade was attacked!" someone shouted in the distance. Whark sulked, riddled with guilt now he knew the name of who he'd assaulted and possibly killed. He reminded himself it was in self-defense.

"GO! Look for him! Whark Dimmerk, he has brown hair, average height…" They continued giving an exact description of his appearance.

Examining the crack again, he knew it'd be tight, but his bigger issue was the barbarian on the other side. His only advantage was the element of surprise. Adjusting his line of vision, Whark saw part of Karg River, some large boulders and part of some equipment. He couldn't quite tell what it was yet.

As the guards approached from behind, his time was up. Placing his right hand in his pocket, he grabbed the now empty vial of sulfuric acid. With focused accuracy and precision, he tossed the vial so it rotated in a narrow motion, allowing it to squeeze through the crack without hitting the obsidian wall. It soared right over the guard's head and landed on the ground about six feet in front of him. The guard immediately placed his hands on his deadly weapon.

With a few steps, the guard investigated the mysterious object. Whark leapt forward and exhaled all his air to squeeze his body through the opening. He immediately silenced his urge to scream from the sharp edges of obsidian piercing his skin. Fortunately, it only lasted a few seconds and Whark now stood a few feet behind the barbarian.

He evaluated his options. An escape by Karg River wouldn't go unnoticed and he'd be quickly caught. Running around the other side would lead to a dead end. Whark looked down, remembering their environment, and grinned.

He couldn't win in a fight against the guard, but he did have stealthy reflexes. He quietly knelt and used both hands to pick up a boulder large enough to knock down his opponent, yet small enough that he could lift it.

He heaved the boulder at the guard who was still bent down examining the vial. There was a moment of absolute silence as Whark watched the event unfold. The guard never turned around and as the boulder descended, it met with the back of his skull. His head flung forward and face-planted into the cracked, empty vial of sulfuric acid. Once again riddled with guilt, Whark knew he'd just killed for the second time.

With the threat removed, he focused on the glistening metal covered by debris. With a naturally curious mind, Whark removed some of it to unveil his new, unexpected plan – a motorized buggy completely enclosed to handle the elements. He jumped inside and feverishly looked around for keys when he noticed two guards approaching the crack in the castle wall.

Whark's hands trembled as he felt around, a careful eye on their position. They examined the fallen barbarian, then gazed upon the vehicle, but not before he quietly hid into the seat. Whark's stomach sank. The guards placed their hands on their swords and walked toward the vehicle. Suddenly remembering the windows were blacked-out for the sun, Whark took a breath and surveyed his surroundings. He was embarrassed to notice the keys on the passenger seat beside him.

The guards jumped from the roar of the ignition and Whark felt a wave of relief knowing he'd escape. Tempted to open the window and gloat at the guards, he knew the fight was far from over. Brugōr's men wouldn't stop until he was captured.

Whark put the buggy in drive and floored it across the desert landscape. He followed the obsidian wall around toward the front of the castle grounds and drove parallel to the Karg River. A wave of panic rushed over him. He knew if they couldn't find him within the castle, they'd travel to his home. He needed to reach his family first and seek shelter. Remembering the quorian sprawled across the floor, he desperately wanted to save him but knew he wasn't able to do so yet.

16

The thought of Neetri, a Savior, surviving the confrontation with the Divinity King excited Lady Vixa. She'd been certain that such a powerful force would've vanquished her. If it hadn't been for Fravia, she wouldn't have known to check whether the page from the Klai Chronicles was still intact.

As Quorian Ruler, she was always treated with respect due to her title, but that didn't mean everyone agreed with her beliefs and leadership. One such doubter was Lucemia, Fravia's mother. She desperately wanted to see Lady Vixa empower others, especially other females. She wished for her to act and use her voice, instead of the complacency she'd witnessed. Though Lucemia maintained respect, Lady Vixa always sensed her disdain.

Lucemia raised her daughter to form her own opinions, yet it proved challenging when Fravia consistently heard her mother's disapproval of Lady Vixa. She felt pressured to share her sentiment, but held onto her independent opinion. When she befriended Smolar, she'd occasionally learned of the ruler, resulting in a different perspective than her mother. She felt all quorians were different and no one should be scrutinized or judged, regardless of their position in the community, due to personal expectations or perceptions.

"Thank you, Fravia. I appreciate your knowledge, your wisdom, and your willingness to think freely," Lady Vixa said.

"Of course." Fravia smiled. "My mother raised me to be a free-thinker. I'm not sure it *always* worked out as she intended."

"A parent should welcome their child's unique mind instead of trying to duplicate their own." Lady Vixa admired her maturity. "My apologies, but after learning what you informed me of, I must check on Neetri. Maybe I can still connect with her."

"Of course." Smolar glanced at Fravia, hinting they should leave.

"You are more than welcome to stay, if you'd like," Lady Vixa blurted out. "Both of you."

Though excited they could stay, Smolar was envious of Fravia's immediate warmth with Lady Vixa. He'd spent years yearning for it himself. Remembering her recent revelation, he couldn't rid the lingering resentment.

"Thank you!" Fravia said, trying to minimize her excitement.

Lady Vixa closed her eyes, channeling the Klai's Eye charm she had given to Neetri, wondering if anything would appear.

The Divinity King. The Lost Sphere. The Barren Land. Life. Death.

Uncertain what it could be, she kept an open mind. Her surrounding sounds slowly drowned away as her tightly shut eyes began to reveal a new picture. Unable to make out what it was, the sound blared through instead.

"Stop playing with your dick already! We gotta go."

Lady Vixa wondered where the vaguely familiar voice came from. The peculiar, blurry shape shook violently and then started to come into focus as the sight panned up to reveal the individual wearing Klai's Eye around his neck.

How is this possible!? Lady Vixa wondered. In front of her stood a familiar man, tall and slender with dark hair and dark brown eyes.

Mont…? Lady Vixa tried to recall his name.

"I can't fucking believe she stole it from us," another familiar voice shouted.

Isn't that…?

"I know, Vanilor. Can't do anything about it now, though. What's important is he knows the job's done."

"You're right, Morty, you're fuckin' right. We did it."

Mortimer and Vanilor...those were the men Neetri had chased. Where is she? How did they obtain the necklace?

"Now that he's got the Novalis Rod and that...creature, we can meet with Brugōr and claim our reward." Vanilor grinned.

"Creature..." Mortimer whispered with contempt.

Creature!? Are they referring to Promit?

"It'll be nice to put this behind us." Mortimer sounded defeated, drained. Exhausted.

"And see what's next." Vanilor patted a displeased Mortimer on the back as they exited the bathroom.

The two men walked out into the peculiar tower with a winding staircase around the perimeter. Shrenka and the guards were gone.

"Who do you think that man was?" Mortimer asked.

"I'm not sure, but hopefully they find him. Little fucker was creeping his nose around shit that didn't concern him."

"Didn't care enough to go after him though?" Mortimer chuckled, attempting to lighten the mood.

"Shit, I did more than you did, boy," Vanilor hissed. "Besides, there's something shady about Shrenka. I don't trust the bitch, ya know?"

"She certainly isn't the nicest—"

"Fuck no, she ain't."

Shrenka? Who's that?

Mortimer and Vanilor exited the stairwell and followed the path until they faced the tallest tower in the entire valley – the Kurhal. Mortimer raised his head, squinting in a failed attempt to see the tip.

This world...is astonishing.

As the men approached the entrance, which was surrounded by a massive rose garden with spikes in place of thorns, they were halted by a guard.

"Excuse me." He placed his sword out, stopping Vanilor.

"Excuse *you*. We're meeting with Brugōr," Vanilor insisted.

"He's expecting us," Mortimer added softly.

"What're your names?"

"Vanilor and Mortimer."

The guard scanned a sheet inside the doorframe that listed all expected visitors for the day. "Vanilor Dipythian and Mortimer Hullington?"

"That's what we fuckin' said." Vanilor forced himself into the tower, pushing aside the guard's sword. Mortimer shook his head and followed.

"My apologies," the guard said.

"I'm sorry," Mortimer whispered back.

Kurhal Tower was larger than either man remembered. The floors were glistening obsidian with a red carpet to indicate various paths, and the walls were built with large gray cinderblocks. The main foyer was well-lit by electricity and candlelight, with three elevator shafts on each wall, excluding the southern end they entered from. Guards and unknown individuals passed by Vanilor and Mortimer.

The men walked toward the closest set of elevators and waited for the doors to open.

"Where are we meeting him?" Mortimer asked.

"The banquet hall," Vanilor answered, pressing the button for the thirty-third floor.

Halfway through their ascent, the dark cab illuminated from the light outside. The wall behind them was thick glass, exposing the entire valley below. Both men were mesmerized by the glorious sight, neither afraid of heights.

"Our home is fuckin' stunning," Vanilor said, excited for his life to change.

"There are endless places to explore and hide. Nothing is truly hidden."

Mortimer didn't share the same excitement as Vanilor as he dealt with his own morality from the pain he'd caused. He was ravaged with guilt from the quorian capture, manipulating Michael in Tillerack, and aiding in the death of the unknown assailant coming into The Barren Land.

This place…is massive. How are we ever going to find Promit here?

The two men turned around when they arrived at their destination. They stepped out to what seemed to be an average space. The ceilings were high, the walls were beige and the floors were white. Vanilor paced the room, wondering if there was something awry. Mortimer looked around, his eyes darting in various corners to look for anything peculiar.

"This seems…like a waiting room," Mortimer exclaimed. Suddenly, a shiny, obsidian door in the back corner, which neither man had noticed, slowly creaked open.

"Uhh…are we supposed to…?" Mortimer hesitated.

The door opened all the way, exposing another, more elaborate room with no one to greet them.

"Did that shit just open on its own?" Vanilor asked.

"I…I think we're supposed to go in there," Mortimer whispered.

"You may enter," a dark and nefarious voice said from inside.

Who was that? Lady Vixa asked.

Vanilor and Mortimer exchanged glances and sighed, knowing who was waiting for them.

Finally. Show me the one responsible for this.

Vanilor and Mortimer entered a room massive in every direction – the banquet hall. The ceilings were high, studded with crystal chandeliers, and the space was wide, filled with dozens of circular dinner tables, each with ten chairs and golden centerpieces. Unlike most of the places within Brugōr's castle, obsidian was nowhere to be found. The floor glistened white marble, with gray veins throughout, and all of the walls were draped in a royal, rich blue fabric. The back wall had one single, elongated ivory drape surpassing one-hundred feet. In front of that was a podium with a small, rectangular table beside it of the same decor. There was one dark brown door that resided in the far back, left corner of the room.

This…is one room!? I'd never believe this without seeing it, Lady Vixa thought, appreciative of her inside access.

"What is this place? This shit is sick," Vanilor whispered.

"This must be the banquet hall," Mortimer responded.

The men slowly walked toward the center of the room, unsure what to do. They both heard the eerie voice from earlier, but there was no one in the room.

"H-hello?" Vanilor asked, his voice reverberating throughout.

"Speak with confidence," the nefarious voice replied. Suddenly the back corner door swung open and a large, brute of a man entered. The men could feel the vibration in the floor with each step he took.

"Sir Brugōr," they said in unison as they bowed their heads.

That…is their leader!? Sir Brugōr. He's…huge.

Standing seven-feet tall, his intimidation matched the Kurhal. The leader of The Barren Land was a self-righteous man of brute force, and strength. His muscles were large, skin golden, and his dark-brown eyes perfectly matched the hair on his head and face. Partially covering his physique was the royal armor and black cape, both showcasing the emblem for The Barren Land. Shaped like a damaged spearpoint that pierced an object with a circular center, it represented the castle's regime and everything the region stood for.

"It seems as though you've completed the mission, yes?" Brugōr asked.

That voice… Lady Vixa felt the menace.

While Vanilor and Mortimer had met him numerous times, they'd never felt more intimidated. Mortimer waited for his partner to respond, but realized he was unable to. Brugōr grew impatient.

"Yes," Mortimer murmured. "Yes!" He repeated louder. "The mission's complete. We returned with the creature and weapon."

"Brilliant!" Brugōr sat at a table, inviting the men to sit and talk.

"Thank you, Sir Brugōr. We're excited to return successfully." Vanilor found his voice.

They're all happy...for capturing Promit. Evil. They're all evil.

"How did it feel to capture one of those things? Look at it in the eye?" Brugōr asked, excited at the thought. Mortimer sulked, unable to answer the question.

"It was glorious!" Vanilor shouted.

You monster.

"I remember hearing about quorians, but never thought I'd have the chance to see one up close." Vanilor's excitement was tangible. Mortimer poorly attempted a smirk and glanced at Brugōr, who shared the same excitement as Vanilor.

"Shit! Incredible!" Brugōr shouted, leaning back in his chair. "So…"

Vanilor and Mortimer exchanged glances, wondering what their leader was going to say next.

"Where is it? Where is the quorian? The Novalis Rod?"

"We…" Vanilor looked at Mortimer again. "We thought your assistant Shrenka provided you with everything."

Brugōr slammed his right foot down on the floor hard enough to crack the marble. Suddenly, the back door swung open and a heavily-armored guard approached them. He saluted in place and remained silent.

"Find Shrenka and bring her here," the brute leader demanded. The guard nodded and swiftly left the room. "Now, tell me what happened from the beginning."

Vanilor proudly explained most of the story. With Mortimer's point of view, Lady Vixa knew the two men, though both vindictive, were different. While Vanilor was driven, Mortimer carried a heaviness – shame. He looked around the room, occasionally making eye contact with the men, but he continuously sulked.

"After the other escaped, we decided it was best to return with the one we had,"

Vanilor continued.

That must've been Smolar, Lady Vixa thought.

Brugōr was impressed and delighted with the information. Vanilor hoped it would bring him closer with the regime. As he described the events with Shrenka, he explained their version of the story.

"So you asked to keep the object in your possession and she denied you?" Brugōr asked.

"Yes."

"And you." Brugōr looked at Mortimer. "Do you agree with your partner?"

"Yeah, it's true. We wanted to deliver it to you ourselves, but she claimed, 'it's property of the castle' and belonged in her possession." There was a moment of silence. Vanilor contemplated mentioning the intruder, but didn't want to tarnish Brugōr's perception of him.

Facing the entrance of the banquet hall, the leader looked up to admire the sensual walk of his female companion who'd just entered the room.

"Shrenka. Nice of you to join us. Sit." His voice billowed. Shrenka smiled and followed his orders. Over her right shoulder was the same satchel Vanilor had possessed during the mission.

"Hello, gentlemen. Today's been an interesting day, no?" She smirked. Her long, curly blonde hair flowed over her shoulders and upper back. With dark eye makeup and rich crimson lips, her skin appeared as porcelain. Dressed entirely in black, her upper body was tightly fitted in tulle and her pants were skin-tight leather. If her sharply arched eyebrows didn't express such a sinister expression, Vanilor would've found her more ravishing than he already did.

Shrenka carefully placed the bag onto the table as Brugōr continued to speak.

"Vanilor and Mortimer were just disclosing the details of their successful mission. Everything went as anticipated." He grinned. "Until they arrived here. Care to explain?"

Shrenka exhaled, displeased. "I'd prefer to discuss the matter privately, but since *they* brought it up…" She rolled her eyes. "It seems as though the intruder's name was Whark Dimmerk and—"

"Intruder!?" Brugōr interjected.

"Isn't that what they…?" Shrenka furiously glanced at the men.

"Shrenka." Brugōr's voice deepened. "Vanilor and Mortimer claimed you barred them from holding onto their findings. That you took the Novalis Rod from them, insisting it belonged to the castle." Shrenka was appalled. Not only had her assumption been wrong, but she felt wrongfully accused of harassment. "Let's resolve this, and then we'll return to this intruder *you* mentioned."

"Well, I don't know what *they* told you, but here's what happened." Under the table, Shrenka extended her leather-bound leg toward Brugōr's, grazing it higher and higher. He glanced at her but didn't push away. "The three of us met in the east tower where they briefly explained their success story. They unveiled to me the Novalis Rod and, ultimately, the creature."

Promit isn't a creature! Lady Vixa shouted.

"After the unveiling, it reentered the rod and insisted I hold onto it."

"That's a lie!" Vanilor shouted.

"Hey!" Brugōr yelled. "You explained your story without interruption. Let her do the same."

Vanilor sulked in his chair. Mortimer sat quietly, watching the madness unfold.

"Both men demanded I hold onto the Novalis Rod," Shrenka reiterated. "I allowed them to hold onto the artifact themselves, but they had no interest. All they wanted was their reward." Shrenka gave an evil grin, flaunting her victory. Just as Brugōr was about to respond, she continued.

"Might I just add, I know we need to discuss the intruder, which we can do privately; however, these two men chose to do nothing about it." Brugōr glared at them. Mortimer anticipated her words while Vanilor was enraged. "They stood by as the man fled the tower, insisting that their job was complete." Shrenka felt the power of control over the story, continuously rubbing Brugōr's prominently outlined groin. She flung open the satchel and pulled out the inactive Novalis Rod.

Vanilor, Mortimer and Brugōr all admired the object. Brugōr picked it up, having a special bond with it. With a precise movement, he activated the rod, pointing it toward the ground. A bright light illuminated from the tip as the brown boards began to lower. The true appearance exposed itself – a golden nova at the end of a sturdy rod. Shooting out were grains of yellow sand that extended toward the floor, slowly forming a shape. Suddenly, one more startling light gleamed, forcing everyone to shut their eyes or look away. When they looked again, the Novalis Rod was deactivated and on the floor lay a blue figure.

PROMIT! Lady Vixa shouted. *He's alive!*

Face down on the floor with his arms and legs in shackles, Promit was banged up, bruised and emaciated.

"I can't believe my eyes…" Brugōr was speechless, astounded at their mission.

"We have no form of communication with it," Shrenka admitted.

Brugōr recalled the dishonesty and deception from their discussion moments ago. "Look at this creature on the ground," he insisted. "*This* is why we are all here. All the bullshit about who took what, and when, is nonsense. Some of you are lying to me and I *hate* liars."

"I'm sorry for any miscommunication," Vanilor pleaded. "I can assure you we're loyal and dedicated. We're here with good intentions. We wanted to hold onto the Novalis Rod, but maybe—"

"Lies! Lies. Nothing out of your mouths can be trusted," Shrenka hissed. "Yes, you captured a quorian – outstanding work. That doesn't mean you can return with arrogance and greed." She looked down at the creature. "It's not like you taught that thing to speak or understand us. We've no form of communication with it."

"That is just simply not—" Vanilor tried once again.

"Enough!" Brugōr shouted, forcibly standing, throwing his chair backwards onto the floor. Shrenka quickly retracted her leg. "I will not stand for this any longer. Guard!" When Brugōr shouted, it wasn't the volume that sent chills down the spines of those around him – it was his tone. It somehow managed to deepen, almost from the depths of darkness.

Mortimer noticed an enlarged bulge in the leader's groin. Staring a moment too long, he'd been caught by Shrenka. The two locked eyes until she winked at him and turned away.

The corner brown door opened, and the familiar armored guard approached the table.

Brugōr looked back down at the weakened, tortured quorian. With little movement and slow breaths, he was very much alive.

Monster! Let him go! Lady Vixa shouted, aware her words couldn't be heard.

"This should be a celebratory occasion. You don't realize the importance of this mission. It's incredible you were able to capture him. For that, you'll be rewarded as promised." Vanilor gleamed, looking at Mortimer, who didn't seem as appreciative. "Additionally, there'll be a dinner held here in our banquet room to celebrate this success." Brugōr placed his arms down and for a moment, the room fell silent, as if time stood still. The two men, Shrenka and the guard waited patiently to hear what their leader said next. Brugōr decided to act instead of using words.

In one swift move, he raised his right arm across the guard's neck. The two men hadn't noticed what he had in his hand until they saw the blood. Deep crimson escaped his body. There was a unified gasp around the table. The guard's eyes widened and his body clamored to the ground, bouncing his knees off the marble floor until he collapsed entirely. The guard's right arm tried to reach his neck but his life quickly faded away. Blood continued to pour out from the wide gash.

My word... Lady Vixa was horrified, unaware of the brutality in the Outer World.

"If there's any more disloyalty or dishonesty from you three, your fate will be worse than his." Brugōr expressed a maniacal grin as he spoke.

Mortimer wanted nothing more than to run. If he could have without risking his life, he would have, forgetting the reward. His only option was to remain and wait until he could leave, questioning his actions and morals.

Vanilor remained silent and still, battling between fear and admiration. He was terrified to move or question his leader, aware of the consequences. It was also a reason Vanilor idolized the man. He was ruthless – his actions reflected his own beliefs. Vanilor knew Brugōr's choices were his to make. Surrounded by riches, beautiful women, and a slew of exciting possibilities, he found Brugōr's life appealing. The idea was a pleasant escape from the life he had at home, a deep regret that had slowly eaten away at him for years.

Unlike the two men, Shrenka was only partially surprised. She'd known Brugōr long enough to always watch him. Though he typically kept the obsidian dagger near his ankle, she noticed it was inside his bracer. As the guard's lifeless body lay across the floor, Shrenka didn't feel sorrow or sadness – she was aroused. Grinning and wiggling her hips, Vanilor noticed her movements while Mortimer's head remained down.

Brugōr looked at his woman and smirked, aware of her arousal. "If you'll excuse me, I've some business to tend to. You'll hear from us regarding the celebratory dinner."

"Plans are already underway," Shrenka remarked.

Brugōr grabbed the Novalis Rod and summoned Promit back into his lair. "You'll come with me until we're ready."

Promit…we'll come for you. We will save you.

As Brugōr and Shrenka exited through the brown door, the two men were left alone. Vanilor stood up and made his way toward the exit, battling his emotions.

"You coming? We needa get the fuck out of here," Vanilor insisted.

Mortimer stared at the body on the ground as the blood dried.

Their world's surrounded by monsters. Every one of them is evil. Lady Vixa was sickened by what she'd witnessed.

Carefully walking around the body, Mortimer made his way toward Vanilor when they heard unusual sounds from the back corner. With Shrenka's constant moaning and Brugōr's occasional grunt, it was no secret what was going on.

"Fuck. That man's a machine," Vanilor proclaimed. Mortimer's patience was dwindling. He couldn't stand to hear Vanilor speak of their leader in such a positive light anymore, especially after what they'd just witnessed.

The two exited the banquet room and entered the elevator. The men were riddled with shock and exhaustion.

"Well, what a day this has been!" Vanilor exclaimed with glee.

"I can't with this bullshit anymore, Vanilor. I'm done!" Mortimer blurted out, unable to maintain his composure. He rustled his hair and pulled off the pendant he'd found just inside The Lost Sphere.

No! Lady Vixa shouted. Everything went dark as the transmission ended.

To say the Quorian Ruler was exhausted was an understatement. When her eyes opened, she was relieved to see the comforts of her own home. Being within her city walls never felt so good. She was granted a new, deep appreciation and respect for their city. It was clear to her how fortunate they were to have been secluded, avoiding such evil.

"Lady Vixa?" Smolar asked.

"W-what?" Lady Vixa was caught off guard, forgetting she had allowed Smolar and Fravia to stay. "You're both still here…" She couldn't believe her eyes. "I feel as though I've been under for an entire day. You didn't have to stay."

"Of course we did," Fravia insisted. "We heard what you were saying. We wanted to make sure you'd be okay."

Lady Vixa tilted her head, staring at the two quorians. She had trouble remembering the last time someone had shown genuine concern for her safety. The only person she could recall was her father and that had been a lifetime ago.

When Lady Vixa collapsed on the floor, the two quorians ran toward her.

"Are you okay?" Smolar shouted. He looked at Fravia with worry, though she maintained her composure.

"She's okay. Lady Vixa will be fine." Fravia noticed her breathing. "She's exhausted. She saw more than she was prepared for. The world outside our city is filled with temptation and mystery. Who knows what she just exposed herself to."

17

As Whark explained the situation, Osvita became enraged. She wasn't an angry person, but she was disappointed that her husband would jeopardize their life and well-being. All the years of patience, grit and loyalty she'd given to growing her catering business were at risk due to his actions. It was a realization that Osvita had difficulty accepting, especially since Whark had never helped with her culinary success.

The Dimmerk family knew it was best to leave their home for a few days. While Rexhia gathered some belongings from her bedroom, Whark and Osvita did the same in theirs.

"You're awfully quiet," Whark noticed.

"It's better than fighting."

"I'm really sorry, Osvita. I never meant for any of this to happen." He was genuinely remorseful for his actions but didn't know how to resolve the situation. Osvita didn't dignify his words with a response – she continued to grab clothes and personal belongings. Whark watched as his wife opened her bedside drawer and pulled out a small vial of clear water.

"Do you think it's necessary to bring that?"

"I don't know what kind of trouble you got us all into…" She paused, holding back her emotions. "But I refuse to lose what's left of our past. I've—"

"Okay, okay," Whark interjected. "I understand."

"Oh shit," Osvita muttered, startling them both as she didn't often curse.

"What is it?"

"I just remembered…" Osvita sat on the bed and closed her eyes, maintaining her temper since her daughter was close enough to hear a meltdown. "Before you came home, we had a visitor."

"A visitor? Who?"

"Someone from the Kurhal." Whark felt the weight of her words on his heart. She continued before he could respond. "They requested my catering services for a dinner being held in their banquet room a few weeks from now."

"What!?"

"Shh," Osvita insisted, reminding him of their daughter nearby.

"Well obviously you can't do it. It's just not—"

"We both know when Brugōr requests something…"

"I don't care. Call it off, cancel it. There's no way you can go there *now*," Whark insisted. Osvita understood his point, but was agitated that he'd tried to insert himself in the decision-making of her business.

"I'm not making any decisions right now. Let's just grab our things and go." Osvita took her bag and walked out of the room. She couldn't blatantly lie and say she'd cancel. Though the regime's purpose for booking her seemed suspect, Osvita considered how it could aid in her business. Working for the most powerful and influential person would help her standing. It was the only major territory in the valley she hadn't captivated. She decided to put the discussion to rest, for now.

"Hey, sweetheart, are you ready?" Osvita peeked into her daughter's room.

"Just about, Mom," Rexhia replied, shoving belongings into her bag, hiding a slingshot she'd found a few years ago.

"Alright, let's go."

Rexhia nodded and zipped her bag closed. "We'll only be gone two nights?"

she asked, shutting the light off in her room.

"I'm sure just a few," Whark replied.

"And are we staying the night at Mr. Grum's house?"

"We'll see, darling. First, we plan to just speak with him."

Each with their own bag in hand, the Dimmerks exited their home and locked the front door. Just as they were about to leave, their neighbor spotted them.

"Hey, guys!" Crogin shouted in a friendly tone. Whark planned to ignore him, but Osvita would never.

"Hello, Crogin. Hope you are both well today?" she asked, slowly walking backwards to head off.

"Yes. I just wanted to say thank you for the soup!" Osvita stopped walking – Rexhia followed suit. "Suzmina nearly ate the entire thing. She hadn't slept so good in years. There was something different about it…what was it?"

"A new berry Rexi brought home," she said, smiling at her daughter.

"Well do it again next time – it was scrumptious!"

"Absolutely! Will do."

They were about to continue their journey when he spoke again. "Heading out for the day?" Crogin asked, admiring their bags.

"Osvita…" Whark whispered, as she darted him a piercing stare. Osvita placed her bag down and walked toward their kind neighbor.

"Yes, we are leaving for the night – maybe two."

"Is…everything okay?" He sensed urgency in their departure.

"Can I ask a favor?" Osvita whispered without answering his question.

"Anything for you." Crogin looked beyond her, past Rexhia, and stared directly at Whark. He smiled when his gaze returned to Osvita.

"A few guards from the Kurhal may come by soon looking for us."

"Guards? Are you guys in troub —"

"If they come to you with questions, tell them you haven't seen us today."

Crogin smiled, closed his eyes, and nodded. "Of course. I haven't seen a thing."

"Thank you. I owe you a delicious pot when I return. Please give my regards to Suzmina."

Returning to her family, she picked up her bags and waved goodbye to Crogin.

Grum Lagom had no spouse or children; he lived a simple, comfortable life. He was the type of man who didn't take himself too seriously and always appreciated a good laugh. Whark had never seen Grum show any strong emotional connection. He maintained a lackadaisical attitude in life, which Whark partially envied.

He immediately thought of Grum's home when he realized they needed to flee. It would provide his family with shelter, yet a connection to the goings on at the castle. Grum only lived ten minutes away from the Dimmerks, within the Bazaar.

"So, are we going to talk about what I saw in there?" Whark whispered to his wife, as their daughter led the way, making sure she hadn't heard their conversation. He desperately wanted to discuss it, but Osvita was so disappointed, she hadn't even thought about it herself.

"The quorian..." she replied. "It's...terrifying." She looked at him with deep fear in her eyes.

"His condition wasn't good. He was being held captive by a device. A rod of some sort." He couldn't recall its name. "He seemed young."

"Where'd they find him?"

"They didn't say."

"I wonder if anyone plans to rescue him. If anyone even knows he's here..." She found herself sympathizing for the quorian – a stranger of a supposedly extinct race she hadn't met.

"I doubt it," he claimed. "Rexhia, don't wander too far off," Whark shouted, watching his daughter.

"Hmmm," Osvita said, as a controversial thought came to mind. She wasn't sure if it was worth the effort.

"What is it?" Whark asked.

"Just thinking if we could do anything. My heart aches for that young one."

"He's under heightened security, especially now. I doubt anyone but Brugōr will see him," Whark remarked as they turned right and came to a fork in the road. "Rexhia, come this way, honey. His house is over here."

"Whark," Osvita said, "capturing a quorian isn't something they'll want the public knowing. It's a huge problem. You're possibly their only liability to ensure the quorian remains a secret." Whark felt a rush of fear and panic. Though he knew the severity of the situation, hearing someone else speak the words forced him to accept reality. "There's a good chance we won't be able to return home...for a while."

Whark sighed. "Come, Rexhia. This is his home."

"Fortunately I packed my new knives, just in case," Osvita whispered. She had no history of violence or fighting, but her instinct told her to bring something to help defend her family.

Knock, knock, knock.

"I hope he's home."

"I'm sure he is. The man doesn't do much." Whark remarked.

Knock. Knock. Knock.

The sound grew louder with each thump. Four guards stood outside the Dimmerks' home, awaiting a response. After a minute, it was clear no one was there. While three of the guards stood by the door, unsure what to do next, the commander walked to the adjacent house and knocked. Within seconds, an elderly man opened.

"Hello, sir. Mind if I ask you a couple questions? I'm from the Kurhal," the guard clarified, knowing his rank would intimidate more than a typical castle guard's.

"Sure."

"May I ask your name?"

"Crogin, and yours?"

"Vincent," he answered. "Thank you, Crogin." The guard took out a notepad and began writing. "Does anyone else live here with you?"

"My wife, Suzmina. She is gravely ill and hasn't been able to get out of bed for months now."

"I-I see." Vincent didn't expect such an answer. "Well, I'm here to ask about your neighbor, Whark Dimmerk."

"Oh, yes." Crogin looked over at their house. "Nice man, kind family. Quiet."

"How long have you known Whark and his family?"

"I don't know – we've neighbors for many years. We didn't speak much until my wife fell ill. That's when Osvita, Whark's wife, began making nutritious meals for Suzmina. She's known throughout town for her culinary creativity."

"Do you know where they might be? They don't seem to be home."

"Unfortunately not. I've been tending to my wife all day." Aware he sounded like a broken record, he knew only a monster would disregard her condition.

"Right. Well, if you do see them, make sure to contact us immediately. They aren't to be trusted." Vincent wrote down a telephone number, ripped off the piece of paper and handed it to Crogin.

"Of course." He glanced at the paper. "What did you say this was regarding?"

"I didn't say. Take care." Vincent returned to the huddled guards out front.

Crogin's curiosity grew. "What've you all gotten into?" he whispered to himself, observing their empty residence. Though he was skeptical about the situation, he maintained his loyalty to Osvita. Crogin greatly appreciated all she did for Suzmina.

"Did the old man say anything?" one guard asked.

"Not a thing. He's too busy caring for his dying wife to notice anything."

"For fuck's sake," one guard replied. "Now what? You know Brugōr will have our heads if we come up empty."

"Any ideas?" Vincent asked, looking around. "Hey, you over there." He nodded to the quiet guard, partially secluded. "Any ideas?"

"I don't…I mean, I don't know. We could always ask his co-worker." A couple of the guards laughed, mocking him. The introverted guard was younger, inexperienced and obviously uncomfortable.

"His co-worker?" Vincent asked, waving his hands for the other guards to hush.

"Yes. I believe his name was Grum something."

"Grum…Grum…" Vincent tried to recall the name. "Grum Lagom?"

"Yes. Maybe he'd know something."

Impressed and embarrassed he didn't think of it, Vincent considered it an obvious choice. "Brilliant. Time to visit Grum Lagom." He pulled out his Barren Land Locator (B.L.L.), an electronic rolodex device used by the Kurhal guards. "What was your name again, agent?" Vincent asked as he entered Grum Lagom into the B.L.L.

"Rocky, sir."

"Rocky. Great job." Within seconds, the B.L.L. pinged and Grum's address revealed itself. "Wonderful. The man lives a short distance from here. Rocky, you stay here, guard the residence. Under no circumstance is anyone allowed to enter. If anyone from the Dimmerk family arrives, notify us immediately."

"Will do."

"Let's go, men. This way."

As guests in Grum's home, Rexhia and Osvita sat in his living room, staying within earshot of Whark as he described the events of what had happened.

"Sorry to unload everything on you and bombard your home," Whark said.

"No worries, buddy. I get it." Grum looked at Whark and his family with sympathy. He knew Brugōr would go to extreme measures to ensure secrecy.

"If we could just stay the night, we'll devise a plan and get out of your hair by morning."

"Not sure whose hair you're referring to there, my friend." Grum chuckled as he rubbed his hairless scalp. They all welcomed the much-needed laughter.

Grum explained the bedrooms were upstairs and welcomed them to settle in for the evening. Osvita and Rexhia went upstairs while Whark stayed, thanking his comrade for opening his home to them.

"Don't worry about it, my friend." After a moment of awkward silence, they realized their inability to communicate outside of work. "So, a quorian, eh? I thought they were extinct. I'm not sure I'd even be able to identify one!"

"You know, Grum…" Whark felt his heartbeat in his neck, gazing upstairs as his family settled in. "Just in case something happens to me…"

"Oh, stop." Grum grinned, waving his hand.

"No, I'm serious." The two men made eye contact, understanding the shift in tone. "When Osvita and I moved here thirteen years ago, we agreed to forget our past and move forward with a new future. We found a home, had our daughter, and built a life here. Unfortunately, sometimes our past has a way of smacking us in the face when we least expect it."

Whark's hands shook as nerves ravaged his body. Looking up to make sure his wife and daughter weren't nearby, he turned to Grum.

"We moved here from a city known as The Quo." Whark's mouth was bone dry, eagerly awaiting Grum's response.

"Huh?"

"The Quo is the home of all quorians," Whark revealed.

"I don't understand…"

"Osvita and I are quorians. We used to live amongst our own race before we moved here. Our appearance was bestowed upon us as both a curse and protection, to ensure the safety of our kind." Whark didn't know how to make it any easier to understand.

"This doesn't make any sense. Quorians have been extinct for eons, until the War of Kings." Grum widened his eyes, surprised their conversation had become more awkward than the silence from earlier.

"Unbeknownst to everyone, we survived," Whark revealed.

"Now *that's* what I call a secret." Grum chuckled, trying to bypass what he considered an absurd discussion, but his boss wasn't smiling, so he shifted his tone. "How's it possible to maintain such secrecy for so long? Why'd you leave in the first place?" Just as Whark was about to speak, Grum spoke again. "You know...it was the quorian race that savagely attacked the land many years ago, ultimately leading to their demise...or so everyone thought." He raised his eyebrows.

Whark sighed. "Please, Grum...you have to keep this a secret. We've worked together over ten years now. You know us. I'm telling you this in case something happens to me. In case..." He paused and flinched. "In case they try to go after my family. I want someone to understand the potential danger for them."

Grum sighed, evaluating the situation. What he lacked in emotion, he made up for with intellect. He knew it'd be strange to lie about the accusation and understood Whark's reason to confess, but it was still a bold claim, and oddly timed.

"So the quorian you saw in captivity...did you know him or her?"

"No, there are—"

Knock. Knock.

The two men froze as Osvita approached the landing of the staircase. They all waited, hoping the guest at the door would leave.

Knock. Knock. The pounding reverberated through the home. Grum knew he couldn't ignore it.

"Hello? Yes?"

"My name's Vincent Anders and I work at the Kurhal. We're here to ask you a few questions."

"Oh shit," Whark whispered.

18

"Just a minute! Need to put some clothes on…unless you wanna see all of this." Grum motioned his hands around his body. Rexhia, now standing beside her mother, quietly chuckled. Though there was much he didn't understand, hearing the innocent laughter of a child warmed his heart. He decided to treat his guests as he knew them to be, and not what society had told him they were. Grum grabbed Whark by the wrist and pulled him toward the backdoor.

"Osvita and Rexhia," Whark whispered.

"They won't recognize them. You need to leave. When you hear them enter, sneak around front and go left. Hide in the depths of the Bazaar. *Remain hidden.*" Whark looked past Grum at Osvita and Rexhia standing there. With a tear rolling down his daughter's cheek, they tightly embraced with the intention of seeing one another soon.

"I love you," he whispered in her ear.

"Love you too, Daddy."

Whark released his daughter and stood up to hug his wife. For a moment, he sensed her anger towards him relinquish.

Knock, knock, knock.

"Mr. Lagom! Open this door before we force ourselves in," Vincent insisted.

"You've got to go, *now*," Grum whispered.

As Osvita and Rexhia returned upstairs, Grum pushed Whark outside. He rushed to the front door, exhaled, and opened it.

"Hello…everyone." Grum was surprised by the number of guards at his door. "What can I do ya for?" he said in a cheerful tone.

"Mr. Lagom? Grum Lagom?" Vincent asked.

"It's pronounced Grum, like bum, not groom, like broom. There is a difference, please take note," Grum corrected. "Who's asking?"

"The name is Vincent, head of Kurhal security. We've—"

"Vincent…" Grum interrupted. "Can't say that rings a bell."

Agitated by his demeanor, Vincent continued. "We've come to ask questions about your co-worker, Whark Dimmerk."

"Nice fellow, though not much to say." Grum stood in his doorway, staring at the three guards.

"May we come in?" Vincent asked.

Grum was tempted to joke, but didn't want to cause suspicion. "Of course."

As the three guards entered, Grum looked toward the back door, confirming Whark had escaped. He glanced upstairs as he closed the front door, hoping Osvita and Rexhia had hidden. He assumed the guards wouldn't recognize them, but wasn't sure it was best for them to be in plain sight.

"When was the last time you saw Whark Dimmerk?"

"Today." Grum's tone was free-spirited, almost careless.

"What was he doing?" As Vincent interrogated him, the two other guards surveyed the residence for anything unusual. Grum watched carefully, always aware of their position.

"Working."

Vincent sighed. "Did he do or say anything strange?" Just before Grum could respond, Vincent interjected. "And, boy, your answer better be more than one word," he instructed, waving his index finger at his face.

Grum stared at the finger, then made emotionless eye contact. "Today seemed no different than any other day." He chuckled. "By the way, it's rude to point in someone's face."

"Mr. Lagom, you're aware you work for the Kurhal, right? We could fire you."

Grum looked directly into Vincent's eyes and replied with confidence. "Considering the position you're in, you may want to rethink threatening the only other individual who can maintain the balance and safety of Karg River. You need me more than I need you."

Silence fell upon the room. The two guards were impressed by Grum's wit, but didn't respond. Since his home seemed unoccupied, they both made their way back toward the entrance.

Vincent was aggravated, but knew Grum was right – Karg River needed someone, so he continued the questioning. "When did he leave?"

"Not sure. He performed a calibration due to unbalanced particle levels." Grum could easily lie, so much so he'd sometimes find it difficult to identify the truth.

"Where'd he go?" Vincent asked. The other two guards waited outside the doorway.

"Castle grounds, to check the water supply. He's meticulous about every finite detail."

Vincent revealed a document and handed it to Grum. It was the daily water report that Whark claimed to be concerned about, though the levels were perfectly normal.

"These are the reports your boss claimed to be in poor condition." Vincent paused. "How would you interpret these findings?"

"When were these results taken?"

"They were—"

"I ask this," Grum interrupted, "because logistically, it'd be tough to confirm or deny when Whark actually procured the sample and developed these results. Furthermore, if it was taken after Whark obtained his initial findings, the levels would've already been adjusted."

While the interrogation continued, Osvita and Rexhia remained silent upstairs. They'd been listening to the discussion between Grum and the guards. Osvita was ready to get involved if needed; however, she didn't wish to make matters worse.

"Where's Da—" Rexhia began, but Osvita covered her daughter's mouth. They couldn't see anything, but she didn't want to risk being spotted. Rexhia, on the other hand, didn't seem as concerned and quickly scurried across the stairs to get a better view. Osvita reached out to grab her but was just short. Mother and daughter were now split on opposite ends of the landing. The second floor had some height to it with a total of seventeen stairs connecting the two floors.

Rexhia was small and nimble enough to quietly move and see the group below. While Osvita maintained strict focus on her daughter, something caught her attention in the corner of her eye. It was coming from outside, through the window. Osvita turned her head for a moment and noticed a familiar man, running. *Whark.* He was fleeing in the opposite direction – into the depths of the Bazaar.

Time stood still as her mind battled between two opposing emotions. She understood her husband was being hunted and needed to flee for survival, however she couldn't help consider it cowardice to abandon his family. She thought about her relationship with Whark, from The Quo to their life in The Barren Land. Though they'd experienced a world of hurt and an abundance of joy, her patience was thinning out. She recognized the falsified happiness she portrayed for her family. As she entered the tunnel of doubt and uncertainty, Osvita reminded herself she didn't have the luxury of escaping her reality like Whark. She had responsibilities and her daughter to protect.

"Where do you think we'd find him?" Vincent asked.

"Haven't a clue," Grum said. "Maybe he returned to the river. Maybe he returned home. Hell, maybe he's inside the castle. I have no idea."

Vincent lingered, gazing up toward the second floor. The sound of his next step coincided with a distant thud, but it didn't go unnoticed.

"You know," Grum said, conjuring up a lie, but he was interrupted.

"Alright, Mr. Lagom," Vincent said. "We'll let you go about your day." He made his way toward the exit. "Is there anything else you know which could prove helpful?"

"I make a mean chocolate chip cookie. Most seem to find my recipe quite helpful." Unamused by the sarcasm, Vincent tilted his head and walked outside.

Grum was relieved when the guards left his home, but annoyed they couldn't be bothered to fully close the door. As he attempted to close it, there was resistance. With his second attempt, Grum didn't realize it was being forced open. Suddenly, the door swung, throwing him against the wall.

"He's here, I heard him! Check downstairs again, and upstairs." Vincent shouted from the entrance.

Osvita heard the guards storm the house and locked eye contact with her daughter. She silently instructed Rexhia to hide inside the adjacent bedroom, aware the guards intended to search the second floor. Osvita headed into the bathroom and closed the door. She crawled behind the shower curtain and stood flat against the wall, hoping Rexhia had secured a safe location.

Once the guard reached the second floor, Osvita heard the footsteps and the clanging of his equipment, realizing she needed a plan in case there was a confrontation. The steps grew louder until they stopped outside the door. As she focused on her breathing, Osvita maintained a calm demeanor. There was a loud bang and she jumped.

The bathroom door swung open, leaving just a thin shower curtain between her and her assailant. Osvita looked around for a weapon , but all she could find was a body scrubber on a stick. With another footstep coming closer, she picked it up, gripping it tightly, and prepared to defend herself. She maintained her stance in the deafening silence. Osvita jumped again when she heard the door slam shut.

Once she tracked the sound outside the bathroom, she realized the guard was headed for the bedroom.

Rexhia.

Osvita flung open the shower curtain and raised Grum's bathing tools as a weapon. Walking by a mirror, she realized how foolish she looked. The scrubbing brush couldn't protect anyone, so she placed it down and opened Grum's medicine cabinet.

"Sorry, Grum," Osvita whispered, finding a small pair of scissors. She heard the guard's steps slowly dissipating – she needed to be quick. Osvita opened the vanity cabinet below and noticed a sharp knife on a tray resting toward the front. Relieved, she picked up the knife and noticed the smell of bleach. Osvita wondered why Grum kept a knife in his bathroom, but didn't pass judgement. She knew it could be what saved their lives. If there was any weapon she felt comfortable with, it was a knife.

Osvita carefully opened the bathroom door and noticed the guard to her left had entered the bedroom. She'd no idea where her daughter was, but she needed to act fast. She quietly tip-toed through the hallway, advancing on the assailant.

Downstairs, Grum was appalled. He hadn't expected the guards to barge back into his home. With his vision still blurred, he felt a wave of panic. He needed to make every second count and choose his actions carefully. Grum noticed Vincent was still outside, guarding the residence. One guard was entering his guest bedroom upstairs, while the other was closer, looking toward the backdoor. In a swift manner, Grum pushed himself toward the kitchen, grabbed a wrought-iron pan and quietly approached the guard near the back. The pan required two hands due to its weight. Once he was close enough, Grum gritted his teeth and swung upwards, at an angle, with all his might.

CLUNK!

The sound startled everyone. Though Grum knew the weight of the pan, his adrenaline hadn't allowed him to consider the consequences. Once the pan met the guard's head, he knew he'd cracked his skull and killed the man.

His lifeless body fell forward, smashing his living room table on the way down. Blood pooled around him and shards of glass protruded from his skin. Grum dropped the pan, the sound echoing throughout the house. He couldn't believe what'd happened. He'd maintained a carefree lifestyle, but shortly after Whark's arrival, he'd become violent. A murderer.

"Dexter!" Vincent shouted, looking at the terrified Grum. "Get on your Vin damn knees!" he yelled.

"What's going on down there?" The guard shouted from upstairs.

"This shithead killed Dexter!"

"Fuck!" the guard shouted, both in shock of his partner and from the searing pain in his neck. Standing in front of him was Rexhia in a protective stance with her intricately carved slingshot.

"Gotcha," she smiled. Unbeknownst to him, Rexhia's slingshot was loaded and ready.

"Why you little—" The guard advanced, but quickly came to a stop. Her instincts had her aim for his right eye, which showcased her perfect marksmanship. His head ricocheted back, he dropped to his knees, and let out a roar of unbelievable pain, gaining the attention of everyone in the house. As his knees slammed into the ground, he felt a surge of pain and pressure in his back. Uncertain of his surroundings, the guard collapsed.

Horrified by the sight before him, Vincent couldn't fathom how both of his partners were feared dead in a matter of minutes. Glancing at Dexter's lifeless body and a traumatic Grum, Vincent returned to the staircase to evaluate Roger's situation. He was surprised to see only his partner at the head of the stairs. Vincent gripped the hilt of his sword and ran up, carefully watching the surroundings.

"Roger! Talk to me. Hang in there," he said, cradling his head while examining the stab wound.

"I-I…" Roger couldn't speak without coughing up blood. His condition was rapidly declining.

"Stay with me, Roger. I'm calling for help now." Vincent pulled out his B.L.L. to contact emergency services. He skimmed the screen and initiated the call, however Rexhia's perfect aim shattered the device before anyone answered. She then shifted her aim directly at Vincent.

"Rexhia, no!" Osvita shouted, horrified by her daughter's peculiarly successful violent tendencies. Rexhia abided, but Vincent was so alarmed he lost his traction and tumbled down the staircase, grunting the entire way.

"I didn't shoot!" Rexhia shouted, but the damage was done. Osvita looked down at Roger's arm hanging over the staircase and realized he'd died.

"Stay here, Rexhia. I'm going to check downstairs," Osvita ordered.

As she descended the stairs, she gripped her knife. Observing the guard lying across the landing, she noticed him still breathing but unresponsive.

"Grum," she called out, maintaining her focus, but there was no answer. "Grum!" Silence. Osvita turned and saw Grum curled up on the floor. Concerned for his health, she checked on him – his body shook in response.

"Hm?" Grum replied.

"Are you okay? I called you, but you didn't answer." Osvita was relived.

"I-I—" Grum struggled to speak. "I killed a man." he pointed to the dead body.

"It was self-defense," she replied, justifying his cause while rubbing his back.

"But...was it?"

"Listen. I know it's challenging, but we aren't safe quite yet." She pointed to Vincent who hadn't moved.

"Is he dead too? What about the other one?" Grum asked, relieved he wasn't the only killer.

"Vincent's still breathing."

"Oh." Grum sighed, walking to observe Vincent closer.

"But that one..." Osvita pointed toward the second story.

"Dead?" Grum whispered.

"We needed to protect ourselves."

"*We?*" He turned around, ensuring privacy from her daughter. "You mean to tell me you both killed him?"

"No. Absolutely not. I killed him. Not her. She didn't do anything."

Grum's taste of denial was sweet. Osvita observed her daughter's slingshot, uncertain if she was proud or concerned. She couldn't imagine how or when she'd learned such skills.

"Come down, honey," she asked her daughter as an unresponsive Vincent remained sprawled across the floor.

"Now what?" Grum asked.

"He's seen too much, heard too much," Osvita said.

"No…" Grum walked backwards. "Not again. There's already too much death here."

"I wasn't suggesting —"

"We should tie him up and run," Rexhia interrupted. Grum and Osvita looked at the young girl, surprised.

"No. We should interrogate him. See what he knows. Why don't you—" Osvita started, but her daughter interjected again.

"So we shouldn't be concerned about the tracking device on the locator?"

"The what!?" Grum and Osvita said in unison.

"The electronic device the guard had. Up there." Rexhia pointed toward the shattered Barren Land Locator beside the slain guard.

"Honey, how do you know there is a tracking device in that? How do you know anything about those things?"

"I heard two men talking about it in the Bazaar. The one who gave me those berries, remember?"

"Glimboberries?" Osvita confirmed.

"Yeah!"

"Did you say Glimboberries?" Grum asked in a somber tone.

"You've heard of them? In all my years of culinary experience, I'm yet to hear of this berry." Osvita stopped herself, remembering the more pressing matter at hand. "Never mind, not important right now. If Rexhia's right, then we need to get out of here *now*." Osvita leapt up the stairs and grabbed the device, confirming it was destroyed.

"The man said even if it were destroyed, some signal would still be sent," Rexhia remarked. Osvita and Grum exchanged glances.

"Well, Rexhia, it seems as though we're in the presence of a prodigy!" Grum was still deeply disturbed, but grateful for her knowledge.

He grabbed twine, and with Osvita's assistance, hogtied Vincent in the back corner, using Grum's belt as additional security.

"This should buy us some time," Osvita said.

"But where will we go, Mom?"

"I have an idea…" She glanced at Vincent. "We'll discuss it outside. Grab your things and let's move. You too, Grum."

"Yes," Grum said, mesmerized by what his house had turned into. "I think that's a good idea."

While Osvita and Rexhia gathered their belongings, Grum quickly packed a bag for himself.

"Got everything?" Osvita asked.

"Yup. All ready for our excursion." Grum expressed a kind smile towards Rexhia, patting her on the back. He suppressed the sadness and sorrow for the sake of the young girl.

Osvita leaned forward and whispered into his ear. "Do you have a weapon? Some form of defense?"

"No."

"Grab something you'd use."

Rexhia padded her pocket, securing her slingshot. "I'm ready. What about Mr. Grum?"

"Don't worry, he's coming with us," her mother answered.

"You can't get rid of me that easily. You're stuck with me now, ho ho!" Grum plastered on a smile as he stashed a taser into his bag. Osvita read right through his grin, but appreciated the effort for her daughter. Grum closed the door, locking it behind him as the three left his house.

"So…what's the plan?" he asked.

"Yeah, Mom. What was your idea?"

"You know my co-worker Nigel?"

"Oh yes, I remember him. He's *so* nice, especially to you." Rexhia giggled.

"Rexhia…" Osvita scolded, aware of her daughter's implication. "He lives in the depths of the Bazaar. It'd be a great place to hide considering the winding, narrow streets."

Grum agreed, ignoring Rexhia's comments.

"Are we going to find Daddy first?" Rexhia asked. Osvita was so preoccupied by what had happened, she'd forgotten about her husband.

"I'm not sure, sweetie. Where'd Whark run off to?" Osvita asked, entering the middle of the street.

"We'll meet him in a short while." Grum smiled at Rexhia, patting her on the head. "Don't worry. You'll see your daddy soon."

Rexhia smiled, walking on ahead. For a thirteen-year-old, she was cognizant and clever, however, she still found comfort in the presence of her parents.

"Where's Whark going to meet us?" Osvita asked Grum.

"I haven't the slightest idea. We didn't have a plan. I just told him to run into the depths of the Bazaar," Grum whispered.

"Okay. His safety is the priority. Remaining separate may be for the best," she whispered. Osvita recognized how calm she was with Whark gone, uncertain if she believed her words or if the space apart was a relief.

19

"How'd you meet Giddeom so soon?" Sir Kalvin wondered.

"I've had these visions, experiences. I was in this other place with a large manor," Jacob began. "I didn't know who he was initially, but he formally introduced himself the second time."

"The place you went to…what did it look like? Where were you?" Sir Kalvin asked.

"I refer to it as the manor."

"That's it? Just a manor?"

"There didn't seem to be much of anything else. The manor was massive – the inside was bigger than the exterior let on."

As Sir Kalvin pondered his words, Jacob used the time to evaluate his surroundings. He never expected to be invited into the mysterious royal home. Though deep within the Subterranean Domain, he felt as though he were above ground.

Behind the luxurious golden doors in the hill of the Ersatzian Field was a psychedelic elevator cab filled with warped colors, dizzying patterns and swirling motions. Had the descent into the main foyer taken longer, Jacob would've gotten sick. Once the cab opened, the two men stood in an enormous space filled with shimmering golds, ruby reds and emerald greens. Every area was decadently designed with unique art and sculptures for the prestigious family.

Walking through the hallways, Jacob admired the numerous windows imitating life above ground with views of landscapes, sunlight and animals. It provided an inviting atmosphere for an underground environment. The artificial light illuminated the hallways and rooms as if the sun were gleaming through the land.

The Subterranean Domain had countless luxurious and regal staircases; however, they all descended deeper into the depths of their home. It was on the second grand staircase that Jacob viewed a large, stained-glass portrait of the original leader of Sartica – Lord Lurion. He wondered if his dismal appearance was a reflection of his personality.

When they entered Sir Kalvin's study, Jacob was mesmerized by the insurmountable number of books. The ceilings were at least twenty-feet high with what he thought were hundreds of thousands of books squeezed into the walls. Though not an avid reader, Jacob suddenly felt compelled to browse a library so large it housed four spiral staircases, one at each corner. The study was ornately lit in an organized manner, accentuating certain books or sculptures. The furniture was hand carved and traditionally designed. Jacob enjoyed the earthy musk as it wasn't a common aroma throughout the region.

"Hello?" Sir Kalvin repeated. Jacob anxiously turned his head, uncertain how long he had ignored the leader.

"I'm terribly sorry. Just…admiring your study. It's beautiful," Jacob said.

"It's okay." The leader chuckled. "I suppose we can discuss your visions afterwards. Have you ever wondered what's outside Sartica?" he asked, startling Jacob.

"Not really. My family used to take my sister and me to walk the perimeter, but I never enjoyed it. I know other regions exist though, like Tillerack and Prateria." He instantly realized half of his family had seen regions outside of Sartica and wondered how he hadn't thought about it before.

"Having an awareness of the larger world is a good start."

"Oh?"

"You almost know half of the regions in Diveria. You just named three: Sartica, Prateria and Tillerack." Sir Kalvin stood up from his brown, leather chair and walked toward the books beside the crackling fireplace.

"The land of Diveria." He paused. "You know the origin of its name, right?"

"Of course. It was named after the Divinity King." Jacob nodded, in respect to their deity.

"Precisely." Sir Kalvin smiled. "After the Divinity King and his people defended themselves from the vicious quorian attack, he divided the land into numerous regions for safety." Sir Kalvin skimmed the bookshelf with determination. "Separating the land into ten regions, with each of his ten loyal subjects to lead, he created the outer world known as Diveria." He pulled a tome from the shelf and stood by the fireplace, mystified by the embers floating up the chimney. Jacob wondered where the exhaust was. "History doesn't go into great detail, but at some point the King harnessed part of his power into ten sacred artifacts, one for each of the regions. According to folklore, Divinity went into hiding, unable to leave his inner sanctum." Sir Kalvin returned to his seat and placed the tome on the table between them. "And so begins our journey. Your family's journey."

"My family's journey? How in the world does it relate to the almighty Divinity King!?" A puzzled Jacob looked down at the book, reading the title aloud. "A New Diveria."

"With Divinity, and presumably Giddeom, secluded away in their sanctum, they needed someone to aid in their affairs. *A guardian.*"

Though riddled with anxiety, Jacob's mind raced with questions, doubts, and curiosities. "There's so much I don't understand. You're saying *the* Divinity King is alive and Giddeom works alongside him? Then where are they? Why not present themselves? Do as they please? How could *He* need a guardian?"

"A king will remain, unless he is slain," Sir Kalvin announced, waving for Jacob to calm down. "Protection. He'd watched all the kings succumb to their fate. I imagine he wanted to avoid a similar demise. They now reside somewhere, wherever they invited you to, so the Divinity King can safely ensure order in the world he'd organized."

"But…but…" Jacob tried his hardest to understand the situation. "You said He dispersed some power into ten objects?

"Ten ancient artifacts."

"That doesn't make any sense. If the Divinity King wanted to maintain order, why give away power? He should hold onto what He has," Jacob asked in an almost rude tone.

"I imagine He didn't want to place all his eggs in one basket."

"But wait, *you* are a leader."

"Yes…?"

"So you must have an ancient artifact. You harness some of the Divinity King's power?"

"I do have Sartica's ancient artifact securely locked away."

"What does it do? Do you feel—"

"We're getting off topic, Jacob." Sir Kalvin shook his head. "That's not the reason I welcomed you inside. It's all minuscule compared to the rest of your journey."

"You keep mentioning my journey. How could you possibly know something like that?" Jacob's face turned red as he questioned the royal leader of Sartica.

"Because you told me. The same reason that brought you and your mother to me this morning."

"Giddeom."

"Exactly."

The two men remained quiet. Sir Kalvin maintained a hopeful, subtle grin that his guest would understand the magnitude of the situation while Jacob continued to build up frustration, confusion and anxiety.

"I'm sorry, Sir Kalvin. I don't mean to be rude, but I think this may all be some sort of mistake." The leader shook his head, but Jacob continued. "This all happened because I had a couple visions. Yes, this Giddeom character is strange, but the man hasn't even spoken to me yet. Our communication has been based on telepathy only. There's no way any of what you explained correlates to me, my family or my journey. I'm just a simple guy, who lives with his family in Sartica." Jacob grunted. "I think it's time for us to go. I'm sorry to have wasted your time, Sir Kalvin." Jacob nodded and made his way for the door. "Was it this—"

"Wait!" Sir Kalvin shouted. "Jacob, please."

He slowed down but still made his way toward the door. Sir Kalvin grabbed the book off the table and approached Jacob. "I understand this may be a lot for you. It may seem strange or peculiar."

"I just think you have it wrong. Even if you were right, apparently these...*guardians* have always been women. Seems they missed the mark on this one." Subconsciously, Jacob knew there was some validity in Sir Kalvin's words, but it was too much for him to handle at once.

"I'm afraid I don't have the answer to that...but you know who does?"

"Who?" Jacob replied. "Giddeom?"

"Ding, ding, ding."

"Of course he does." Jacob threw his arms up.

"Here. Take this. Humor me for a moment."

"I don't think—"

"I order you to take it, as your leader." Jacob grabbed the copy of *A New Diveria* from him.

"What would you like me to do with it?" he asked.

"Turn to page two-hundred-and-fifty-four."

"Alright. Two...fifty..." Before he could speak the third number, Sir Kalvin grabbed a larger book off the shelf and smashed it across Jacob's head, forcing him to drop the copy of *A New Diveria* and collapse. Before he touched the ground, Sir Kalvin grabbed him to avoid injury. He lowered Jacob to the ground, gently placing a pillow under his head against the cold floor.

"Have a good visit. Maybe *he* will convince you," Sir Kalvin whispered as he picked up *A New Diveria* and returned it to its proper home.

Standing within the Ersatzian Field, Anna Emmerson was enamored by the fulsome horticulture obstructing the view of the city. Her visual and nasal senses were overloaded. Knowing her son was in safe hands, she admired the nearby rose bushes. As she approached them, she knelt and read the sign.

Rosa Kordesii

The label reminded Anna of her own experience she'd had years ago. She envisioned the open fields, the colorless fire, and the large structure in the distance. She wondered why Giddeom wasn't as persistent with her and how different her life would've been if he had. With the prospect of not having her two beautiful children, Anna knew the choice, or decision, to not involve her was appropriate.

"Hello?" Anna broke her concentration and turned at a noise behind her. Though no one was there, she sensed a presence watching her. She carefully scanned the garden, looking for signs of movement. With no avail, she blissfully admired the roses again until she heard a crackling of a branch.

"Who's there?" She whipped around. "Are you Sir Kalvin's assistant?"

In an instant, Anna felt a strong, firm hand rest upon her right shoulder. She froze. Without moving her head, she lowered her gaze to her bottom right to see a large, masculine hand.

"Hello," a soft, monotone voice said. In one swift move, she spun around and jumped back in surprise. In front of her was a translucent apparition whose body disappeared just past the waist. Uncertain of its gender, Anna noticed the pale white hands and a black cloak covering its face.

"Who are you?" she asked. Anna looked around, but saw no one else.

"Jacob's opaque vision will lead him into an archaic deception," the nameless figure voiced.

"Jacob's what? What about my son?" Anna asked, but it remained quiet. "How convenient, not talking again, eh?" She was annoyed by its presence. As she continued to glare, Anna started to feel strange. "Why speak to me if you didn't wish to talk?"

The apparition lifted its head and revealed its eerie face. As if frozen in time, its permanent grin was accompanied by widened white eyes. Anna slowly backed away, uncomfortable with its presence.

"I'm going to observe the fig tree over there." Anna pointed, walking in the direction. She gazed at the figure again, though its face hadn't changed. Her discomfort increased as she made her way toward the fig tree. With the sensation of eyes still on her, Anna gently turned her head a little. Not seeing the figure, she turned her head completely and realized it'd vanished. She examined the entire field from her view, but saw no one. She exhaled in relief.

Anna turned around to examine the fig tree and shouted.

"Ma'am, I'm so terribly sorry. I didn't mean to frighten you." A kind, gentle woman spoke, trying to calm Anna down.

"No, it's okay. I—" Anna looked around for the apparition. "I shouldn't have frightened so easily."

"My name is Avery, and I'm Sir Kalvin's assistant. I just came by to check on you. Everything okay? Can I get you anything?" She had a nurturing quality. Anna exhaled and chuckled.

"No, I'm fine, thank you. I think…" She hesitated to mention what she'd seen. Avery waited. Anna knew what she'd seen was real, but it wasn't a person. To avoid sounding silly, she changed the topic. "I think this is the most beautiful garden I've ever seen." She smiled.

"Yes, isn't it spectacular?" Avery replied. "Well, if you need anything, please don't hesitate to ask. I'll be on the other side of the field." She nodded, walking toward the opposite end.

Anna thought about the apparition and what it could've been. Its ghastly appearance was unforgettable, but provided no information. Jumbling the words in her mind, she shivered as her memory recalled what he'd said.

Jacob's opaque vision will lead him into an archaic deception.

Anna felt a yearning to speak with her son.

"Excuse me, Avery!?" she shouted from across the field.

"Yes?"

"I need to see my son, *now.*"

Jacob Emmerson clenched his eyes, rubbing his fingers over his eyebrows from the crippling headache. Anger billowed within for his leader who'd unexpectedly assaulted him. Anticipating a view of dusty books amid a dark ambiance from Sir Kalvin's study, what he gazed upon when he opened his eyes was a pleasant surprise.

In front of him was an entire city filled with people, buildings, colors, noise – it was expansive. Some buildings were short, others scraped the sky. Jacob was mystified, unsure of where he was standing. The sun was bright and warm – it seemed closer than normal. Between him and the city was a vast, open field with luscious green grass. He knelt down to feel it – the blades were warm and dry. The aroma of fresh cut grass was potent in the air. Jacob observed his surroundings, turning for a full view. He shuddered and froze when he realized where he was.

"I'm back," Jacob said aloud, and this time he heard his voice. He stepped forward, closer to the manor. "How can this be?" Jacob had vivid memories of his previous experiences, but he was always surrounded by darkness. He felt foolish.

How'd I miss an entire city right under my nose?

"It's because we didn't want you to see anything yet," a familiar voice said from afar.

"Who's that?" Jacob asked, scanning the surroundings. From the left side of the manor walked a familiar man in a tuxedo. "Giddeom? Is that you?" he said, delighted to communicate normally.

"Yes, Jacob. It's nice to see you again."

"It– it's nice to be back. Though I must admit, I cannot believe this is an entire city."

"Welcome to Diad!" Giddeom shouted. "A world within a world. A place where those not suitable for Diveria reside."

"Like the Divinity King?" Jacob replied.

Giddeom sighed. "We needed to take certain precautions before exposing you to the entire city. After matters were confirmed, we properly opened our home to you."

"So I'm not having visions? This isn't just a figment of my imagination or telepathy? You've been transporting me to a different region?"

"Precisely."

"How'd you know where I was?"

"I think the more important question is *why* did I know, yes? Why you are here?" Giddeom suggested.

Trying to find the words, Jacob wanted to use his time wisely, uncertain how long he'd be welcome. "Sir Kalvin and I were just discussing something about a guardian and the history of Diveria." As Giddeom tried to respond, Jacob interjected. "You continuously say *we*. Are you referring to yourself and the Divinity King?"

"Why don't we make our way toward the manor, as you call it, and I'll educate you." Jacob agreed and the two casually walked toward the familiar structure.

"You have many questions, young man. Some which you deserve to know, others you have no business asking. We will sort through them all, and allow you to get comfortable here," Giddeom said as they ascended the staircase. "To get things started, could you please open the door?"

"Sure?" Confused why Giddeom didn't do it himself, Jacob wrapped his hand around the silver doorknob and turned, sensing the familiar engravings. When he retracted his arm, Jacob noticed a sudden movement in his palm, as if a spider had run across it.

"What is…?" Jacob asked, noticing a small string of illuminated shapes appear within his palm.

"You've officially received a key to our home, granting you access to freely come and go."

"But I was able to enter the last two times without any key."

"That's because I let you enter. Always be mindful of perception." Giddeom grinned.

Entering the manor, Jacob was once again stripped of his anxiety and worry, liberated and euphoric. His surroundings appeared identical to his prior visit, except others acknowledged him with a friendly wave or a polite smile. Still, Jacob couldn't help but sense the others weren't as welcoming as they appeared to be. He sensed their judgement and confusion.

"This mural…" Jacob exclaimed, still mesmerized by its substantial size.

"This is the essence of why you are here," Giddeom said, stopping in place. "Sir Kalvin may seem nice and means well, but can be too involved." Giddeom paused for a moment, took a deep breath, and began his speech.

"Jacob Emmerson, you've been summoned to Diad because of your lineage. You come from a long line of women who've accepted their fate to secure and protect the sanctity of the Divinity King and the world of Diveria. As you may know, eons ago, the Divinity King coordinated and facilitated the world you know as Diveria. Ten leaders for the ten regions, each with the task of maintaining order, governing their land and aiding their community to flourish by the grace of the Divine.

"To aid in their leadership, The Divinity King partially harnessed his power and created ten ancient artifacts, each with their own unique abilities. They were strategically dispersed amongst the leaders as a reminder and warning – power always comes at a price." Giddeom took a moment to let the information settle as he gazed upon the mural.

"Every emblem upon this mural represents each of the ten regions under Divinity's rule. If you notice the emblem on the bottom left,"—Giddeom pointed—"the one with the beige orb, that represents your home of Sartica." Jacob nodded, already aware. "Now down this hallway, there are a total of ten individual doors, plus a set of double doors at the end. As you can surmise, each door represents its own region, excluding the double doors."

"Ten?" Jacob questioned. "I only see nine – three rows of three."

Giddeom smiled. "Look in the center. You'll notice an emblem atop another, larger one." Jacob looked in amazement, surprised he didn't notice it before. "Ten," Giddeom repeated. "The nine smaller ones represent those amongst Diveria while the larger, centered emblem is designated for the realm Divinity created – Diad."

"This realm? He *created* it?" Jacob was astonished by the King's exemplary power.

"Sure did."

Jacob was speechless. While there was much he wanted to say, he didn't know where to begin. Instead, he followed-up on something he'd seen during his first visit. "When I first arrived, I saw a doorknob wiggling, but it was locked. The second time I came here, I noticed it was the door with the dark brown orb. Where does that represent?"

"Dark brown. The emblem located on the top left?" Jacob tried his best to visualize it at that height.

"I believe that's the one."

"That…is The Barren Land. It's actually located near Sartica."

"Really? I've never heard of it…"

"I suspect there'll be much you've never heard of." Giddeom glanced down the hallway, eager to continue.

"What're behind the doors? Are there people? Why would I see it wiggling?" Jacob asked.

Giddeom smirked. "I'm not entirely sure you saw them wiggle," he said in a confident tone. "Behind the doors are a means for teleporting to the corresponding region. This is where you shine – why you were brought here." Giddeom stepped closer to the hallway and stopped partially between it and the mural, focusing on the important matter at hand. "Jacob, you are here to become the next guardian. The connection between us and the other regions, ensuring the safety and security of the ancient artifacts, while preserving the legacy of the Divinity King."

"This is where I have many questions. I've spoken to my mother and—"

"Let me stop you right there," Giddeom interrupted. "I know I haven't made it clear, but you are not, under any circumstances, to discuss *anything* involving Diad. Not your mother, not a leader, not a lover. No one." There was an awkward pause as Jacob hated being reprimanded. "Do I make myself clear? Going forward, not a word."

"I-I...I didn't know." Jacob realized how challenging the request would be, but planned to abide by it. "As I mentioned, I spoke to my mother and learned about our unique lineage. She didn't know much, but I'm assuming my great grandmother Edith was the last guardian selected? It doesn't make sense why two generations were skipped and now it's fallen upon me, instead of following the tradition of my sister, Catherine."

Giddeom gazed around, in search of an adequate response. "Becoming the Guardian of Emblems is a title that requires pure acceptance and refined awareness between both parties. There are certain requirements which must be met and acknowledged. If two generations of guardians were skipped, the focus should be on the work that has gone undone, instead of logistic reasoning."

"And my sister? Why not her? Why me?"

"Catherine…" Giddeom stalled, uncertain how to answer his persistent question. "You are, and will continue to be, more available than her."

"But how—"

Giddeom raised his hand. "It appears it's time for you to head back."

"What? Return…to Sir Kalvin? How do you know? Why? I have so many—"

"Don't fret, Jacob. You'll return very soon. We're in need of your assistance. After all, there're two generations worth of cleanup to be done." Giddeom smirked.

"If there's so much to do, then why—"

"And remember, not a word to anyone. Not even a poised leader like Sir Kalvin and his manipulative diction."

"Promise," Jacob replied.

"See you soon." Giddeom hissed those final three words and snapped his fingers. Shockingly loud, it startled Jacob, forcing him to open his eyes. He found himself back in Sir Kalvin's home, on the floor, with the same headache he'd felt earlier.

"So what should I tell her?" a woman's voice said.

"It'll be another twenty minutes. Reassure her that Jacob's well and we're just finishing up," Sir Kalvin insisted.

"Okay. She's being persistent, just so you know."

"It's fine. She'll be fine."

Jacob sat up holding his head, using the chair to steady his balance. "Wait," he grunted. "I'm awake. Are you—"

"Jacob! Nice to see you're okay." Sir Kalvin smiled. Jacob darted him an angry look but said nothing to him.

"Sorry. Are you talking about my mother?" he asked the woman.

"Yes. She has been asking about you. I'm Avery, Sir Kalvin's assistant. Are you okay?" She looked at Kalvin with concern for his safety. "Can I get you —"

"No, I'm okay," Jacob mustered, staggering to stand. "I'll come with you.

We're done here anyway." Jacob stumbled toward the front door. Avery offered to help him but he managed to walk by himself. "I'm okay, thanks."

"Wait! Jacob, there's still much we need to discuss. It's not safe to—"

"There's nothing more to be said here." He turned around, locking eyes with Sir Kalvin. "I believe you already knew that." With those final words, Jacob turned around and walked out of the study with Avery.

20

Since meeting with Lady Vixa, Fravia and Smolar began to perceive her differently. While Smolar knew she had a good heart, it was Fravia who was pleasantly surprised. She empathized on the parental connection between Lady Vixa and Lord Erko. It reminded her of her own parents, and the expectations they'd placed on her.

They'd always wanted her to follow them in medicine. Lucemia often took the time to teach her daughter certain resources for healing properties. Fravia thrived on knowledge, welcoming the time spent. Her fear was that her mother would mistake her interest in knowledge for a passion in medicine.

"All you need to do is evenly apply the Frinkle Flakes across the wound, and it'll heal before the day's end." Reagor demonstrated on an injured quorian. While Lucemia focused more on research, her father worked with quorians to heal their ailments.

The patient moaned.

"Does it hurt?" Fravia asked.

"Oh no. It feels nice. Soothing."

"Brilliant," Reagor said. "There are some mint chips within the flakes to help ease the discomfort."

After a couple layers were placed on the quorian's arm, he thanked Reagor for his patience and time.

"You're most welcome. Thank you for allowing my daughter to watch the application of this newer medication." After the patient left, Fravia helped her father clean up until she looked at the time, realizing she was late.

"Oh wow, I need to head out. Sorry for running, Dad." Fravia kissed her father goodbye on the cheek. "Thank you for inviting me to view your new discovery."

"Where are you running off to?"

Fravia hesitated, but knew she couldn't lie. "I've offered my services to help prepare for the Blue Diamond Jubilee."

"You're going to help? That's kind of you." Reagor chuckled. "Does your mother know?"

"No, and I plan to keep it that way." Fravia's tone was stern. Though she hadn't admitted her time spent with Lady Vixa, she felt comfortable being a little more honest with her father.

"Understood, my dear." He smiled as his daughter left the room.

As Fravia gathered her belongings and said goodbye to her mother, she noticed a hand-drawn map, lazily covered, on the table. Fravia knew it was their personal map of Diveria, but would never acknowledge it. Though never discussed, she knew at a young age what her parents were secretly involved in. They had found and used every herb, plant and liquid within the city for their personal apothecary, and they yearned to explore other options.

Fravia caught her father coming home late one night from an *excursion*, and overheard a conversation he had with Lucemia. They discussed the path toward a vast, open desert. It was obvious they'd been sneaking outside the city and exploring the Outer World. Even at a young age, Fravia knew the severity and ramifications of the situation if others found out. It was strictly forbidden to leave the city. She considered it reckless and selfish, but they were also her parents. She'd decided to look the other way, ignoring any signs of their illicit activities.

It was because of this that Fravia had learned about the Enchanted Gate and its history.

As she made her way towards the Belvase on the twenty-seventh floor, where the Blue Diamond Jubilee would be held, she quickly rerouted to the twenty-fourth floor. Unsure if Smolar would be home, she heard rumbling inside after a few knocks.

"Hey, Fravia! How's it going?" he joyfully answered.

"S-Smolar. H-Hi! How…uh, how's it going?" Smolar, unfazed by her stutter and hesitation, continued to stand in the doorway with nothing but a towel around his waist, still dripping water from his apparent shower.

"Sorry, I didn't want to be rude and not answer, but just stepping out of the shower." He genuinely smiled. "Come in. Just give me a minute to change." Fravia immediately welcomed herself in.

She hadn't often seen Smolar shirtless. The water droplets falling from his hair onto his glistening muscles yearned to be admired.

"I didn't mean to interrupt. I was just on my way to the Belvase and thought I'd stop by. See how you were after the meeting with Lady Vixa." Fravia remained standing until Smolar entered the room fully clothed.

"Never an interruption, Fravia. Always a pleasure having you around." Fravia smiled, yearning for such words. Smolar's actions never implied he wanted more than friendship, but his words did. It left Fravia in a precarious situation. She didn't want to risk their friendship if she misunderstood the situation. "Things are well, though. My head's been spinning since our meeting. How're you? How've you been?"

"Not terrible. The same. Curious about a lot."

"Wait, I just realized…Did you say you're heading off to the Belvase to help with the Jubilee?" Smolar asked.

"Yes…" She paused. "After our time together, I had a new perspective on who she is and what it must be like in her position. I empathize with her upbringing and her parents. She seems…*different*."

"I've never seen this side of her and we lived together. The discussion we had before you arrived was my proof. She genuinely apologized for her demeanor in the past. It was a conversation I didn't know I needed to have until it was over."

"That's lovely to hear, Smolar. I'm really happy for you both," Fravia replied, following an awkward silence. "Well I can let you resume your day. I'm sure you—"

"Oh," Smolar interrupted with a disappointing tone. "Well, I was actually going to speak with Lady Vixa about the plan to rescue Promit. Maybe…well…"

"What is it?"

"I was going to suggest that maybe I could join you at the Belvase, then we could visit Lady Vixa together? Your willingness to support her is inspiring."

Fravia excitedly agreed, welcoming any time spent with Smolar.

The two friends made their way to the Belvase. Most of it was open, with space to host events and social gatherings. There was an abundance of decorations for annual parties; however, a Blue Diamond Jubilee was rare. Due to the unique nature of the event, a theme would be chosen in honor of the ruler and the preparation team was to execute it.

As the duo walked onto the Belvase, Fravia looked out at the glorious view of their city. "We're so lucky to live in such a majestic place."

"Yeah."

"Do you doubt the beauty?" Fravia spun around and displayed her beauty as she asked. She typically wore cloaks and robes that cinched at the waist with a glamorous belt and glistening necklaces.

"No doubt this view is glorious," he said, looking her up and down with a smile. He shifted his attention up, admiring the moon. "I can't help but imagine what's out there. The world is much bigger than just our city."

"It's much bigger…and dangerous," Fravia said.

"Yeah…" With the loss of his parents and never feeling a sense of home with Lady Vixa though, Smolar always yearned for something more. "The reward from danger can be greater than that of knowledge."

"You really want to leave The Quo one day, don't you? Actually leave and possibly not return," she asked. Fravia knew he enjoyed the idea of exploration, but it wasn't until that moment she understood how deep his passion went.

"Yes. I'd love nothing more than to see all of Diveria. Why would I need to return? I have no real family here." Fravia wondered why those closest to her had more interest in the Outer World than their own city, which she was devoted to. Deeply upset by Smolar's desertion, they were interrupted by a boisterous voice.

"Hello, hello!" he shouted. "Why…if it isn't Ms. Fravia and Smolar. How're you two doing?"

"Greetings, Mr. Kladimazoo," Fravia replied. The pair were acquaintances of Ludwig Kladimazoo. Fravia knew him as much as she knew everyone else within The Quo. Smolar knew him from the time he'd lived under Lady Vixa's roof. With his jovial voice, his exorbitantly round physique and elongated mustache, he was easy to spot amongst a crowd.

"What brings you both by?"

"Well…I was recently inspired to come and see if I could offer any help in preparation for the Blue Diamond Jubilee. On my way here, I ran into Smolar, who decided to tag along."

"Splendid! Incredible!" Mr. Kladimazoo shouted.

"It'd be an honor to help." Smolar smiled at them both, but only Mr. Kladimazoo returned the gesture.

"Well how about you follow me toward the food station and we can discuss. I need to check a few things."

"Wonderful," Fravia replied, following Mr. Kladimazoo and disregarding Smolar.

"Hey, hey," Smolar whispered. "Is everything okay?"

"Don't worry about me, I'm fine," she insisted.

After Smolar and Fravia witnessed her collapse, Lady Vixa allowed herself some time to rest, but only for a short while. She cleaned up her appearance and prepared herself for two important visits – the Grundimmers' home and the Deallius residence.

Starting with Promit's family, Lady Vixa visited his father and sister once more. Her initial cover story of Promit and Smolar on a secretive mission for the city bought her time for Neetri to successfully return. With her new-found clarity and pride, Lady Vixa sided with honesty and started a new era of her reign.

Mr. Grundimmer's demeanor hadn't changed when Lady Vixa visited, and she was uncertain if that was for the better or worse.

"I've come to admit a hidden truth about your son, Promit," she admitted. The two spoke alone as his daughter, Bindetta, wasn't home.

"Eh, what about him?"

"It seems as though Promit and his friend had gotten into a situation," Lady Vixa informed him.

"Yeah…he's foolish."

Lady Vixa told Promit's father the truth. Everything and everyone that was involved. From the escape and the chase to their attempt to retrieve him and a current plan to rescue him. The only information excluded was any mention of Neetri being summoned and the appearance of the Divinity King.

"So my son escaped under your watch and you haven't saved him yet?"

"That's correct," Lady Vixa revealed, preparing for a justifiably difficult reaction.

"And you want me to keep this secret, as to not alert others in the city?"

"Yes. It'd only make matters worse. Maintaining secrecy allows us to focus our efforts on his return."

Though he wondered who she meant by *us*, that wasn't Mr. Grundimmer's concern. "What's my secrecy worth to you?" He raised an eyebrow.

Lady Vixa was floored. She'd prepared for anger, disappointment and shame, not for a parent disregarding his child. Putting her emotions aside, she reassured him that he'd be compensated for his cooperation and could expect an enchanted gift later in the day. She left his residence and hoped her next visit that day would go a little smoother, though she didn't have high expectations.

Lucemia and Reagor Deallius were known throughout the city for their medicinal talents. They were well versed in healing properties using various herbs and plants with some enchanted water, graciously allowed by Lady Vixa. With tension between the two, she'd hoped to relinquish any residual angst and work together.

As she knocked on the door of their eleventh-floor home, Reagor stood up to answer while his wife cleared off the living room table. Planning their next secret excursion to accumulate berries from a faraway region, they needed to secure the path to travel along. Reagor quietly approached the door, peered through the looking hole and jumped backwards.

"Just a minute – I'll be right there!" he called out as he stepped toward his wife and whispered, "It's Lady Vixa!"

Lucemia rolled her eyes, placing the rest of their exploration equipment away. "Well…go open it."

"Oh, Lady Vixa! What a pleasant surprise," Reagor said in an overzealous volume, bowing. Like Fravia, his ability to successfully lie was dismal. Lucemia's brutal honesty rarely placed her in situations where she'd have to lie.

"Lady Vixa." Lucemia bowed. "To what do we owe this visit?"

"Hello to you both. I'd like to have a discussion with you in private. Is your daughter here?" Lady Vixa looked around.

"Fravia? No, she left not too long ago. She was actually…" Reagor remembered her participation in the Blue Diamond Jubilee should remain secret from Lucemia. "She was actually in a rush. Just missed her, sorry. Should she be here?"

"No. Actually, it's better that she isn't. May I come in?"

"Of course," Lucemia proclaimed and sat down. "Please take a seat."

Lady Vixa couldn't help but admire the surrounding objects. Though most of their personal belongings were family heirlooms, decor and family portraits, there were a few peculiar items that stood out. To her right, high up on a shelf, was a stone fragment of a plant leaf or flower. Not too far away was a small vial of sand behind a family portrait on the table. Not knowing the origin of either object, she knew they couldn't have originated within the city. It filled Lady Vixa with additional confidence, but made Lucemia uncomfortable.

"So, what did you wish to discuss, Lady Vixa?" Lucemia asked. Reagor took a seat beside his wife. Lady Vixa sat with remarkable posture, her robes covering her entire body except her silver shoes.

"I'd like to start by apologizing for any trouble, inconvenience or disappointment I may've brought you. I know we've shared the room a few times and there's typically tension between us," she said, staring at Lucemia. "Due to some recent revelations, I wanted to personally meet with you and say it's time for a change. It's time to take action and do what's necessary to help our city thrive."

"Oh wow, Lady Vixa. That's wonderful to hear," Reagor said joyfully.

"Happy to hear," Lucemia remarked, unfazed by her words.

"Certain events reactivated my drive and vision. I'm seeing our city in a different light for the first time in almost one-hundred years. While I won't have another hundred left, I plan to use my time wisely as your ruler. Interestingly, your daughter is partially to thank."

"Fravia? What has she done?" Lucemia wondered.

"She's been working closely with my...well, with Smolar. You may remember him when—"

"Yes, we know Smolar. He's very kind. Fravia is very fond of him," Reagor said.

"Those two helped open my eyes and see things differently."

"Oh really? How?" Lucemia grinned.

Lady Vixa relaxed her posture and disclosed everything that had happened, beginning with Smolar and Promit's first escape from The Quo. The story took more time than it did at her previous meeting. Lucemia and Reagor were instantly captivated with a growing concern for Promit's safety. With every sentence Lady Vixa uttered, they both hoped to hear the resolution that he was brought home safely. Unfortunately, such an ending never arrived as she wrapped up her explanation. Since there was an ulterior motive with this meeting, she excluded no details. Lady Vixa asked for their secrecy at the start of their conversation, but re-iterated it once more before unveiling the startling revelation.

"We understand. Nothing will leave these walls," Reagor reassured.

"Absolutely." Lucemia's tone slightly changed.

"In an attempt to resolve the situation and return Promit home, I summoned the help of a Savior." She paused. "I…assume you know of them?"

"You summoned…?" Reagor started.

"Of course," Lucemia confirmed.

"Well, in short, Neetri, the Savior, was captured by the Divinity King. I presumed she was dead but…" She smiled. "It was actually Fravia who taught me how to ensure she didn't perish. She's a knowledgeable young quorian." Her parents nodded as she continued. "Anyway, I don't believe he noticed *my* presence, but his…was terrifying."

"*The* Divinity King? As in…?" Reagor started to ask.

"Yes. The executor of all quorians," Lady Vixa confirmed. "While I wish the outcome were different, we gained pertinent insight into Promit's attackers, who sent the orders and Promit's status."

"Dare I ask…but where are Promit and Neetri now?" Lucemia wondered.

"That's why I'm here. While we've gathered a lot, there's still much we're missing. We know nothing of Neetri's location. Just that I lost communication with her outside The Barren Land. Promit's being held deep inside the same desert region." Reagor instinctually grabbed his wife's wrist, but she moved her hands, trying to downplay his startling reaction.

"Oh gosh, okay." Lucemia stood up. She found the discussion peculiar, but acted coy. "That poor boy. What's his condition? I'm assuming you're asking us to aid in his recovery upon his return?"

"Eventually, yes, but there is a more pressing reason."

Reagor and Lucemia glanced at one another, concerned about the direction of their conversation.

"Considering the honesty I bestowed upon you both, I was hoping you'd return the favor. I'd like to speak with you regarding the findings from your explorations that've gone on for years under the radar."

"What?" Reagor reacted.

"I'm sure there must be—" Lucemia started.

"I've had my suspicions. When Smolar and Promit accessed the Enchanted Gate twice, I realized others may be actively using it. While I still don't understand how you two obtained the key to activate it, I found others' excursions that were in the log. Most of them taken a week before an announcement of a new medicine."

"A log…" Lucemia whispered.

"Let me just say, I greatly appreciate your time, work and risk to gain knowledge and resources for those in our city. It's a dedicated and loyal job to take on. With that said, I'm concerned for possible diseases and parasites that may enter from those who leave without any quarantine or safety protocols. The Outer World is a tumultuous place. May I remind you Lord Horlix, the creator of the Enchanted Gate, died while roaming the Outer World." She paused, reminding herself why she was visiting Fravia's parents. "I'm bringing this up in hopes to learn from what knowledge you may have so our next mission can be successful.

First for Promit, then Neetri." Lady Vixa's words were sharp and decisive.

Reagor was speechless, his mouth open. Lucemia contemplated denying her claims, but knew it was a losing battle. She looked at her husband and he nodded.

"We're willing to do anything necessary to bring one of our own home and recover a Savior." Lucemia expressed a genuine smile. "Just promise me one thing."

"Yes?"

"Promise you won't reprimand us for exploring in the future," she said in a stern tone. Regardless of her answer, Lucemia still planned to help.

"Lucemia, Reagor, if you can help save them, I promise to discuss plans to help facilitate your explorations. The Outer World is a dangerous and unknown realm for us, but the sooner we can learn more about it, the more prepared we can be to handle whatever may come our way in the future. With the Divinity King aware of our existence…I'm afraid to think of what could happen."

Fravia and Smolar were both surprised by how much preparation was needed for the jubilee. Though plenty left to do, they had to say goodbye to Mr. Kladimazoo after seven hours, six hours longer than Smolar had anticipated.

"Wow, they really have their work cut out for them," he remarked.

"Yes, they do," Fravia responded coldly.

"Are you sure everything is okay?"

"You just don't get it," she replied, grunting.

"Get what? Please explain it to me."

"We've been in each other's lives for five years and it's somehow meaningless to you."

"What? That's not true."

"You'd have no problem leaving this city and everyone behind to explore your fantasy life." After a brief silence, she continued. "Then go. Why're you still here?"

"You know it's not safe out there for us."

"Shame that thought didn't come to mind when you and Promit escaped."

Fravia widened her eyes, aware of her harsh words. Smolar darted a piercing look at her, infuriated. They both stood in silence, neither one willing to apologize or admit fault.

"I'm heading to Lady Vixa's," she continued. "See if she has an update. Come. Don't come. I don't care." Fravia had no desire to see Smolar, and partially wished for him to go home. Her loyalty had switched towards Promit and, shockingly, Lady Vixa.

"Well, technically, I was already going to visit her before—"

"Fine," Fravia interjected. "Just be cordial while in her home, out of respect."

"Fine," Smolar replied.

"Fine."

The two didn't speak another word on their way to the Quorian Ruler's home.

Smolar was completely blindsided by their argument and didn't understand where her anger had come from. He was initially willing to have a discussion, but that moment had long passed.

Fravia knew her communication was off-putting, but she felt justified in her emotions. She'd been in love with Smolar for years, and he'd never once acknowledged it. Always friendly, he never showed any affection or expression of love toward her. Hearing his desire to leave without her consideration was devastating. She was disappointed in herself more than she was with him.

Unfortunately, Fravia didn't have time to unravel everything with Smolar. Promit was in danger, a Savior was missing, and they needed to coordinate a rescue plan. Upon their arrival, Fravia knocked on the door as though it were Smolar's head. He clearly understood the message.

"Well, isn't this a pleasant surprise. Both of you, please come in." Lady Vixa greeted them into her home and, to their surprise, she had guests.

"Dad? Mom!?" Fravia exclaimed.

21

The last thing Fravia expected to see were her parents standing in Lady Vixa's home, especially her mother. Fravia looked to Smolar, who was just as shocked, but turned away, recalling the fight they'd just had.

"Fravia, my darling. Perfect timing," Lucemia expressed with love.

"What're you both doing here?" she wondered, darting glances between her parents.

"Lady Vixa reached out to us and we had a long chat. She told us about the…situation, and asked for assistance."

"Assistance? But you—" Fravia looked at Lady Vixa.

"We've discussed our differences and understand one another more." Lucemia smiled. "It's lovely what open and honest communication can do." She glanced at Lady Vixa. "Not to say we'll never disagree again." Both ladies smirked.

Fravia was impressed. It was more than she could have expected. She hoped if Lady Vixa requested their assistance, her mother would help, especially with a fellow quorian in danger. She knew her mother was kind, but breaking bread with their ruler was a different scenario. Fravia didn't know how their conversation went, but it didn't matter. She remained quiet, happy to see her mother's change of heart.

"That's beautiful." Fravia smiled. As the shock subsided, her focus shifted again toward the reasoning. "So, you know about *everything*?"

"Yes," Lady Vixa replied. "Once I confessed it all, we were able to discuss a rescue plan."

"I think it's about time we fleshed out this plan and got the ball rolling," Lucemia suggested.

"Yes," Lady Vixa agreed. She waved her arms, inviting everyone to take a seat.

The Deallius family sat beside one another, with Smolar on a single plush chair. He and Fravia's eyes met; hers were filled with disappointment, his with sadness and frustration.

"A fellow quorian and Savior have been taken from us. Though we need to save them both, our priority is to bring Promit home first, then Neetri and prepare for what may come," Lady Vixa spoke confidently. "I've devised a plan and each of you play a pivotal role in his rescue, either being away on the mission or preparing for his arrival. While I wish I could rescue him myself, it's not wise for me to leave." Everyone nodded in agreement. Losing their ruler without a successor would be detrimental to their civilization. "Once he's home, prepare yourselves. Change is coming."

Lady Vixa walked toward her desk in the corner and grabbed three small charms. "I know the Blue Diamond Jubilee is near to celebrate my one-hundred-year reign, but I'd like to adjust that notion. I'd like to welcome a new era for our city. Our race's next phase." She paused, her excitement shifting to concern. "It's only a matter of time until word spreads of our existence. Though initially concerning, I've concluded it's for the best. We've been forced into suppression for too long, and it's time for that to end. During the mission, I'll be in contact with the ground team while meeting with quorians throughout the city. I'll announce my plans for exploration at the Blue Diamond Jubilee to reclaim our rightful place in the Outer World, honoring our eternal King Klai."

Smolar was utterly surprised by her enthusiasm. The ruler he'd known, the same who was once his guardian, had changed. He wasn't sure if it was Promit's capture, Neetri's disappearance or her willingness to listen to others, but Smolar was elated. Though everyone in The Quo showed her respect, he knew they'd begin to express love and adoration, something she'd yearned for.

Fravia and Reagor were enlightened by their ruler's words. They'd each already seen a difference in Lady Vixa, but her speech was further demonstration. Within the Deallius family, no one was more surprised than the matriarch, Lucemia. Though late in her reign, Lady Vixa had finally begun to show a new representation of the Quorian Ruler, starting with the acceptance of exploration and an overhaul of The Quo.

"Give me your hand," Lady Vixa said to Smolar. "This is a Pendant of Perception, one of three I possess. Though all three allow us to communicate with one another, only this one allows me to view where you are; see what you see. With regards to Promit, I know you feel great responsibility and disappointment. I also know you couldn't pass up the opportunity to leave The Quo and aid in his return." She sighed. "Do you acknowledge the risk and accept the task to accomplish greatness for our city?"

"Yes," he said without hesitation. "I'm bringing him home, no matter the cost."

Lady Vixa smiled, knowing his mother would be proud, and placed the pendant into his hand. It reminded her they still needed to speak privately.

As he examined it, Lady Vixa walked toward Reagor with a smile.

"Reagor, due to your extensive knowledge of the Outer World, I have to ask; do you acknowledge the risk and accept the task to accomplish greatness for our city?" Lady Vixa held her hand out with her second Pendant of Perception.

"Dad!?" Fravia burst out.

"Is there a problem, Fravia?" Lady Vixa asked. Her tone still startled everyone as they adjusted to their *new* leader.

"Are you sure he's the best to go?" she respectfully rambled. "I volunteer to accompany Smolar on the excursion. My father may have more knowledge than me, but he also has a responsibility to The Quo. There are patients here who need his services." Fravia darted an empathetic look at Smolar. Though she wouldn't admit it during a feud, she couldn't fathom the one she loved wandering through the Outer World alone. Fravia's suggestion warranted a moment of silence. They knew she'd made a good point.

"I know it was never something we spoke about at home," she said to her parents. "You both may have thought everything was secret and private, but honestly...I've read and reviewed much of your work. The maps, the regions, the paths, the descriptions, the weather conditions...everything. I may not remember it all, but who can?"

Lucemia and Reagor didn't know whether to be proud or angry. Though she was far from a child, it was touching for them to see her morality and courage. In particular, it was the first time Lucemia saw a part of herself in her daughter.

Smolar, on the other hand, was uncertain about the turn of events. He and Fravia were in the midst of a fight, and though he was certain it'd dissipate soon enough, he wasn't sure it was best for her to accompany him.

"I can't argue your reasoning," Lady Vixa said, breaking the silence. She glanced at Lucemia and Reagor, then back at Fravia. "Fravia Deallius, do you acknowledge the risk and accept the task to accomplish greatness for our city?"

"Consider it done." Fravia's certainty was palpable. Lady Vixa placed the second Pendant of Perception into her hand, gripping it tightly while looking at Smolar.

"There's just one pendant left," Lady Vixa announced. As the only unaddressed quorian remaining in the room, Lucemia adjusted her posture in anticipation. The two females made eye contact and their newly enlightened leader smiled. "With the final pendant, I'd like to introduce you to someone," she announced. Those in the room gasped, their eyes darting at one another. Lucemia cocked her head curiously.

"There's someone else here?" Smolar asked.

"Rhugor!" Lady Vixa shouted. "Can you come down, please?"

The other four quorians, in unison, whispered the name under their breath, with an upwards inflection.

Rhugor?

Heavy footsteps sounded from upstairs, slowly approaching. With each step of his descent, Rhugor's weight vibrated the Quorian Ruler's home.

Thud. Thud. Thud.

The mysterious quorian approached the final step and the group turned to observe him.

"Everyone, I'd like you to meet Rhugor Horwick. He is the third quorian who will join you on your excursion across the Outer World and into The Barren Land." Lady Vixa's revelation rendered them speechless.

Rhugor hesitantly entered the room, standing taller than most quorians, except Lady Vixa. He wore a leather vest cut off at the shoulders, exposing his muscular, slate-colored arms. It was form-fitting around his torso and his waist was tight, extending down to two strong, burly legs, mostly covered in leather. While everyone evaluated his physique, Fravia was smitten by his aposematic appearance, but intrigued she'd never seen him before.

"Hello. It's great to meet you." His voice was deep, mysterious.

"Wait," Lucemia interrupted, "you're going to send my daughter out there with a stranger?"

"What Rhugor lacks in familiarity, he more than makes up for in strength," Lady Vixa replied. "Additionally, I think it's more important to have you remain in the city. When Promit returns, I want to be adequately prepared to heal any wounds. I've seen the poor condition he's in." The reminder of Promit's status resolved any concern within the group.

Lady Vixa walked toward Rhugor and held out her third and final Pendant of Perception. "Rhugor, do you acknowledge the risk and accept the task to accomplish greatness for our city?"

"Gladly." He reached out and accepted the pendant.

With the three individuals chosen, Smolar looked to Fravia in astonishment, but she was too focused on Rhugor. He noticed her eyes wander up and down, admiring his physique.

"So," Smolar exclaimed loudly, jolting Fravia and everyone else in the room. "Lady Vixa, how does this pendant work? It's tiny." All three of them admired the beauty of their pendant, but questioned its ability. Though the Pendant of Perception was small, it bore weight. Smolar and Rhugor examined the luxurious, silver pendant, uncertain of its unique symbol, but Fravia smiled, immediately aware of its meaning.

"This is the ancient quorian seal, isn't it?"

"My, my." Lady Vixa grinned. "Your knowledge continues to impress me." Fravia proudly adjusted her posture. She looked at Smolar with a smug expression, then flirtatiously smiled at Rhugor, who smiled back in admiration.

"Yes. This is the oldest of quorian seals. The Q represents our people and K our beloved King Klai. These pendants have been enchanted, granting me access to your senses. What Smolar sees, I'll see. What you all hear, I'll hear. While I improve my enchanting abilities, which I've neglected to use, these are by far my finest concoctions. Just pin the pendants behind your ears. It'll grant telecommunication access between us all." Lady Vixa smiled at Smolar and Fravia, aware of their concern.

"Lady Vixa," Fravia began, "this is great preparation and discussion, but…" She hesitated, not wanting to cast doubt. "What's the plan when we arrive to The Barren Land?"

"Right," Smolar agreed, reassuring Fravia. "How do we find Promit? What about The Lost Sphere? How do we get in?" Everyone in the room gazed upon their ruler for answers. Lady Vixa sat down in a luxurious chair beside Smolar and revealed her plan.

"Fravia, Smolar and Rhugor will use the Enchanted Gate to transport into the

Outer World. After speaking with Lucemia and Reagor, it seems safest to use Sartica as your destination." Everyone huddled as Reagor rustled a few of the maps on the center table, bringing their amateur depiction of Sartica to the center. "The gate will grant you access to this point." Lady Vixa pointed toward a bundle of numerous bumps sketched around the perimeter of the region.

"What's that?" Smolar asked.

"They're known as sand dunes. They surround the perimeter of Sartica, with reports of certain portions moving. Some rotate in a circular motion while others just sink in a pit. It's imperative to watch your step," Lucemia explained. Fravia was proud to see her mother as they locked eyes and smiled.

"Once you pass the exterior, you'll be in the open world of Diveria. Little is known about the world between regions," Lady Vixa revealed, looking to Reagor for a more detailed description.

"Those who have ventured out have described unique individuals, strange creatures, unusual sensations."

"Unusual…sensations?" Rhugor asked, his ivory eyebrow arched.

Reagor hesitated. "Some…have said they sensed a presence watching them, like they were being followed. There's never been evidence to prove it – no sound, no footprints, no marks. Just a hunch." The room remained silent until he continued. "Some brushed it off, others blamed it on aimless wanderers. A few, however, adamantly felt it was the Divinity King himself, watching what goes on throughout his wrongfully claimed territory."

"Don't be silly!" Rhugor smirked. "That's ridiculous."

"Ridiculous or not, I refuse to take the risk. That's why each one of you will be granted metamorphic potions. I'll dispense them at the time of the mission."

Atop Lady Vixa's desk was a small, black velvet canister. She picked it up and stood beside her chair. "This brings me to the final enchantment for the mission," she announced, holding the canister in one hand and rubbing her necklace in another.

Smolar had always admired the amulet around her neck. It was a large teardrop ruby, rich in color and heavy in size. Her necklace was made of silver, as was the holder for the gem.

"This is the Amulet of Eymus. Gifted to me by my father before his death, it's been around my neck since I was a child. It's my most prized possession." Lady Vixa looked at Smolar. "I don't think you've ever seen me without it?"

"No, never."

"Well that ends today." With a swift tug, Lady Vixa inhaled and pulled the amulet away from her body, breaking the clasp at the back. As she exhaled, the Quorian Ruler felt lighter. "Here is your weapon to destroy The Lost Sphere. It contains pure, raw emotion. Pain. Sadness. Sorrow."

Lady Vixa placed the amulet into the canister, then into Smolar's hands. "I've seen what's inside The Lost Sphere. When you arrive at its base, toss it into the storm. Disrupt its peaceful containment, release the ferocity that lives within and watch The Lost Sphere crumble to the ground. Reveal The Barren Land and everyone who lives within, granting them the freedom that quorians will soon achieve." Lady Vixa stared at Smolar's clenched fist for just a moment longer before gazing into his eyes. "*Only you* can successfully handle and activate the necklace."

After an intense, silent moment, Smolar lowered his gaze as Lady Vixa returned to her chair. Lucemia and Reagor were both touched by her emotion and impressed by her leadership. Rhugor, Fravia and Smolar were in deep contemplation about the plan.

"Once you enter The Barren Land, you must reach the tallest tower in the region. That was where I last saw Promit. It'll be up to you three to make it happen." She turned and made eye contact with each quorian as she spoke to them. "Rhugor, you personify brawn, courage, and strength. Fravia, your knowledge and wisdom are well beyond your years. Smolar, my dear Smolar, your pure heart yearns for the resolution of Promit's safe return." Lady Vixa paused, looking between the three brave explorers. "Use your gifts and harness your strengths. While you'll never be alone on this journey, its success will depend upon your cooperation with each other and yourselves."

22

After completing the mission, Vanilor Dipythian returned home to his wife, Cordova, and their twin children. Unaware of the job before his departure, Cordova wasn't pleased with his time away, but he convinced her. Though uncertain of the reward's amount, Vanilor explained Brugōr's promise of financial freedom. It's what fueled her to push through being alone with her six-year-old twins for the couple of weeks. Even a mother's unconditional, endless love becomes tested under such circumstances.

Days after his meeting with Brugōr, a Kurhal guard arrived at the Dipythians' home with a small bag of jinugery, the currency across Diveria, and a check. Vanilor nearly fell over when he noticed the amount. He secretly placed the check into his pocket and flaunted the bag of jinugery to his wife and children.

"Look at what we have here!" Vanilor shouted in excitement. "This is only the beginning of it."

"Holy! You weren't kidding!" Cordova was elated. Raised in a poor household, she wanted her children to have a better life than she had. She embraced her husband as tears of joy rolled down her cheeks. "You did it," she whispered.

"I can't believe it's over," he said. "They're waiting for me to pick up the rest. Might as well secure it and bring it home, right?"

"Absolutely."

"I'll be back shortly," he said, handing the jinugery to his wife. The energy heightened within the household – a much needed change from the stress and angst that'd been lingering while Cordova struggled with her twins alone.

Vanilor expected to feel guilty lying about the entire reward, but such emotion never arrived. Placing the check on the seat beside him as he drove away, he considered the choices he'd made in recent years. Before he'd laid eyes on a quorian, before he accepted Brugōr's mission and before having a family.

Back then, Vanilor had been single and steadily working as an entry-level guard for the castle. He was thirty and thriving. While tending his post at the entryway of the castle grounds, Vanilor's innocent eyes gazed upon a stumbling man with a skinny, yet striking, woman. They passed by the drawbridge, walking away from Karg River. Being the only guard on duty, he kept a close eye on the couple.

As the man staggered, leaning on the woman, he shouted obscenities at her. Vanilor resisted the urge to intervene. It wasn't until the drunk slapped her across the face, bringing her to her knees, that he marched over. Vanilor drew his sword to the man's neck as he prepared to kick the defenseless woman.

"Don't make this your final move, ya drunk fuck," Vanilor warned.

"The fuck did you—" The wasted man tried to confront him, but failed. Vanilor slightly withdrew his sword, flipped it mid-air, gripping the blade, and swung the hilt directly at the back of the drunk's head. Both Vanilor and the woman heard a crack as the disorderly man collapsed. Looking down at the frail, injured woman, he prepared to help her when he heard a distant yell.

"Wooooo!"

Vanilor turned and saw Brugōr exiting the castle grounds. "You! Young man. Come here." He looked around, unsure if he was speaking to him. "Yes. You, for fuck's sake." His armor clanged from laughter. Vanilor made his way toward the leader.

"Hello, sir."

"What is your name, boy?" Brugōr asked.

"Vanilor Dipythian."

"I see you've left your post here for...that," Brugōr stoically exclaimed. Just as he was about to defend his actions, the brute approached him and whispered, "I admire your eagerness to claim what's yours – may it be women, wealth or wine. Harness your inner greed." Vanilor had expected to be reprimanded not praised.

"Go." Brugōr nodded toward the woman.

"Sir?"

"Go. Tend to your needs. Sow your seed. I'll have another guard release you. Tomorrow morning, meet me on the twenty-fifth floor of the Kurhal to discuss a promotion." Brugōr retreated to the castle grounds surrounded by guards. Vanilor was exhilarated, proud. He desperately wanted internal access to the castle's regime and, with some luck, he'd found his way in.

He returned to the frail woman to ensure her safety. She claimed he'd saved her life and wished to reward him. While he had no intention of forcing himself on her, she insisted on thanking him in the only way she knew how. The two wandered around the back of the castle for her to express her gratitude. Vanilor lay sprawled out on the hot desert sand, moaning at the sensation of the mysteriously striking woman atop him. He couldn't help but consider her his good luck charm.

As quickly as she appeared to him, she was gone.

After their brief, euphoric encounter, Vanilor's life shifted. Brugōr promoted him to be a personal spy for the castle, assisting in various jobs within the region and, eventually, across Diveria. He found great fulfillment and happiness with his new role. Working directly with Brugōr gave Vanilor hope he could do more, maybe even become leader. Vanilor wasn't sure where he'd end up, but knew he wanted to have power and control.

Wandering the castle grounds one night, his gaze fell upon a familiar figure in the distance. Vanilor wasn't certain but he wondered if his sight was fooling him.

My good luck charm.

He walked over and spoke with the familiar woman, whose name he never learned.

"I'm with child," she proclaimed.

"I-I can see that. Congratulations…"

"And to you."

Riddled with disbelief, Vanilor asked how it could've happened. The woman, who revealed her name as Cordova, explained how she hadn't had relations with anyone except him some time ago. Vanilor wanted to ignore her, discredit it, but the tone of her voice resonated within him. He knew she spoke the truth.

Vanilor had never let anything or anyone get in his way of achieving power and success, but he realized having a child could solidify his legacy. It'd continue his bloodline. Hiding his reason for excitement, he reassured Cordova he'd do the right thing. The two eventually married and, to their surprise and his disappointment, ended up with a pair of twin girls.

When Vanilor stopped daydreaming, he found himself in front of the bank. Ready to make a deposit that would change his life, he accepted a revelation he'd long ignored. Vanilor's family hindered his ability to gain power and wealth. Up until the successful mission with Mortimer, which required him to leave his family, he'd sacrificed his dream over the last seven years. He knew his happiness had vanished, and sensed his legacy was tarnished without boys.

With the check in hand, he decided his skillful tactics allowed him to risk his life for the hefty reward and felt he deserved to enjoy it – alone. Vanilor planned to open a private bank account, gather some belongings, and go visit a friend until he decided where he'd begin the next phase of his life.

Mortimer Hullington hadn't slept well since returning home. Any time he closed his eyes to rest, he envisioned the suffering quorian, the presumed death of their assailant, the stranger being hunted for snooping on their meeting with Shrenka, or the horrific murder of Brugōr's personal guard. Though deeply disturbed by them all, it was the manipulation of Michael in Tillerack that frequently appeared. He acknowledged how ludicrous it was to consider murder secondary to manipulation, but there was something about Michael that he couldn't forget. It went beyond the unexpected kiss, which he hadn't yet unraveled. Mortimer questioned his feelings toward the man, but disregarded it since they'd been strangers. The suppression halted his own analysis of his internal struggles.

Filled with regret and shame, Mortimer knew his friendship with Vanilor was over. He felt it was made clear in the elevator after their meeting with Brugōr and Shrenka. He didn't understand how someone could cause such harm without regret or reflection.

Mortimer was trapped with the nightmares, and hadn't left his house since he returned from the castle grounds. His only visitor was the guard that delivered his reward. The check remained on the corner table with the bag of jinugery on top – untouched. He refused to take the reward for his own profit, but didn't know what to do with it.

Stagnant in life, Mortimer decided to leave the house. He thought interaction with others in the valley might help. Though he had no plan to keep the jinugery, he thought it best to secure it in the bank until the appropriate time. He hoped to be quickly inspired so he could rid himself of the blood jinu.

After a quick rinse and a fresh outfit, Mortimer grabbed the reward off the table and departed. He deposited the check into a new bank account for ease, and held onto the bag as proof. He then traveled to Karg City, located in the southern end of the valley, west of the Karg River.

As a computer engineer, he spent most of his time working alone, ensuring happiness came from within and not from others. The biggest project he'd worked on, which forced him to work alongside others, was the creation of the Barren

Land Locator. At the time, it brought Mortimer pleasure to help the welcoming leader and express his gratitude. He eventually realized it was how Brugōr ruled. He'd welcome degreants across Diveria and ensure their comfort. Once the newcomer felt a sense of pride and debt to Brugōr, they'd offer up their personalized services – accounting, metalwork, culinary, etc. After Brugōr benefitted, he'd forget the individual and move onto the next target.

In Mortimer's situation, however, he was never tossed aside. The castle regime had him readily available when they needed support or assistance in their system. He was blinded by their willingness to include him in their circle – it was intoxicating. It was how Mortimer was coerced into the quorian mission, though he wasn't aware at the time.

He knew the only way he'd find forgiveness would be to rectify the problems he'd instigated. The quorian, Michael, the meddler, the death of the guard. Mortimer vowed to himself to try his best to resolve these issues. The assailant outside of The Barren Land was the only exception. It brought him sadness that some blood would forever remain on his hands, but hoped it wasn't too late to rectify the four other lives he'd affected.

Reflecting too much on recent events, Mortimer lost himself in Karg City. Uncertain where he'd parked his car, he decided to grab a bite and drink somewhere appealing. Across the street from where he stood was a bright blue sign.

Cristal Caverns.

Mortimer hadn't heard of it before, but if the aroma coming from within was anything to go by, he'd enjoy it. Fortunately, he remembered to grab his satchel, now resting across his chest, which held his wallet and the bag of blood jinu.

As he entered Cristal Caverns, he was surprised it was less of a restaurant and more of a bar with mellow music. To his left was a small lounge with plush couches, chairs and community tables. Ahead was a bar filled with patrons eating and drinking. Mortimer eagerly grabbed an open stool at the end. Beside him sat a broad-shouldered man eating a steak, grilled vegetables and potatoes.

"What can I get ya?" the bartender asked. Mortimer looked at the surrounding drinks, considering his options.

"I'll take a double whiskey, and keep the bottle close." He smiled. Both the bartender and the patron beside him expressed a look of shock.

"Alright, man. Coming up." The bartender rolled his eyes, having enough experience to know how his night would end.

"That kind of a day, eh?" The broad-shouldered man smirked.

"That kind of a week," Mortimer corrected, grabbing a menu.

"Can I get you anything else, boss?" the bartender asked, placing his drink in front of him.

"Just lookin' now."

"Alright. I'll check back in a bit." The bartender returned to the drunk patrons.

"Don't order the steak and potatoes. Not that great," his bar neighbor suggested. Mortimer curiously looked at the chatty man.

"Ah, alright. Thanks. I'll take note…"

"Franklin. Franklin Novack."

"Mortimer Hullington."

"Nice to meet you, Mortimer." The two shook hands, and Mortimer was startled by his tight grip. He was a burly man, built like a tank, with brown hair, brown eyes, thick glasses and olive skin. Though on a barstool, it was obvious Franklin stood tall.

Mortimer tossed back his first drink as he and Franklin talked. The conversation was light – the weather, work, areas within the valley. After he'd ordered and finished his second double whiskey, Mortimer was buzzed. The alcohol coursed through his veins, allowing his guard to fall. When the bartender asked once more what he'd like to eat, Mortimer insisted upon the baked chicken breast with a loaded baked potato and vegetables.

"Would you like a drink, Franklin? Third round's on me."

"Sure. Why not?" He looked over toward the bartender. "Hey, Tom! I'll have what he's having. Put it on his tab." The bartender nodded and shared a smile.

"Oh, you know him?" Mortimer asked.

"Yes. Very well. We used to..." Franklin hesitated, attempting to read Mortimer. "We used to know each other well. Haven't hung out much lately."

"Ah. I see."

"Do you *really* see though?" Franklin wondered.

Mortimer smiled, slightly more confident in his assumption. "Loud and clear, buddy." He raised his glass to toast and winked.

"It's always nice to meet family," Franklin replied, as they clinked glasses amongst the noisy, drunken crowd.

"Well...not quite family. Not yet? I don't know. That's a small part of the reason I'm here." Mortimer wasn't sure if it was the whiskey, the pressure or the comfort he felt from Franklin, but for the first time, he opened up about his recent experience with Michael.

Their conversation lasted longer than he could recall. They shared stories and experiences, though Franklin did most of the talking. By the time he finished his whiskey, Mortimer knew he'd had too much.

Tom informed the two it was closing time and they offered him the untouched whiskey Franklin neglected to consume, which he kindly accepted. Mortimer paid the tab and they exited the bar together.

"Where'd you park, Mortimer?"

"Morty. Call me...Morty. All...my friends do," he said, stumbling over his words, and his feet. "If I had...friends."

"You have one friend, Morty, and his name's Franklin Novack! Remember that!" They exchanged smiles.

Realizing his new friend was too intoxicated to drive, Franklin appreciated having slowed down his own alcohol intake.

"Thank you, Franklin. You're ve-very...kind." Mortimer nodded as he began to walk away in search of his vehicle. "It's been a pleasure—"

"The pleasure's all mine, Morty, but our night isn't over yet."

"No?" Mortimer stopped, curious.

"You don't know where your car is, and even if you did, you shouldn't be driving. Let me drive you home and you can pick the car up in the morning." Franklin's voice was kind, but stern. He was adamant about the decision. Mortimer didn't want to impose upon his new friend, but decided he was right.

The two men hopped into Franklin's vehicle and fastened their seatbelts.

"Alright. Where do you live?"

"In the Outer Limits, across Karg River." Mortimer pointed at the windshield, unaware that location was in the opposite direction.

"Alright." Franklin smirked. "Wonderful. How about you plug your address in." He pointed to his navigation.

"Technology…isn't it a son of a bitch?" Mortimer remarked, following his instructions. Franklin laughed.

Mortimer admired the nightlight as he rested his head against the window. Though the streets weren't as busy as during the day, he was impressed by how many people roamed around. He wondered what life must be like as a nightwalker.

After observing the streets, Mortimer's eyes browsed the interior of the car, starting with Franklin. Though still lackluster to Michael, he chuckled, admiring his new friend's appearance.

"Everything alright, buddy?" Franklin asked, noticing Mortimer's wandering eye.

"Absolutely. Just…thank you for bringing me home. It was for the best." They exchanged smiles. Pulling his leaded, intoxicated eyes away, Mortimer noticed a generic folded up piece of paper in the cup holder. When he grabbed it, Franklin startled, shouting for him to hand it back as he unintentionally swerved the car.

"What?" Mortimer sneered, continuing to unravel the paper.

"Seriously, man, don't piss me off." Franklin's tone changed. By the time he was finished speaking, Mortimer had unfolded the paper, confused by its contents.

"What is it?"

"Nothing, now give it." Franklin grabbed it out of his hands and shoved it under his seat. Mortimer wasn't sure what had piqued his curiosity, but he didn't mean to upset his new friend.

"What's the Anti-Regime?"

"Forget you saw that."

"What if I can't?" Mortimer blamed the alcohol for his confidence. "What if I have questions?" He smiled. "What if I'm interested?"

"Interested in what?" Franklin questioned.

"Learning more about that flyer."

"You don't know what you're talking about."

"Then why don't you tell me?" At a quick glance, Mortimer had noticed mention of an Anti-Regime with The Barren Land's emblem upside-down, crossed out in red. "What if I told you I'm not happy with the castle regime?" He paused. "What if I told you I'm looking for a way to right some wrongs?"

"What wrongs could you've possibly caused?"

"One capture, one, possibly two, deaths, another probably fleeing for their life and putting stress to another whom…I really connected with, and miss."

"Michael?" Franklin asked, which Mortimer confirmed with a simple nod. "Mortimer, my friend, you are one complex son-of-a-bitch."

"You have no idea." Silence fell between the two men.

"Well, it appears we've made it," Franklin announced. Mortimer sighed, disappointed to be home already.

"Please. Tell me."

"Fine, but you didn't hear it from me." Franklin pulled the piece of paper out and tossed it back at Mortimer. "It's called the Anti-Regime. A secret society, within the valley, who're against everything the castle regime stands for."

"A secret society…with flyers?" Mortimer grimaced.

"Yes, exactly." Franklin rolled his eyes. "I thought it was a ridiculous idea—"

"So you're a part of it?" Mortimer interrupted. Franklin clearly hadn't intended to admit his participation. "I'll take that as a yes."

"I've been once or twice," Franklin replied.

"So if I wanted to learn more…?" Mortimer reviewed the flyer.

"You'd have to go into the depths of the Bazaar."

"But where?" Mortimer asked, sensing the Anti-Regime could be his solution.

"I can't say anymore, but take the flyer." Franklin smiled. "Maybe I'll see you around soon."

Exhausted, Mortimer nodded, exited the vehicle, and the two said goodbye.

"The Anti-Regime. The Bazaar…" he said aloud. Mortimer sensed it was his answer, and decided he'd attend the meeting in the upcoming days to try and learn more about the group. Until then, he entered his home, placed the flyer in his satchel and tossed it onto the table. Exhausted by the idea of having to pick up his car the following day, he collapsed on the couch. Just as his eyelids began to relax and his mind wandered off, a heavy knock sounded at the door.

"Mortimer, you home?"

Vanilor, he thought. Mortimer had no desire to see the man.

He knocked a few times more. "I see your car is gone, are you there? Please answer if so."

Mortimer wanted to distance himself, but there was an unusual desperation in his voice. Had he begun to feel remorseful for what they had done? Exhausted, and anticipating a hangover, he answered the door.

"Hey, pal," Vanilor said. "You look like shit."

"What'd ya want?" Mortimer replied.

"I have a favor to ask. I'm heading out for a bit, but just need a place to crash for the night. Do you mind?" Mortimer wanted nothing more to do with the man, but he hesitated with an answer, as an idea came to mind.

"Only on one condition. I'll need you to bring me to my car tomorrow morning."

Vanilor walked in with his bags, accepting the terms. "What the fuck happened to it?"

"Nothing. I just need to pick it up in the morning." Mortimer didn't wish to speak about it any longer. "Where are you off to?"

"Just…away. I need some time."

"And Cordova? The kids?"

"How about we make another deal. I won't ask you about your car, how you've gone into hiding or your recent mood swings, and you don't ask about my plans, ya know?"

"Sounds great to me," Mortimer replied, though disturbed why he didn't wish to speak of his family.

"I'll just crash on the couch, if that's alright with you."

"That works. I'm going to head upstairs to bed. I'm beat."

23

Nigel Hatherton was experimenting with recipes when he heard a knock at the door. His one-story home was quaint, charming and inviting, but yearned for a woman's touch. Not expecting any visitors, Nigel curiously approached the door.

"Hello?" His voice was gentle and calming, but masculine. He peered through his magic mirror, pleasantly surprised his boss was standing at his front door. Uncertain who the others were with her, he glanced around the house, evaluating the cleanliness of his home.

"Hey, Nigel, sorry to bother you!" Osvita replied.

"Never a bother," Nigel said as he unlocked and opened the door. "It's always a delight to see you, Osvita."

"You're too kind, Nigel." She blushed. "This is—"

"Little ol' Rexhia? My you've certainly grown up!" Nigel gleamed.

"You've got it! It's been a few years since you've last seen her." Osvita smiled as Rexhia waved hello. "And this is Grum Lagom, a co-worker of my husband." The two men kindly shook hands. "May we come in?" Osvita asked, with a sense of urgency.

"Of course, please." Nigel welcomed them inside, locking the door behind them.

A loud bark came from the back room and out ran a small ball of fur.

"Chowder! Calm down, girl." Nigel's attempt to ease his whippersnapper down was futile, as Rexhia had collapsed to the floor, in awe of the dog.

"Aww, hi, Chowder!" Rexhia exclaimed. "Ahh, you are just adorable! Mom, look at her!"

"She's now distracted for the next hour or so." Everyone chuckled.

"Sorry for the mess. I was just having a little fun in the kitchen. I do have some muffins made if you'd—"

"Muffins!?" Grum questioned.

"Please, they're on the counter. Help yourselves. There are plenty of beverages in the fridge. Drink what you'd like." Nigel was a considerate host. While he hadn't met Grum before, he considered anyone who knew Osvita a friend. The three adults wandered toward the kitchen and Rexhia remained on the living room floor.

"So what brings ya'll to my neck of the woods?" Nigel asked.

"Neck of the woods?" Grum wondered as he shoved half a muffin into his mouth.

"Never heard of that expression before? It means, what brings ya'll here, into the depths of the Bazaar? People don't just wander here without a purpose."

"Well…" Osvita glanced at Grum devouring the muffin. He appreciated quality home-cooking.

"Is everything okay, Vit?" Nigel's concern grew.

"Well, I don't know exactly," she replied, looking at her daughter, ensuring she was preoccupied with Chowder.

Nigel read Osvita like a book, so he stood up and took action. "Hey, Rexhia, why don't you go to the living room table with Chowder and split a freshly-baked muffin?" Nigel grabbed one, poured a small cup of juice and brought them into the living room for her to enjoy. "Chowder is on a diet, so try to make it no more than three pieces." The two laughed as he patted her on the shoulder and returned to the kitchen.

"Thank you," Osvita replied.

"Of course." Nigel smiled. "So tell me what's going on. How can I help?"

She sighed, lowering her voice. "The short version is my husband's being hunted by the regime for something he witnessed within the castle. He escaped, but not without being seen. To ensure secrecy, Brugōr sent guards to manage the situation. Their initial priority was him, but I believe it's extended to us. Before I found out, they requested our services for a celebratory dinner at the castle." Osvita broke down, resting her head in her palms. Nigel instantly embraced her, reassuring her everything would be okay.

"*They* requested your services?" he asked, aware of it being a goal of hers, but Osvita's face displayed disappointment and fear. He sighed and changed his focus. "Where's Whark now?"

"He fled for safety," Grum replied. "We assume he's in the depths of the Bazaar, but haven't found him yet. Osvita suggested we come here to get off the streets momentarily."

"Okay…okay," he said, patting her back as she calmed down. "Let's start from the beginning. Tell me everything and we can figure out a plan." Nigel suggested, glancing between Grum and Osvita.

"I'll go check on Rexhia and let you two discuss," Grum said, leaving them to it.

Though Osvita trusted Nigel, she had reservations about disclosing everything to him. He always had a strong opinion about Brugōr and his regime, which was her reasoning for not discussing Whark's work often.

Osvita composed herself enough to explain what had happened. She admitted every detail, but omitted the truth about their identity. She was already overwhelmed and couldn't handle the emotional stress of Nigel's reaction.

Grum's hunger was satisfied when he entered the living room to join Rexhia and

Chowder. Though they'd been together for a short period, he'd felt a connection with Osvita's daughter. They'd experienced a life-changing situation. As traumatic as it'd been for him, he couldn't imagine its impact on a thirteen-year-old girl. He wanted to bring laughter and light into her life.

Grum Lagom first married in his early years, but the love quickly faded and the two parted ways. The relationship with his second wife was passionate and beautiful until they learned she was unable to conceive children. Although they had options, their disagreements and arguments ultimately led to the demise of their marriage.

After a long time and relocating into The Barren Land, Grum eventually found himself in another serious relationship. Unfortunately, the two never reached marriage after she adamantly confessed her unwillingness to conceive children. Exhausted and older, Grum relinquished his vision of having a family. He'd wasted too much time on the expectation. Acknowledging his critical flaw wasn't easy, but eventually, Grum learned to accept his biggest regret. It wasn't until the Dimmerks bombarded his home and he spent time with Rexhia that his parental desires flourished again.

"Chowder really likes you." Grum smiled. "I can tell."

"You really think so?" Rexhia asked.

"That's what he told me earlier." Rexhia and Grum exchanged laughter as she continued to pet Chowder.

"How're you doing, Rexhia?"

"I'm good, Mr. Lagom."

"Call me Grum," he said with comfort. "What happened at my house was scary though, and can be overwhelming. Did you want to talk about anything?"

"It…was shocking. I didn't expect it. I'm glad we're okay…and I hope Dad is too," Rexhia sulked.

"I know your dad well. He's smart, cunning. He wouldn't want you to worry," Grum comforted her. "Besides, from what you showed back there, looks like you're one tough girl."

"Well…" She patted her pocket, felt her slingshot and took it out.

"This…is yours?"

"Mmhmm, meet Sohnora," Rexhia said with an innocent tone.

"That's a beautiful name. Where'd you ever find something like this? It's glorious." The frame of the slingshot glistened a majestic cobalt with subtle white strips throughout. The handle was carved out of a dark, rich oak, thick enough to provide a secure grip. The band was a pristine white, as if it were brand new, never used.

"I found it at home. Mom didn't know I snatched it, and I didn't plan on keeping it." Rexhia rubbed the slingshot. "But then something strange happened. When I used it for the first time, we had perfect aim."

"We?"

"She helps me aim. I couldn't do it without her," Rexhia admitted.

"Is that so?" Grum smiled. "Mind if I look at her? I'll be careful."

"Of course." Rexhia handed Sohnora over for him to inspect. Though he wasn't knowledgeable in weapons, he was mystified by its beauty.

"Do you mind if I try?"

"Oh yes! Please!" Rexhia jumped up. It brought her great joy to see Grum interested in the slingshot. They stood across the room and agreed upon a spot in the couch to aim for.

"Have you ever used one before?" she asked.

"A couple times, but it's been years."

Rexhia handed him a marble, he placed it in the band, and shut his right eye to aim. They agreed upon hitting a button in the backing of the couch. With all his focus and determination, Grum aimed slightly above the button. With Sohnora in his right hand, and the band in his left, he held his breath and released the marble.

"Oooh!" Rexhia shouted. "So close!" Grum grinned and placed his index finger to his lips to lower their voices.

"Close!?" Grum whispered. "I almost hit the wall." The two laughed in unison. "I won't tell if you won't," he said, winking at her.

"Deal."

"Okay, your turn. Show me what you got."

Rexhia grabbed the marble, held Sohnora and stood in the same spot as Grum. With a similar stance, she held the slingshot in her right hand and the band in her left. Grum realized Rexhia shut both of her eyes. Nervous she'd damage Nigel's home, he attempted to stop her, but it was too late. His shoulders raised up, anticipating a crash. Rexhia and Grum's gaze followed the marble and watched as it perfectly hit the center of the button they'd agreed upon, falling gracefully onto the couch.

"But...your eyes were closed."

"I told you. I've perfect aim every time. *She guides me.*"

"But...how? I just don't..." Grum picked up the marble and handed it back to her. "Try again, but this time, switch hands." Rexhia placed Sohnora in her left hand, the band with the marble in her right. With a grin, she shut her eyes and released once more. Grum watched the marble fly across the room, landing directly in the center of the button.

"Want me to try anything else?" She chuckled.

"I...just don't understand. Have you spoken to your parents about it?"

Rexhia's demeanor immediately shifted as she picked up the marble. "No..."

"Why not?" he asked as they both sat on the couch. Chowder jumped up to join them.

"I don't want them to get angry or stop me. I'm not using it all the time. It's just a special thing I enjoy having. It's mine," she said. "It's easier to talk to you about it than my parents." Her words warmed Grum's heart.

"I appreciate you saying that, Rexhia. Please know you can always talk to me about anything." He paused with a perplexed look. "Didn't your mom see you use it at my house?"

"Yes. I was worried she'd ask me, but she hasn't yet. I'm not sure if she forgot or is too busy."

"You're probably right." He glanced over at Osvita and Nigel. "Regardless, it's your decision to make and I won't say anything. You can trust me."

"Thanks, Grum. You know…I haven't spoken to anyone about this before. It's nice."

"Of course." Grum wondered what else she could be hiding. He decided to share something about himself. "You know…I have a secret ability too."

"You do!?" Rexhia perked up.

"I can make things disappear," he said, waving his hands as if presenting a magic trick.

"Oh yeah? Can you make me disappear?"

"Your mom wouldn't be too happy if I did that, ho ho!" He winked. "But tell ya what, find yourself a piece of chocolate, an old flower or a banana peel, and I'll show you just how powerful my abilities really are." Grum gleamed as Rexhia laughed.

Osvita entered the living room with Nigel, warmed by the sounds of her daughter's laughter. "How's it going, you two? Or should I say you three." Osvita felt a weight had lifted off her shoulders after confiding in Nigel.

"Looks like Chowder's really become enamored by you." Nigel smiled. It brought Osvita joy to be surrounded by happiness, even if just for a moment. Though she'd hoped to see her husband soon, she reminded herself that he was the one who ran away.

"We're doing well, aren't we?" Grum asked Rexhia. "We were just chatting and getting to know Chowder." While she continued to play, Grum stood up, asking Osvita and Nigel how they were.

"Not bad, considering. I told Nigel what'd happened since we left our home up until now. He generously offered to have us stay here as long as we need until we have a plan or find Whark." Somehow, Grum understood her words well enough to know she didn't divulge the deeper secret of their identity.

"That's very kind, thank you." Grum nodded. "Though with food like yours, you may want to be careful. I'll never want to leave – ho ho!"

Suddenly a firm knock on the door startled everyone, except Chowder who barked.

"Chowder! Stop it, girl," Nigel said. "Coming, just give me a moment. Trying to manage my dog." He chuckled. An unsettling feeling was left in their stomachs as they hoped to not relive what'd happened at Grum's house. Osvita motioned at Grum and her daughter to head toward the back of the house.

"Guards wouldn't enter the depths of the Bazaar," Nigel whispered. "Word would spread before they arrived if that happened." Osvita sensed Nigel wasn't kidding and wondered how he'd know that.

"After what we experienced, we can't be too safe."

"I understand."

Knock, knock.

Nigel grabbed Chowder and answered the door. When it opened, much to his surprise, he was greeted by a familiar face.

"Heya, mate! You coming to the meeting?" a woman asked. Though Osvita couldn't see her fully, she noticed her broad figure and heard her voice.

"Oh, boy, that's right now? I've lost track of time…" Nigel shut the door a little behind him for privacy. "I'm not able to make it. Something's come up," he insisted. The visitor tried to peer inside, but he stood in the way. They laughed at one another, understanding each other's tactics.

"Hm. Alright, Mr. Hatherton." She snickered. "I'll make sure to let Lazarus know."

"Rude," Nigel hissed.

"We'll see if I let you in next time," she said sarcastically. The two exchanged smiles as he closed the front door.

Osvita didn't want to pry about personal matters, but her curiosity prevailed.

"What was that about?"

"That was just my neighbor, Kimber," Nigel replied, though with hesitation. She darted him a look.

"Oh." Osvita's tone changed, unsure why the unexpected guest's appearance rattled her. "Please don't change any plans for us. Go about your day. Seems like she really wanted you to join her."

"It's okay." He smiled. "With everything that you've gone through, I'd rather be here…with you…all." Nigel stumbled, causing a guilty smile on Osvita's face. There was an awkward moment of silence between the two.

"What meeting was she inviting you to?" Osvita quickly changed the subject. Nigel hesitated, as the question proved to be more awkward than the silence had been.

"A local community meeting," he replied. Just then, Grum slowly entered the room with Rexhia behind him.

"Nothing of concern, I presume?" he asked.

"Nope, just a friend of mine."

Rexhia returned to the couch to play with Chowder and her toy. Grum instinctually followed her, as if she were his own child. Osvita smiled at their companionship, happy that her daughter had someone to talk to.

"Nigel, who's Lazarus?" Osvita wondered.

"Huh?" He heard her question, but needed to think of a quick lie.

"Your *friend* mentioned a Lazarus. Is he just another friend?"

"Yes, just another friend." Nigel knew he wasn't a great liar, as did Osvita.

"Hopefully it isn't Lazarus Docaras, ho ho!"

"How do you…?" Nigel whispered to himself as his knees nearly buckled.

"Who's that?" Osvita wondered.

"He's the one who runs the Anti-Regime here in the depths," Grum replied, seemingly disinterested in the topic. Nigel remained silent.

"The what?"

"The Anti-Regime. You haven't heard of them?" Grum assumed everyone had. "It's an underground society that stands against Brugōr and his regime. The castle's aware of their existence, but never considered the group a threat," he explained as Osvita glared at Nigel. "I've always considered it public knowledge, but I suppose it's because of working beside Karg River," Grum continued, though no one was focused on him anymore. He returned his attention to Rexhia and Chowder.

"Nigel…" Osvita said carefully.

"W-Wh-What?" he stuttered, knowing he wouldn't be able to turn this around.

"What's Lazarus's last name?" She made sure to ask a question he couldn't talk his way out of.

Nigel didn't answer.

"Nigel?" Her tone was stern, though she wasn't upset. Osvita knew his disdain for their leader; she even agreed in certain areas, especially now.

"Fine," he admitted. "The woman who rang was Kimber. She's a fellow member of the Anti-Regime."

"And you two were going to attend this meeting?"

"Yes."

"So…you're a part of the elusive Anti-Regime? Never thought I'd meet a member." Grum was pleasantly surprised. He had preconceived notions on what members looked like and Nigel didn't match the visual.

"Can you all please keep this a secret?" Nigel asked without begging. "This sort of information shouldn't get out."

"What do ya say, Rexhia?" Grum asked.

"Secret's safe with me!" she replied.

"We're good over here," Grum joined. Everyone looked at Osvita, awaiting her reply. "I'm sure Osvita feels the same way, yes? Especially with how generous he's been to open his house to us, right?"

"Tell you what," Osvita announced. She had no intention of revealing his secret, but wanted to use the situation to gain knowledge. "Bring me with you to the meeting, and your secret's safe with me."

"Osvita Dimmerk…are you blackmailing me?" Nigel chuckled, knowing she wouldn't betray him.

"Never," she said, grinning and flashing him a wink. "I just…" Osvita walked over to Nigel and whispered, "Maybe someone there would know of Whark? We haven't any clue where he might be."

Nigel knew going to a meeting in search of someone wasn't a great idea, especially with a newcomer, but he always wanted to appease Osvita. "Fine." Nigel looked at the clock, trying to recall the time of the meeting. "I think it starts soon though, so we better leave."

"You're going to their meeting?" Grum stood up.

"I figured it could help us find my husband," she whispered, glancing at her daughter, still amused by Chowder.

"Be careful," Grum warned. "I know I said the castle doesn't take them seriously, but that doesn't mean you shouldn't. If they learn about your ties to the castle…"

"Don't worry. I'll stay close to Nigel the entire time. We'll be back before you know it," she said. "Do you mind—"

"She's in good hands," he said with a smile. "It's been such a delight getting to know your daughter. She's incredibly smart and witty. Since I never had the chance to have a child myself…" Grum glanced at Rexhia, realizing he had changed topics. "Anyway, you two should get going, don't worry about us. We'll be good, right, Rexhia?"

"I'll take great care of Chowder too," she said.

Osvita kissed her daughter on the head. "I love you, cookie. Be good for Mr. Grum and take care of Chowder for Mr. Hatherton. We'll be home shortly, maybe an hour or two?" She looked to Nigel.

"That should work," he replied. Nigel turned to Rexhia and knelt down. "Thank you for watching Chowder for me. On the kitchen counter, there's a container of dog treats. Why don't you grab one to give her after we leave?"

"Will do!"

As Rexhia hustled into the kitchen, Nigel whispered to Grum. "If for any reason you need protection, I have a gun in my bedroom closet. Top shelf." Nigel pointed in the direction of his bedroom for clarification.

When Rexhia returned, Osvita gave her one last goodbye and the two headed out for the meeting. Not a moment after the door shut, Grum turned to Rexhia and asked, "Can we try Sohnora once more?"

"Great! Then afterwards, maybe you can show me the special disappearing ability you have with banana peels and chocolate?" The two laughed.

24

The depths of the Bazaar were narrower, more consuming, than the perimeter. Structures appeared taller, as they were commonly built into the walls. Though the sun still reached the floor, the gorge constricted the streets. It was the chilliest part of the valley. Such conditions made navigating the depths difficult unless familiar with them. Due to the lack of visitors, there were far less vendors than the outer market, resulting in a more serene and silent part of the valley. The locals cherished their peacefulness, but anyone unfamiliar to it found it eerie.

Besides the architectural differences, many residents within the depths took pride in their exuberant flair and flamboyant appearance. With flashy colors and glistening gems, clothing was a form of expression. Popular hair colors included purple, light blue and even polka dots. Some individuals even used animals, whether dead or alive, as part of their fashion.

When Osvita and Nigel arrived at the Skull and Bones Grill, they were greeted by a familiar face. Kimber stood over six-feet tall, with a pale complexion, disheveled neon-yellow hair, a furry white vest that exposed her toned arms, and the same material around her waist – its length leaving little to the imagination. Her legs were long and strong with shredded leather shoes.

"Well, well, look who changed his mind…" She glanced toward Osvita. "And with a new face, no less."

"Hey, Kimber. I apologize for before. Some unexpected guests arrived, and I was looking out for our secrecy."

"Such a priority you decided to bring a non-member to our meeting?" Kimber wondered.

"Come on." Nigel's tone was borderline flirtatious, his eyes begging for sympathy.

"Alright, alright. Cool it." Kimber put her hand up. "You're lucky I like ya, but some advice: flirting won't get you anywhere, honey. I'll never fuck you." Osvita's jaw almost dropped. "Too risqué for you?"

"Can't blame me for trying." Nigel smiled. "Kimber Jones, meet Osvita Dimmerk. She's my boss back in the valley. She'll be staying with me for a few days."

"Pleasure to meet ya." Kimber eyed her. "You could really express yourself with a body like that. Don't you agree, Nigel?"

"Okay, okay…Let me not waste any more of your time. We'll head in, if you don't mind," a flustered Nigel insisted.

"Hold it. No offense, darlin',"—she turned back to Nigel—"but how do I know she can be trusted? We can't just let anybody in."

Nigel looked at Osvita with an apologetic expression. "Her husband's being hunted by the regime. By Brugōr personally."

"Nigel!" Osvita shouted.

"Is this true?" Kimber stared at her with widened eyes.

"Yes," she said with a heavy sigh. "We've been on the run."

"Shit, that's awful." Kimber recognized her discomfort from their conversation. Sympathizing for Osvita's situation, she welcomed them both inside the meeting with a reassuring smile.

"I'm sorry to disclose your personal life,' he whispered as they entered, 'but it was the only way she—"

"I understand."

The grill had been transformed from a restaurant to a meeting hall. All tables, chairs and booths were moved toward the perimeter, leaving a dozen small, bar-height tables with enough space for four. The room was filled with members, most of whom were creatively dressed. They both smiled as they walked toward an open table in the far back corner.

"Stay here, I'm going to find my friend and ask if he's seen your husband."

"You're going to leave me here? Let me come with you," Osvita pleaded.

"It's best to meet him alone. Just stay here and I'll be back shortly. You're in good hands." Nigel smiled. Osvita knew he'd keep her safe.

As he vanished into the swarm of people, Osvita admired the elaborate fashion, unique decor and carefree energy. Feeling as though inside a rainbow, she observed the room until she noticed a shimmering wall covered in jinugery from patrons. Most of them had writing on it – names, dates, random words, etc.

"Such a neat idea, don't you think?" an unfamiliar voice asked. Osvita turned to see a tall, slender man with brown eyes and smooth tan. His attire was similar to hers – typical in appearance for her, nothing dramatic.

"Very much so." She slowly returned to the table where Nigel had left her.

"Do you know when the meeting's scheduled to begin?" he asked, following her.

"Hopefully soon."

"Sounds good," he replied, followed by a moment of silence between them. "Sorry. I haven't attended a meeting before. This is all foreign to me."

"Me too." She smiled, comforted to not be alone. "I'm here with a friend of mine who stepped away for just a moment."

"Another newbie? I didn't think I'd be so lucky." The man smiled and put his hand out to shake. "Nice to meet ya. My name is Mortimer. Mortimer Hullington."

"Nice to meet you Mortimer, I'm Osvita Dimmerk."

"Call me Morty," he replied.

Nigel felt bad leaving Osvita, but knew it was best to talk to the founder of the Anti-Regime privately. As he walked through the crowd, he turned around and paused for a moment, admiring the one he loved from afar. He understood the predicament, but couldn't ignore his feelings toward her. Ever since they began working together, Nigel envisioned a life with Osvita, his heart filled with forbidden love.

As Osvita admired the corner wall of jinugery, Nigel resumed his focus and entered the back room. Though it wasn't spacious, there were still a couple dozen people awaiting the meeting. Surrounded by stovetops, refrigerators, and other restaurant supplies, Nigel gazed around to find the familiar face.

"Nigel? Is that you?" a voice said in the distance. Nigel's eyes couldn't find the man, though he knew the voice. "Over here, fool," he said with a chuckle. The two made eye contact.

"Lazarus! Look at you," Nigel shouted exuberantly, looking him up and down as he approached. Typically in formal attire, Nigel was surprised to see him in casual appearance.

"Nigel Hatherton, I'm glad you made it." Lazarus adjusted his wavy, grey-ish hair in the mirror before standing up to greet his guest. "And not with much time to spare."

"Wouldn't miss it," Nigel reassured him.

"I'd hope not. This is going to be a groundbreaking one," Lazarus teased and whispered into Nigel's ear. "We're finally going to take action. The time has come."

"Take action?" The two huddled toward a secluded corner, giving the founder space.

"We've received an exorbitant donation from a newcomer. We can finally execute our strategic plan without financial strain. I'll announce it during the meeting. We just need to coordinate a few final details." Lazarus's excitement was palpable. Nigel respectfully shared his emotions, but quickly shifted the subject to Osvita.

"Let me know when you'd like to talk, but until then, I have a question to ask." Nigel's tone was stern.

"Shoot," Lazarus replied, returning to his chair to approve his look for the meeting. He moved his large hands across his prominent jawline, rubbing his well-groomed grey stubble.

"You haven't happened to meet someone by the name of Whark Dimmerk, have you?" Lazarus didn't react to the question. "Laz?"

"Name's familiar. How do you know him?"

"He and his family are in hiding from the regime after something happened."

"If he's missing, then where's his family?"

Nigel hesitated to answer, but the leader repeated himself, maintaining eye contact.

"They're…with me. They were nearly caught when Whark had to flee, but they managed to escape." There was a moment of silence until both men spoke at the same time. Lazarus insisted Nigel speak first. "Though the husband is their primary interest, his wife, my boss, was requested to cater a special event within the castle. Hardly a coincidence, she knows Brugōr always gets what he wants."

Lazarus perked up, aware of Nigel's profession. "You mean to tell me this is your boss's husband?"

"Yes."

"And you're invited to be inside the castle grounds?"

"Well, yes, specifically the banquet hall, but I'm not sure how she plans to handle their request."

Lazarus's gaze fell, deep in thought.

"So…if you happen to hear anything about Whark or his whereabouts, please let me know." Acknowledging Lazarus's lack of interest, Nigel turned around, but then the leader spoke.

"Say, Nigel…"

"Yeah?"

"What's her name?"

"Who?"

"Your boss. Whark's wife."

"Osvita."

"Right," Lazarus said sarcastically, aware of Nigel's widened smile. "I'm sure it's a challenging task to manage. Being a talented business owner, especially for a woman, I'm sure she'd want to further her success. Has she spoken to them since?"

"I'm sure anyone in her position would find it difficult," Nigel said, unappreciative of the misogynistic comment. "Considering they're hiding, I doubt she's made contact. She's worked diligently to build her reputation and career within the valley. I'd imagine she'd want to follow through, but is concerned for her safety."

"Then don't cancel," Lazarus suggested. "You'd be with her for the job, yes?"

"Yes, but entering the Kurhal while being hunted is not—"

"What if I can ensure the safety of you both?" Lazarus stood again. "I think there's a way you could help us *and* make your lady happy."

"She's not my—"

"Yes, I've heard you *say* that too," Lazarus mumbled, rolling his eyes. He took Nigel into a back office, shutting the door behind them. They were surrounded by a myriad of filing cabinets, random decor, and a large desk with two chairs. The desk was filled with unorganized papers, a pair of glass pig paperweights, an abacus beside a calculator, and a dusty telecommunication device.

"What's going on?" Nigel asked, darting his eyes around the room.

"Destiny has spoken. Everything has fallen into place to execute our plan."

"What plan?"

"The one I'm about to tell you, and ask to help facilitate," Lazarus announced.

Nigel always supported the Anti-Regime since he joined two years ago; however, he hadn't seen their founder act in such an erratic, militant manner.

"Just me?" he asked, aware of the answer.

"And Osvita," Lazarus added. "Let me explain everything first, you'll see."

"We can talk, but I want to make one thing clear. My loyalty is with Osvita – her safety is my priority." While he hadn't spoken to Lazarus in such a manner before, Nigel sensed his compliance was imperative to execute the plan.

Lazarus's face turned cold, his lips pressed together. "Noted," he said, emotionless.

"If you live in the outer limits, how'd you find out about this meeting?" Osvita asked her new friend.

"An acquaintance. He drove me home after one too many in Karg City when I noticed a flyer in his car." Mortimer remembered Franklin's name, but excluded it from the story. He didn't find it fair to out another individual's identity. He didn't want to be outcasted for being a snitch.

"A flyer?" Osvita shouted, realizing her volume. "Why the hell would a secret group make flyers?" she whispered to him.

"I wondered the same damn thing." He laughed.

"So where's your acquaintance?"

"That's…a good question." Mortimer surveyed the room. Preoccupied with correcting his recent wrongdoings, he hadn't thought about Franklin attending the meeting. "Maybe he's here, maybe he isn't, but I don't see him. What brought you here?" he asked, catching Osvita off guard.

"My friend needed to speak to someone here. How about you?"

Mortimer hesitated. He wondered if there'd ever be a time he'd be comfortable sharing his past.

"Michael," he unintentionally murmured.

"What was that? Michael? Was that your friend with the flyer?"

"Sorry. No, that wasn't him." He quickly searched for a response. "I'd like to right the wrongs of my past." Mortimer plastered a smile on his face.

As Osvita prepared to answer, Nigel interrupted the conversation.

"Hello," he said, darting between the two. "Sorry to have left you."

"It's okay." Osvita smiled. "Morty Hullington, meet Nigel Hatherton." The two men shook hands. "This is his first meeting as well."

"Incredible! I hope you enjoy," Nigel said with a smile. "I'm sorry to run, but we should get going." Nigel glared at Osvita.

"Leaving already? The meeting hasn't started yet."

"Did you learn anything about Whark?" she asked.

"Sorry to be nosey, but did you say Whark?" Mortimer asked, remembering what Shrenka had said at their meeting with Brugōr.

"Why? Do you know him? Do you know where he is?" Osvita asked in desperation.

"Unfortunately no, I haven't met him. Just heard his name before—"

"Ahem." Lazarus's voice echoed throughout the room as he tapped the microphone. "Hello?" The entire room fell silent as their eyes gazed upon the founder of their group. "Brilliant. Hello, everyone, and thank you for joining today's meeting. Let me tell you that it's going to be an exciting one."

"We should head out," Nigel suggested. "It was a pleasure to meet you, Mortimer, but we must be going," he whispered.

"You sure? Seems like an important meeting."

"I've been to these enough times to know Lazarus says that about every meeting." He chuckled. "Ready to head out?" Nigel asked Osvita. She preferred to stay, hear what the excitement was about, but she felt the eagerness in his voice.

"Sounds good, let's go. It was lovely to meet you, Mortimer. Hope to see you again soon."

Nigel and Osvita made their way toward the front door. He and Lazarus made eye contact once, nodding in unison, and then exited the Skull and Bone Grill, waving goodbye to Kimber guarding the doors from within.

"So," Nigel inquired. "What did you think of the meeting?"

"It was…nice?" She chuckled. "I mean, I was in a crowd of strangers. I only talked to that one man, Mortimer. He seemed like a nice guy, but we didn't stay long enough to hear anything. What was the hurry?"

"I'm glad you liked it." Nigel paused for a moment, aware of the conversation he needed to have. "I didn't intend to rush you, but I gathered the information we needed and thought it better to leave than stick around. Though the meetings are secure, there's always a risk involved."

Osvita appreciated his warm tone and watchful eye. "Thank you for thinking of me."

"Of course." Nigel exhaled. "There *is* something we should discuss."

"Is it about Whark?" Osvita stopped walking.

"Kind of? You know that man you saw at the podium, with the silver hair?"

"Yes."

"That was Lazarus Docaras. He's the founder of the Anti-Regime," Nigel whispered. "He's the one I spoke with when I left you alone."

"Well, I'll be damned."

"When we spoke, he mentioned the Anti-Regime received a hefty donation and it was time to execute a long-awaited plan, but their tactical operation has one missing component."

"And that would be…?"

"A way in," Nigel whispered. "Lazarus needs an inconspicuous way to enter the castle grounds with access to the Kurhal."

"That's certainly a flaw in his plan. But what does any of this have to do with finding Whark?"

"Well, Lazarus said he hasn't seen Whark. At least not yet."

"What? Then why go on about all of this?" She sighed in disappointment and aggravation.

"No, please listen." Nigel grabbed her hand and locked eyes. They both felt the spark, but didn't acknowledge it. He wanted to profess his love for her, but knew he needed to reveal more pertinent information. "Lazarus asked us to cater the event, bringing him in as an associate. We wouldn't have to do anything else but the job that was asked of us by the regime."

"But why—"

"After the plan is executed, Brugōr will lose control over the valley. Your husband would be the last thing on his mind. Plus, Lazarus said if we agreed, he'd inform all members of what happened to Whark and seek assistance in his return." Nigel's voice was hopeful, reassuring.

"You're out of your mind. That'll never work. I don't even know what this Lazarus has planned. We'd be in the middle of danger, especially with Rexhia. *Rexhia.* I'd never allow her—"

"Osvita…" Nigel insisted she calm down. "Let me just tell you that I didn't agree to anything. We don't have to do it. I told Lazarus that my loyalty was to you and your safety. I said we'd discuss it, but there was no guarantee."

She appreciated Nigel's understanding, especially since it was something Whark lacked.

"I don't even know the guy. How does he, or you, expect me to trust him?"

"I've known him a while. He's good. Quirky, but good. Since I've known him, his mission has been to take down Brugōr and his regime. We're in good hands. I trust him."

"Enough that you laid out my entire situation to him. To someone I hadn't met. A stranger." Osvita knew her delivery was harsh, but felt justified.

"You're right. I shouldn't have revealed anything to him. This is a personal matter, but please know I had the best intentions. He's a great ally and resource, and I thought—"

"Look…you've been nothing but helpful, sweet and welcoming. I'm sorry for being on edge. This is all overwhelming. I've been on the run with my daughter and a man I barely knew, my husband is missing and we can't go home. This is just…" Osvita tried to fight back the tears, but the barrier broke. They rolled down her cheeks until caught by Nigel's smooth hands.

"Oh, Vita…" Nigel said, as he embraced her tightly. It was a hug Osvita didn't realize she needed. Ever since Whark arrived home and warned her, she'd been suppressing her emotions – staying strong for Rexhia. Though they stood in the middle of the alley, in uncharted territory for Osvita, she felt safe in Nigel's arms. She sensed a new emotion rising to the surface. One she had denied for a while, but couldn't fight off any longer. She had a forbidden adoration for Nigel.

"I…I…" She battled the words as the tears continued. She didn't trust herself on what she may say next, so she shifted gears. "Let's head back." Nigel released his embrace as she pulled away, wiping the tears from her cheeks. "I'll calm down by the time we return to your home. It'll be good to let this settle and we can revisit the conversation."

Nigel was happy with her response. He had feared an automatic denial to what he proposed from Lazarus. Instead, he was left with hope and more time to spend with Osvita.

Lazarus Docaras always enjoyed speaking at a meeting – he found comfort in front of others. Admired and respected amongst the group, he yearned to provide his members with hope and excitement. While the Anti-Regime accomplished small mishaps and schemes against Brugōr, Lazarus eagerly awaited executing a more disastrous plan, permanently changing the valley's foundation. When he learned of the large financial donor, he knew it was their moment to strike. The moment he'd been waiting for.

"My oh my…" Lazarus whispered to himself as he returned to the backroom. Members wanted to discuss the strategy he had laid out in his speech, but he ignored them for now. He had announced their huge financial donation was from

Mr. Mortimer Hullington, which made him an instant celebrity. Everyone flocked to ask questions and thank him after the speech.

The plan had two phases.

Phase one involved members of the Anti-Regime ascending the bluffs behind the castle grounds, along the northern-most end of Karg River, and wedging dynamite into the bedrock. The explosion would cause significant destruction to the Kurhal and the castle grounds. More importantly, it'd provide a distraction for the more devastating, second phase.

Lazarus planned to infiltrate the castle grounds, access Brugōr's power, and destroy The Lost Sphere, granting freedom to everyone within the valley. He maintained secrecy on how he'd accomplish the task or by what means, but he was confident in his knowledge.

While members of the Anti-Regime had questions, most of them were excited, having been personally harmed or losing loved ones at the hands of Brugōr. Lazarus knew it would bring much needed excitement back into the group.

As he headed toward the back office, he waved at the members following him and shouted, "Please give me a moment. I'll return shortly to answer any questions you may have. In the meantime, please head out front and grab a celebratory drink!"

The members roared in excitement and followed the command. Lazarus swung the door open, quickly shutting it behind him and locking it. For just a moment, he stood there with his eyes closed, relishing in his accomplishment.

"It's here. It's finally here. The time is now," he said aloud.

"Lazarus?" a voice whispered.

"Hey! Did I say to come out?" Lazarus punched the man in his abdomen, then kicked him behind the knee. The man collapsed. "What if someone were with me?"

"I-I'm sorry. It's just so tight under—"

"Shit. You could've ruined everything just now. You do exactly what I say, when I say. That's the only way you'll see your wife and daughter again. Got it?"

"Right." Whark nodded.

"Alright, I'm heading out to answer some questions. Once they leave, I'll come back and escort you."

"I have one question before you go."

"What is it?"

"Did Nigel come across a little…"

"A little what? Spit it out." Lazarus's patience grew thin.

"Do you think he's fucking my wife?" Whark blurted.

"Naw." Lazarus chuckled. "Not yet at least." He expressed his wide grin once more before heading out and closing the door.

As Whark stood there in the room with office supplies, he heard Lazarus lock the door from the other side and wondered if he had been too trustworthy too quickly.

25

The last week had left Jacob with a wealth of knowledge to ponder. His inability to communicate with anyone but Giddeom ignited his depression and anxiety. His severance had run out and with no hope of a future employer, Jacob's life was on the verge of an unexpectedly permanent change. He'd normally calm his nerves in the comfort of home; however, it no longer seemed to work. The only place Jacob knew he could ease his anxiety was at Lotus Lake.

One warm, sunny morning, Jacob invited his sister, Catherine, to join him. As the two walked along the white, sandy shore, Jacob explained what he could about the job proposition, hoping for advice. He felt it was imperative to speak with someone with an unbiased viewpoint.

"So you were offered a job by someone…doing a task you cannot say…in a location you cannot disclose…for an unknown amount of time?" Catherine laughed, rubbing her belly.

"Precisely," he smiled, admiring her baby bump.

"How'd you feel when you were talking to them? What vibes did you get?"

Jacob couldn't mention the exuberant sensation from inside the manor, but he also wanted to be honest. "It was euphoric. They made sure I wouldn't be anxious or nervous."

"That's good."

"Yeah. I felt that way all three times I met with them."

"Three times?" Catherine stopped walking. "I hadn't realized how much interaction you'd had. That speaks volumes."

Jacob. We need you. He heard the familiar voice in his mind. He shut his eyes and shook his head.

"Jacob?" Catherine asked.

He continued the conversation as if he'd heard nothing. "Maybe if our great grandmother Edith were alive." He paused. "She was the last person to accept the role and it came with its problems."

"But she was rarely around family. We grew up hearing the stories."

"From what I've been told, it seemed as though she felt fulfilled by her work. Always happy the few times she was around family and friends."

"But would you be okay with that? Being away from us." Catherine eyed her belly, reminding him of her baby-to-be.

Jacob pondered what his life would look like without frequent visits with family. His parents would grow older and his future nieces and/or nephews would grow up barely knowing him. He also realized his chance of companionship would diminish. Though he didn't have a desire for children at twenty-three, he wasn't certain he was prepared to make a final decision either. His life would be unlike that of anyone he knew. Then he considered what the role of guardian meant.

He was to ensure the safety and security of ancient artifacts, while preserving the legacy of the Divinity King.

Jacob wasn't sure how he could forgo such a prestigious position, regardless of whether he didn't understand why he was chosen. He grew up in a world that praised the Divinity King as a deity. Jacob wondered what his family would think if they were privy to such information. Turning his back on the role meant turning his back on the Divinity King. He'd seen aggressive violence for expressing far less disrespect toward their king. He wondered what the punishment could be, if one existed, for such disobedience.

Suddenly, he realized there was only one choice if he wished to maintain his sanity. Ignoring Giddeom's request to become the guardian meant he'd never know what his life could've been. He was shown a glimpse of a larger world that made him curiously uncomfortable. His mind had been unexpectedly opened, impossible to reseal. He'd be riddled with regret; something he refused to incorporate into his life.

Jacob. It's time for you to return. He heard the same voice again – Giddeom.

"I think I'll have to be." Jacob lowered his head, not in shame, but in acceptance. He understood the decision that he'd already made, though he was late to the realization.

"It saddens me to think you'll miss out on momentous family events."

"I'll still be there for most of them. It's about time management."

"Just promise me you'll be there for the crucial moments, little bro, like the birth of my child. Never forget the importance of family."

"Of course. I promise." The two shared a smile and tightly embraced.

"Sounds like you've made your decision. Just don't let Mom and Dad know you told me."

"Thank you, sis. I couldn't have realized it without you." Jacob knew she didn't provide him with an answer, but it was through their discussion that he was able to accept his fate. "By the way, Mom already knows. We've discussed it. The only one who doesn't know is Dad."

"Really?" Catherine paused, disappointed to have excluded their father. "You should really tell him. It's not fair to leave him excluded."

"I plan to soon."

Jacob. You can't continue to ignore me. His patience was diminishing.

"Why now?" he whispered under his breath.

"What?" Catherine asked, but Jacob shrugged it off. Giddeom didn't respond.

276

The two continued to stroll along the sand as the sun warmed the region. They discussed Catherine's pregnancy and her meticulous preparation for the child. Aware they'd spent a majority of their time discussing his matters, he didn't want to be insensitive to hers.

Genuinely enjoying their conversation, Catherine and Jacob lost track of time. They were scheduled to meet the rest of the family for an ultrasound gathering and needed to leave. Since they had arrived in separate cars, Jacob saw his sister safely back to hers and bid her a brief goodbye.

Jacob. Close your eyes. Return to Diad.

"Not now, please," Jacob whispered aloud. "I have to meet my family."

Walking to his car, he tried to ignore Giddeom's words. He attempted to call his mother, but there was no answer. Jacob hesitantly called his father, but he didn't pick up either.

Racing along the beach and speeding down the highway, Jacob tried to calm down. He turned his air conditioning on high as he felt his body temperature rising. It was a reminder that his anxiety wasn't managed. He recalled the euphoric feeling he had while inside the manor, wishing he could bottle the essence up.

Frantically focused on the next exit, Jacob hadn't noticed what was happening up ahead. A sedan driving in the center lane veered into a semi-truck's path in the fast lane. Both vehicles slammed on their brakes, but it was too late and the sedan swerved.

It wasn't until Jacob heard the crash of the sedan rolling on his side that he turned his head. Frightened for his life, he sharply turned the steering wheel as the sedan rolled directly at him. The shock of the accident forced him into another lane without looking, but cognizant drivers hastily reacted and avoided a secondary collision.

Having been conveniently forced onto the exit ramp he had planned to take, Jacob acknowledged the horrific reminder to slow down and focus. *I could've been killed.*

When he finally arrived at the office, Jacob noticed his family standing outside, relieved to see the viewing hadn't begun.

"Hey!" Jacob shouted, exiting his car. "Sorry for being late. Why's everyone out here?"

"They're backed up," Anna explained. "It's alright. Calm down. The woman said it would be another twenty minutes until they'd be ready."

Jacob. He instinctually shook his head, trying to rid his mind of Giddeom's voice.

"Everything alright?" Anna asked.

"All's well," he replied, happy no one commented on his tardiness. Once he noticed his sister had safely arrived, Jacob greeted his parents, Catherine, his mother's sister, Cynthia, and Andrew with his parents.

After a few minutes of chatter, Jacob found himself in a discussion with Anna, Cynthia and Catherine, while Andrew spoke to his parents and Ben stood guard, waiting for the office to invite them inside.

"You feeling okay, little brother?"

"Yeah, just didn't want to miss the show." Jacob chuckled.

"We wouldn't let that happen," Catherine said. They discussed their morning activities up until that point. Anna mentioned shopping, though she secretly purchased items for her future grandchild. Cynthia Halverson offered motherly advice to the mother-to-be. Catherine discussed her morning sickness that followed meeting her brother, causing her to be late. Fortunately, the nausea had subsided in time for their appointment.

"Speaking of which, I need to use the restroom," Cynthia said, heading inside the office.

"Jacob told me about his possible new job," Catherine whispered.

"Oh?" Anna raised her eyebrows.

Jacob chuckled and shot a glance at his mother. He didn't quite know how to comfortably address the situation yet. Anna and Jacob had already discussed it after their meeting with Sir Kalvin. It had been a short conversation. He mentioned the secrecy, his inability to discuss matters further and the possibility of accepting the position. Anna understood the situation and respected his boundaries. She knew her efforts would be futile and didn't want to upset her son, but was relieved to see he was honest with his sister.

"We can talk about that another time. Today's about you."

Just then, Catherine's phone rang. She read the name and expressed a look of shock. "Hm. Sorry, guys, I should take this," she said as she walked away. "Hello?" she asked in the distance, walking further on.

"So you told Catherine everything?" Anna confirmed.

"Not as much as we've discussed, but I was as honest as I could be."

"That's nice to hear, son. Sounds like you made a decision."

"I think so."

"Just be careful, my son."

Anna wanted him to make his own choice, but in the back of her mind, she was still bothered by the presence she'd met in the Ersatzian Field. Its haunting, frozen grin made her shudder, its words engraved in her memory. *Jacob's opaque vision will lead him into an archaic deception.* She hadn't told him about the visitor, and wasn't sure if she ever would.

"I will," Jacob responded with a smile. "The position isn't something I could pass on, in good faith."

"Honey, I knew the job was yours the moment you told me about it. I'm just glad you're aware."

Jacob. Your family will understand.

"No," he muttered to himself, violently turning his head to the left.

"Son, are you okay?"

"Yeah, I'm fine," Jacob said, though his mother didn't believe him.

"Will do. It's great to hear from you and we'll talk soon about traveling,"

Catherine said, returning to her family. "Goodbye, Michael." She turned her phone off and placed it into her pocket.

"Everything okay?" Anna asked.

"Oh yes. That was an old friend of mine. I'm not sure if you remember him. Michael Grinshaw? We met back in Tillerack."

"Wasn't that your boozin' buddy?" The siblings laughed.

"I remember you phoned me drunk one night with him." Cynthia laughed, returning to the group.

"Oh, Catherine." Anna's judgement was palpable, but Catherine still laughed.

"We'd drink way too many beers, but somehow awoke early without struggle or worry. He just had some questions about inter-regional travel since—"

"Hey, it looks like they're ready," Ben shouted to everyone. "Come on, let's go."

"How exciting! You guys ready to meet the new addition to our family?" Catherine put her arm around her mother and aunt.

"You have no idea," Anna gleamed with excitement.

"Hell yes!" Cynthia shouted.

"Absolutely! Let's—" Jacob keeled over, suddenly stricken with a severe headache starting from his right temple to around the back of his head. Although his eyes were forcibly shut, all he could see was Giddeom's face.

Jacob. I know you can see me. Come. We must speak. His voice was stoic and loud; impossible to ignore.

Please. I cannot right now. It must wait. Leave me, Jacob thought to himself. He assumed Giddeom received the message since his face disappeared and the pain subsided. When Jacob opened his eyes, everyone was looking at him.

"Are you alright?"

"What's wrong?"

"Do you need to sit down?"

He was bombarded with questions. Though they were genuine, he wanted to be ignored. His anxiety began to rise.

"I'm okay. I just had a splitting headache, but it's gone now."

"Are you sure you're okay to come in?" Catherine asked, rubbing his back.

"Absolutely. I refuse to miss this."

"As long as you're okay…" she said, concerned for her brother's well-being.

As everyone gathered to enter the building, Anna and Jacob glared at one another.

His eyes confessed the truth.

Hers said, *I know*.

The miniature theater was inviting and comfortable for their group of eight, plus the physician scheduled to perform the ultrasound. The lights were dim and soft, allowing the massive screen in the front of the room to be the focal point. The walls and vaulted ceiling were white, helping to maintain a tidy and clean environment. It was expected from any medical office, especially one with a prestigious legacy. It was the unofficial viewing location for the royal family. While it wasn't public knowledge, Anna mentioned it to her daughter when she was younger. Knowing the excitement it'd bring her mother, Catherine selected the company in honor of her.

As everyone carefully picked a plush, red velvet viewing chair, Catherine and Andrew sat in the back center of the room, toward the luxurious, reclinable seat for the mother during the examination.

"Mom, come sit next to me," Catherine said.

"I was coming up there whether you asked me or not. I'm not missing a moment of this."

"I'm right behind you, Nan," Cynthia said. Partially raised by Anna given the age difference, *Nan* was one of her first words, securing it as her sister's nickname. The two were extremely close, though their parents had them ten years apart.

The two shared a smile. Anna was consumed with excitement to see her first grandchild, providing her with a kind of love she didn't know was possible. Catherine was elated to see the excitement in her mother's face. Up until that moment, she hadn't been entirely sure how her mother felt about their pregnancy. With a genuine smile, Anna sat down beside her daughter, hands clasped in anticipation.

Ben sat behind his wife, close enough to his family, yet allowing Anna and Catherine their moment together. Jacob sat a few seats over from them, along the side of the room. Andrew's parents were seated in the first row, directly in front of Anna.

"So, are you to do the examination yourself or...?" Ben shouted, uncomfortably loud, hoping for a chuckle from the group.

"Dad!" Catherine shouted. "The doctor will be here soon."

"You know you can't take your father anywhere." Catherine chuckled with her mother, cherishing their genuine laughter.

Jacob. This isn't how this works.

He tensed up, hoping the voice would go away.

I'm not going anywhere. Not until we talk.

Jacob slouched, shut his eyes and rubbed his face. *Just give me an hour or two. We can talk then.*

There was no response.

He opened his eyes and looked directly at Catherine, who'd happened to be staring at him. She expressed a look of concern, but he assured her everything was fine with a wave of his hand.

Jacob. Giddeom repeated. Jacob wondered if their struggle would become his new normal.

Jacob. Jacob. Jacob. His tone was more stern, his volume louder. Jacob didn't know how to quiet the voice in his mind. He started to question his sanity as his anxiety soared.

Suddenly, the door swung open and a brunette woman in business attire and a white lab coat entered the room.

"Good afternoon, everyone." She smiled. "Catherine and Andrew, it's lovely to see you two and your entire family."

"Hi, Dr. Navanth," the parents-to-be said in unison. As the physician walked toward Catherine and Andrew, Jacob squirmed in his chair quietly.

Jacob. Jacob. Jacob. Giddeom's voice grew louder as Jacob struggled between his sense of reality. He slumped his body into the velvet chair, covering his ears.

"Before we begin the examination, I'd like to discuss a couple things so the mommy and daddy to-be, and everyone here, can better understand what we see."

As Dr. Navanth began her speech, Jacob wondered if it was a good opportunity to sneak out for a few minutes to address Giddeom. After multiple failed attempts, he couldn't bear to listen to his voice for the duration of the exam.

"When you look at the image and see..." Dr. Navanth continued. It was all Jacob needed to hear. He quietly scurried low to the floor, out the side door and through the main lobby.

Jacob. Jacob. Jacob.

"What do you want!? I can't live like this!" he shouted, running toward his car for privacy to avoid looking mad.

We need you here. Giddeom's volume lowered, his tone relaxed.

"Well right now, I need to be here."

Your presence here is more important. I need you here. They need you here.

"What do you mean, they? Who?"

Come here. We must discuss.

"How would I even—"

Look at your right hand. Open it.

Jacob curiously followed his instructions. To his surprise, the engravings from the manor's doorknobs were etched on his palm. Mystified by the glowing inscriptions, Jacob widened his eyes as they swirled and moved around. He became enamored by its appearance, ignoring his surroundings. As the glow of the markings brightened, he watched a small, white ball of energy form above his palm.

"Giddeom...what is—"

Last we spoke, I mentioned you'd freely be able to travel between your home and ours.

Captivated by its appearance, Jacob was startled when the levitating sphere burst, instinctively shutting his eyes. He sensed the warmth from the light, providing a similar sensation as the manor. He knew it was his means of transportation between the two regions.

He thought about his family, and the ramifications of leaving. It was impossible to return to his seat with Giddeom's constant interruptions, but he also knew it'd be an argument if he deserted his family. Aware that there'd be more difficult decisions in the future, Jacob thought about Edith and the challenges she must've faced.

When he opened his eyes, his gaze fell upon the manor. Diad was slowly becoming a comforting place for him.

Jacob was mindful that he was no longer sitting in his car. With a heavy sigh and long exhale, he walked toward the manor in search of Giddeom. He wanted to have the discussion as quickly as possible to return home, resuming the joyful moment his family was fortunately sharing together.

As the family sat together, in anticipation for the visual of the baby in-utero, few wondered where Jacob had run off to. Catherine was disappointed, but didn't allow it to affect her excitement. Andrew and his parents noticed, but remained quiet. Ben and Anna observed their son leave. Cynthia stood up to check on him, but Anna stopped her.

"He'll be back soon. I'm sure of it. Sit down, you're going to miss it," she insisted.

Something within Anna told her she had probably lied about their son's return. Whether it was mother's intuition or her knowledge of his situation, she felt his swift exit involved something more. Something secretive. Anna hoped he'd tell Ben sooner than later to avoid withholding the secret from him.

"Just going to check a few things before we begin," Dr. Navanth said. They remained in silence as she poked and prodded the device around Catherine's abdomen. There was a sudden heaviness in the air.

"Is everything okay?" Catherine whispered to the doctor, but she was too focused to respond. She glanced at her husband with a concerned look as they gripped each other's hand.

"Is there something wrong, doctor?" Anna blurted out.

"I'm clumsy with this probe sometimes…" Dr. Navanth said. "I'm…I'm going to grab an associate. I'll be right back." The doctor rushed toward the exit.

26

"Giddeom?" Jacob shouted inside the manor. "Where are you?" He'd normally never shout in such a large space, but he attributed it to the euphoria rushing through his body. As he paced toward the back, near the mural, others nearby silently stared at him. "Giddeom? You called for me, I know you're—"

"I'm right here. No need to cause a scene, my child." Giddeom appeared from the illuminated grand hallway just left of the mural of emblems.

"Everyone," he shouted, halting the room. "If I can have your attention for just a moment." Giddeom approached Jacob, who found the irony in being scolded for causing a scene. "I'd like you all to meet our next guardian – Jacob Emmerson."

The energy in the room was lackluster. Some people smiled, others nodded, but most continued about their tasks. Normally terrified of attention, Jacob felt awkward as everyone in the room didn't seem to care. Regardless, he returned his focus to Giddeom.

"I'd like to go back to my family soon, so can we chat quickly?"

Giddeom smiled, extending his arm, inviting him down the grand hallway.

"My boy, you are with family." Disappointed in the lack of a reaction, Giddeom continued. "One of the hardest parts about this honorary position is the balance between your time. Every guardian before you struggled with the same aspects. It will be no different for you."

"Every guardian?" Jacob asked. "I know you knew my grandmother, but exactly how long have you been here?"

"Long enough to know how to manage these situations. Long enough to see history rewrite itself. Long enough to know and see our family over the generations." Giddeom sneered. Jacob stopped walking.

"With all due respect, my family is *my* family. I'm sure I'll spend a lot of time here, but the two aren't the same."

Giddeom didn't respond.

Jacob knew his demeanor was different inside the manor's walls and he wanted to be respectful, but he also wanted to clarify his loyalty. He expected a shift in the relationship with his family, but he didn't appreciate Giddeom's assumptions.

As the two reached the end of the grand hallway, passing the doors housing the regional gateways, they approached a set of silver double doors Jacob hadn't noticed before. Giddeom turned to open the right door and welcomed the guardian to enter.

"And what makes them your family?" Giddeom asked, closing the door behind them. Jacob became too distracted by his surroundings to immediately answer.

The two stood in a cylindrical, open room with a luxurious, twenty-foot-wide crystal chandelier hanging from the ceiling. At the opposite end of the room was an altar with another set of golden double doors. There were two other doors within the room – one to the left and another on the right.

"They're…family. I grew up with them. They raised me. We share similar experiences, characteristics, and environment. They're my blood," Jacob said. "What's behind—"

"You did grow up with them around you. Your parents raised you, but it isn't accurate to say you share the same experiences, characteristics and environment. All four of you have experienced different events in your lives, endured your own hardships. Those situations mold you into the person you've become. Though you may share some traits, each of you are different from one another." Giddeom paused, considering Jacob's final explanation. "And your environment..." He chuckled. "Your mother was born and raised in Prateria, while your sister traveled to Tillerack for five years, returning a completely different woman."

Jacob wasn't sure if he was more annoyed at Giddeom analyzing his every word or shocked at the amount of information he knew of the Emmerson family. *What a silly question to ask anyway*, he thought. *What makes them my family? They're my family!* he wanted to shout. Jacob remembered how he used to communicate with Giddeom telepathically, wondering if he could sense his frustrations.

"How do you know all this information about my family?"

Giddeom chuckled. "Those you choose to surround yourself with become your family, regardless of whether blood is shared. Time reveals your true family as your heart latches on, whether you invite it or not."

Jacob grunted. *He isn't wrong*, he thought.

"You are my family, Jacob...and I am yours." Giddeom's blackened eyes pierced through him.

"We barely know one another," Jacob insisted. "If I spend enough time here, and..."

"No," Giddeom interrupted. "You don't get it." He placed his hand on Jacob's shoulder, jolting his body back as a burst of energy rushed through Jacob's veins. There was no pain or discomfort, but his eyes slammed shut as visions began to appear.

At first, all Jacob saw was Giddeom's face. As his field of view widened, he noticed a woman and two children nearby. Giddeom approached them, kissing the woman and hugging the children. *Giddeom had a family*, Jacob thought. It was the first time he observed the Divinity King's associate without his regular tuxedo. He was dressed in a flowing, tan shirt, a brown band wrapped around his waist a few times as a belt, and dark brown pants tucked into his black boots. His presumed wife had kind blue eyes, brown hair topped with a bonnet, a long brown dress with an apron and black shoes with large, silver buckles. The children wore similar clothing. *They seem happy*, Jacob thought. Suddenly, the scene vanished into smoke and a new, concerning image appeared.

A man resembling Giddeom lay on the ground in a pool of blood, a spear pierced through his chest. Beside him stood a man with black hair, a bright red coat, covering his neck down to the back of his knees, tight white pants, black shoes and a black cane in his left hand. He looked regal, wealthier than Giddeom's family. His back was facing Jacob, hiding his face. The stranger slammed the bottom of his cane down once, hard enough that Jacob felt the vibration. The man turned around and looked directly at him. Jacob gasped.

Giddeom!?

Instantly, the scene vanished into smoke. He was starting to see a pattern.

Jacob's next vision welcomed the return of the woman and children from before – Giddeom's supposed family. Time had passed as they'd all aged. The woman still wore raggedy clothing, but they were well-kept. She lay on the ground with her arms bent at the elbows, hands resting on opposite shoulders. Her eyes were closed, her skin was white. She looked peaceful. Jacob noticed the kneeling children beside her. Upon closer examination, he realized they were crying.

She died, he thought. Jacob sympathized with the children as they mourned their mother. As quickly as the scene changed, so did his emotions. Once again, everyone vanished into smoke and Jacob prepared for what the next vision brought him.

In front of him stood Giddeom, in the red coat, with his left hand on the shoulder of a woman in front of him. Just then, Jacob's field of view shrunk. All he could see were their faces. It confirmed to him the man in red was Giddeom and the woman beside him was his daughter. Though she appeared older, she had similar features from the previous scenes. Giddeom hadn't aged at all.

It seemed time began ticking in overdrive. The woman's face quickly aged and then vanished, though Giddeom remained still, appearing the same. After a few seconds, another woman's face appeared. Starting off young, she continued to age like Giddeom's daughter. Eventually, the woman vanished and a third appeared in a similar fashion.

Jacob watched the frenzy of faces appear and then vanish just moments later. Though some aged more than others, he realized all of them were women. Jacob shifted his attention to Giddeom, whose gaze was locked on his.

These are all the previous guardians, he thought to himself. Just then, the scene froze. Time stood still. Jacob looked at the woman and recognized her. *Edith.*

Time progressed until she eventually vanished. Aware that he followed her, Jacob eagerly awaited what was next. He wondered if the ride was over or if he'd make a cameo. Much to his surprise, everything went black. Just as he lowered his head, his surroundings illuminated for a moment. As the lights flickered, Jacob noticed Giddeom in the same position with another person beside him. There was only a silhouette, but it was clearly a woman.

As the lights continued to flicker, the scene became distorted. Jacob frantically tried to make out any details, but his attempt was futile. Blackness returned for a few seconds until a new scene revealed itself. He was staring at himself, with Giddeom's left hand on his right shoulder. Jacob smiled, causing the entire scene to shatter like a broken mirror.

As his eyes opened, Jacob found himself back in the room, just past the double doors. With no one in sight, he turned around and startled himself when he noticed Giddeom in the distance. His perfect tuxedo had changed into the red coat attire, with the black cane in his left hand.

"Veracity wasn't meant to be concealed," Giddeom said with a confident smile.

"Did you…?" Jacob paused. His mind analyzed the visions he'd experienced, processing and acknowledging the meaning behind them all. "Are we…?" He pointed between himself and Giddeom. "So you were…"

"Yes, I had a wife and children," Giddeom replied. "Yes, we are related. I'm a very, very, *very*, distant grandfather of yours." There was hesitation with the second response, having never admitted that detail to another guardian before. "And finally, yes…I was killed." His hands were palm-side up, widening in front of him, as if to present a gift below. His head lowered and to the side, aware of how absurd it must all sound.

Jacob sighed. "There is just so much I don't understand."

"It'll take time to grasp the world in which you now live. Your eyes have been opened, your mind extended. Whether you like it or not, there is no turning back. It's important to accept that."

Jacob took a moment to organize his thoughts, which Giddeom could no longer read now that the guardian had learned of his lineage.

"So all that talk about family earlier…you were talking about yourself. How time spent here with you…is with family."

"Yes."

Though he found it strange and concerning, Jacob sympathized with Giddeom's yearning for family. He considered being alone in a different realm would be eternally lonely.

"But you died. That was your body slain on the ground. A spear penetrated your chest."

"Specifically, it was a perfect shot through my heart, but yes, I died."

"So…you're a ghost?"

"It's a bit more complicated than that."

"Oh! I get it now," Jacob said, nearly interrupting Giddeom. "That's why you can't leave Diad. That's why I'm here. That's why there's even a guardian in the first place. You can't leave."

"You're starting to put together the pieces. I'm impressed." Giddeom smiled. "I'm proud."

"There was one scene in your show I didn't quite understand."

"Which was that?"

"The section with the flickering lights."

"I'm sorry…what?"

"You know, between my grandmother's appearance and my own? There was a part where the lights flickered and someone stood next to you, but I couldn't tell who it was," Jacob said, trying to recall the image from his memory. There was no smell or sensation to help, only what he saw.

"You must be mistaken," Giddeom said. "That's not part of the presentation. I think you're just overwhelmed. There's a lot of information being thrown at you." He could tell Jacob wasn't satisfied with his response, so he decided to shift the topic. "Jacob, I think now is a good time to discuss why I called you here in the first place."

Giddeom approached Jacob, who, until that moment, had completely forgotten about his family, and where he was at the time he returned to Diad.

"Shit," Jacob remarked. Not one to curse, he grabbed his left wrist and then looked around the room. "What time is it?"

Giddeom chuckled and waved his cane around counterclockwise above his head. Just then, Jacob noticed numerous, ornate objects appear on the wall around the room.

"This should come in handy," he said.

"Clocks," Jacob whispered to himself. He walked to the wall and looked up at one of the clocks, realizing they were all similar in appearance – covered in gold, all gears exposed. There was one unique difference between them all. "The orbs…" Jacob noted.

"Correct. As you can see, none of them are labeled. An orb for each region. You'll become familiar with them soon enough." Giddeom's words resonated within Jacob as he walked around the room, trying to identify the orb belonging to Sartica. He wandered the perimeter just over half-way until he found the orange orb.

"This…is Sartica, correct? It's 2:45pm."

"Brilliant," Giddeom replied. "That's one down."

"How much longer do you think we'll be?" he asked, keeping a calm composure. He thought about his family and assumed the viewing was near its end. Though he was unable to stress about it, he felt bad for missing it.

"That ultimately depends on you."

"Okay, so let's have it."

"As I mentioned during your last visit, we are in need of your assistance."

Then you should have let me stay longer last time, Jacob thought. He actively stopped himself from saying the words aloud and replied with a simple 'yes' instead.

"The Barren Land is a region near Sartica." Giddeom walked toward the clock with the dark brown orb in the center and pointed. It read 9:15, though didn't specify morning or night. "Do you know anything about this region? Have you heard of it before?"

"No, nothing." Jacob realized all the clocks had different times. He wondered how it was possible and why it was necessary, but decided against asking another question.

"Known to the locals as *the valley,* The Barren Land…*welcomes* those who've been exiled from their home or any degrant wandering throughout Diveria." Giddeom grinned. "Surrounding the entire region is a barrier known as The Lost Sphere. Comprised of sand, rocks, and miscellaneous debris, it's an impenetrable force which appears to stop anyone from entering…or exiting."

"Why would a supposed welcoming region sustain such an uninviting and dangerous perimeter?"

"We're not entirely sure, but your focus isn't to pass judgement or question morality," Giddeom said. "The leader of The Barren Land goes by Brugōr. If any particular vision comes to mind from just his name, it's probably correct."

"It's not my job to pass judgement," Jacob replied. Giddeom smirked.

"Yes, well…he's a brute force – both strong and intimidating. Brugōr demands respect."

"Seems like this valley isn't as inviting as it seems." Jacob glanced back at the clock of Sartica with an orange orb. *3:05.*

"Inviting or not, your assistance is needed in The Barren Land." Giddeom walked Jacob over to the opposite end of the room with the closed golden door.

"Deep in the valley is a group known as the Anti-Regime and their momentum has been building. They've devised a plan to overthrow Brugōr and his loyal companions, while also attempting to obtain their ancient artifact – the Transcending Tablets. Your duty, as guardian, is to meet with Brugōr, inform him of the plan, and help ensure the safety of the artifact. The Transcending Tablets must not be captured, removed or destroyed."

"So…you want me to enter The Barren Land, find this intimidating leader, get him to listen to me about the planned attack against him, and then help defend the object at stake?" He chuckled. As a non-confrontational person, Jacob hadn't had any physical altercations in his life.

"Glad to see you understand. Any questions?" His serious tone caused a shift in Jacob's mind. The weight of the situation and Giddeom's expectation felt heavy upon his shoulders.

Jacob felt a sense of urgency. It was an unusual sensation without anxiety or stress. *Why would the Divinity King support such a ruthless leader?*

"Giddeom…" Jacob chose his words carefully. "I don't mean any disrespect, and maybe I'm naive, but I grew up admiring and loving the Divinity King. He provided us with everything we have, ensured our safety and longevity. Why would…" Jacob didn't want to use the word *you*, and accuse the king of anything malicious, "…*it* be deemed worthy to protect such a sinister leader?"

"Everyone has their justifications. Everyone has a past," Giddeom explained. "He's a strong man who demands respect and maintains a protective forcefield around the region. That doesn't prove he's sinister. His reasons could be warranted." There was a moment of silence between them until Giddeom repeated a familiar line. "Don't pass judgement or question morality."

Jacob understood why the phrase was often repeated, but it was growing old. He knew there'd be numerous moments he'd need to be reminded of his field of scope. Unsettled, Jacob didn't want to question it again. He couldn't bear to hear Giddeom repeat the same words, so he asked a question which he found to be more prudent.

"Considering I've never fought anyone in my life, how exactly am I expected to protect an ancient...relic?"

"Artifact," Giddeom corrected.

"Ancient artifact. How in the world do you expect me to do that? The sheer thought gives me anxiety." He thought for a moment. "Well, it would if I could feel anxiety here." Jacob realized he still hadn't received an answer from Giddeom as to why the manor caused such emotions to vanish.

"This is where your foundation for our trust really begins."

"Begins? Disclosing our connection or the fact that you're dead didn't count?"

"Those two facts have less repercussions for you. You have guardian's blood coursing through your body. You have been chosen. Something very special happens when the guardian is in close proximity to an ancient artifact." Giddeom walked toward the golden door and placed his hand on it. "This door was commonly accessed by every guardian before you, the last being your grandmother, Edith. It's the only portion of this place I cannot enter. It's strictly reserved for our guardian."

Jacob admired the door. He instantly considered it his safe haven. Though he didn't need one now, his subconscious told him it would come in handy soon enough.

"Each of our historic guardians had their own, unique relationship with us and their method of performing the tasks. It varied upon the individual. Your grandmother, for example, conveniently battled with her temper. When in the presence of an artifact, she harnessed her fury and molded it into an effective, unique fighting style. It proved to be quite successful in guarding the artifacts."

"My grandmother...was a fighter?"

"A warrior. A great one." Giddeom's eyes wandered, reminiscing on Edith's legacy. "Others, however, used more subtle, yet effective methods. There was a guardian named Octavia who was incapable of lying. While she spoke well, her words were often silenced for the harm they brought others. When in the presence of an ancient artifact, her mind filled with knowledge and her words became powerful, crippling anyone in her way. She could crush the heart of someone with one sentence."

Silence fell between the two men before Giddeom continued.

"Many years ago, there was Jamila, a soul whose beauty shined brighter than nearly anyone else I'd met. Her heart and mind were filled with the purest of thoughts and wishes. Unfortunately, most pushed her aside due to their perception of her physical appearance. When she became guardian and presented herself in front of an artifact—"

"Let me guess," Jacob interrupted as he cleared his throat, mimicking Giddeom's tone and mannerism. "Her physical appearance shined as brightly as her soul had and she was able to make any man or woman fall in love with her." Jacob smiled, proud of his performance. Giddeom squinted his eyes in response.

"Not quite. Jamila was able to command anyone she pleased. Fetch her a drink, have someone walk away from the ancient artifact...kill."

Jacob raised his eyebrows with no response.

"So, Jacob, that brings us to you and your question. How do *you* think you'll be able to defend the ancient artifacts?"

He contemplated the question before answering. Jacob considered numerous flaws he recognized within himself: *weak, cowardly and lazy*. He knew one stood out to him more than the rest. It became clear to him in recent days, since he was stripped of it every time he entered the manor.

Anxiety.

"I'd guess it has something to do with my anxiety and stress."

"Brilliant," Giddeom proudly replied.

"Unless I plan to worry someone to death or stress a guy out in aggravation, I'm not sure how that helps me." Jacob's anxiety had only brought him more angst and negativity. He couldn't fathom it in a positive light.

"What your mind considers a vulnerability, your body will exploit for strength. Unfortunately, I'm unable to assist you any further."

"What!? How am I supposed to practice? Shouldn't there be time for me to train and prepare for my journey?" Scenes from action movies flashed through Jacob's mind.

"If I could help you, I would," Giddeom reassured. "We're on the same side here, Jacob, but unfortunately I'm not able to predict your future." Giddeom slowly lowered his gaze. "I have my predictions on what you may be able to achieve, but you have to go in with a clear mind, free of any impressionable thoughts."

Jacob felt abandoned. His life had been turned upside-down. Unaware of his family history, unsure how his life would change and uncertain what he could one day encounter, he panicked. It was the first time inside the manor he could feel the slightest sense of anxiety. Though the euphoric state was still mostly present, it startled him. He wondered if his nerves had reached such a plateau that he was beginning to break the barrier.

"Jacob," Giddeom said. "I know you'd like to return to your…familiar family." He smiled reassuringly. "I won't take any more of your time. There's only one thing left for you to see before you leave."

Jacob's mind was spinning with the details and realizations. "What?"

"It's customary for the guardian to leave a personalized, detailed letter for her successor."

"You mean….my great grandmother left me a letter?"

"Yes." Giddeom was hesitant to respond. It was the first time Jacob witnessed any uncertainty from him.

"Okay…"

"I've never been privy to the letters since I don't have access to your sanctuary. I'd assume it's normally filled with wise words and sentiment." Giddeom stalled once more.

"Normally…?" Jacob wondered what Giddeom was struggling with. "Why do I feel like there's something you're not telling me?"

"There's not," Giddeom said with finality. "But if you have any questions or if she mentions anything strange, know you may come to me. I'm here to help."

"Thank you," he replied, though remained unsettled by Giddeom's tone.

Giddeom clapped his hands and plastered on a smile. Jacob tasted his insincerity. "I'll leave you to explore what's behind the golden door. With the engraving of the main door etched in the palms of a guardian, you'll be granted access."

"Thank you for your patience, Giddeom." Jacob smiled, though he still had numerous unanswered questions. He began to feel a deeper appreciation for his new-found relative and wondered what his mother would think if she knew.

Giddeom walked toward the double doors the two had entered through. Instead of opening them to enter the grand hallway, he turned into a plume of smoke and vanished. Jacob was astonished. He had no idea the man had such an ability, making him wonder what else he was capable of.

"Just when you think you know someone…"

Unaware what could reveal itself behind the golden door of his soon to be sanctuary, Jacob cautiously placed his palm on the doorknob. There was no pain or sensation.

Click.

With his hand still on the doorknob, Jacob felt it turn and tug open from the other side, as if someone were in there.

"Hello?" Jacob asked. The golden door only opened a couple inches on its own until he had to push it entirely. It proved quite challenging. Though golden in appearance, he hadn't expected it to be made of solid gold.

He didn't believe what he was looking at when the door fully opened. He turned around, confirming that he remained in the same space when speaking with Giddeom. What he saw was beautiful. The entire back wall of his secluded, private sanctuary had an incredible view of Diad, as if on the top of a mountain. He entered to look closer, and instantly felt a heaviness again. His anxiety and stress had returned. He wondered how the euphoric feeling dissipated, reminding himself there was still much to learn.

Jacob shut the door behind him and slowly made his way to the glorious view. His gaze focused on the beautiful city, though his peripheral vision was quickly making notes of the interior. There were buildings of various shapes and sizes, all taller than he had ever seen before. While some parts glistened in the sunlight, most of the structures were covered in greenery, shrubs and flowers. Rooftops had large trees and shrubs while vines swirled around buildings, crawling around the windows as if to consume them. Jacob hadn't seen such a sight before.

As he approached the window, he looked down and was quickly startled. "How am I this high!?" he chirped, jumping back. Born and raised in Sartica, the highest he had ever been was atop a sand dune in the outskirts of the region. Standing inside his sanctuary, he quickly realized that he may suffer from a fear of heights.

Taking a few steps back, cautiously observing the city below, he saw open streets with people walking, green fields with children playing, and pets freely roaming. He raised his gaze toward the horizon and noticed the entire region of Diad was surrounded by water. He wondered if it was an island or just a big shoreline.

Jacob turned and focused his attention on the interior of the room, immediately reminded of houses he'd see along the shore of Lotus Lake in Sartica. The tones were soft and warm. The space was open and simplistic. The room felt private, safe.

The ceilings were high, triple the height of Jacob. There were only a few pieces of notable furniture. A large couch overlooked Jacob's breathtaking view with a table in front of it. A plush sofa chair sat in the far corner with wooden arms thick enough to support a large cup of coffee. On the opposite end of the room, near the golden door, stood a wooden desk with intricately carved legs. The chair looked uncomfortable and old, but Jacob assumed they were antiques. He walked toward the center of the room and admired a table toward the left, particularly the familiar carving along the top.

"It's the mural…" he whispered to himself. The precise mural that hung in the entryway was etched into the beautiful elder wood, all ten emblems. He felt it was too delicate to ever place anything on top of it. Then he remembered Giddeom didn't have access to the room, no one did. This was Jacob's own space in the region of Diad.

"The letter!" He frantically looked around for signs of a letter from his great grandmother. Startled by the loss of euphoria and the view, he'd forgotten about Edith's personal note to him. Jacob walked over to the desk beside the golden door and abruptly stopped, unsure how he didn't notice anything earlier.

In the right corner was a glass orb, the size of his fist, sitting atop an envelope. All he did was stare at it, his body frozen. He tilted his head, curiously, sensing a peculiar energy emanating from it. The glass orb was clear, showing the envelope through it. The center was crimson, about the size of a marble. As Jacob reached out to pick it up, he sensed a vibration from it.

"What…?" He recoiled his hand. "What are you?" he asked, chuckling at how strange he must look. When he stretched his hand out again, the crimson liquid swayed. Jacob jumped back. He glanced around the room, confirming he was alone.

Jacob decided to try a faster approach. Standing upright with his eyes focused, he jolted his arm forward to grab the orb. Seconds before he would've made contact, the crimson liquid swayed right and the orb glided in the same direction.

"How the hell'd you do that!?" Jacob shouted. His pulse raced, nerves and exhilaration bubbling within him. He leaped toward the left side of the desk to catch it, but he was yet again too slow. It glided with ease toward the right side of the desk, covering the envelope once more.

Jacob had an idea.

With a grin on his face, he reached for the orb, expecting it to move; however, instead of sliding toward the left again, it levitated upwards. He froze, momentarily forgetting his idea, as he questioned the concept of gravity. He refocused and snatched the envelope instead of chasing the orb.

As he retracted his arm, the levitating object collided with it.

"OW!" Jacob shouted, dropping the envelope back onto the desk. He rubbed his forearm as the orb lowered itself back onto the envelope, guarding its contents. Jacob began to sweat as his heartbeat increased. He wished his sanctuary provided him with the euphoric feeling. He missed being able to numb that part of him. Looking down on the orb protecting Edith's letter, Jacob became angry.

"You son of a bitch," he said quietly as he lunged forward to grab the orb with all his strength. It floated upwards once more as Jacob crashed into the desk. The moment he grabbed the exposed envelope, the orb found its target and caused a loud crack on impact with his forehead. Jacob shouted once more in pain, unintentionally releasing the letter. The orb resumed its position atop the envelope. Jacob stood back to witness the scene, holding his forehead with his lightly injured right arm.

"What the fuck are you!?" His frustration had begun to dictate his language. "How does an inanimate object do this?" he asked, feeling nauseous as his heart continued to beat fast, coursing searing blood through his body.

Suddenly, he witnessed a sequence of events in his mind, as if it were a memory. He watched as he extended his right arm just right of the desk, which the orb followed. Then he extended his left hand to trail behind and pushed it away, smashing it against the wall. The vision continued as he grabbed the envelope with his right hand, spun around, and curled his body into a ball, protecting the letter. The orb crashed against his back once in an attempt to reach the envelope, but when it failed, it collapsed to the floor. The red liquid reverberated as it bounced on the ground.

Jolting back to reality, Jacob looked at what was in front of him. The orb remained on the envelope. *What was that?* he wondered. The vision seemed as though he was a stranger looking down on himself and the orb. It was an odd sensation he didn't quite understand. Jacob wondered if the orb had hit him on the head too hard.

He didn't know why the vision had happened, but it did end with him obtaining the letter so he decided it was worth a shot to recreate the scenario.

Standing in front of the desk, both arms slightly out as if prepared to wrestle, Jacob recreated the scene. He stretched his right arm out and the orb floated right off the desk. Anticipating the movement, he brought his left arm around, increasing the speed once the device moved. For the first time, Jacob touched the orb, using his left hand to push it. Though it was smooth, he was surprised that it was warm. He inferred it was heavy because it required more strength than he'd expected to push it away. Eventually the orb smacked the wall, causing Jacob to pause for a second.

With his left arm still extended out across his chest, he quickly grabbed the envelope and turned around. His upper body lowered as he wrapped himself around the envelope, which was pressed firmly against his abdomen. Holding his position, he tightened his body, anticipating the orb's final attempt. Just as he was about to turn around to observe, he felt the impact between his shoulders. It hit hard enough to make his upper body nudge forward, but his feet remained planted on the ground.

After the collision, Jacob heard the echoing sounds of the orb collapse on the ground. He turned to examine it, placing the envelope behind his back. *It worked.*

The orb was on the ground and the crimson liquid was still. Jacob wanted to place it back on the desk, but didn't dare to take the chance. Instead, he sat across the room, in sight of the now stagnant orb, and studied the envelope.

"My Dear Great Grandchild," Jacob read aloud. He delicately opened the envelope, placed it beside him, and unfolded the single piece of paper.

Hello my darling,

It seems you've successfully achieved your first encounter with one of the ancient artifacts. Congratulations! I'm confident Giddeom has spoken to you about them, though not this one in particular. Though this artifact is unique in its appearance, it exudes the same ability onto you as the rest of them. What that ability is, I cannot say. Every guardian has their insecurity converted into their biggest strength. It's for you alone to seek and extrapolate that inner strength.

Writing this to you is challenging because I, unfortunately, have not, nor will I ever, meet you. Reflecting on my personal experience, I remember having a difficult time in the beginning. It was a long time ago now, but it can be a struggle. I tried my best to spend time equally between home and Diad, where you are now. Eventually, I learned that it was best to relinquish the burden and embrace my destiny as guardian. Once I accepted that decision, life seemed to flow easier.

It's difficult for me to suggest, especially being a woman, but it's probably best to avoid having children, if you haven't already done so. I deeply love my family and children more than anything, but I have an obligation here in Diad. This needs to be my priority, and that has been the toughest choice of all. If by chance you have already done so, then my only advice would be to accept your fate sooner rather than later.

I wish you well on your path as the Guardian of Emblems. I'm incredibly proud of you for acknowledging and accepting what some would call a choice. Always believe in yourself and the abilities you possess over others, regardless how it may appear. Remember to embrace what you may consider your weakest trait, as it'll be your saving grace.

Guardian Di

Jacob carefully lowered the letter, aware he'd cherish the piece of paper his entire life. It was a part of his family's legacy, one that others weren't privy to reading. Though excited to have been included in this secretive side of his family, he was disappointed in being unable to discuss it with others.

Across the room, his gaze landed upon the orb, motionless on the floor.

"So," he said aloud, defiantly, "you're one of the ancient artifacts, eh?"

Jacob placed his letter down as he stood up and stared at the object. He recalled Giddeom telling him about a unique ability that would come to fruition. Now Edith's letter mentioned an ability that allowed him to overcome the artifact and obtain the letter. Jacob had expected some magical strength, invisibility, or maybe the ability to fly.

Then, for the first time, he had clarity about something within Diad.

"I get it," he said talking to the orb. "I understand it now. The ability being different for each guardian. '*Every guardian has their insecurity converted into their biggest strength*,'" he repeated the words of his great grandmother. "This manor suppresses my anxiety and stress, allowing clarity for my tasks here. This room, this sanctuary, removed it to harness that emotion, embrace the inner worry. When you tried to defend yourself, I could nearly feel my heart leap out of my chest from the anxiety. The emotion led me to having the vision, allowing me to retrieve the letter." Jacob remained silent for a moment, continuing to stare at the frozen orb.

"Ancient artifacts convert my anxiety and worry into a heightened awareness and precognition," he said. "I envision what's about to happen moments before it does, whether to defend myself or reveal what actions I need to take. Right?" He laughed. "Why am I talking to an inanimate object?"

As he began to turn around, there was a sound. Jacob jumped, startled by the sudden bubbling red liquid in the center of the orb.

27

Sitting in the heart of Restaurant Alley was Draka's Diner, a popular establishment maintained by Draka and Birvena Jruk.

"What can I getcha, Fravia?" Birvena asked.

"Just a Hironchu sandwich with a side of spider-fries." She smiled, handing over the menu.

"And how about you, hun?"

"I'll take the Wiggly Riggly and an aliquo, please," Smolar replied, thanking her.

The two sat across from one another outside Draka's Diner. Their meeting at Lady Vixa's had surprised them, and their argument moments before complicated matters. Neither had spoken for days since then.

"So," Smolar began, "how've you been?" His tone was genuine, his expression concerned. The time had brought him a whirlwind of emotions, struggling to navigate through them. He was excited to be involved in Promit's return. It was his priority as the guilt had weighed heavy on him, though he tried to suppress it. Smolar hoped if Promit safely returned home, other issues could be resolved too.

Aside from his hopeful excitement, he'd continued to envision the glances exchanged between Fravia and Rhugor. He knew Rhugor was a stranger, but it was apparent that she was smitten. It caused a visceral reaction for Smolar. *He was jealous.*

His only experience with jealousy was as a younger quorian, after his parents died. He'd see families walking, filled with cheer and laughter. He yearned for the return of his mother's loving touch or his father's reassuring voice. His ability to feel genuine happiness for others was hindered by his own bitterness and resentment. Smolar would've given anything to have them back in his life. His love for them was deep and powerful, yet the pain for their loss was insurmountable.

Though the scenarios were opposite in severity, he identified a similarity, resulting in a crucial, yet crippling, realization.

I love Fravia.

Looking at her from across the table, Smolar knew he couldn't ignore his longing affection toward her. Whether eating in Restaurant Alley, praying at the Enchanted Reservoir or solving a mystery in the quorian library, he cherished the time he'd spent with her. Even sitting across the table, having an awkward conversation, there was nowhere else he'd rather be. His heart had relinquished the complacency from his mind.

Due to his traumatic past, Smolar had never experienced a relationship before. Grieving his parents, while living with the Quorian Ruler, didn't make him a popular commodity. Though he tried to seek companionship, he was met with constant failures, so he surrendered. Accepting that he'd unexpectedly found love caused him a sense of awkwardness.

He felt it was inappropriate to confess during their cumbersome meeting. And remembering the excitement on Fravia's face at the sight of Rhugor filled him with doubt, uncertain when, how, or if it was too late for the discussion.

"I've been okay," she replied to his initial question. "Just preparing for what's to come."

Disappointed in herself, Fravia had spent their time apart questioning the love she had for someone she considered a close friend. Withholding her emotions for three years, she hadn't seen any signs that Smolar's heart aligned with hers. There were multiple occasions Fravia felt she'd given him ample opportunity, but he'd always fallen short. Though she wanted to confess her love for him, the reality terrified her.

She knew their friendship would forever change if he didn't feel the same. Even worse, Fravia feared she'd be the one to sever the beautiful relationship, unable to withstand the pain of being in the friend-zone. She'd rather sustain their current bond than risk losing it entirely.

But their latest disagreement had caused a shift.

Hearing the quorian she loved for three years yearn to escape his city and everyone within it crippled her. Being an extremely smart and patient quorian, Fravia could understand his desire to explore the Outer World, but his insensitivity enraged her. With no indication of interest, she became enlightened. Fravia was relieved to have concealed her emotions and protected her vulnerabilities. She considered it time to open her heart and mind to other possibilities.

Unfortunately, the looming journey with him made it difficult. Though her parents had experienced the Outer World, she couldn't fathom her father injuring himself out there. Just as troubling was the notion of Smolar impairing himself without anyone there to help him. While she questioned her future emotions, she couldn't ignore the love billowing deep within.

Aside from saving Promit, the only excitement she anticipated was spending more time with Rhugor, the strange quorian she'd never met before. His strikingly handsome features awakened her stagnant state. A fresh new face was exactly what she didn't know she needed.

"How're you doing?" she asked.

"The same. So much happened that evening, it almost seems like a blur." Silence fell between the two until Smolar spoke again. "I'm excited to help bring

Promit home. I'll do whatever it takes to make it happen."

"Yes. The sooner we bring him home, the better." She sighed. "I never anticipated leaving the city. It's overwhelming."

"Even with what your parents have accomplished?" Smolar asked, aware of the sensitive topic.

"Yeah. Maybe one day I would have, but certainly not this soon. I love our city so much. It's a glorious, majestic place." Fravia contemplated making a snide remark about Smolar's eagerness to leave, but decided against it. "I suppose I've read so much about the Outer World from books and my parents that I've satisfied my curiosities."

"Don't you wonder what else is out there though? Beyond what information is available here. We couldn't possibly know everything."

"Great knowledge comes at great cost. I'm content with the balance I've achieved, but I guess that'll change."

"I have to ask…why volunteer? If Lady Vixa planned for your father to go, why step in?"

"I wouldn't be able to live with myself if something happened to my dad and I did nothing to stop it. He's nimble and wise, but he's not a fighter."

Smolar shrugged. "Neither are you, and neither am I."

"Yes," she said, aggravated by his attitude, "but I'm in a better condition to endure this journey than he. Besides, he should be here helping quorians in the city. Others can't afford to have him gone for days, or possibly worse. It's the best of two bad options."

"I'm sorry," Smolar blurted out. "I didn't mean to say you weren't a fighter." He paused. "It's very noble of you."

Fravia sighed as their food arrived.

"One Hironchu sandwich with spider-fries for Ms. Fravia,' Birvena announced, "and the Wiggly Riggly with aliquo for…"

"Smolar," he said with a smile.

"Nice to meet you, hun." Birvena raised her eyebrows at Fravia, as if to say she was impressed by her friend. Fravia politely smiled, rolled her eyes and thanked her. As the owner of Draka's Diner walked away, Smolar took a sip of his drink for courage and changed the topic.

"That strange fellow Lady Vixa introduced to us...That was a surprise." Smolar watched her subtly smile at the mention of Rhugor. His heart felt heavy.

"Certainly was a surprise. I'm shocked I've never seen him before."

"There're so many quorians throughout the city. You could have but just don't remember," he said stirring the Wiggly Riggly soup. It was light brown due to the beef broth with potatoes, vegetables and chunks of meat. Three thick green leaves rested on the side of the bowl to use as miniature wraps. The dish was a complex blend of savory and sweet, exactly what Smolar had in mind.

"I'd remember him if I had seen him before," she said, smiling. Her words momentarily halted his position.

"Oh? Why's that?" he rebutted. Fravia held up her Hironchu sandwich, a vegetarian delicacy, to take a bite but stopped from his snide question.

"Because of his striking features," she exclaimed with a smirk.

"Whose striking features?" a deep, familiar voice asked close by. Fravia and Smolar turned to see Rhugor, their new companion, walking toward them.

"Rhugor!" Fravia shouted, overjoyed by his presence.

"Jeez." Smolar rolled his eyes. "Hi, Rhugor, nice to see you."

"Please join us," Fravia invited him, grabbing a nearby chair to add to the table.

"I don't want to intrude on—"

"You're not," they said in unison. Neither one was particularly happy with the conversation and welcomed the distraction, one more than the other.

"Eat with us," Fravia said in a jubilant tone. "The three of us are in for an incredible, life-changing journey—"

"And hopefully life-saving." Rhugor's voice exuded strength, yet it was gentle.

"Absolutely," Fravia replied as Smolar agreed with a mouthful of soup. "We should get to know one another since we'll have to depend on each other."

"Well *hello* there!" Birvena said, impressed by Fravia's attractive company. "What can I get started for ya?"

Rhugor admired what Smolar and Fravia were eating. "I'll take the soup and sandwich, please." His smile was charismatic, charming and infectious.

"You got it."

"You enjoy your food, eh? Gotta bring extra for the trip." Smolar sarcastically smiled. His eating habits obviously had no effect on his pristine physical condition.

"They both look appealing, so why not try both?" Rhugor patted Smolar once on the back, showcasing his strength. His body ricocheted forward, but he tried to hold his position.

"Would you like the other half of my sandwich? I can take your half when it arrives," Fravia offered.

"No, I couldn't. There's no—"

She put her hand up. "I insist. We'll be really close, really soon, so don't mention it." The two exchanged smiles as Smolar's jealously boiled within.

"So sorry, hun." Birvena said from behind. "I never asked if there was a drink I could get ya?" Rhugor looked at Smolar's aliquo. "An aliquo would be great. What'ya say?" He looked at Fravia. "Let's have a toast?"

She giggled. "Wonderful."

"Oh! Ms. Fravia, what're you toasting to?" Birvena raised her eyebrows.

Fravia looked at Rhugor, then Smolar, then back at Birvena. "To new friends!"

"How lovely! I'll be right back with that for you!"

While awaiting her return, the inquisition of Rhugor began.

"So where do you live, Rhugor?" Fravia asked.

"In a small establishment on the seventh floor. It isn't much, but it's mine."

"Do you have any family?" Smolar wondered. "Parents, children?"

"Nope." Rhugor paused, startling both Smolar and Fravia. "I've never had a proclamation nor a desire for children. They're sweet and all, but not sure it's a lifestyle for me."

"And your parents?" Fravia followed-up.

"They died long ago."

"I'm so sorry."

"My condolences," Smolar genuinely remarked. He instantly felt a small connection due to their shared pain.

"Much thanks, but it was expected. My parents had me later in life and they were older." Rhugor paused, then smiled. "I believe I'm older than you both."

"Just how old are you?" Fravia's tone was borderline flirtatious.

"*Older*," he said, avoiding an exact number. "How about you two?" It was the first question Rhugor had asked either of them.

"I'm thirty-five, Smolar's thirty-three," she replied.

"Here we go!" Birvena surprised them with three fresh aliquos. "I know you have one already Smolar, but I grabbed you a fresh one. You can't toast on a nearly empty glass. It's on the house!" She dispersed them and wished them all well.

Fravia, Smolar and Rhugor raised their glasses and smiled.

"To new friends," Fravia toasted.

"To Promit's rescue," Smolar added.

"To the unexpected." With Rhugor's words, the three new friends clinked their glasses as another familiar voice was heard.

"Well this is a pleasant sight."

"Lady Vixa!" Fravia exclaimed.

Rhugor immediately stood up in respect. "Hello, Lady Vixa." He bowed his head.

She looked over at Smolar who was just finishing his sip of aliquo.

"Hi, Lady Vixa," he mustered.

"Oh, please, it's okay," she said, instructing Rhugor to sit down. "I didn't mean to interrupt."

"No interruption at all. Would you like to join us?" Fravia asked.

"Thank you, but I can't. I actually came here to speak with Smolar." Lady Vixa looked at him with a kind expression. "There are some things we should discuss before your departure."

"Sounds good." Knowing the discussion that needed to be had, Smolar tossed back the freshly made drink and stood up. "It's been nice chatting, Rhugor." Smolar seemed unintentionally disingenuous as nerves settled in for the looming discussion. "Talk soon, Fravia."

"What do you think that was about?" Rhugor asked, as Lady Vixa and Smolar departed.

"I'm not sure," Fravia said, her eyes focused on them walking away and her mind wandering. "But it may have to do with Smolar's parents." She questioned her words the second she said them aloud. It wasn't her place to reveal his past, even though it was publicly known and Rhugor would find out eventually if he didn't already know.

"What happened?"

"They died when he was young and the conversation was recently brought up again."

"What a tragedy, for him and his parents," Rhugor responded. Fravia found his reaction to be underwhelming and peculiar, but rushed to change the subject.

"So, you're really not going to tell me how old you are?" She smiled as she nudged him and he laughed.

"Some things should remain a mystery." He winked and sipped his drink.

Smolar's heart raced as he anticipated the discussion of his parents with Lady Vixa. Since their deaths, he'd always felt disconnected from The Quo, fueling his eagerness to explore the Outer World. With a heavy heart, he didn't often discuss the events from that night. It wasn't until his visit to the quorian library, specifically the Hall of Antiquity, that he was faced with the intriguing question.

What really happened to your parents?

"Why don't we head up top?" Lady Vixa suggested, ascending the staircase. "Remember when you first moved in? You used to love coming up here."

"I really did," Smolar admitted. "It's magical. There's nothing else like it."

"I used to always come with you, but eventually stopped," she reminisced.

"Until you trusted me." He chuckled, as did Lady Vixa, until her smile dimmed looking out over the city.

"I know your mother and father wouldn't have forgiven me if I let something happen on my watch." Lady Vixa had maintained a calm demeanor, but recent events had changed that – changed her. Apprehension flowed through her body. "It would've all been for nothing," she murmured.

"I'm sure they'd be appreciative of your willingness to take me in."

Lady Vixa looked at Smolar with a nurturing, yet sympathetic expression. "You and I haven't really spoken much about what happened." She paused, lowering her head, then turned toward the edge of the thirty-first floor once more, overlooking bright lights and humid air from the Enchanted Reservoir at the base. "Do you have any memories of it?"

"Not really," he responded, standing beside her. "It's all a bit fuzzy, and most of what I recall is what you've told me. It's difficult to recollect what I actually lived through versus what I've been told."

"Try," she urged him.

Smolar shut his eyes and remained quiet while Lady Vixa continued to gaze out over the city. She noticed the Belvase was nearly prepared for the Blue Diamond Jubilee. Though she hadn't had time to meet with much of the community yet, she informed a few notable quorians, one being Ludwig Kladimazoo, the chairman of the Jubilee. The two had had a brief conversation regarding her plans to broaden the horizons for quorians and that she'd like to have an announcement regarding the matter. Lady Vixa informed him that it wasn't secretive, hoping to spread the news via word of mouth.

"I remember..." Smolar said slowly, refocusing the Quorian Ruler, as he grasped visions from his mind. "I remember hearing noises in the house, murmuring in another room, but I couldn't understand. It nearly felt like a dream." He opened his eyes and looked at Lady Vixa. "Then I remember you waking me up. You told me something had happened, that I should gather some clothes, and follow you home."

"You couldn't hear any conversations?" Lady Vixa asked, but he shook his head.

"Why?" Smolar asked, his tone stern. "You know, I assumed you invited me here to finish our conversation about my parents. I told you about my experience in the Hall of Antiquity and the title of the book which appeared to me."

"*What Really Happened To Your Parents?*" they said in unison.

"Exactly," Smolar said, waiting for a response. "So I have to ask...what happened to them?"

Lady Vixa knew the time had come. Smolar had accepted a dangerous task, and she felt he deserved to know the truth, just in case.

"What you remember is real and true," she began. Smolar noticed the pinky finger on her right hand was shaking. He'd never seen her tremble before. "Your remembrance of that night begins with those murmurs because you were,"—she hesitated, searching for the proper word—"protected. You were protected from your surroundings." Smolar expressed a curious look as she continued. "In fact, everything about that night was for your protection."

Lady Vixa turned her back on the city below and gazed up at the Great Quorian Seal. The bright moonlight shined upon them. Smolar admired the clear sky and the twinkling stars when Lady Vixa unleashed a whirlwind of a story.

"Long before the events of that night, an apparition appeared to me here, on the thirty-first floor. It somehow passed through the Great Quorian Seal from the Outer World into our city. Considering the monstrosity of enchantments on the seal, King Klai himself couldn't cross it if he wanted to. Dressed in a black cloak and ghostly in appearance, its skin glistened white. Unable to identify the gender, I tried to examine its face, but it was carefully blocked by the hood. The apparition proclaimed a very specific prophecy about the future of our civilization, one that couldn't be ignored." Lady Vixa paced, carefully assessing Smolar's expression.

"As you know, I've bore no children and don't intend to lie beside a male companion. With that in mind, certain precautions needed to be taken to ensure a proper and secure succession. The apparition explained your safety was of the utmost importance and that you should remain in a safe haven. The second request was a bit more precarious. It insisted you remain in the care of the Quorian Ruler to familiarize yourself with the lifestyle."

Smolar's mind analyzed what Lady Vixa slowly revealed to him. He was puzzled by who the apparition was, angry they didn't consider his parents safe enough, and wondered how Lady Vixa was involved in their deaths. However, Smolar's curiosity was piqued at the prospect of being the next Quorian Ruler.

"Unfortunately, this needed to happen without any inclination on your end. The apparition urged extreme measures were necessary to ensure the execution of—"

"The execution of my parents? Did it murder them? Who is this apparition that you blindly listened to?" Smolar blurted out, surprising himself. His forehead began to sweat as his body temperature rose. He was enraged that she had possibly played a role in his parents' deaths.

Lady Vixa wanted to address the question, but continued with her explanation. "It urged certain extreme measures to ensure the execution of your safety and experiences, but I vehemently refused. I couldn't bring myself to such destruction," Lady Vixa reassured Smolar. "I just couldn't do it. Unfortunately, the apparition saw no other way. It insisted that the death of your parents allowed the opportunity for you to live under my roof, with the Quorian Ruler."

"So the apparition was the intruder you mentioned. The one who murdered my parents." He was relieved to know Lady Vixa hadn't committed the deed.

Somehow, he trusted her words, her eyes, though she had a history of lying.

"Not exactly." She hesitated, frightening Smolar. "When I declined the suggestion, the apparition informed me it wasn't actually a choice. It was an order. Two days later it was to return to ensure your parents' were gone.

"The countdown had begun and there was only forty-eight hours to devise a plan. Much deliberation and contemplation was had, but there weren't many options outside of the apparition's request – only one. With only a few hours remaining, I met with your parents. Apparently the apparition had visited them a few days prior with its demands, but they ignored it. The love your parents had for you was too strong."

Smolar found himself holding back his emotion. He had never heard another quorian reference the love his parents had for him. It was heartfelt and nourishing in a way he didn't know he required.

"Considering the situation and the timeline, it was collectively agreed to execute the only other option we had. I rushed home and conjured up a few enchantments. One was brand new to me, and I had to make it twice. In the meantime, your parents spent their final moments gathering up some belongings and protecting other sentimental objects." Smolar's eyes widened, captivated by her every word. "They were ready when I returned and the three of us quietly entered your bedroom. I activated a silencer enchantment around you, ensuring absolute silence while asleep. This was your final moment spent with your parents."

Lady Vixa approached Smolar. While she'd never seen him cry, his eyes were red from fighting back the tears. "Smolar, let me just reassure you that your parents unconditionally love you, and forever will. You were their everything. Seeing you in bed, peaceful and safe, reaffirmed the plan we had put into action. Unfortunately, time was ticking and we had less than an hour before the apparition would arrive. With tear-filled eyes, your mother and father gave you one final kiss. I still remember the smile you had when that final contact was made."

Smolar lost the battle. His emotions won. Tears rolled down his face, heartbroken by the love lost from the only family he had ever known. Years of suppressed emotions flooded out. He wanted to curl up into a ball, but Lady Vixa reminded him the story wasn't over.

"While still surrounded by the silencer enchantment, your parents and I quietly left the house with their belongings. We descended to the fifth floor, the three of us moving swiftly, knowing the apparition's arrival was near." Lady Vixa took a breath, excited that the story was nearly over. "I pulled back the curtain to reveal the Enchanted Gate, an inactive portal which hadn't been used in years – though we both know how inaccurate that is now," she added in an attempt of slight humor.

"With the key in my hand and bags in theirs, your mother, father and I wished each other farewell and good luck. The Enchanted Gate activated as I stepped back to see your parents for one last time. Your mother had pain in her eyes, but knew their actions were in your best interest. With her hand on her stomach and your father's arm wrapped around her, they both gave one final nod before leaving the city, forever."

Though Lady Vixa hadn't yet said the words, the story was over. The message was clear. She cautiously awaited Smolar's reaction, her heart fluttering.

Smolar looked up, stunned. The saddened, battered face with streaming tears morphed into confusion as he tightened his eyebrows. After taking a few steps, Smolar looked back at her, his face shifting once more to judgement and aggravation.

All these years, he'd been told his parents were murdered, possibly in a brutal manner. He'd felt alone, isolated and without a place to call home. The events of that night fifteen years ago had shaped him into the quorian he'd become. But now his loyal confidant, the Quorian Ruler, who was once his guardian, had lied about it all. She was as close to family as Smolar could ever expect, and he had just been royally betrayed.

"You mean...to tell me..." Smolar's eyes sharpened, piercing into Lady Vixa with anger and disdain. "My parents...are alive? Is that what you're telling me?" He stepped toward her, but she remained still.

"Yes, my dear."

"Say it. I want to hear you say it," Smolar demanded. He'd never spoken to her in such a tone.

"Your mother and father are alive."

Time stood still for him. All Smolar heard was the hum from the Enchanted Reservoir below and it took every ounce of resistance to not push the Quorian Ruler to her death. He'd never felt so betrayed. The hot blood coursed through his body like fire, yet his skin remained icy to the touch. He didn't know whether to run, scream, fight or end it all.

Smolar turned his back on Lady Vixa and looked out over the city, deep in thought. Through the pain, he acknowledged it was a pivotal moment in his life and contemplated his two options. He could be boisterous with his anger, unleashing a fury of words and thoughts. Though it'd be cathartic, it could result in regret and forced apologies. Smolar had no intention of apologizing for anything. The second option was to maintain his composure – show no emotion.

"Where are they?" he asked through clenched teeth.

"I-I don't know. I'm terribly sorry for such an answer, but we had no time," she pleaded. "We had to make sure the apparition no longer sensed them in the city and that you remained safe. Once they passed through the Enchanted Gate, they were never heard from again."

"Why didn't you follow them? Why didn't you cast an enchantment? Why—"

"To save their lives. Of course we needed to keep you safe, but the apparition didn't intend to hurt you. It was there to ensure you followed the designated path that'd been chosen for you. Your fate."

"We make our own fate. No one can tell me what I'm destined to do. It's up to me to make it happen!" Smolar shouted. "Why are you telling me this now? Just before our mission to rescue Promit."

"You're heading out into a dangerous world, not typically welcoming of quorians. Who knows how things will go, but you deserved to know. You should have known years ago, but it wasn't my call to make."

"And it's your call now?"

"Nope. Not even a bit. I've been frightened to tell you in case it returned, but it's gone on for far too long. The prophecy's been fulfilled. You were kept safe and lived with me for numerous years. You needed to know in case someone out there knew something, or if something happens to either one of us."

Smolar walked toward the entrance to Lady Vixa's home as she eagerly awaited a response. There were more questions to be asked, and details to learn, but he wasn't sure he could hear anymore without breaking his composure.

"Smolar?" Lady Vixa asked, hoping to continue the discussion and ensure his mental status.

"I can't manage any more tonight. I'll see you just before we leave on the mission, but know this: *I will* return with Promit, then leave to find my parents. *They will* be found."

With those final words, Smolar walked out of her home, slamming the door behind him. Lady Vixa watched him head toward the descending shaft.

Gazing up through The Great Barrier, she wondered if she was right to be concerned for the apparition's return. She remembered the unique enchantment she had cast upon his parents. It'd been the only time she'd ever attempted it. The Quorian Ruler hoped it'd successfully worked for their safety, but knew Smolar wouldn't recognize them if so. A shapeshifter enchantment was intended to last a lifetime, allowing them to be welcomed by another region and deter the apparition from finding them.

Looking at the glistening moonlight which shined down upon the city, Lady Vixa wondered if Smolar's parents were still alive and if a reunion was even possible.

28

Knock, knock.

An exhausted Lady Vixa answered her front door, aware of the significance of the day.

"Good morning!" a jovial Fravia greeted.

"Fravia, Rhugor!" She smiled. "Hello to you both. How are you feeling?"

"Nervous. Excited," Fravia answered, peering inside.

"Ready to get out there," Rhugor replied as Lady Vixa stepped aside, welcoming them in.

"Are we missing someone?" Fravia asked.

"Smolar? I was hoping he'd be with you," Lady Vixa replied.

Fravia nodded, expressing a look of aggravation. Placing her backpack down, she let out a sigh. The last time she'd seen Smolar was when he'd left with the Quorian Ruler. Each of them knew the time and day to meet at Lady Vixa's home for their departure, so Fravia was disappointed in his tardiness.

"Let me see what's going on. I'll be back," Fravia informed them. As she exited Lady Vixa's home and entered the elevator, she wondered what'd gotten into Smolar. Rescuing Promit was his greatest priority and she didn't think anything could waver his determination.

When she approached Smolar's home, she knocked and heard the eerie creak of the door ajar. Fravia gently pushed it open further.

"Hello? Smolar, are you there?" she asked, not wanting to intrude. There was no answer. "Hello?" she repeated. Fravia pushed the door completely open, revealing a startling scene.

A frightening chill rushed down her spine at the sight of Smolar's nearly destroyed home. Tables were upside-down, upholstery torn open, chairs knocked over, clothes everywhere and papers lining the floor. His place had been ransacked.

"Smolar! Answer me! Are you in here!?" Fravia shouted, darting between rooms, trying to find him. His kitchen had utensils everywhere, pots and pans thrown across the room. Though the sink was empty, the faucet was pouring out water, which she turned off. With the entire house silent, Fravia called out for Smolar again, but still no answer.

When she entered the bedroom, her heart nearly dropped. His bed had been flipped over, a pair of shoes sticking out from underneath. "Smolar!" she yelled, running toward him. *He needs to be okay*, she thought. *This cannot be happening.* Fravia tried to lift up the bed but it was too heavy. She could barely move it at all.

She tried to lift if just enough to look underneath and see Smolar's condition, but when she did, she fell backwards, releasing her grip on the bed. The shoes had been situated as though he was underneath, but no one was there.

Fravia panicked. If he wasn't home, he had either been taken away or had left. She feverishly returned to Lady Vixa's home, envisioning scenarios on what could've happened.

Maybe someone was upset with Smolar and caused a fight.

Maybe someone burglarized him for a family heirloom or enchantment.

Maybe someone knew of our mission and wished to stop us.

Lady Vixa and Rhugor jumped when Fravia barged into the Quorian Ruler's home.

"What happened?" Rhugor asked.

"It's Smolar. He's gone missing. His house,"—she paused to breathe—"His house is destroyed. Everything's upside-down."

"Just breathe," Rhugor said, consoling her with his hand on her shoulder.

"There was no sign of Smolar?" Lady Vixa asked. Fravia gave a perplexed look, surprised by her underwhelming response.

"No. No one was there. I shouted, but no answer."

Lady Vixa looked around her room pensively. She raised her right hand, elongating her slender index finger to her nose.

"I may know where he went," she said, dashing out from her home.

"Where!?" Fravia asked, but it was too late. Lady Vixa had already left, closing the door behind her.

After his discussion with Lady Vixa, Smolar was enraged. He was rarely an angry person, so with his inexperience, he unleashed his pain in the safest, most private place possible – his home. When he arrived, he locked the door behind him and immediately cried out a single yell. He made his way into the kitchen, destroying something after every few steps. First it was the smaller objects, like a glass vase and a picture frame. Moving onto bigger items, he shoved his bar cart to the ground, breaking the glass contents. Just before entering the kitchen, he noticed his rocking chair on his left. He'd never liked it, but Lady Vixa cherished them, so he bought one during a time he was impressionable. He stomped over, lifted it above his head and slammed it to the ground. It was built out of wood, one of the most valuable materials in The Quo. A few pieces broke off, but Smolar wasn't satisfied. He wanted it shattered, so he picked it up and hurled it down again, repeating this until all that remained was a pile of splinters.

Catching his breath, Smolar turned toward the kitchen where he grabbed his largest, sharpest knife. For a split second, he felt a surge of energy from wielding a weapon. Though he wasn't a killer, he sensed the possible urge to kill their

Quorian Ruler. It startled him. As quickly as the thought entered his mind, he forced it out. He returned to his living room to continue his destruction, lashing out on his couch and a plush sofa chair, knocking them both over, tearing the upholstery.

His next destination was his bedroom, which was where he released the brunt of his anger. Smolar destroyed parts of the wall, tore up the majority of his clothing, then flipped and destroyed his bed. Nothing was left untouched. His emotions were so strong, Smolar had no recollection of the energy or weight of anything he destroyed.

After nearly complete destruction, Smolar collapsed to the ground, letting out a roar of exhaustion and pain. His breathing nearly caused him to hyperventilate, but he maintained his composure. As he gazed around the living space, he was reminded that his house had never felt like a home. It was a stable place to live, but it was emotionless. He realized there was only one place he'd ever felt comforted by, a place he'd called home.

Having never entered his childhood home since that night, he wondered if anyone else had. Smolar didn't have a key, but he wasn't about to let a lock stop him. He went around the side of the house where his parents used to have a garden full of luscious vegetables. After fifteen years of neglect, all that remained were beds of dirt where the plants used to thrive. Smolar remembered the exact location to dig, in the corner closest to the front door.

As his hand buried deeper into the dry, malnourished dirt, he felt the icy hard key and swiftly pulled it out. The aqueous solution from the Enchanted Reservoir was still contained within it, ensuring it was still activated. Smolar returned to the front, unlocked the door, and entered his past, traversing through the events that formed him into the quorian he'd become.

He was immediately greeted by the familiar smell of jasper flowers, a common aroma for his mother. It was warmth and comfort. As he gazed into the home, Smolar envisioned numerous memories from his childhood. Moments spent in the living room, meals cooked in their kitchen, dinners had in the dining room. Though mesmerized by his surroundings, he headed toward the back of the home, where his life had forever changed – his bedroom.

Unable to withstand the overwhelming feelings, he allowed himself to release the pent-up emotion. Tears silently rolled down his face as he lay on his dusty bed. There was no exaggerated weeping, no resistance. Just tears.

Exhausted from the destruction he'd caused earlier, he shut his eyes and welcomed the tranquility of his childhood. Just as he was about to fall asleep, he recalled the gentle tap of Lady Vixa on that night to escort him out. He rolled over to rest his eyes for a short while, as if he were eighteen again and nothing had happened.

Smolar lost track of time, but was aware of the significance of the day.

It was time to save Promit.

He felt the gentle touch on his shoulder again and shuddered. He knew it wasn't a memory. Furious at the possibility of strangers entering his childhood home, he was now ready to attack. He stabilized his body and perfectly executed a roll while lunging toward the assailant, but the figure moved faster and he collapsed to the floor.

"What're you doing here?" the voice asked, though Smolar knew exactly who stood over him.

"Revisiting the life I had ripped from me."

"Okay, enough," Lady Vixa said sternly. "I sympathize with your pain and frustration but you're living the life you were meant to have. Nothing was ripped away from you."

"You don't understand," Smolar tried to defend himself, but she wouldn't allow it.

"No, *you* don't understand. Your parents and I sacrificed our lives to assist in the greater good. Neither one of us expected such a shift. Change is the primary constant in our lives and without its acceptance, we suffer." Lady Vixa paused, and though he wanted to speak, he only stood up and looked down at his bed with painful eyes.

"The greater good," Smolar whispered to himself. "You know, when we spoke, I was so startled at my parents' fate, I hadn't addressed the other half of what you revealed." He turned around to meet her gaze. "Why did the apparition ask for *me* to be safe? For *me* to familiarize myself with the lifestyle of the Quorian Ruler? Am I, in some way or for some reason, your successor?"

"Maybe. The apparition never specified, but that's my perception." It had bothered Lady Vixa that the apparition never went into detail regarding the prophecy. Fortunately its presence never returned, but it also barred her from asking any further questions.

"I shouldn't have had to lose all who loved me to fulfill a prophecy I never asked for." Smolar appeared broken, battered. Lady Vixa was surprised by his underwhelming reaction to her admission.

"I know it's difficult to look beyond your parents, but you must see the bigger picture. Causing destruction from your despair will lead you toward an angry future. She went to your home, you know, to check on you, and returned terrified for your safety."

"She?" Smolar looked up, puzzled.

"Ms. Deallius." Lady Vixa paused. "You can't say you've lost all your loved ones, Smolar. It's belittling to those who care for you. Fravia has loved you for a long time now. It's apparently clear to everyone but yourself." Smolar tried to interrupt, but Lady Vixa continued. "You lived with me for nearly ten years, under my supervision and care. Of course there's a nursing aspect which grew over time." Lady Vixa wasn't one to say *I love you*, even with her father, but she had other ways of expressing the concept.

Smolar raised his thick eyebrows in shock. He had always cared about Fravia but it wasn't until recently that he acknowledged his love for her. Seeing her with Rhugor reminded him how she'd acted with him in the past. He was never aware of it at the time, but hoped it wasn't too late. Smolar questioned Lady Vixa's opinion of Fravia's love for him, but appreciated the gesture. He was, however, completely stunned to hear her expression of personal emotion. Smolar had never heard the Quorian Ruler speak in such an emotional state. She hadn't said the words, but he understood her meaning. Though filled with anger, he was touched.

"Let's be honest, Smolar. Even if your parents had died, their love for you would've lived on, just like I know my father's does. I still feel Lord Erko with me occasionally, and though our relationship had its strains, I allow it to empower me, not belittle me. Fortunately for you, both of your parents are still alive. Though they are somewhere in the Outer World, I know their love for you has only grown."

"I'm happy for you with your father, but with all due respect, Lady Vixa, I'm the reason my parents were forced out of their home. Had it not been for me, they could've stayed here, resumed their lives, and remained safe. It's my fault they were forced to leave into a dangerous world, unprotected." Smolar exhaled, defeated. He imagined his parents leaving the city, afraid, sad and, though they had each other, they were alone. "It must've been terrifying."

Lady Vixa sympathized. Though she couldn't do anything to bring them back, there was one parting gift she could give him.

"Smolar, there's something I'd like to do. Though we must begin preparations for your departure, this is important and won't take too much time. As I mentioned, on the night of the incident, I encapsulated you in a silencer enchantment. It stopped you from hearing, seeing or feeling anything during that period. I'd like to unveil those moments and return those memories to you."

Without waiting for his approval, the Quorian Ruler closed her eyes and waved her hands, fluttering her slender fingers and her long, ivory hair floated upwards. Smolar tensed in anticipation.

As quick as the clear bubble appeared from nothing, it burst and disappeared. Lady Vixa's hands and hair slowly lowered as she opened her eyes. Staring at

Smolar, she knew the words and sensations were being returned to him. Standing there with his back arched and eyes closed, she noticed a tear roll down his left cheek.

Lady Vixa quietly left the residence, allowing Smolar his privacy. She needed to return home to the guests waiting for her. There was an excursion to be had, a quorian to rescue. As difficult as the timing was, Lady Vixa was relieved for Smolar to know the truth and experience their final goodbyes.

She wondered if the apparition would return, displeased with her choice, but she was too preoccupied to focus on it. Too much had happened and was yet to come.

As she returned to her home, Lady Vixa knew it wasn't her choice to reveal Smolar's past, but before she could consider her options, her front door swung open.

"Lady Vixa!" Fravia exclaimed. "Sorry, I didn't mean to interrupt your thoughts. I had a feeling you were outside and I thought I'd check. Is everything alright?" Fravia looked around. "Where's Smolar?"

Rhugor walked up behind her, displeased that their third companion was already causing issues before the mission had even begun.

"He should be here soon," Lady Vixa responded. She confidently strutted into her home, hoping her demeanor would limit the number of questions asked.

"So he's alright?" Rhugor asked.

"He is. He will be. Him and I had a discussion that had some repercussions. I'm confident Smolar will arrive soon and we can begin your departure. Are the two of you ready?"

"Ready and raring to go," Rhugor said boldly.

Fravia smiled. "Yes."

"Perfect." Lady Vixa reached into a drawer from her desk and pulled out a small pouch. "All that's left is to give each of you two metamorphic potions. I've perfected an enchantment that'll allow you to appear as a typical degreant. I'll warn you that it may not be the most pleasant, as it does bring upon change on a molecular level, leaving no trace of the quorian race behind. Rest assured, you'll return to a quorian once more with the second vial. One to change, and one to revert back. Simple." Lady Vixa placed the pouch back on her desk and turned. "Just don't lose the second vial," she said with a smirk.

"What about your Amulet of Eymus?" Fravia asked.

"It's in Smolar's possession."

"Are you sure it's best for him to hold onto it?"

"Respectfully, my lady, I have to agree. Smolar's actions are questionable and your amulet is pivotal to this mission's success," Rhugor added.

"Be gentle on Smolar. Have patience. He's of great importance and ultimately the only one who can activate my amulet," Lady Vixa proclaimed. "To mention that which should not be said, had it not been for their innocent adventure, Promit would still reside within our city, safe. The burden of guilt he carries is warranted." Fravia raised her eyebrows and Rhugor looked as if he wanted to speak, but Lady Vixa continued. "Smolar needs our support more than ever during this time, and I'm confident you'll both provide that for him on this journey. All three of you play an important role and the mission will be a failure without you working together." Lady Vixa turned, locking eyes with the figure behind her. "Don't you agree, Smolar?"

"I do, Lady Vixa," he said in a monotone voice. As Smolar entered the room, a bag atop his back, he acknowledged both Rhugor and Fravia.

"Smolar! It's great to see you're alright. I was worried after seeing your house," she said.

Smolar smiled. "Sorry to have frightened you. It wasn't my intention to—"

"You finally made it. We've been waiting on you to depart. Hopefully you're all ready to go," Rhugor said smugly.

Smolar's emotional state was teetering. The burdens he carried drained his energy; however, the gift of the unveiling from Lady Vixa brought him much needed love he'd nearly forgotten was possible to feel. He knew it wouldn't take much to break his spirit and mental stability, but he refused to allow Rhugor to break him. *He isn't worth it.*

"Yup," he replied with an insincere smile. Fravia witnessed their interaction, immediately sensing she may need to be the voice of reason between the two males along the journey.

"What happened to your home?" she asked.

"Alright," Lady Vixa interrupted. "You three will have plenty of time to discuss matters after you leave, but let's get this show started. Shall we?" Her skinny fingers whimsically poked the air while the three stared. After a few seconds, small fireworks appeared in the middle of the living room, all shapes and colors. While they didn't last long, all three were impressed, particularly Smolar. She'd never used her abilities in such a way before. It was clear to him she had been working on her craft, improving her knowledge. When the display ended, Lady Vixa continued her speech.

"Smolar, do you have your Pendant of Perception? Fravia and Rhugor have already confirmed they do."

"Yes, Lady Vixa." Smolar reached into his bag, pulled out the pendant, and attached it to his right ear.

"Then here are your metamorphic potions. I explained them to Fravia and Rhugor, but essentially this one turns you into a degreant while the other changes you back to a quorian." She handed them over and placed them into his bag. "I have one final set here, and that's for Promit."

"I'll hold onto them," Fravia insisted.

"Splendid, and the Amulet of Eymus?" Lady Vixa asked, returning her focus to Smolar, who exposed part of his chest and pulled the amulet forward, displaying it for everyone to see.

"Right here."

"Excellent."

"I guess it's time then. To the fifth floor we go!"

"Are you doing alright?" Fravia quietly asked Smolar, as they made their way to the Enchanted Gate.

"Yes, there's just been a lot going on lately." Various topics had flooded his mind in recent hours, one being his relationship with Fravia and how Lady Vixa mentioned the love she had for him.

"What was your discussion about? Your parents?"

"Mhm."

"What about them?" Fravia asked, uncertain if he'd answer. Knowing what had happened to them, she considered the story finite. "Was there something you hadn't already known?"

"Yeah, but let's talk about it after we leave. We're nearly there." His voice was kinder than before, at ease. Fravia appreciated it.

As they arrived on the fifth floor, Restaurant Alley was nearly empty. Most of the eateries weren't yet open, which was what they'd hoped for. Since the Enchanted Gate was an archaic part of their city, unused and forgotten about, it wasn't ever heavily protected. As the group approached it, they were startled to see a forcefield surrounding the area. Its energetic waves glistened purple, distorting the view of the other side.

"What's that?" Fravia extended her arm out, sensing the energy without contact. She, Smolar and Rhugor stopped, mystified.

"It's my Preservation Ensorcellation. Conjured up with a rare stalagmite deep within the Enchanted Reservoir, the barrier ensures preservation of its contents from the outside world."

"This hasn't always been here though," Rhugor said.

"No. This is something I manifested last night."

"But why?" Smolar wondered. "The Enchanted Gate has been accessible to everyone for years without any interest. Why change that now?"

"The Blue Diamond Jubilee is around the corner. Once you return home with Promit, I'll announce our mission to expand our exploration into the Outer World. Our time of hiding will end, and our gate must remain protected during that heightened emotional announcement."

"Plus, the Divinity King knows we exist, so we need all the protection we can get," Fravia reminded them.

They all nodded in agreement. Smolar and Rhugor were excited for the new age for quorians. Fravia, though eager, felt a knot in her stomach. It worried her more than she wanted it to, but she tried her best to put her feelings aside.

"How do you gain access to the gate?" Rhugor asked.

Lady Vixa opened her palm and revealed three small stones.

"Moonstones," Fravia said, astonished. Some of the rarest material to find within The Quo, moonstones were generally considered a myth. Grown from a plant known as the Lunarc Vine, they were rare to find during the Age of Kings and none were known to have still existed. The moonstones were dusty white, perfectly rounded and seemingly smooth. Though the stone was solid, pulling it from the Lunarc Vine resulted in a short permanent thorn-like projection.

After being instructed to each take one, Lady Vixa explained they must prick their finger with the thorned tip, until their whitest blood expelled onto the stone, and then throw it into the forcefield.

"The Preservation Ensorcellation feeds upon the moonstones."

"Feeds? That *thing* is alive?" Rhugor asked.

"It may not be a breathing organism, but it does have the ability to grow."

"You really improved your enchantment abilities," Smolar said, being the first to follow the command. He pricked his left index finger, squeezing slightly, until the ivory blood revealed itself. He grazed the moonstone against the blood, ensuring a sufficient amount resided on it, then threw it into the forcefield. It immediately illuminated a royal blue hue, identical to Smolar's pigmentation.

"Did it just…grow?" Fravia asked.

"Told you it could."

With confidence, Smolar walked straight into the Ensorcellation.

"Wait!" Fravia shouted, but it was too late. His body had completely vanished. She tried to look through to the other side, but it wasn't possible to see anything. Fravia was next to prick her finger and throw the moonstone at the barrier. This time, the Preservation Ensorcellation noticeably expanded in size, causing Lady Vixa, Fravia and Rhugor to take a step back. It illuminated a soft blue hue, similar to her pigmentation.

"I…hadn't expected that." Lady Vixa was stunned, and glanced at Fravia, who looked puzzled.

"What was that about?"

"I don't know…" Lady Vixa rubbed her chin and gave her a pat on the shoulder. "Be safe out there. Watch after Smolar, but allow them to keep you safe. We can't have anything happen to you." Fravia gave her a perplexed look. "Your parents just started to approve of me," she said, trying to lighten the mood. "I don't want to give them a reason to hate me again."

Fravia smiled. "Thank you." With those final words, she hesitantly walked into the Ensorcellation.

"Guess it's my turn," Rhugor said. He jammed the moonstone into his arm, digging around for a minute. After pulling it out, he wiped on the excess blood and threw it at the Ensorcellation. While the color shifted to a powder blue to match his pigment, nothing else changed.

"Take care of them," Lady Vixa instructed, her eyes focused.

"Yes, ma'am." Rhugor pulled out his short dagger and leaped into the forcefield.

On the other side, Smolar, Fravia and Rhugor stood in front of the Enchanted Gate.

"Are you all ready?" Fravia asked.

"Let's do this," Rhugor responded. They looked at Smolar, awaiting a response in the awkward silence. Just as Fravia was going to ask again, he spoke two words, gently but with vigor.

"For Promit."

29

Osvita maintained a heavy heart after the Anti-Regime meeting followed by her discussion with Nigel. After her husband escaped without any contact or return, she was concerned for his safety. Then, after one Anti-Regime meeting, she was given an opportunity from an influential person: Lazarus. By agreeing to facilitate his entrance into the castle grounds, Lazarus reassured them he'd find Whark by whatever means necessary. Unfortunately, it required her to dive into the lion's den – the Kurhal.

Fleeing from the regime with her daughter had its struggles, but it brought her comfort to know she could watch over her. Osvita considered their journey had brought them closer. For the first time, she was able to see her daughter as her own person and not just her innocent, perfect child. She also found joy in seeing her daughter's relationship with Grum flourish.

Leaving her during a tumultuous time seemed impossible, and a choice she would've never made. But with limited options, Osvita knew agreeing to Lazarus's plan was her family's best chance to return to normalcy. Choosing to do nothing would result in regret – something she refused to endure again.

Ever since Osvita and Whark left The Quo and found shelter within The Barren Land, she did what was needed to progress in life. She felt it unnecessary to focus on the struggles of the quorian life she'd left behind. Instead, she suppressed her emotions. It had worked perfectly until the facade around her began to crumble from her husband's curious mind.

Immediately following their return home from the Anti-Regime meeting, Nigel noticed a sealed envelope attached to the front door with two letters in the top right corner.

O.D.

Looking around for anyone who could've left it, the two entered his home with the envelope in hand. A short discussion with Grum notified them of a knock at the door while alone with Rexhia. Fearing for their safety, the two remained silent until the visitor left the property and refused to open the door to investigate.

Tearing open the envelope, Osvita read aloud the contents of the letter to the group. It revealed that she, her daughter, and any accomplices with her were pardoned for their crimes and actions. Furthermore, it insisted she uphold the invitation to cater the dinner as requested.

"This seems awfully convenient." Osvita glared at Nigel, recalling his conversation with the Anti-Regime leader.

He knew exactly what she was referring to. "Lazarus had no idea we'd show up. Especially with your arrival. Besides, he's talking to everyone as we speak."

Osvita knew he was right, and it didn't help her curiosity, but being pardoned for what had gone on brought her immense relief. Though completely shocked, the seal on the Kurhal stationary was undoubtedly authentic.

"Maybe they learned about what happened at my home," Grum suggested. They all expressed a puzzled look. "Vincent."

"My word…I completely—"

"Forgot about him?" He chuckled. "Me too, ho ho! It just struck me. He must've survived and informed the castle. Having requested your services, they probably assumed you'd be here, or at least be in contact with Nigel."

"You know…" Nigel realized, "if they thought you'd be here, they could've stormed my home. They could've chosen violence, but they didn't."

"You think Shrenka sent this? Brugōr himself!?" Osvita wondered.

"Doesn't matter who it was, all that matters is what it says," Nigel explained.

Osvita unexpectedly felt a surge of relief from the discussion as her curiosity eased with a reasonable explanation. She was grateful for the break in stress and worry. Looking deep into Nigel's eyes, Osvita appreciated his presence and patience, uncertain if she'd be as strong without him by her side.

With the air lighter in the home, the two spent over a week preparing for the lavish banquet. Fortunately, he'd been ready for such an event. His quaint home was filled with various meats, an abundance of vegetables and enough sugary ingredients to satisfy Grum for a month. He went to the local market only once for certain spices and miscellaneous items.

While they weren't in the comfort of their own home, Osvita and Rexhia enjoyed the change of pace. Though she missed her husband, Whark had no culinary interest. She'd never been able to experience the euphoric feeling with him like she could with Nigel. Expressing her creativity through food had always been cathartic for Osvita. To Nigel, she just had a passion for cooking, but she knew it provided the perfect escape from her haunting past.

"Hey," Grum said, giving Osvita a reprieve from her thoughts. "Is there anything I can do to help out?" He surveyed the messy room. Flour coating the table, parchment paper strung out like a tablecloth, raw meat sitting beside the range, bowls of chopped vegetables in numerous locations, and dishes covering nearly every open space.

"Oh, Grum, you're already doing so much. Rexhia has really grown fond of you, I can tell. It's almost…"

"Almost?"

"It's refreshing to see," she replied. "Whark and I each have our own beautiful relationships with her, but she's different with you. Being her parent puts up an automatic wall between us, one that I wish didn't exist."

"Then dismantle it like I do with freshly baked brownies," Grum whispered. "Ho ho!" he exclaimed in a louder tone.

Osvita smiled. "If only it were that easy. Must be a parent first and her friend second."

Though receiving the pardon, the four of them mostly remained indoors for safety. They enjoyed dinners and played a variety of games, providing them with a false sense of normalcy. Though aware it wouldn't last, everyone allowed themselves the disconnect from reality. With a private backyard, Grum and Rexhia spent most of their time outside with Chowder. Though Osvita and Nigel occasionally joined them, they'd remain inside cooking and baking.

When Nigel left to gather supplies, he used that time to meet with Lazarus to confirm their plan. He insisted that he arrive at his home two hours before they depart for the Kurhal. Despite having the freedom to leave, Nigel never wasted time outdoors. Not only did he want to ensure his guests' safety, but he cherished the time they had together. He found himself living the life he'd dreamt of and he planned to enjoy every moment, even though it had an expiration date.

After Rexhia and Grum had excessively played with Chowder in the backyard, the three of them found themselves taking a mid-day nap. Osvita watched as the three of them slept under a large blanket, her heart warmed by Grum's kindness.

"How's it going?" Nigel whispered from behind, grazing her arm.

She smiled. "Great. I couldn't be happier," she blurted out. "I mean, this is just the calm we all needed before the possible storm."

"Good." Nigel was enthralled to have successfully made her happy. "You know you're more than welcome to come over anytime." His voice was low, deep, but gentle. They locked eyes, gazing deep into each other. Osvita felt a heaviness with every breath as they stood in silence, confident her heartbeat could be seen in her neck.

"I…" Osvita battled between the thoughts in her mind and the sensation in her heart. She loved Whark. They shared a connection that couldn't be broken, but she couldn't deny the crippling energy with Nigel. Her body was screaming to lean forward and kiss him, but her mind insisted against it.

Staring at the woman he loved, Nigel felt the excitement through his body. He'd always respected and admired Osvita, never wanting to cross a boundary. He didn't want to ruin what they had, because he sensed it would be the most he'd experience. But sensing the spark between them, there was no denying that Osvita, at least in that moment, felt the same way he did. Nigel's heart raced as he questioned whether to lean forward for a kiss. His entire body was yearning to do so, but his mind halted him.

Finally, a decision was made. Unable to contain the sensation, Osvita leaned forward and gently kissed him. Following their hearts and ignoring their minds, the two allowed themselves to enjoy the pleasure of what they longed for. No guilt, no shame. Just happiness.

After what seemed like an hour, yet somehow just one second, Osvita and Nigel pulled apart. Glancing into each other's eyes, they felt as though they were teenagers again. Excitement and anxiety passed through their bodies as they both made a poor attempt to hide their gleaming smiles.

"Well…" Nigel broke the silence.

"We should get back to the food." She chuckled.

He smirked. "Right. Of course."

Neither acknowledged the kiss, but sensed it was welcomed and enjoyed. Moments later, Grum entered the room.

"Is Rexhia asleep?" Osvita asked, unaware if he'd witnessed their kiss.

"Ho ho, she's fast asleep." Grum smiled. "I told her to slow down on those glimboberries."

"Glimboberries?" Osvita questioned, still unfamiliar with them. "I must—"

"Let the girl rest," Grum suggested. "She could use it. It's one of the best natural relaxants after all."

"What?" Osvita peeked outside and saw Rexhia in a deep slumber.

"You've really never heard of them?" Grum was surprised that a culinary veteran such as Osvita hadn't heard of the delectable fruits, but then he remembered how uncommon they'd become in recent years. Being in The Barren Land for a while, he remembered a time when glimboberries were a staple in households. Sold by the bundle, they'd be consumed as a sweet, after-dinner dessert to aid in a good night's sleep.

As the younger generation entered the region, outnumbering the older civilians, glimboberries slowly stopped selling, and a stigma surrounded those who consumed them. They were considered lazy, unambitious and unintelligent. With a system of capitalism within the valley, the plummeting demand forced harvesters to stop spending their resources on them, causing them to become a rare commodity.

"No, strangely enough…" She paused. "Rexhia came home with some before everything happened. It caught me off guard, but we tossed them aside."

"Came home with them, eh? For free?" Osvita nodded. "Well that is one kind salesmen, ho ho!" Grum explained the history of glimboberries within the valley. Osvita was surprised, yet intrigued – both at the history and his vast knowledge.

"Oh, Grum,"—she smiled, grabbing a couple of freshly-baked chocolate chip cookies—"I have a favor to ask." She handed him both cookies, still smiling.

"Bribing me with cookies, eh?" He chuckled. "You've gotten to know me well!" Grum chomped down, forcibly chewing and moaning at the sweet, delicious taste.

"When Nigel and I leave for the Kurhal tomorrow—"

"You want me to watch Rexhia?" He finished her sentence, chuckling. She blushed, embarrassed that he'd perceive her as a bad mother.

"I promise, this will be the last time," she insisted.

"I hope…" He struggled to speak through his mouth filled with cookies. Osvita sighed. "…not. Sorry, those were just too good." He laughed. "Your daughter is an incredible young girl who will one day be a fierce, cerebral woman. I consider myself lucky to spend what time I can with her."

"Aw, thank you, Grum. That…makes me happy to hear." Grum heard the uncertainty in her voice and briefly explained his previous wives and how he missed out on having children.

"I had no idea," Osvita said as they embraced. Grum welcomed the compassion, as it was a side of himself he didn't often share.

"Thank you," he replied as they parted. Just then, a staggering Rexhia entered the kitchen.

"Hi, Mom," she rubbed her eyes, yawning.

"Sleep well, darling?"

"Guess you enjoyed those glimboberries, huh?" Grum's mouth opened wide as he cackled at his own question.

"Yes, I did. I was just…so tired."

"It's okay. Clearly those berries helped you get the extra rest you needed."

"Hey, everyone!" Nigel shouted as he entered the kitchen. "Looks like the party's in here." With twenty-four hours remaining until the banquet dinner, most of the work had been completed. There were just a few finishing touches to make before they could rest.

"So when are we leaving for this dinner tomorrow?" Rexhia asked.

Nigel and Grum exchanged glances and then turned to Osvita.

"Oh, honey…" she replied. "I thought it was understood that only Nigel and myself can attend the banquet. Unfortunately, I'm not allowed to bring you along this time."

"But—"

"Now, darling, Grum is going to stay here with you until Nigel and I return. We should only be gone for half the day, but it'll probably be late. The following day we will organize our next move and find your father."

"I don't need a babysitter, Mom."

"I think your mom intends to have you babysit me," Grum chimed in with a wink.

"Exactly." Osvita smiled. "I've seen what you can do with that slingshot." Rexhia's jaw dropped open.

"But....ho—"

"If you decide to become a mother one day, you'll learn all our secrets," she said with a chuckle. "I'll always be watching you, no matter where I am. Always remember that. Now, do you think you could watch Grum and Chowder for us?" Osvita asked once more.

Rexhia reached into her pocket, pulled out her slingshot and smiled. "We certainly can!"

For the remainder of the evening, Osvita and Nigel worked together finishing up their menu for Brugōr's banquet.

"How're you feeling?" Nigel asked, knowing it wouldn't be easy to enter the lion's den with her husband missing.

"Fine," she replied, shrugging. "I'm looking forward to this being over."

"You'll get through this. I know you can," he insisted, resting his hand on her shoulder. Osvita turned around and stared at him. It lasted only a few seconds, but Nigel felt her linger. Every time their eyes met his heart fluttered. Though they both envisioned the kiss they'd shared, neither one acted upon it a second time.

"Thank you," she responded. "I wish I could just go back to the way things were. Back before life got so complicated."

"Life is as complicated as we allow it to be."

Though Nigel was referring to her home life with Whark, Osvita was struggling with the reminder of the life she once had in The Quo. Aware of the quorian in captivity, she couldn't help but reminisce. For the first time in a long time, as she and Nigel wrapped up their final preparations, Osvita thought about her life as a quorian.

Her friends. Her marriage. *Her son.*

The following morning, Rexhia awoke to the sound of clanging from downstairs. Her eyes widened with energy, remembering the conversation she had with her mother the night before. She reached under her pillow to feel Sohnora, uncertain how her mother knew about it and her ability to wield it. Rexhia momentarily questioned Grum, but was confident he hadn't broken her trust. Even though Osvita admitted it was an ability that mothers possessed, she didn't buy that excuse.

Because of her upbringing, Rexhia had a difficult time believing what wasn't tangible. She'd been raised to defend herself, to be independent and work for her achievements. The idea of *magic* or *special powers* only existed in fairytales. She considered her handling of Sohnora a skill, liberated to use under proper circumstances. Rexhia was relieved to sense her mother's trust, treating her like an adult. This reminded her how poorly Grum handled the slingshot, which gave her an idea on how to spend their time together.

Directly under her bedroom, on the main level of the house, Grum was fast asleep. None of the noise from the kitchen woke him. Just one of the perks of a deep sleeper.

Nigel Hatherton was wide awake, sipping on his morning coffee, anticipating the day ahead. Though nervous for the outcome, he had confidence that Lazarus's plan would work out in their favor. Regardless, he made it known that his priority was Osvita's safety. If he felt they were in danger, he'd ensure their escape, at risk of the mission's success, and relish in his moment to be Osvita's knight in shining armor.

Looking around his kitchen full of tools and dishes, Nigel began strategically packing his car. Though confident it'd all fit inside, losing the space from two passengers made it a challenge. As he made his way toward the front door, Osvita appeared from the hallway. Nigel glanced at her natural beauty longer than appropriate.

"Morning, Nigel."

"Osvita!" he shouted, overcompensating for the prolonged glance. "How'd you sleep?"

"Like a baby. It was marvelous. You good?"

"Just energized for the day." Aware of Osvita's stress, Nigel tried to bring exciting energy to the event, and have her focus on the culinary aspect.

"It'll be exhilarating when it's over."

"Certainly," he agreed. "I'm going to prep my car for the pack. Coffee's made, and an egg casserole is in the oven. Please help yourself."

"Splendid, thank you. Oh, Nigel," she urged, just as he turned to walk toward the front door. "Maybe calm down on the coffee? We don't want to seem too out of sorts. Our reputation is on the line."

"Of course."

It was the first time since their arrival that Osvita stepped into the leadership role, which felt awkward for her still under his roof. When it came to their work, Osvita reigned supreme with her culinary talent. The unfamiliarity of feeling uneasy about it was foreign to her, which ultimately made for the awkwardness of the situation. Regardless, it was how their professional relationship was and must continue to be.

Though Rexhia woke up before Grum, she couldn't help but think about what her mother had said. She suddenly felt the need to nurture him. It was the first time she had the urge to provide care for another person. Both Rexhia's parents were in great health and she hadn't known anyone else in her life who could benefit from her care. Though independent, Grum was alone. She knew their flourished bond under chaotic circumstances would be greatly appreciated.

While sitting in the living room, showering Chowder with love, Rexhia noticed Grum exit his bedroom and head into the bathroom. Knowing the organized mess in the kitchen, she quickly poured him a fresh cup of hot coffee and grabbed him two muffins. As he entered the living room, Grum stopped to greet the smiling child.

"Good morning, Grum!" she said cheerfully, holding out the steaming cup of coffee.

"Well, hello there. Is this for me?"

"Mmhm." She nodded. "Mom and Mr. Hatherton have the kitchen upside-down right now. They're packing for work, so I grabbed you a cup of coffee and some muffins so you don't have to deal with the mess."

"Ho ho, that's very considerate of you."

"That's my sweet angel," Osvita said in passing.

"And you even remembered that I liked my coffee black."

Rexhia smiled.

Though Grum had just woken up, he offered his assistance to load the car, but Osvita and Nigel politely declined. They had a particular system for packing, so he remained on the living room couch with Rhexia, Chowder between them.

There was a knock on the door and Grum and Rexhia noticed a muscular arm extending inwards.

"Hello?" he asked. Grum guarded Rexhia as she slumped into the couch. Chowder let out a small bark. She quickly calmed him down, but the unknown man peered inside making eye contact with Grum.

"Can I help you?" he asked without movement.

"Well, hello there." The mysterious man smiled widely. His chiseled face and striking gray hair were a unique look. "I'm looking for—"

"Laz! There you are. Nearly perfect time," Nigel interjected, both smiling as they shook hands. Grum lowered his guard as he realized the stranger wasn't a threat. He was never one to assume the worst of people, but after his experience inside his home, he wondered if that'd change.

"Marvelous," the gray-haired man said.

"Lazarus, I'd like you to meet Grum Lagom, a co-worker of Whark." Just as he finished his first introduction, Osvita entered the room. Nigel turned around to formally introduce her. "And *this* is Osvita. Over there is her daughter Rexhia."

Lazarus politely made eye contact with everyone.

"It's a delight to finally meet you, Osvita. Nigel has told me all about you. Riveting." Gazing down at her daughter, Lazarus chose his words carefully. "I very much look forward to assisting you on this complex, unified cuisine. I'm certain it'll be the talk of the valley."

"Thank you," Osvita said, smiling politely. "Lazarus will be assisting us to cater the elaborate event," she said to her daughter.

"But I thought you said only you and Nigel could go?" Rexhia asked, curiously gazing at Lazarus. "Can I come?"

Grum assisted in the only way he knew how. "Hey, Rexhia, what'd ya say we go play with Chowder outside for a bit and let these boring folk focus on work?" Knowing her mother's mind was made up, she sighed, jumped up and joined Grum toward the backyard.

"Does Lazarus look familiar to you?" Rexhia whispered.

"Not particularly. Do you recognize him?" Grum glanced as she shrugged her shoulders.

As the two played outside, Lazarus, Nigel and Osvita finished packing up the vehicle. With little time left, Osvita and Nigel went to say their goodbyes, while Lazarus waited in the living room.

"Thanks for holding down the fort while we leave," Nigel patted Grum on the back and smiled. "It's comforting to know Rexhia and Chowder are in good hands."

"Ho ho, of course!" Grum replied joyfully before gazing around the yard. "Just kick some ass tonight," he whispered.

"Hm?" Nigel replied. Worried he'd misspoken, Grum widened his eyes until Nigel winked with a chuckle.

As he called Chowder over to express his love, Osvita approached her daughter.

"Now remember what we spoke about. You're the warrior of the house tonight, so stay alert. Keep your guard up and whatever you do, *do not* unlock the door for anyone. No one is to enter or leave Mr. Hatherton's home." Rexhia nodded. "Do you have your slingshot nearby?"

"Sohnora doesn't leave my side," she said patting her pocket. "We're always together."

"Sohnora?"

"It's her name. My slingshot."

"That's a peculiar name…" Osvita pondered. She wanted to ask more about it, but knew they had to get going. Before she could utter another word, Rexhia spoke.

"Mom, I really like Mr. Lagom. He's like a fun uncle."

Osvita chuckled, "I can see that. I'm happy you're both bonding so well. He always wan—"

"And Mr. Hatherton. He's *very* nice, Mom. He reminds me of Dad."

"Oh? How so?" Osvita asked in disbelief.

"The way he looks at you. He's got a twinkle in his eye. I've seen that in Dad sometimes, but Mr. Hatherton's eyes seem stuck on you." Rexhia's words bore a heavy weight. Osvita planned to respond when her daughter continued. "I miss Daddy. When will we see him again?"

She sighed. "I know, dear. I do too. Once this banquet is over, we'll see him again."

"Hey, Vita," Nigel said behind her. "You ready?" With a nod, Osvita gave her daughter one more kiss on the head and held her tightly, expressing her love. As she and Nigel walked inside, she took one more gander at Rexhia and smiled.

"Looks like it's just us two, kid," Grum said.

"I guess so, but something doesn't make sense," she said in a curious tone.

"How so?"

"Mom's been cooking my entire life. It's her passion, and I know she's worked a lot for her success. When she first accepted the job, she was excited, but then everything changed. We left our home for yours, were attacked by guards from the Kurhal, and the rest…well, you've been there for all that. She has enough success that she didn't *need* to take the job, but…she went. Regardless of the pardon, she went into the lair of the beast with Nigel and that…unusual fellow. Something doesn't add up."

Grum couldn't believe what he had heard. The cerebral, yet innocent, thirteen-year-old girl was showcasing and embracing a new side of her, and he was intrigued.

"Grum?"

"You either have everyone fooled or you are wise beyond your years," he said, nearly breathless. She stared back with a perplexed look. "You've portrayed yourself as a sweet, young girl with little to no interest in your parent's lives. Though I knew you were extremely bright, it's common and expected for a thirteen-year-old child. Adults are boring," he said with a wink. "When you first showed me Sohnora, I knew you were different. Unlike most children, I knew there was depth to you, but uncertain of the extent. You're completely aware of your surroundings and in-tune with nearby conversations."

"It's no different than what my mom does to me," she insisted. It was obvious Grum was confused. "My mom's constantly changing how she treats me. Sometimes I'm her precious baby who can do no wrong, and also do nothing adventurous at all. Then, there are the times she embraces my inner adult, allowing me time to explore and speaking to me like I'm a grown-up. I understand she's my mom, so I'm always respectful, but if she can change how she acts then why can't I?" Rexhia held her chin up high, proud of her actions.

Grum stood speechless, impressed by what he'd heard. If a parent can treat their child differently, then why not allow the same privilege to the child? He was most impressed by her controlled patience to hide her observations and opinions.

"You're remarkable, Rexhia. Your ability to stay vigilant and uphold such composure isn't an easy task. I'm not sure how your mother and father would feel, but I think it's really cool."

"Thanks!"

Having never shared such secretive information about her personality, Rexhia was elated. She threw herself onto the grass and showered Chowder with an abundance of love and kisses.

30

After his revelations in Diad, Jacob Emmerson returned to the empty parking lot of the ultrasound office. He knew he'd upset his family, but his travel proved worthwhile – learning of his great grandmother, Edith, and the ancient artifact she'd left for him. Spending time in Giddeom's region allowed him to appreciate Sartica more; however, he knew being there more was an inevitability that he'd chosen to accept.

Opening the gate to the house, Jacob was startled to see nearly his entire family there.

Did they call everyone in fear of my safety?

Did I overshadow Catherine's day with my disappearance?

Have they been trying to find me?

Hesitantly exiting his vehicle, he walked toward the front door, feeling his right pocket for Edith's orb. After his struggle and acceptance with the ancient artifact, it miraculously miniaturized itself, allowing Jacob to keep it on him. Strangely enough, it brought him peace. Uncertain if it was the connection with a family member or being in possession of a mystical object, it helped ease his nerves.

"Hello?" he asked as he entered, but there was no answer. Hearing faint murmurs, Jacob followed them toward the back of the house. An abundance of boxes had been laid out across the floor – diapers, formula, baby blankets, onesies, a car seat, baby books. "Hello?" he repeated as he entered the kitchen.

"Jacob! There you are!" Anna jumped up. Everyone turned and looked with a similar, reassuring reaction.

"You're okay!"

"Where've you been!?"

"Hey, everyone." He waved at the room. Both he and Andrew's parents were there, plus Catherine and Cynthia.

"Hi, Mom," he said as she embraced her son for a moment, before whacking him behind the head. He flinched.

"What were you thinking? What's wrong with you." She looked him up and down to ensure he wasn't harmed.

"It's a long story," he said, rubbing his head, "but I can explain later." Jacob greeted everyone with hugs, smiling, until he approached his sister sitting at the kitchen table. "I'm really sorry for leaving. I hadn't intended to be gone for so long."

"It's alright," she replied, waving one hand and rubbing her belly with the other. There was an eerie calmness in her tone.

"So, do we know the gender yet or is it too early?" Jacob asked. "Will I have a nephew or a niece?" The room fell silent. Jacob sensed they were center stage, everyone anticipating her response.

"Well, Jacob, it's certainly not too early to tell." She looked up at her husband, and then over toward her parents with an unsettling look.

"What's going on?" Jacob asked. "Is everything okay?"

"Yes," she said, placing her hand on Andrew's, which was resting on her shoulder. She smiled. "We'll be having a baby girl."

"That's incredible! Congratulations!" Jacob was elated and quickly embraced her, but sensed there was more. He stepped back and surveyed the room. "What the hell's going on? Why's everyone acting so strange?"

"There's something else," Catherine admitted. She raised her eyebrows and rolled her eyes, expressing a look of disbelief. "After you walked out, the doctor revealed some startling news."

"Okay. Are you having twins or something?"

"No, no twins. Just the one girl, but…it seems my due date was off a bit."

"A bit?" Ben said with a chuckle. Anna hit his arm to say *shut up.*

"You were expecting her in, what, six months? How off were they?" Jacob knew dates commonly changed and couldn't comprehend what was so startling.

"The date is sooner than expected."

"How soon?"

"Next week?" She shrugged. "Maybe two?"

"What!?" Jacob shook his head violently, then glanced around the room. "But you just told us—"

"I know," Catherine interrupted.

"We're all just as shocked as you," Anna said.

"What's important is that she is very healthy. All signs are good and she's nearly fully developed," Cynthia added.

"But…how's this possible?" Jacob asked. "How come you don't look nine months pregnant?"

"We're not entirely sure. They're not entirely sure either. Ultrasounds were done, bloodwork was ran, but everything checked out," Catherine admitted.

"After we left and noticed you were still gone, we came home with Anna and my mom," Andrew said. "Everyone else ran to a couple stores to purchase some of what you probably saw walking in. Seems we have less time than expected to prepare." His face expressed a jovial, carefree disposition, but Jacob noticed the stress in his eyes. *Who wouldn't be stressed to know their two- or three-month-old baby would arrive in a week?*

Guests eventually dispersed as the night lingered until it was just the four

Emmersons and Andrew.

"We should probably head home. Andrew's passed out on the living room couch. It's been a long day," Catherine said, rubbing her belly. "It's going to be a hectic week considering this child can arrive any day now…" Just as Anna was about to hug her daughter goodbye, Jacob interrupted.

"If you don't mind…" He hesitated. "I know it's been an emotionally draining day, but I just wanted to mention something."

"Can we discuss this tomorrow?" Catherine asked.

"I may not be around tomorrow. Actually, I may not be around for the next few days." His response grasped their attention. Ben, Anna, Catherine and Jacob all sat down at the kitchen table. It had been the first time in a while just the four of them were together.

"Did something happen? Everything alright?" Ben wondered. Jacob glanced at his mother, quietly smiling. Understanding one another, she knew the topic of discussion.

"Everything's okay." Jacob gazed around the room. "This may seem random, but do you remember Great Grandmother Edith?"

"Of course," Anna said. Catherine acted surprised by his words, but expressed a reassuring smile.

"How can I remember her if I never met her?" Ben said with a smile. A poor attempt at a joke.

"Well…you see, this is the difficult part."

"We're here for you," Catherine supported, aware of the looming discussion.

"I'm not at liberty to reveal much. Dear Edith wasn't often around because of a role she had. A responsibility she accepted. It wasn't a typical job with regular perks and a flexible schedule."

"Sounds like she should have bargained for more job perks." Ben chuckled again, but Jacob just rolled his eyes.

With a long exhale, he officially informed his entire family of the news, though it was only new to his father. "It seems as though I may have fallen into the same situation, acquiring her same responsibilities."

"What responsibility is that? What job did she have?" Ben asked.

"I can't say. This responsibility…this job position, for whatever reason, has fallen upon me. It requires me to be away from home for long periods, and sometimes without notice."

"So that's why you disappeared during the appointment?" Ben asked. "Here I thought you ran to get some pizza," he said, which Jacob rolled his eyes even harder at. "No, but seriously. I'm glad to see you found a job. Sounds like they recruited you?"

"It was a mutual agreement. I'd like to think we met halfway."

"Can you tell us if they pay well? Are the benefits good?" his father asked.

"They're certainly taking care of me. I even have my own office." Jacob knew he couldn't give any information, but figured his sanctuary could qualify for an office. *It's not like I showed them the ancient artifact in my pocket*, he thought.

Mother and daughter gazed at one another, sharing a comforting smile.

"Anna, did you know?" Ben inquired, noticing the look between the women. "You too, Catherine?"

"I-I…"

"You knew." Ben's tone flipped, staring at his wife.

"Jacob and I hadn't spoken about it, but I had my suspicions," she answered.

"You know how we share unique experiences in our dreams," Jacob said, pointing to his mother and himself. Both Catherine and Ben nodded. Jacob explained that they'd had brief discussions about his visions, until he was told everything needed to remain secret.

"How are you employed by someone in a vision? Is this all just a figment of your imagination? Are you feeling alright, son?" Ben looked toward Anna. "Maybe we should have him see a specialist?"

"It's…difficult to explain, especially when I can't give any details." Jacob found himself in a precarious place. He yearned to discuss his role as a guardian. It was exhilarating, yet concerning; he was eager, yet anxious. Their discussion was a reminder that being guardian was more than just handling Giddeom's tasks. It'd be a challenge to balance two lives.

"Right now, you're talking nonsense." Ben became frustrated. He didn't like being excluded, especially when he couldn't understand why. "You can't tell us where you'll be spending your time because someone in a vision told you to keep it secret?"

"It wasn't a vision. I physically went to…"—Jacob paused, trying to find the words—"their office. Their flagship location was beautiful. It's a massive stone building with a beautiful entryway and colorful flowers I'd never seen before. Just breathtaking," Jacob said, remembering his first time visiting the manor. The excitement, the uncertainty, the curiosity. "But when I went inside, I just couldn't believe what I saw…" Noticing his father's unamused face, he shifted gears. "Anyway, my point is that I've been there. I've met my boss, who was very informative, dapper in appearance. I even met some co-workers and was given my first assignment." Catherine cocked her head, perplexed by the new detail.

"When's your first assignment?" Anna asked. It was the first time she'd spoken since they sat down.

"Immediately. I have a meeting tomorrow, but then I expect I'll have to tr—" Jacob stopped, realizing he was about to say *travel*, implying more than they needed to know. Fortunately, he recovered quickly. "I'll have to try and get a move on right after."

"Just tell me one thing," Ben said. "Are you doing anything illegal? Are you involved with corrupt people? Drugs? Sex? Is this work dangerous?"

Jacob didn't know how to honestly answer the question. Considering the region of Diad was home to the Divinity King, he didn't foresee corruption or anything illegal, but danger seemed possible. His response had to be a complete lie to satisfy his family.

"Of course not, Dad. I swear to the Divine that I'm not selling drugs or doing anything like that." Jacob smirked, aware of the irony.

"Good," his father said, seeming pleased enough. "Well, I guess there's nothing more to say. If you can't discuss anything further, then we're good. You're employed, you're getting paid and you're staying safe. Just try to let us know when you'll be away, that way Mom doesn't worry and I can have what would've been your dinner." Ben smiled before wishing his family goodnight and heading upstairs. "I'll see you tomorrow, right?"

Jacob nodded, reassuring him he didn't plan to leave in the middle of the night.

Remembering her husband was fast asleep on the couch, Catherine followed suit. "I should really get going." She stood up, hugging her mother and brother, neither of whom seemed eager to end the conversation. As she was about to exit the kitchen, she stopped and turned around. "Hey, Jacob," she started.

"Yeah?"

"That boss of yours, the dapper one…" She thought for a moment, closing her eyes, focusing. "Was he dressed in red?" Jacob shuddered in his chair enough for his mother to notice. "Does he have a cane?" He knew details couldn't be revealed, but he hadn't considered someone would correctly identify them.

"Uhh…" Jacob struggled for words, knowing he'd already answered the question, but he tried to recover. "Now that you mention it, he did. Does?" He chuckled. "Sorry, I've met him a few times. At first, he didn't, but the last time I met with him, he did." He stood up, extending his neck slightly. "How do you know?"

Since his experiences began, Jacob had wondered why a tradition exclusively meant for women suddenly changed with him, a man. *Did she meet him and decline? Had Giddeom tried to connect with her, but failed?*

"I'm not sure. When you explained things just now, an image of this man appeared in my head. Like a memory. Deja-vu." Catherine pondered, then tossed her arms up and chuckled. "Maybe I've just seen him along the streets of Sartica," she said shaking her head. "It's been a long day. Time for us to head out. In case you leave tomorrow, little brother, good luck on your job. I'm really happy for you." The two hugged and she left the kitchen. "Just don't miss the birth of your niece!" she shouted from the dining room, waking up her husband.

"What was that about?" Anna asked. "You jumped when she asked you about your…boss," she said with a grin. "I assume you're referring to Giddeom?"

"Shhh," he said, looking around. "I shouldn't have said anything. You probably know more than you should, but what's done is done. You can't tell anyone anything about our discussions."

"Don't worry, I won't. But was she right?"

"Has she said anything to you about having visions?" Jacob asked, avoiding the question

"Never."

"I just don't—" he stopped as he heard a familiar voice.

Jacob. The time is now. Come.

"Already!?" Jacob grunted.

"What?" Anna asked.

"Sorry, but I'm being summoned. *Work.*" Jacob rolled his eyes, gathering his belongings.

"But I thought your meeting was tomorrow?" Her voice was filled with disappointment. He gave his mother a kiss on the cheek.

"So did I. I'm sorry." As the two hugged, Jacob felt guilty. He knew his mother wanted to discuss more, but those days had ended. Even if Giddeom hadn't called, the days of confiding in his mother were over.

"Great Grandmother Edith asked me to say hello," he whispered into Anna's ear. He knew it'd probably be frowned upon, but he felt justified since her letter instructed him to do so.

Anna's mouth hung open, her face in disbelief.

"Jacob…" She paused as her eyes watered up. "How did you—"

"I have to go, Mom. See you soon."

"Love you, son."

Jacob didn't waste any time returning to his sanctuary, inside the manor. It appeared the same as when he left it, reassuring him of his privacy. He took out Edith's miniaturized orb and examined it in the palm of his hand. Suddenly, it's size enlarged to what it originally had been. Jacob jumped back, forcing the orb to levitate in front of him and slowly lower to the ground.

"Hello again." Jacob smirked, feeling foolish addressing an inanimate object. He was entranced by the red, viscous fluid swirling at its core. "I wonder if you'd go unnoticed if I brought you along with me."

He felt at ease with the artifact in his possession. He didn't know what the journey to The Barren Land would entail, but thought a sense of familiarity in a strange place would prove helpful. "What could I put you in…?" he said, glancing around the room.

"What!?" a bold female voice said with a unique accent, frightening Jacob.

"Who's there? How did you get in?" he asked. His eyes darted around the room for an intruder.

"Down here. I believe you referred to me as Edith's Orb." The orb slowly floated up from the floor as Jacob's eye's locked onto it.

"You've got to be kidding me."

"Afraid not, Jacob Emmerson." Her voice was stoic, affirmative. "My name is Anitta, and you're not locking me inside anything."

31

Traveling through The Enchanted Gate was underwhelming for Fravia, and overwhelming for Rhugor, who got sick to his stomach. After allowing himself a moment to recover, the three quorians regrouped and consumed their metamorphic potions. With no sensation, pain or discomfort, Smolar, Fravia and Rhugor's appearances changed, allowing them to travel inconspicuously in the Outer World.

Smolar's royal blue pigmentation transformed to light cream and his white hair turned blonde, as the rest of his features slightly changed. Most noticeably was the increase in height to stand nearly six-feet tall. The only familiarity that remained were his eyes, which changed from white to a familiar royal blue.

"Smolar? You in there?" Fravia asked.

Mesmerized by her transformation, he hadn't even acknowledged the question. Her soft blue tone quickly changed into a silky umber, her flowing hair jet black. Her once petite frame strengthened as her muscles toned and her height extended to a few inches less than his. Fravia's soft blue eyes were all that remained of the quorian they once recognized.

"Well the potions clearly worked, regardless of how ridiculous we seem." Both Fravia and Smolar chuckled, which eventually turned to laughter. It was a much-needed reprieve from the pressure – joyous and rejuvenating.

Smolar tried to put aside his frustration with Lady Vixa, his love predicament with Fravia and curiosity of his parents' whereabouts. Though the thought of meeting them constantly came to mind, he knew he needed to remain focused if they planned to be successful. He also remembered he may be the next Quorian Ruler, which was the reason his parents were forced to leave.

"We look so different," Fravia said. As their laughter eased, she looked around for Rhugor, uncertain where he'd gone. "Rhugor?"

"Rhugor?" Smolar said, still with a slight chuckle. "Where'd you go?"

"I'm…I'm back here." They both followed the voice into a dimly lit corner. "I think something happened…"

"We can't see you. Come out," Fravia said.

Immediately, a quorian's blue eyes looked up at them with concern. They were unexpectedly low to the ground, especially considering how tall Rhugor was.

"Why're you on the floor?" Smolar asked.

"I'm not." Rhugor's voice remained deep, but there was a hypnotic sense in his tone. Fravia found it tempting and alluring, while Smolar thought it was distrustful and devious.

Rhugor slowly walked out from the shadows, exposing his new form. Fravia stepped back, startled by his appearance while Smolar froze in place.

His once tall body was now stretched out horizontally as he stood on four legs. He was bigger, muscular. Thick, red-and-gold fur covered his body that looked silky smooth in the light. They admired his unique facial markings, but most intriguing were his large ears with long hair extending off the tips.

"What…what are you?" Smolar asked.

"A…golden lynx." Fravia looked closer. "Could it be?"

"What in Klai's name is a golden lynx?" Smolar asked.

"Is it dangerous? Am I…dangerous?"

"Well…it's a dangerous beast. Strangely enough, I heard of them from my parent's work. There was a drawing of one – looked very similar to you, Rhugor. They are fast, cunning and capable of destruction."

"I was fast and capable of destruction before. I didn't need to be turned into an animal for that."

"We're in a new world now. Maybe you're capable of more here as a lynx than a human."

"Human?" Smolar asked.

"That's what we look like. The majority of those in the Outer World are humans."

Considering her explanation, Rhugor decided to test out his capabilities. He darted off as fast as he could down the narrow cavern. Though he stumbled at first, there was no denying his increased speed on four legs. Returning to where his comrades stood, he noticed a large boulder beside them. With a strong kick from his two back legs, Rhugor catapulted it against the wall.

"Jeez…" Smolar was intimidated.

"Oh wow!" Fravia said with excitement. Smolar admired her overzealous reaction, wondering if he'd been too late to express his love for her. Turning around, heavily breathing, the two quorians jumped back in surprise.

"What is it?" Rhugor asked.

"Your eyes…" Fravia was hypnotized by their beauty. "They're golden!"

"Really?"

"Wait," Smolar urged. He and Fravia watched as they slowly returned to blue. Explaining what had happened, the group realized his eyes changed during his time of strength and haste.

"Well this is going to be fun." Rhugor grinned, exposing his razor-sharp teeth and large fangs.

After accepting their new looks, the three of them walked down the cavernous hall, poorly lit and full of repetitive rock formations. Seeing light in the distance, they all hurried.

"That must be it!" Smolar shouted.

"Let's go!" Rhugor yelled and took off with Fravia and Smolar trailing behind, unprepared for what was next.

Exiting the cavernous hall, they stood atop a sand dune, surrounded by dozens more in every direction. All three of them immediately felt the heat emanating from the desert world around them. The sky was a soft blue, reminding Fravia of her quorian roots.

The land of Diveria spanned as far as their eyes could see. Smolar wondered if it was the same destination his parents had taken so many years ago. He quickly shifted his focus and admired the sight for what it was. Though he'd explored the Outer World before, both times led him into a dark forest. He'd never experienced such a jarring sight, but it only further proved his passion for exploration.

"Which way do we go?" Rhugor asked, adjusting to his four legs on the plush sand.

"Hello?" A muffled frequency echoed in all their ears. "Can you hear me?" Lady Vixa asked, all three of them hearing her voice through their Pendants of Perception. Her skills had improved, but the quality was poor.

"Hello!" Fravia shouted.

"Yes, we made it!" Smolar replied.

"Did you purposely turn me into a golden lynx?" Rhugor asked, causing Fravia and Smolar to smirk.

"A what!?" Lady Vixa sounded just as surprised as they were. "Unfortunately, I didn't have enough time to perfect the enchantments. Your alternative appearances were meant to help assist you in your roles during the mission." Faint chuckling could be heard through the devices from everyone but Rhugor.

"Then I suppose I'm meant to tear Promit's capturers limb from limb," Rhugor said, followed by a ferocious roar.

"And yet, you could also come off as being our cuddly, innocent cat." Smolar enjoyed the subtle dig to his cohort.

"There ain't nothing innocent about this look."

"Okay." Fravia called them both to order. "Focus. Lady Vixa, which direction are we heading?"

"Observe your surroundings so we can evaluate."

Fravia wondered who she meant by *we*, but then realized it must have been her parents. They were the true guides and knew the land better than any other quorian.

Smolar panned around to let the Quorian Ruler see through his eyes.

"Many sand dunes," Rhugor said.

Fravia tried to make out anything in the horizon, but the sun was so bright. Her eyes had a difficult time adjusting to the light.

"Sand dunes," Lady Vixa repeated. "The city is south?" The group heard their ruler speaking to Fravia's parents.

"Behind us!" Smolar shouted and they all turned around. "It looks like a city, though we can't see much of the inside. Looks like it's open to the elements."

"That can't be The Barren Land…it must be…"

"Sartica," Lucemia interjected, confirming Fravia's assumption. As the three adventurers turned to admire the strange region, they were all stunned by its monstrous size. They all realized how small The Quo was by comparison.

"With Sartica in front of you, turn left to get to The Barren Land," Reagor informed the group. It brought Fravia great pride to hear both her parents providing essential insight.

"That'll gives us a general idea of the direction, thank you. How hard could it be to spot a large spherical dust storm around the perimeter of The Barren Land?" Smolar made a valid point and Fravia agreed.

"What is that in the distance?" Lady Vixa asked. Everyone looked around, but there was nothing.

"What do you mean?" Smolar asked.

"Up in the sky, off in the distance," she said.

"Is that…a large cloud?" Rhugor slowly walked in the corresponding direction to get a better look.

"Where?"

"I don't see anything."

"Yes, there's a large plume of smoke or a cloud. You two don't see anything?" They both shook their heads. Rhugor wondered if his vision, like his agility and strength, had improved.

"Yes!" Lucemia shouted. "We've speculated that could be another region. We don't have enough information on it yet."

"But…it's so high. Who could live up there?" Rhugor wondered.

"Maybe one day we'll find out," Lucemia said.

"For what it's worth, if you can see the floating cloud, then travel with it on your right. Stay along that path to eventually find The Barren Land," Reagor informed them.

"Sounds like we have a path," Smolar said. "We should get going."

"We'll check in with you all in a bit," Lady Vixa said. "But if you need anything, call to me. I'll remain connected, though inactive for communication until necessary."

"Be safe out there, honey!" Reagor shouted from his end. His words pierced Smolar like a dagger to the heart, a painful reminder that his parents might've said the same if given the chance. He was eager to get this mission going.

First, save Promit.

Second, find his parents.

Traversing through the sandy dunes seemed surreal to Fravia. Reading fables and stories was exciting, but physically experiencing a new world changed her perspective. Her passion for reading was strong, and though she'd never stop, she sensed a yearning to explore the unknown. She found it terrifying and exhilarating.

"Do you still see that floating plume, Rhugor?" Fravia asked, unable to visualize it herself.

"Yup, it's still up there. I wonder what it is."

"I wonder how far it is," Smolar added.

"It's just there…floating. If it's really as far as we're assuming, then it must be a large city. To see it from this far away. I—"

"STOP!" Fravia shouted. Smolar and Rhugor froze. "Look!" As the three of them stood atop a sand dune, she pointed down, noticing the movement in the sand. Though slow, it was notably rotating.

"Didn't your mom mention whirlpools in the sand?" Smolar recalled.

"It's best to avoid them," Fravia insisted.

The group carefully walked around the whirlpools, one after the other – increasing speed as they approached, slowing down as they walked away.

"They sense us," Fravia acknowledged.

"As if they're alive," Rhugor added.

With a curious mind, Smolar, who was slightly ahead of the pack, tossed a pebble from his pocket into the swirling sand. As it began its descent, they noticed a force from within the whirlpool pulling the object down into its center rapidly until it vanished.

Suddenly, all the surrounding whirlpools activated at full speed and the environment around them shifted. The air came to life as winds turned to gusts and the three quorians balanced to avoid danger.

"What's happening!?" Fravia shouted, covering her face.

"We have to get out of here!" Smolar grabbed her arm and shouted at Rhugor to follow. "Watch your step." Smolar surprised them all with his tactical ability to see between the whirlpools, dodging left and right. Their faces took a beating from the forceful grains of sand. Only Rhugor was protected by his fur coat.

Smolar managed to see freedom as they darted between the death traps.

The split-second distraction led him directly into the spiraling storm. He desperately tried to stop but failed. Fravia felt Smolar release his grip, causing her to squeeze tighter, preventing him from falling into the mysterious pit.

With the deafening gusts, Smolar and Fravia locked eyes and without words expressed their gratitude for one another. For the first time in a while, the two shared a sweet, loving moment, unfortunately tarnished by the surrounding danger.

Rhugor rushed toward them, reminding them of the urgency to keep moving. As they veered right, toward what appeared to be an opening between two whirlpools, the gap narrowed too much by the time they reached it.

"Did they just..." Smolar halted. The three of them stood still as the two neighboring whirlpools collided into one, the sound loud enough to make the ground shake.

"They're growing!" Rhugor shouted. Fearful, he sensed his eyes beginning to transition from quorian blue to a rich golden hue.

"Run!" Fravia yelled.

"Left!" Rhugor shouted. They all ran blindly in the direction, trusting him, but the opening quickly closed again. Fravia observed her surroundings. She considered the possibility that if they collided together, then maybe they'd separate too, but they had no such luck. Smolar remained still, unable to see a way out. The sound of the roaring whirlpools distracted them. Had it not been for their pendants, he wouldn't have been able to hear Fravia and Rhugor, let alone his own thoughts.

The pendants. Lady Vixa. He felt foolish for not thinking of it earlier. Smolar pressed the button on his Pendant of Perception.

"Lady Vixa! Are you there?" he shouted, glancing at his cohorts.

Rhugor pressed against him harder, struggling to find a way out of the mayhem. When Smolar noticed Fravia curled up, shivering in fright, he ran and wrapped his arms around her.

"We'll get out of this, Fravia." Smolar attempted to reassure her they'd be okay, though it looked grim.

"Lady Vixa!" Rhugor pleaded. They all had their backs to one another, Smolar's arm still around Fravia as they braced for impact.

"I'm sorry to have put us in this position. I shouldn't have…" Smolar stopped as he felt Fravia's hand on his thigh, reassuring him. Once again, he found himself riddled with guilt. His actions brought harm, or worse, and there was no way out.

"Smolar!?" A voice came over the Pendant. "Fravia. Rhugor. What's—" Lady Vixa shuddered and froze in horror at the sight around them.

"Lady Vixa!" Smolar shouted. "We're trapped in a maze of swirling sinkholes in the desert and—"

A force from behind knocked Fravia over. She moaned in agony as the jagged grains felt like daggers throughout her body.

"Smolar!" she shouted, but there was no response.

"Where did he go? Smolar!" Rhugor shouted, but still no answer. "They were right here. What could've—"

"What's happening!? Who was that?" Lady Vixa panicked, only visually connected to Smolar's Pendant of Perception.

"Who was who!?" Rhugor mustered the words out before he, too, vanished. Fravia felt his soft fur bristle against her body as he was taken away.

"Rhugor!" Facing the reality of death crippled her. It wasn't a fate she'd been prepared to face. Tears rolled from her eyes, but were swiftly blown away by the gusts.

"I'm sorry Promit…I love you, Mom. I love you, Dad." She paused for a moment, attempting one more time to look out in front of her, but it hurt her eyes too much. "I love you, Smolar."

"Hold onto your pendant and never let it go. We'll get you out of there," Lady Vixa insisted. Then in an instant, with her hands and knees buried in the sand, Fravia was pulled in one direction and she yelled a terrifying scream from the depths of her soul.

Within seconds, the gusts were gone, and the sand was calm – it was eerily silent. Fravia felt the warm sun beating down on her skin. She opened her tightly sealed eyelids, and gazed upon the figure beside her, stunned.

"Hello there." The voice was unknown to her, but soothing, nearly too relaxed after the chaos they'd just experienced. "You okay?"

"Fravia!" Smolar shouted from a distance, approaching her.

"Glad to see you made it," Rhugor said, his tail leisurely wagging, his eyes slowly returning blue.

Off in the distance, the roaring of the whirlpools were heard. Everyone glared at the deathly maze, watching as the rumbling relaxed and the circumference of the spirals shrunk. The three of them all knew that death had been imminent, but somehow a stranger had appeared to save their lives.

"You...saved us," Fravia whispered. The stranger beside her was extremely pale and uncomfortably thin, yet she appeared healthy, strong. Her long black hair was pulled back in a tight ponytail, revealing a gentle face with silver eyes.

"You're lucky I was nearby and saw you in time. All of you," the stranger added, glancing at Rhugor and Smolar. "What're you doing out here?" She offered Fravia a hand up as she admired the stranger's full suit of armor. Thin and durable, it exposed every minuscule curve of her body.

"We're degreants," Fravia lied. Smolar and Rhugor blindly nodded in agreement.

"Why're you so close to the regional border. You should know better than to take the risk," the stranger said. Fravia glanced over at her cohorts in need of help for an answer. Noticing a Pendant of Perception glistening in the sand, Smolar swiftly picked it up, put it on, and turned around with his head down, hoping to not let the stranger see the device.

"We're from the north and haven't explored the south much," Rhugor answered. "We were fascinated by the spiraling sands and before we knew it, we were trying to avoid death. Thank you for coming to our rescue...?"

"Sam. Just Sam." She exuded confidence and power.

"Thank you, Sam," Rhugor finished.

Fravia took a moment to admire her surroundings. From outside the perimeter of Sartica, they were able to see the open world of Diveria without any distractions. With only a couple individuals far off in the distance, they were alone. Unlike the confines of The Quo, the Outer World smelled clean and fresh. With a gentle breeze, she smelled the fragrant plants warmed by the sun.

The land was rich in wildlife and horticulture. A variety of colorful plants came out of the ground. She noticed that most of them had prickly spikes, but if she looked carefully, there were many colorful flowers too. Behind Sam, Fravia noticed quite a bit of movement. Small creatures of all sizes were scurrying around. Some tried to remain hidden, while others seemed to enjoy the sunlight. Four legs, two legs and even no legs, she couldn't believe the variety of animals cohabitating with one another.

The blazing heat from the sand beneath her feet jolted Fravia back to reality with a few burning questions.

"It's desolate here, no one's around. How'd you know we needed rescuing?" Fravia wondered.

"Good timing, I suppose. I was nearby when I heard the ruckus." Sam's voice was androgynous.

"How'd you manage to carry each of us, one at a time, effortlessly?" Though she appreciated being alive, Fravia's suspicion grew.

"I've experienced stickier situations in my time, so I know how to manage," Sam replied with a smile, sensing Fravia's curious tone. "How'd someone from northern Diveria end up on the perimeter of Sartica? Where are you headed?"

Fravia wasn't certain she wanted to reveal their destination and hesitated with her response.

"The Barren Land," Rhugor replied. Fravia darted him an angry glance. "Have you heard of it?"

"Of course…" Sam peered at them. "I've seen it a few times in my travels, though never dared to tackle the challenge of its protective barrier."

"The Lost Sphere," Smolar added, returning from his moment away from the others.

"Yes, precisely." Sam stood tall, examining the exhausted trio. Though she couldn't identify it, there was something about the group she found peculiar. She knew if they came from the north, they would've passed The Barren Land on their way to Sartica. Also if they were truly degrents, they'd know better than to wander the perimeter of a region. Regardless, Sam wasn't there to cause problems. She had enough turmoil that she didn't need to get involved with three strangers.

"Look!" Rhugor shouted. "That hefty cloud in the sky is larger than before." Smolar and Fravia looked in the direction Rhugor pointed.

"Well look at that…"

"I see it too," exclaimed Fravia.

"You're talking about Azjura?" Sam wondered.

"Azjura? That's the name of the cloud?" Fravia asked, hoping to remember it to inform her parents later.

Sam chuckled. "It's the name of an expansive, yet cruel, region." She glanced at it and winced. "I should be going. You all stay safe out here and good luck on…whatever it is you're trying to do." Sam gave them all one final, judgmental look. With the snap of her fingers, she vanished before their eyes.

"Whoa."

"Who in Klai's name was she!?" Smolar asked.

"Someone you'd prefer to befriend than have as an enemy," Fravia said, turning to Smolar. "Where'd you walk off to earlier?"

"Lady Vixa. She was still trying to communicate with us." Fravia and Rhugor had completely forgotten about their communication after being saved by Sam.

They both reached behind their ears and quickly realized why.

Their pendants were gone.

"Oh no," Rhugor said sounding worried.

"The winds from the sands must've blown them off," Fravia explained.

"Ahh, that makes sense. She wasn't able to view my surroundings anymore, so mine must've been destroyed. This one must be one of yours."

"Well thank Klai we still have one left after that fiasco. What did she say?" Fravia wondered.

"I told her what happened, the stranger who helped us, and that we're safe, considering. She was alone, and decided not to worry your parents," he informed Fravia.

"Brilliant."

The three of them took a moment to gather their bearings. To their surprise, no one had sustained any injuries.

"*That* was close." Smolar walked toward Fravia with a deep smile and appreciation for her safety.

"Too close," she added. "If Sam hadn't come to our rescue, I don't know what—"

"Best to not think about it," he interrupted. She agreed.

Smolar took a long look at his friend of five years, one of the strongest female quorians he'd known. Recently accepting the feelings he had for her, he was uncertain she still felt the same way, though Lady Vixa confirmed it. Smolar wasn't sure if it was their brush with death, her altered appearance, or both, but having the discussion with Fravia seemed easier now than ever before. He knew it was time.

"I had a revelation recently, and I've been unsure if I should tell you or not." Smolar sounded courageous, certain of his goal. "Well, I mean, I wanted to talk to you about it, but I didn't know how."

"Hm?"

"The other night when I spoke with Lady Vixa…She mentioned a bit of information that surprised me." While it was easier for him to address the topic, it was still as difficult to utter the words.

"Oh? What's that?" Fravia's eyebrows raised.

"Apparently a few years ago—"

"Jeez, Smolar. Just spit it out!" she shouted, smiling. Rhugor, who sat off in the distance, privately licking his paws, turned around at the commotion.

"I love you," he muttered. It was done. The words had been said. For the first time in Smolar's adult life, he had exposed a vulnerability. It took leaving The Quo, being near death, and a stranger named Sam, to help him gather the courage to utter those three little words. His face froze, nervous for her reaction.

"Oh, Smolar," she responded. Her cheeks turned a hint of red through her darker complexion, her smile gleaming from ear to ear. "For years I was scared and wondered if the feelings were true or not…" She grimaced at him. "But I was right."

Uncertain if it was her long-awaited anticipation or the exhilaration of what had just happened, Fravia leaped forward and tossed her arms around Smolar. The two embraced, long enough to make Rhugor uncomfortable, sighing as he turned around.

Afterwards, Smolar pulled back from her, gazing into her familiar eyes. They both chuckled, aware of the unfortunate timing of their metamorphic potions. His instinct was to kiss her. The timing would've been perfect. Unfortunately, it seemed strange to him for their first kiss to be with their altered appearance.

"It's funny," she said, giggling.

"What is?"

"I've had these feelings for years and when we finally have *the* discussion, our appearances are nothing as they should be."

"I know. I want to kiss you, but…" Smolar hesitated, and she clearly understood.

"Oh just do it already!" Rhugor shouted from afar, looking at the two, no longer fixated on his paws. "There will be plenty of time to kiss as your regular selves."

It was the push they needed. The two looked at each other as their heads leaned forward and they shared their first, long-overdue kiss.

All the angst and bickering the two recently had floated away as the excitement and happiness ignited between them. Fravia was intoxicated to finally have what she hadn't thought was possible, while Smolar was relieved to successfully admit his truth.

Though it didn't last nearly as long as their embrace, Rhugor felt inclined to remind them of their mission.

"We should get going. The sooner we complete the mission, the sooner we can go home and lose these awful appearances." He looked around, confirmed their direction, and began to walk.

Gazing into each other's eyes, Smolar and Fravia smiled as they embraced hands, walking behind Rhugor toward their destination – The Barren Land.

32

"I see an Osvita Dimmerk and Nigel Hatherton, but I don't see anyone by the name of…Victor Surazal," the guard at the castle drawbridge mentioned.

"You'd better check again," Lazarus mumbled from the back seat, agitated.

"Sir, can you please call your supervisor to clear us. We're catering the event tonight and must start the preparations." Nigel spoke in a gentle, polite tone, which the guard appreciated.

"The banquet dinner!? Why didn't you say so," he said joyfully, grabbing the telephone.

"Well *he* seemed chipper about the event," Nigel whispered.

"Chances are he'll be attending," Lazarus suggested. "A majority of the guest list is comprised of staff members and their families."

"Alright, all clear," the guard announced. "Just head down, stay right, and follow the path to the garage. Shrenka will be waiting for you."

"Thank you very much, sir." Nigel nodded. Sealing his window shut, Lazarus let out a long sigh. "Everything alright back there?"

"Yes," Lazarus said in a worrisome tone. Nigel glanced over at Osvita, who sat nervously quiet as they entered the belly of the beast. "It's just…Shrenka."

"She's Brugōr's companion, right? What about her?" he asked, but before

Lazarus could respond, Nigel asked Osvita if she was okay.

"I'm fine," she said softly. "Just a bit nervous being here, you know?"

"Don't worry, we were pardoned," Nigel reassured. Their eyes met for just a few seconds. "I won't let anything happen to you. This is just another ordinary job. We prepare, serve, and leave." Whether it was his words or his smile, Osvita's nerves settled just enough to ease her breathing.

"Thank you," she replied.

Lazarus stared at them both, observing the notable chemistry. Nigel wanted to inquire about Shrenka, but didn't want to ignite Osvita's nerves.

"There's nothing we should be concerned about with Shrenka, right?" Nigel asked Lazarus with a peculiar look in his eye.

"No. I'm sure Shrenka has enough preoccupying her mind that she won't be too concerned with *the help*," Lazarus said sarcastically. "But we should keep the conversation to a minimum. Avoid small talk, the pardon, dinner details, and such."

"That's smart," Nigel agreed.

The silence was deafening inside the vehicle as they slowly followed the bend through the castle grounds. The only noise was the crackling of the gravel beneath them. Behind the wall seemed like its own city, even though it wasn't large enough to sustain an entire civilization. With such narrow paths, Nigel drove cautiously so as not to hit the occasional guard or random structure.

"You can feel the heat from the buildings," Osvita said. Nigel turned the air conditioning higher. As an influx of people walked nearby, a few gazed inside the vehicle, making eye contact with Nigel and Osvita. Lazarus did his best to mask his face.

After a small bend to the left, the three of them gasped in unison when they arrived at Brugōr's home – the Kurhal. Though they'd seen it from afar, the view up close was unlike anything they'd seen before. The tower was taller, more intimidating. Glistening in the sun, the reflection from the iron made it difficult to stare at from certain vantage points and it was impossible to see the top.

"Now *that* is a tower," Nigel said, staring up in astonishment.

"Just imagine if it were to fall over one day." Lazarus chuckled at the thought.

"Why would you say that now of all times?"

"Thankfully I'm not afraid of heights," Osvita said, shrugging.

"Well I am," Nigel revealed.

"What?" Osvita turned her head sharply.

"Are you kidding me, Nigel? You didn't feel it important to mention this earlier?" Lazarus snapped. "You knew what this mission entailed."

"It's fine. We'll be inside the building and I won't be looking out any windows," Nigel said, mostly to convince himself.

"Ignore the tower," Osvita suggested. "Look at the base. It's…glorious. It's the first splash of color I've seen since we've entered."

Surrounding the entire base of the tower was a garden filled with lavish roses of every color and an aroma that permeated the vehicle. The flowers spanned out approximately fifty feet from the tower with the only opening being made for the main entrance.

To the left of the tower, they noticed a seductive woman with blonde hair wearing an exotic dress that barely contained her voluptuous breasts. She informed them where to park. As they slowly passed by the garden, a minor detail caught Nigel's eye.

"Wait…what's that?" he slowed down further, pointing at the roses. Both Lazarus and Osvita gazed in the direction.

"Are those…?"

"Thorns," Lazarus confirmed.

"Thorns!? They're spikes. They're as large as us," Nigel exclaimed.

"It's the prettiest death trap in the valley," Lazarus added. "Look alive. Show's about to begin."

As they pulled into the parking zone, Shrenka's clear unwillingness to smile set the tone for their arrival.

"Good day." Nigel smiled and stepped out of the vehicle.

"Hello," Shrenka said in her shrill tone. "Right on time. I like punctuality."

"We try to stay on schedule," Osvita said, exiting the car. "Hello, I'm—"

"Osvita, I presume." Shrenka nodded. "Always nice to see another woman in charge."

Lazarus murmured a quick hello as Shrenka observed him exiting the car.

"No need to carry anything. The guards will bring all your belongings up to the kitchen for you," Shrenka said, motioning to Lazarus.

"Very generous," he remarked, rummaging through the trunk of the car. "Just a few fragile items I'd like to carry myself." He tossed the objects into a backpack and closed the trunk. Lazarus focused his gaze on his surroundings instead of Shrenka, avoiding eye contact.

"There's plenty to do today, so I don't have much time. Follow me and I'll personally escort you to the banquet hall kitchen."

Osvita and Nigel were astonished when they entered the Kurhal. The space was vast as murmurs echoed off the cinderblock walls.

"Thank you for hiring us for the event," Osvita said.

"You've become well-renowned within the valley," Shrenka said without stopping or turning around. "It'll be a memorable night, and Brugōr expects nothing but the best."

"Of course," Osvita replied. Though she sensed the pressure, it brought her joy to know she'd been known within the regime, regardless of her opinion of them.

Lazarus continued to hide his face from onlookers as they walked to the northern wall and entered the elevator. When he separated himself in the back corner, Shrenka darted him a curious look until Nigel distracted her.

"So what's the dinner for?" he asked.

She stared at the elevator doors and answered. "It's a celebratory event to honor the success of an important mission. A…revelation of sorts. It'll be quite a show."

"A revelation?" Osvita recalled the job offer, which had been followed by the unexpected arrival that led to her husband's manhunt. She thought about Whark, wondered where he was and if he'd tried to find them or was simply waiting for them to find him. She remembered how startled he was to have seen the captured quorian. Though she knew the dinner and the quorians were probably linked, hearing Shrenka's explanation confirmed her fears. Osvita reminded herself it was just another job and to stay focused, hoping she wouldn't have to witness what Whark had.

When they entered the banquet hall, Nigel's stomach sank, nearly stumbling over his own feet. Osvita caught him.

"You okay?" she whispered. Shrenka continued walking as she explained the space.

"The windows…" He shuddered. "I'll be fine," he whispered.

"Keep your head down," Osvita suggested. They scurried behind Shrenka, not to disrupt the flow. Unfortunately, the door to the kitchen was along the back wall of windows, proving difficult for Nigel to approach.

"And here's the kitchen. Your space for the evening," Shrenka said with delight. When the door opened, they saw the floor to ceiling windows from the dining room continued into the kitchen. When Nigel entered, he turned left, placing his back against the entire valley. Osvita tried to downplay his noticeable fear. She was mesmerized by the ornate and elaborate decor of the appliances and equipment. Vaguely familiar with a kitchen setting, Lazarus acted his way through the moment, seemingly interested in the most simplistic tools.

"This kitchen is stunning. Beautifully designed and organized," Osvita remarked. Focusing on her culinary craft eased her nerves.

There was minimal black inside the kitchen, unlike everywhere else she'd seen on the castle grounds. All the countertops were white quartzite, with specs of glistening minerals embedded into it, showcased by the sunlight. All the cabinets were a pristine white, as were the appliances, but any knobs, buttons and accessories had vibrant colors that popped nicely. There were two long and wide islands housing numerous ranges, ovens, washing stations and food preparation areas.

"It's very nice, but it's so bright with all the windows and white everything." Nigel held back indigestion at the thought of their height.

Shrenka darted him a look, but ignored the comment. "They should be up with your stuff soon. Guests will begin arriving in a few hours. I left the itinerary on the counter there." She pointed near Osvita. "Just make sure to stay on schedule," she said through her gritted smile. It was the first time they'd seen any attempt at happiness on the woman's face. "Good luck."

With those final words, Shrenka exited the kitchen. After thirty seconds of quiet observation, Lazarus peered through the door and into the empty dining hall.

"Okay, now's my time," he said.

"*Now?*" Nigel wondered. "She just left. You don't want to get caught."

"The fewer people who see me the better. Once countless guards arrive with your belongings, it'll be difficult to swim under the radar or prove I was ever here to begin with." Both Nigel and Osvita agreed. "I placed a few random items in the backpack I found from the car. No idea what they were though. I'm going to quickly change and get to work," he said, removing clothes from the bag.

With Osvita and Nigel toward the entryway of the kitchen, Lazarus immediately began to disrobe without warning. It seemed his shirt melted off his body to expose his muscular pecs and intricately contoured abdominal muscles. The hair on his chest was much less than that on his chin, but the silver color glistened in the sunlight. Even though Nigel wasn't looking, he instinctually turned around when he realized Lazarus was removing his pants. His eyes met the windows, and even worse, the distance beyond. Nigel lunged over, fighting the urge to be sick from fear. For just a moment, Osvita was mesmerized by Lazarus, who was blissfully unaware and focused on the task. Her concentration broke to tend to Nigel.

"You really gotta get ahold of that my friend," Lazarus said, sliding his pants on as the belt buckle clanged.

"I'll be fine," Nigel muttered after a deep inhale. "I just…I just need to face my fear, get over it, and move forward." He stood up and slowly walked toward the windows with his head down. "I'll look out, admire the beautiful view, and acknowledge our safety from his kitchen. Then I'll get to work." Nigel slowly raised his head and looked out to the valley. They were high enough that he could see the upper level of The Barren Land and The Lost Sphere.

Osvita and Lazarus both watched him tackle his fear, seemingly with ease. They exchanged glances, impressed by his courage and eagerness to overcome it. It was in that moment that Lazarus understood just how much Nigel was willing to sacrifice to ensure Osvita's safety. He was impressed.

"Alright," Nigel said. "I don't love it, and it puts a pit in my stomach," he said, turning around, "but I think I'll be alright." He attempted a wide smile and walked away from the windows. Lazarus wondered if Nigel forgot about what members of the Anti-Regime were going to do later on, but didn't wish to remind him and ruin his courageous moment.

"Good," Lazarus remarked. "Now I must head off. Good luck, you two. Just do what you do best and it'll be over before we know it." He scurried toward the door and vanished, leaving Osvita and Nigel alone to tend to their work.

The two sorted through the space, organizing what they could. Sifting through containers, utensils, spices, herbs, and miscellaneous devices, Osvita and Nigel were pleasantly surprised with what was available to them. Eventually, numerous guards entered the kitchen to deliver all their belongings. Platters filled with cured meats, pastries ready to be baked, and a couple large vats of soup were just some of what they'd brought with them.

Soon enough, the room was empty again, leaving Nigel and Osvita alone.

"It's showtime," Nigel said with a smile. "Let's shine."

33

Osvita and Nigel had been hard at work for hours preparing the courses to be dispersed. While it was an unusual circumstance, Osvita found solace in her culinary skills. She was pleasantly surprised no one had mentioned her husband and the manhunt throughout the valley. Regardless, she didn't falter and remained focused on the task at hand with Nigel by her side.

Like clockwork, guards dressed in butler and maid attire arrived five minutes before the first scheduled course at 6:00pm. Impressed with their impeccable timing, Osvita explained the first round of appetizers as each of the servers grabbed a tray and napkins for guests to enjoy. As they walked away, she felt the familiar sensation of nerves in her throat. Though confident with the menu and execution of their food, the first course always made her the most nervous. There was only one chance to make a good first impression.

"They're going to love it," Nigel said, aware of her concern.

"I hope so."

"They always do." The two shared a smile. Nigel reminisced of the kiss they'd shared in his home. Though tempted to experience it again, he considered it'd be in poor taste. "First course down, just five more to go!"

With a chuckle, Osvita turned around as she made her final preparations to their

Jinto Nut and Citrus Salad, while Nigel finalized the Goat Pepper Soup. As he managed his crippling fear of heights, she sensed and appreciated his nurturing demeanor. He said her safety was his priority and it was alluring to her for Nigel to execute his promise. She glanced at him, focused on the soup, wondering what it'd be like if they could kiss without hassle. Osvita momentarily contemplated a life with him by her side.

Out in the banquet hall, servers passed around hors d'oeuvres as guests began to enter. Though over one-hundred-and-fifty men and women were expected to arrive, the dinner was a private event. The guest list only consisted of workers from within the castle. From personal guards to the cleaning crew; engineers to chefs.

As the men and women entered the room, decadently dressed in their best attire, they hadn't been officially told of the purpose for the gathering. The simple invitation stated there'd be a 'grand party' in celebration of an official announcement. There were whispers and assumptions, but no official word from the regime. Some wondered if it was a wedding announcement between Brugōr and Shrenka, others jumped to the conclusion of a baby. There were a few, however, who heard of the slight mishap of a quorian captive. Regardless of the rumors, there were two guests who knew the reason – Mortimer and Vanilor.

The two hadn't spoken to one another since Vanilor fled and spent the night at Mortimer's home. They parted with a quiet understanding that they'd arrive at the banquet separately. The guilt and shame of what had happened haunted Mortimer so much he no longer wanted to associate with him. He also knew arriving with his ex-partner provided a potential risk for the plan. Excited to see the regime literally and figuratively crumble, there was one resolution within the region Mortimer needed to handle himself – saving the quorian. Once he corrected his wrongful acts, he'd escape the sphere of The Barren Land and head to Tillerack for his final redemption.

Vanilor, on the other hand, yearned for the inner-most, powerful circle. Thriving at the success of others fueled his greed. Even with the newly accumulated wealth, he felt there was more to acquire. Unlike Mortimer, Vanilor wanted the attention and praise in front of others. Uncertain of what he'd do after the banquet, he subconsciously knew he wouldn't return home. Regardless of the hefty reward, he justified his neglect. Unfortunately, the tarnished gift of abandonment leaves a scar on the souls who receive it.

The hall began filling with guests who devoured the initial round of finger foods and cocktails. The sounds of laughter and chatter were heard throughout the entire floor of the Kurhal. Worried he was late to the party, Vanilor feverishly walked into the dining hall. To his relief, he realized it had only just begun, replenishing his excitement. With a sense of entitlement, he snatched a drink off one platter, grabbed food from another, and began conversing with others in the room. With his knowledge of Brugōr's regime and concern for his image, Vanilor spoke only to higher ranking individuals.

Servers returned to the kitchen to replenish their trays while others headed to the bar for a new round of drinks. Osvita and Nigel eagerly handed them freshly-prepared platters to disperse. She asked each server the consensus about the food, and not one bad remark was made. Everyone loved the flavors, especially in combination with Brugōr Brew, the specialty drink cleverly created by Osvita. It was a simple drink consisting of a red ale, chopped prickly pear, and a splash of sparkling wine.

As the second and third platters made their rounds, Shrenka entered the room to a gracious welcome. She surprised everyone in her elegant, crimson dress. The bodice was tight, cinched at the waist, her arms covered in a red lace, while her lower legs were exposed with a small train. Though her ruby-studded shoes shined bright enough to damage the retina, it was her minimally covered cleavage that attracted the eye. Her breasts were squeezed so tight that they'd graze her chin if she looked down. She became the eye candy for almost everyone at the party.

Those who weren't smitten by her were aggressively jealous. Her look was topped off with the tips of two spikes from the Kurhal's rose garden, both intricately placed in her hair.

Shortly after Shrenka arrived, Mortimer quietly crept in beside a group of people. Compared to others, his appearance was lackluster. He was tidy and well-kept, yet had no desire to formally dress for the occasion. Where most of the room gathered in smaller groups of familiar faces, Mortimer headed directly to the bar and ordered a whiskey neat. He found an empty table near the kitchen door and room height windows, mesmerized enough by the overlook of the valley to distract from the hatred of everyone in the room and the chaos that was to come.

By the time Brugōr made his presence known, most of the guests were a couple drinks in with the first course of food nearly finished. There was no formal introduction when he arrived. The room slowly noticed he'd entered, spreading like wildfire. Guests all lowered their drinks, overzealously smiled from the booze, and then clapped to praise their fearless leader. Among those were Vanilor and Shrenka, both of whom stood and clapped proudly. Brugōr made eye contact with them both and nodded. Remaining seated in the corner was Mortimer. Seemingly oblivious to his surroundings, he paid careful attention to every detail his ear detected. He figured Brugōr would be too distracted by the praise to notice his ignorance.

As he sat down at the table reserved for himself and Shrenka, Brugōr contemplated his plan for the evening. He wanted to use the event to celebrate the success of his top-secret mission. Not only did he hope to display the existence of the quorian race, he wished to maintain the control of their growth.

Aware of King Klai and their history, Brugōr wished to show them a *safe* space for growth and enlightenment, hoping to be considered a hero amongst the race, placing him in a controlling position. He found power over an entire race more desirable than having authority in one region.

Osvita and Nigel glanced at one another when they heard a roar, aware that Brugōr had arrived. She looked down at the itinerary and noticed it was time for the second course – the Jinto Nut and Citrus Salad. The familiar pool of servers readily appeared. While Nigel explained the intricacies of the meal, Osvita prepared to serve the third course, knowing guests typically consumed the salads quickly or ignored them entirely.

As their works of art were carried into the banquet for consumption, Osvita was pleasantly surprised by how peaceful the evening had been. They'd managed to stay on schedule and the guests enjoyed their masterpieces. Unfortunately, she also knew there was a shift looming, waiting to ravage the night. She tried her best to stay focused, because anything outside of the kitchen was out of her control, nor was it her responsibility.

On the other side of the wall, Vanilor was shocked to see Mortimer alone. He hadn't seen him come in, nor did he say hello. He knew they'd become distant, but was hurt by the disrespect. Vanilor felt as though Mortimer wanted nothing to do with him or what they'd done.

Why come at all? he thought.

As he teetered at the idea of approaching him, Mortimer turned his head and looked directly at Vanilor, locking eyes. The two momentarily ignored their surroundings until Mortimer plastered on a crooked smile and raised his glass. Hurt and disappointed, Vanilor scowled. He raised his glass too, just before turning back toward the crowd he'd surrounded himself with. Unfazed by Vanilor's reaction, he looked back out over the valley.

I'm sure going to miss this view.

"Ahem." The microphone echoed throughout the room. "Hello." A high-pitched tone reverberated. Everyone shuddered, covering their ears. "Fuck!" Brugōr shouted. "Can someone fix this piece of shit?" One of the guards jumped up and ran toward the speaker. After a slight adjustment, he nodded at their leader to try again.

"Hello." Brugōr halted. "Alright. Seems as though we've sorted out the feedback." He proudly stood up straighter to recite his speech. "Today is an evening to be remembered. I've invited my most loyal and trustworthy staff to this celebratory dinner for a special announcement."

The entire room was still, everyone eager to hear what had been so important for their leader to host such a luxurious event, especially with all the rumors going around. Though slightly muffled, Nigel and Osvita heard his speech through the wall as they continued their prep.

"As the leader of The Barren Land, it's my responsibility to ensure the safety of our community and our valley. We're fortunate to have people from all over Diveria here, helping to bring together various cultures and diversities."

Many guests darted confused looks at his words. He'd never welcomed newcomers to share their experiences. They knew he'd insisted upon everyone forgetting their old lives and starting new within The Barren Land.

"In an effort to maintain a safe and stable environment, we regularly monitor the surrounding regions for foreign threats. Over the years, we've encountered numerous IOIs, individuals of interest. Some creatures, some people." Brugōr paused, taking a sip from his self-named brew. "Most recently, however, we stumbled across a unique find. Something no one anticipated. Unlike most circumstances, we knew of this particular find, but history told us it was impossible."

Brugōr motioned toward a guard near the door who nodded and walked out of the room.

As Brugōr continued his speech, Osvita listened to every word, her heart fluttering in anticipation. It was no secret to her what Brugōr was referring to, and she sensed he was about to reveal it to the room. Her stress and anxiety built, knowing the existence of the quorian race was meant to remain a secret.

"Everything alright, Vita?" Nigel asked.

"Ye-yeah…" She hesitated. Not only did she fear the reveal of the quorian existence, but she grew concerned for their safety, specifically the one they'd captured. Her old life, a world she'd buried for years, was suddenly being unraveled, and she had no means by which to stop it. There was much she wanted to do, yet the only action she could safely take was to continue cooking. It was the first time she loathed being in the kitchen.

With all her patience, Osvita forced herself to continue the task at hand, clinging on to Brugōr's every word. As servers re-entered the kitchen to hand out the third course of Goat Pepper Soup, she froze, focused on her ravaged mind.

"Vita?" Nigel asked. "Osvita? Ready to serve the goat soups?"

"Yes." She looked at the servers. "Bring those out to the guests. When you return, I'll give you Brugōr's and Shrenka's portions."

"But its customary to serve them first," a server replied.

"This is a delicacy from my home, outside of the valley. They deserve a perfected portion with an opulent topping. I just need a few more minutes to execute it." The servers darted looks at one another, hesitant to deliver food to others before the head table. "Go on," Osvita insisted and they followed.

"What're you talking about?" Nigel asked when they left. He knew she was lying, especially since she'd told him the valley was the only place she considered home.

"It's important to make an impression. Their dishes need to be perfect."

Nigel sighed and continued his preparations as she took the two bowls to the back of the kitchen. When he wasn't looking, Osvita grabbed the pouch of glimboberries. She initially wanted to unload them all into both soups, but Shrenka's words brought up hesitation.

Always nice to see another woman in charge.

Osvita wondered if she was as rude and cruel as Brugōr, or if she was under his command. She decided to give her the benefit of the doubt and poured just half the pouch into one soup. Though she wasn't privy to the agenda, Osvita contemplated if her actions would hinder anything they'd planned. She decided the sedative effect of the glimboberries could only help. Not only could it stop him from revealing too much, but it could make the job of the Anti-Regime easier.

Hiding the remaining glimboberries, she returned to Nigel just in time for the servers to return.

"I hope you have Brugōr's portion. He didn't say anything, but he looked furious."

"His majesty's bowl is ready. *This* one belongs to him, and this to Shrenka. With a beautiful figure such as hers, I doubt she will consume as much," she said, explaining the discrepancy in the amounts.

As the final portions of the third course were dispersed, Nigel and Osvita began preparation for the fourth course, a pasta dish. Knowing they had extra time between courses, he checked on the sauce while she peered through the door. Focused on the server at the head table, she watched as he correctly placed the larger portion at his seat and the smaller at hers.

"What're you doing?" Nigel asked.

"Nothing." She pulled away, closing the door. "Just wanted to get a glimpse behind the curtain." She smiled, content with her participation. They worked in silence while listening to Brugōr explain the commonly accepted version of the Age of Kings.

"No matter your origin, we all know the history of the Divinity King," Brugōr said sternly as guests wondered why they were having a history lesson. Osvita walked toward the kitchen door, carefully listening to every word. She knew what *others* considered to be true history, but for some reason, hearing Brugōr announce it to a filled room infuriated her. She felt her heartbeat in her throat.

"It was because of his strength and valor that we're all here today, living in the incredible land we now call Diveria," Brugōr proclaimed. Osvita hoped for him to gluttonously eat the soup, welcoming the glimboberries into his system.

"Vita?" Nigel asked, but she didn't respond, captivated by Brugōr's speech. She peered through the door once more.

"It's widely known and accepted that those quorian creatures, along with King Klai, were expunged during the War of Kings." Brugōr smiled at the faces around him. The guard he motioned toward earlier re-entered the room, wheeling in a large, solid metal container. He wheeled it all the way through the room toward Brugōr. Everyone's attention went from their leader to the delivery.

"What's inside?"

"Was there a historical find?"

"Is this part of his presentation?"

Eventually the guard stopped and stepped aside, allowing Brugōr to approach.

"Today is a day that you will all remember. A day that will astound you and, eventually, all of Diveria. A day that will change history." Brugōr placed his hand flat atop the cage.

Enthralled by his speech, Osvita couldn't look away as Nigel snuck up behind her to watch.

"We recently launched a mission and sent two brave recruits outside the safety of our valley. They traveled very far, to an undisclosed location, in hopes of finding one of these quorian creatures," he said, grinning. "Thanks to the skill and tactfulness of Vanilor Dipythian and Mortimer Hullington, it is with great honor and prestige I welcome you to gaze upon the first ever seen quorian creature!"

"Mortimer!?" Osvita whispered, startling Nigel as he recalled meeting a man of the same name at the last meeting.

With the press of a button, pieces of the solid container seemingly melted away and transformed into a barred cage, revealing the quorian within. There was a unified gasp in horror and fright as everyone laid their eyes upon the first quorian to ever be seen since the Age of Kings.

"What is that thing?"

"It looks like a savage beast."

"Please, Divinity, protect us."

Inside the cage, the ravenous quorian violently shook and howled. His eyes were red, hair partially gone and his once perfect sapphire blue pigment was blotchy with white spots. He seemed enraged and ready to kill. All of the guests watched in horror – some jumped out of their seats.

Vanilor looked at him, first in shock, then adoration. He barely recognized the creature from when they first captured him in Tillerack. No longer was he tame and timid.

Across the other side of the room, Mortimer kept his head down in shame. In that moment, he regretted being in the banquet hall. He wanted nothing to do with Brugōr or his regime. Capturing the quorian was one of the four wrongs he wanted to correct, but now, in his opinion, he was publicly shamed for committing the awful act. It took every ounce of effort to not get up and walk out. He reminded himself of the bigger plan and what needed to happen.

Osvita instinctively leapt forward, but Nigel stopped her. No matter how hard she tried to break free, it was no match for his strength. Then, for just a moment, she locked eyes with the prisoner and time stood still. As she remained motionless, the quorian's anger subsided. Lasting only a few seconds, he turned his head and became enraged within the confines of his cage again. Though their shared moment had been brief, the entire room witnessed it. Osvita went from being the invisible cook to a quorian whisperer.

The quorian's anger jolted the room out of their trance, regaining their focus, but Brugōr's eyes were still on her. As she lowered her gaze, Nigel pulled her back into the kitchen for safety.

With his back to the kitchen door and his disconnect from the room, Mortimer was delayed in the shared moment. When he realized something had happened, he turned around but only saw the sway of the door closing.

"What the hell was that!?" Nigel whispered.

"I can't believe…they captured…" Osvita's mind raced, surprised by the quorian's condition. Whark had informed her of his weak, neglected disposition, but not the rage.

"What the hell was that!?" Nigel repeated.

"He's just a poor—"

"No, not him. I feel terrible for him, but you…him. There was a moment there. It was like…it seemed like he recognized you."

"I—" Osvita paused. She was stunned he showed sympathy, but she didn't know how to answer his question. She'd felt it, that shared connection with the prisoner. The only explanation she could imagine was that the quorian saw through her facade. Osvita pondered if she should come clean to Nigel and admit her truth.

"I—" she stuttered. Brugōr had begun shouting, but she stopped listening to the words. It'd become a distraction. Nigel knew Osvita well enough to know she was hiding something, but also knew they were in a dangerous situation.

"Didn't Brugōr say the name Mortimer earlier?" he asked, changing the subject.

"Yes… that conniving little…What is he doing? Just what is he trying to pull?" she wondered.

"Did you see him?"

"No…" She tried to think. "Why commit such a heinous act for the regime and then join the Anti-Regime? Is he a spy? Is the entire plan compromised?"

"I…I don't know. Maybe it's another Mortimer?"

Suddenly, the kitchen door swung open and both Nigel and Osvita jumped in fright.

"Excuse me," a server said.

"Y-yes…?" Osvita replied.

"I've been given strict orders from Brugōr that he'd like to skip the next two dishes and jump ahead to the second to last course." The server placed the two half-eaten bowls of Goat Pepper Soup on the table. Osvita eyed Brugōr's bowl and noticed some glimboberries remained. She wondered if he'd consumed enough.

"Of course," Nigel answered, nudging Osvita. "You can tell him it will just be some time."

"Actually, you both can. He requested your presence at the table."

34

Confined to the icy, steel cage, Promit was enraged by his surrounding world. Whether it was his frustration with Smolar, his disappointment in himself, or the anger he had toward the race tormenting him, he considered it poetic that only one human knew his name. He was no longer Promit, the shy and timid quorian. He'd been changed, uncertain of who he'd become.

When he was first captured by the two men, Promit's world was transformed from a massive, deciduous forest to a small box of a room. All walls, including the ceiling and floor, were padded with a bright yellow material. With no idea what had happened, Promit was alone, scared, and struggling to maintain his sanity.

In what seemed like an eternity, he was forcibly removed from the psychotic confinement. Surrounded by three humans, Promit identified the two men as the assailants who captured him. Observing his body, he noticed his cachectic figure plus the shackles around his wrists and ankles.

Out of nowhere, one of his original captors had launched over him and tossed his body toward the door. There was chaotic shouting and angst, but Promit remained still in terror. Uncertain where he was or what was happening, all he envisioned was home. He missed his family, no matter how unloving or rude his father might've been.

After tensions eased, Promit observed those standing above him. He learned the woman had more control than the two men. While the shorter man and she continued their words, Promit made eye contact with the other man multiple times. He didn't know why, but the same man who aided in his capture was filled with sorrow. Promit sensed it in his eyes – it was palpable.

With one swift kick, the shorter man heaved his foot directly into Promit's stomach. The pain seared throughout his body as he curled into a tight ball, trembling in fear and agony.

"I hope Brugōr tortures the fucker. Let's go, Morty." Vanilor stormed off, unfazed by his actions. Promit turned his head, ambivalently, and made eye contact with Mortimer again.

I'm sorry, Mortimer silently mouthed, following Vanilor out of the room. Promit was alone and afraid with the woman – Shrenka.

"Well, well...a quorian. I can't believe it." Her voice was shrill and cold. Promit remained on the ground, chained and in pain. "Don't act a fool, now. Your race is quite...enlightened. I know you understand me, so let's save us both some time." She paused, looking out a window. "And torment, hm?" She turned toward him. "What do you say?" Promit had never seen a scarier smile plastered on a face before.

"I..." he mustered.

"Yes?"

"I...where am I?" he asked. Shrenka chuckled.

"No, no, dear. That's not how this works." She paced the room with her hands behind her back and her head held high. "You see, you are what we call a peasant. Our feeble detainee. I ask you the questions and you answer them. Follow the rules, I spare you from torture. Remain silent, prepare for mental and physical misery. Lie to me, and I will find others like you and kill them all."

Promit instantly learned there was nothing kind or understanding about the woman. He wondered if he'd been safer with the two men.

"What is your name?" she asked.

Terrified of her initial warning, Promit answered with the truth. "P-P-P-Promit…"

"Good, good, Promit. What a unique name." She grimaced. "Are you really part of the quorian race?"

"Yes."

"Do you know what that means?" she asked, and he shook his head. "Do you know of the history of your race?"

"Yes…Do you?" Promit asked, shrieking as she approached him.

"Obviously, you know your tone was a mistake. I'll let that slide…but only once. Don't test me," she hissed. "Do you know of the implication for your existence? Do you understand what that means?" Shrenka smiled.

"No…"

"You're living proof that the one and only Divinity King is a deceitful liar. His claims of historic victory would crumble at the sight of your existence." Shrenka's face flushed red with excitement, confident she'd manage the situation better than Brugōr could.

It wasn't until that moment Promit realized the importance of his presence in their world. It brought him a sense of safety as others clearly wanted him alive.

Before Shrenka could ask another question, there was a knock on the door. In a frantic rush, she grabbed the Novalis Rod and summoned him back into his concealed space.

Time ceased to exist in the padded room – it felt uncomfortable, eerie. After his first release, Promit had no idea how long he was in there. He would've believed anything he was told, frightened by his dependency. The second release was awfully familiar with the same three faces, plus one, intimidating addition.

The first time Promit laid eyes on Brugōr, he knew to tread lightly. He knew that the brute could abolish anyone in his way with minimal effort.

"I can't believe my eyes," Brugōr said. His deep, menacing voice was etched into Promit's memory.

"We have no form of communication with it," Shrenka revealed. Sprawled on the floor, terrified, Promit couldn't fathom why she'd lie. As they continued their discussion, he tried to make eye contact with her but she refused. Recognizing the man with the sorrowful eyes, he glanced at him, but his attention was elsewhere.

Promit noticed another new face join the group. The lackluster man who stood before them was not as daunting as Brugōr, to which he was grateful. His presence was shortly lived due to his ghastly murder. Promit shuddered, fighting back the frightful scream he wanted so desperately to let out. The man's neck had been sliced open. Through the horror and shock, Promit noticed the color of their blood was red, strikingly different from their white blood.

"If there's any more disloyalty or dishonesty from you three, your fate will be worse than his," Brugōr proudly proclaimed, plastering the same evil smile Shrenka made the last time he saw her.

The death of the unnamed stranger jolted a reality check for Promit. His concern quickly escalated, recognizing the irrational and erratic behavior. Promit turned to see Brugōr pick up the Novalis Rod and summon him back into his timeless realm.

Upon his third chance at freedom, Promit found himself alone in a room with just the brute himself.

"Do you understand me? Does any of what I say make sense?" Brugōr asked.

Promit refused to give the murderer the satisfaction. He sensed it'd be smarter to keep him pleased, but he'd also learned there was a huge advantage in tricking those around him. Unless mentioned, he pretended Brugōr had no knowledge of his communication with Shrenka.

"Don't make me regret this…" he warned, before kneeling to remove the quorian's constraints on his wrists and ankles. He knew it was risky, but Brugōr hoped it would build trust. Unshackled and partially free, Promit remained on the ground, weak and berated from his host. He continued for about an hour, asking a plethora of questions.

"Are there others like you? Where are they?"

"Tell me where you came from."

"Do you have friends? Family?"

Promit stood his ground and remained silent. Still, Brugōr's curiosity lingered. He had an unsettling notion that the quorian understood him, but chose not to answer. It was time to up the ante.

"I know you didn't travel to Tillerack alone," Brugōr said. He immediately noticed the quorian react with a head turn, stopping midway through to hide, but it failed. Brugōr sensed he was being lied to. "Listen to me, you little shit, I'm warning you. If you do not comply and assist me in what I ask, you and all your kind will suffer."

Promit remained still, as if he were alone in the room. If he wanted to get out of his situation alive, he needed to consider the circumstances. The only advantage he had over his enemies was the secrecy of communication and comprehension. Confident the wretched man was clueless of The Quo's location, Promit knew he was more valuable alive than dead.

"I won't repeat myself," Brugōr warned, but Promit stood his ground. The brute walked off and quickly returned with a small device in his hand. Promit glanced at it, unsure of what the small, metallic box was.

"You see this?" He held up the silver, square cage, big enough for just a worm. Without warning, he hurled the box at Promit.

While he turned to protect himself, the unexpected happened. In motion, the miniature container grew into a larger, barred cage big enough to fit a human, or quorian. Before Promit could comprehend what'd happened, it was too late. Without pain or pressure, he was confined to the metal cage. The top and bottom were solid titanium while the four walls around him were comprised of thick, cylindrical bars. He wrapped his hands around them, happy to see and feel through, but frightened for what had just happened. Suddenly, his timeless chamber seemed more appealing than the vexatious cage.

"Don't say I didn't warn you." With one button, Brugōr's voice fell silent, as did the rattling on the cage from Promit. He smiled wider, pressing the same button again. "Sound Propagation Elimination. For when you become a nuisance and I don't care to listen to your feeble words, which you'll eventually utter." Brugōr approached the cage, sticking his index finger inside. Promit hurled forward in an attempt to grab it, but missed. Brugōr laughed in pity.

"Now for the fun part." Brugōr pressed the button, deafening the sound for Promit. That was the moment Promit knew he'd rather be in the padded room. He had more fear seeing his surroundings without any control or sound. It was unnerving. The brute had somehow managed to mute any noise Promit made.

Brugōr momentarily disappeared, returning with a satchel in his hand. As Brugōr reached inside, he remembered to disable the Sound Propagation Elimination, allowing the quorian to respond or act accordingly. Seeing him press the button, Promit tested his curiosity with a small tap against the cage.

Clink.

With their communication enabled, Brugōr reached inside his satchel and pulled out an unusual stone orb. Promit didn't understand the purpose of the object on display, but the brute's sneer implied a significance. As Brugōr continued to proudly showcase his possession, Promit recognized its markings and identified the object. His eyes widened.

The key to the Enchanted Gate, he thought. *How is this possible!?*

"Seems I have your attention now." Brugōr smiled. "Care to speak?"

Promit opened his mouth as the abusive leader anticipated his first communication with the quorian race. Deciding on what to say and how to respond, he sensed Brugōr required his assistance, yearning for answers. Slowly closing his mouth, without uttering a word, Promit maintained his leverage and smiled.

"You little shit..." Brugōr scowled. "You'll fucking regret defying me."

With the snap of his fingers, Promit's entire world went black, as if his eyes were closed. There was nothing he could do. Promit was encapsulated in deafening silence and eternal darkness.

Left with his thoughts in a sensory deprivation chamber, Promit's sanity began to slip away. His stress and fear heightened with continuous thoughts.

Will I ever get out of here?

Did he breach The Quo?

Maybe he didn't need me. Maybe it was a warning.

Are they even trying to find me?

Is anything worth fighting for anymore?

Promit thought about his deceased mother, leaving him with his father and sister. He deeply loved his sister and helped take care of her when possible, but his father wasn't nurturing. He was only interested in what benefitted him. Promit wondered if his family knew about his disappearance and what they thought.

Are they worried? Are they helping?

He realized the possibility Smolar had returned to the city and remained quiet. He didn't want to doubt his friend's morality, but he began questioning everything and everyone.

What if he didn't escape? What if they captured him? Left him to die?

He'd been so focused on his own predicament that he hadn't considered the possibility Smolar didn't escape. Promit hadn't heard anyone acknowledge him, but he questioned whether they would. He knew everything was a mind game, and he'd become an active participant.

The jarring possibility that no one knew his whereabouts jolted Promit back to reality, focusing on his sanity. He took charge. Uncertain how long he'd be in the blackened chamber, he sustained his mental stability, knowing it was crucial to survive. Hopeful he'd see Brugōr and the light of day again, Promit prepared a non-confrontational plan of attack. He knew the brute wanted information, so putting his sanity at risk could compromise Brugōr's perception of Promit's knowledge he desperately wanted.

The next time he was released from his deprivation chamber, Promit was stunned not to have a private, one-on-one conversation with Brugōr. As bright daylight illuminated his surroundings, he recoiled, protecting his eyes from the sharp adjustment. Even his quorian vision struggled to adjust. As he began to visualize his surroundings, Promit watched as an entire room of humans stared at him. He was the center of attention, and he couldn't have been more uncomfortable. Closing his eyes, he reminded himself of what he needed to do and the risky position he was in.

That's when the rage began.

He acted berserk, shouting as loud as he could, banging on the caged walls, slamming his feet against the titanium floor. Promit realized the Sound Propagation Eliminator was activated. He felt a sense of defeat but knew he needed to continue. He may have been silenced, but he wasn't hidden.

Just then, his eyes fell upon a stranger. A stranger with a familiar presence. *Her eyes*. He couldn't explain it, but Promit felt at home with the individual. They locked gazes for a few seconds until he allowed his fury to consume him once more.

35

Jacob didn't know whether to scream, run or sit and discuss with Anitta, his great grandmother's artifact.

"Who the…what the—"

Knock, knock

"It's Giddeom. I know you've arrived. Come out so we can discuss the final preparations for your departure." Jacob's eyes widened, uncertain what to do with the talking orb.

"You have questions. We'll talk after. I'll become small again. Into your pocket I go," Anitta instructed. "Only you hear me. Remember when you speak." Edith's orb shrunk to the size of a marble once again. Jacob picked Anitta up, placed her in his pocket, and hurried toward the door.

"Hey," Jacob answered, as Giddeom looked him up and down.

"Everything okay?" he asked, peeking inside his sanctuary.

"Yeah, just getting used to transporting from home to here," he said. "Shall we go?" Jacob walked past Giddeom, shutting his door behind him. He was so distracted by Anitta, he'd forgotten about the euphoric sensation. It was just what he needed to shift his focus away from the stress and toward the task at hand.

"Yes…we shall." Giddeom abruptly turned around, unamused by Jacob's casual eagerness. The two headed toward the double white doors, leading to the grand hallway.

"So...The Barren Land. I suppose it's time to meet Brugōr."

"Correct. Find Brugōr and ensure the safety of the Transcending Tablets from the Anti-Regime. Afterwards, you can scurry away and return here to meet with me," Giddeom informed him.

"Where can I find Brugōr?"

"He resides in the tallest structure within the valley known as the Kurhal. You'll know it when you see it. Find him there and he'll know where to go." Giddeom stopped in front of one of the doors within the grand hallway.

"The Kurhal. Got it." Jacob welcomed the lack of anxiety, allowing him to focus.

"Here we are." Giddeom held his arm out to the door in front of them. "Through this door, you can enter The Barren Land."

"Finally," Jacob said. "I've been curious about these doors since I first arrived here."

"Now that you have the mark of the guardian, you may enter. Inside you'll find the portal to The Barren Land and the appropriate armor to aid in your journey. Good luck, our guardian."

Gripping the doorknob tightly, Jacob felt a click in his hand as the door unlocked for him. The time had finally come. Smiling at his ancestor one last time, Jacob wondered if he felt confident in his ability to accomplish the mission. Pushing his curiosity aside, Jacob focused on the task at hand: The Barren Land, the Anti-Regime, Brugōr and the Transcending Tablets.

As he entered, the door immediately shut and locked behind him. The space was dark and eerie, but only served one purpose. The portal in the middle of the room was large, in the shape of a bent arrow with the tip touching the ground. Through it, Jacob heard the howling of wind. Standing just inches away from a portal to an entire region confirmed how *mystical* Diad was.

401

Before entering, Jacob stepped back and observed the rest of the ancient cave. The walls consisted of rock formations, minerals and stones. It was dark, but the flickering flames against the walls lit up the space enough to see the room was empty, with one exception.

The left side of the wall housed a glass cabinet, with a single outfit to change into. A brown shirt, tattered at the sleeves, a pair of black pants and some black shoes.

This is my armor? This is supposed to protect me!?

Being alone in the sepulchral room, he realized it was the perfect time to ask his new companion some questions. He reached into his pocket and placed a marble-sized Anitta onto the ground. Within seconds, it grew into its regular size.

"Giddeom said I'd find my armor here, but all I see is a pathetic excuse for protection. What I have on now would protect me more."

"Blended protection," Anitta said. "It's important."

"You know," he said, feeling frustrated, "it'd be a lot easier if you used your words." Aware of her possible knowledge, Jacob grew tired of interpreting cryptic messages.

"Of course. Though it may not protect your physical body, it *will* help you blend in with others in the region. It'll prove to be vital within the valley."

"Thank you. I suppose that's something…" Jacob said kindly. He opened the glass case and changed into the armor displayed for him. Surprisingly enough, when he put the clothes on, the sizes adjusted perfectly to his physique.

Form-fitted and ready to go, Jacob stared down at Anitta on the ground.

"Never thought I'd feel so alone." He sighed, pocketing the orb once more. "Thanks for being here. It's helpful to have someone to talk to."

With one deep breath, Jacob walked into the portal. His skin felt slippery as he submerged into what felt like jelly. Uncertain what else to expect, he slowly walked until he noticed the bright sun on the other side. Eventually, the hardened, cavernous floor softened and Jacob looked down to a familiar sight – sand.

The Barren Land slowly appeared as his eyes adapted to the change in brightness. Surrounded by exceptionally high, narrow walls, Jacob turned around to view the portal, but it had vanished. Panic rushed through him, uncertain how he'd return to the transportation room in Diad.

"Where did...?" Jacob whispered, reaching his hand out where the portal should have been.

"Touch it," Anitta said. "The portal's still open, but remains hidden." Following her instructions, he was surprised to see she was right. When he placed his hand on the wall of the gorge, he penetrated it. Jacob felt the familiar cool, gelatinous sensation and immediately retracted his arm, looking around to ensure privacy.

"Thank you," he said under his breath.

"Let's get going. The Kurhal isn't far. I can sense it." Anitta's words resonated with him. He appreciated having a partner, even if it wasn't human.

Jacob followed the curved, narrow pathway into the vast valley of The Barren Land, stopping in astonishment. Vague memories of exploring the Sartician perimeter didn't compare to his view. Admiring the large birds flying overhead, he noticed the upper level of the region as the smoldering sun neared the edge of the valley wall.

He noticed the Karg River to his right, expanding between opposite ends of the region. It was so long he couldn't see where it ended. In the far-left corner was the Outer Limits, and the City of Karg was in the far-right corner, with an open gorge to his immediate right. Unaware of their names, there was only one structure he had been made aware of.

The Kurhal

Directly on the other side of the river stood Brugōr's tower, surrounded by the castle grounds. Though Jacob hadn't visited The Barren Land before, Giddeom had mentioned his tower was the tallest in the valley. His anxiety flared up as he ventured right, toward the river, which took longer than expected.

How will I get in?

Where's the artifact located?

What if Brugōr doesn't believe me?

As questions filled his mind, Jacob tried to concentrate, giving Giddeom the benefit of the doubt.

Being my first mission, he wouldn't throw me into the lion's den. He's family. I was given one instruction – defend the artifact to protect the emblem.

He continued to talk through his nerves. With a deeper awareness of his anxiety, deeper trust in Giddeom, and ultimately the Divinity King, he sensed his stress levels declining. The sun was setting across the valley when he finally reached the river.

Water surged out from the wall with a strong current. He assumed there would've been a means to cross, but he was wrong. Being wider than he'd expected, jumping or swimming wasn't feasible. As he looked around to evaluate the situation, Jacob realized his best option was to climb the rock formation along the wall to cross the river. Though fitness wasn't his strongest attribute, he persevered, reminding himself of the purpose for the trip. As he was about to ascend, Jacob checked his helpful sidekick, which triggered an idea.

"Hey, Anitta," he said. "You levitate all the time. Think you can bring me across to reach the castle grounds?"

"If someone were to see you levitating, we'd have bigger problems. You found a solution to cross, so we should continue on."

"I thought you were here to help me—"

"Make no mistake, I am, and I will. Something tells me you'll need my assistance, but first you must overcome this small bump in the road." Anitta's stern, yet encouraging words, made him realize there was no discussion to be had. She wasn't someone he could order around.

"Fine," he forfeited, beginning his climb up and over the river. Fortunately, he didn't need to climb very high. He was nervous, but knew a fall wouldn't lead to his death. He was more concerned with jeopardizing the plan and getting caught in an unexpected predicament.

Fortunately, his rock-climbing lesson quickly ended as he lowered himself onto the other side, sighing in relief when his feet firmly met the rugged terrain. His timing couldn't have been better. Just seconds later, Jacob heard a subtle hum in the distance. In fear of being caught, he took shelter behind a corner pillar of the castle wall, slamming his body against the obsidian.

"Sorry," he whispered to Anitta.

"It'll take more than that to destroy me, but try to remember me next time, alright?"

"Sure." He chuckled, enjoying her unique personality. Peering around the pillar, he witnessed a group of vehicles approach the river. Concerned that they'd seen him, Jacob turned around and moved onward.

He followed the blackened wall, passing a shinier, newly-repaired section, until it curved around near the front. He assumed it was the main entrance but stopped when Anitta spoke up.

"Don't go any closer. It's probably not a good idea to enter through the main doors."

"How else are we to enter? There were no other passages." There was a short moment of silence before Anitta replied.

"There's always another way." With her advice, Jacob slowly retraced his steps.

"The wall is far too high for me to climb...unless you could levitate me over?" he said with a smile.

"It'd raise many questions if those inside noticed a stranger standing on the wall of their castle. You'd be instantly killed," she said, expressing her disappointment in his inability to think through a suggestion. Jacob began to wonder what purpose she served, yet knew she was right.

"Okay then. Should I press on a certain brick for a part of the wall to open up in some sort of secret doorway?" His sarcasm didn't go unnoticed.

"This isn't some sort of magical fairytale land."

"Isn't it though? By the way—"

"Take me out and I'll see what I can do."

Sighing, he placed the shrunken orb on the sandy floor. Instantly, Anitta returned to her normal size and levitated toward the top of the castle wall. Jacob felt useless without her nearby.

"Anything?" he whispered as she rapidly darted around, hidden from those inside.

"Let's try something," she exclaimed, lowering down to his level. "This section of the wall is different." Jacob scurried toward her. "The wall itself is thinner and abuts the Kurhal. I'd like to try and work with you to activate an intangibility power."

"You'd like to *try*?" Jacob asked. "And an intanga-what?"

"Intangibility. Travel through matter, atoms. Since the wall abuts the tower, we'd just need to successfully pass through once. A thinner wall makes for easier success." Anitta hovered in front of one particular spot. "This would be the spot to use."

"Okay," Jacob said hesitantly, trying to grasp the idea. "Can't you just make it happen?"

"Has Giddeom become so lazy he no longer explains how ancient artifacts work?"

"Well…he mentioned when I'm around an artifact, a unique ability would emerge. That something would happen to assist in my duty as guardian, but he couldn't tell me what. He said it would be for me to—"

"Yes, yes. We know that. It's how you were able to obtain Edith's letter from my possession. I assume you're able to envision your opponent's move slightly before they act. It's quite an incredible ability – one I haven't seen in a while. What I'm talking about is the bond between guardian and artifact. Something special happens when they are symbiotic. Take us for example. The more we work together, the stronger our bond becomes, and the more we're able to achieve."

Jacob stood in shock. "Giddeom didn't mention anything of the sort. He never even mentioned you."

"I would hope he didn't mention anything."

"Why?"

"I'm the ancient artifact for Diad. Giddeom doesn't know of my location. I don't know what he's been told, but I know the previous guardians maintained secrecy. It's to ensure a balance of power over the mystical region. I thought Edith would've told you this in the letter."

"She didn't mention anything either." Jacob sighed. "Seems to be a common theme."

"I'm sorry…" She paused. "But to get back to our predicament, I'd like to see if we could achieve intangibility. If it doesn't work, we find an alternative route. If it does, you'll have saved us hours, and possibly your cover." Anitta took advantage of his fear in disappointing others. With noise billowing in the distance from the vehicles that arrived, Jacob decided.

"Fine, let's try."

He walked toward Anitta and placed his hands on the wall. The brick was cold, slightly damp, rigid. Without speaking, he looked at her with disappointment.

"You can't expect it to just happen. You have to work for it. Close your eyes, imagine a doorway, see yourself walking through, feel it."

"Uhh…okay."

"Your mind is important, but we live in a physical world. Envision your physical response."

"Alright."

"Once you have the vision,"—she paused for suspense—"punch the fucker as hard as you can." For the first time, Jacob heard a faint chuckle in her voice.

"Did you just…was that…?"

"What?" She lowered her levitation. "Please don't tell me you're one of those easily offended types. I'll have you know most civilians in The Barren Land curse, so if you plan to fit in, you better suit up, buddy."

"I was referring to your laughter. It's the first time I heard you chuckle…"

"Us artifacts are capable of emotion. I don't know why that's always so shocking."

Jacob awkwardly chuckled, changing the topic. "And I may not curse, but I'm not offended by it. It's just not common where I'm from."

"Good." They heard a crash in the distance. Jacob turned around and Anitta hid herself. "Rule number one, kid. When you hear a loud noise, react in the opposite direction. Don't turn around, exposing yourself. You're a sitting target and would be dead right now." Fortunately, no one was approaching them. There was a momentary commotion that quickly settled down.

"Noted," Jacob replied.

"Alright. Let's try this again. Stand in front, adjust your posture, and envision what you expect to be there. When you're ready, and be certain you're ready, punch through the brick with all your might."

"Okay…"

"Whatever you do, do *not* anticipate any pain or what would happen if it doesn't work. That'll only lead to a broken hand, rendering you partially useless for this mission."

"That's not helping."

"Don't say I didn't warn you."

Jacob shut his eyes and focused, proving to be more challenging than he'd anticipated. He thought about what would happen once they entered, the possibility of fighting, and the group of people who had arrived in the numerous cars. Even when he did focus on just the obsidian wall, his mind automatically thought about the pain he'd endure, but he fought the urge, listening to Anitta's advice.

He envisioned the wall as a gelatinous material, similar to the portal. Instead of breaking down impenetrable stone, Jacob created a portal into the castle grounds on the other side. It was an idea his imagination ran wild with. His heart fluttered with the excitement of such potential. The idea of passing through barriers across Diveria thrilled him.

With his eyes still shut, Jacob pictured the castle interior – high ceilings, obsidian walls, elaborate decor, guards everywhere. That was when he hurled his fist forward with all his force, minimally grunting.

"Oh dear," Anitta said, her orbicular appearance floated closer to the wall.

"D-did I…did I do it?" Jacob asked, his eyes still closed.

"You did…something. Open your eyes," she insisted. Jacob cracked his eyes to see an astonishing, yet uncomfortable, sight. In front of him was the same blackened brick wall; however, half of his arm was consumed.

"Whoa…"

"Can you move your arm?" Anitta wondered. Jacob wiggled his fingers, confirming that he wasn't stuck. With hesitation, he pulled his arm out slowly. There was the slightest resistance, but no pain.

"It feels…weird. Like the portal I used to get here."

"This is interesting. Typically, the doorway is made visual to the naked eye. In this case, you've managed to keep the path hidden, yet still accessible." He was startled by what he'd accomplished with Anitta's assistance and encouragement. "This is miraculous, Jacob. You did a splendid job."

"I couldn't have done it without you, Anitta." Jacob gleamed. For the first time, he felt a sense of confidence and fulfillment in his role as guardian.

"Yes, well, we should get going," she suggested. Foreign to compliments, Anitta levitated toward the wall with Jacob following.

Once again, his eyes took a moment to adjust from the bright sun of The Barren Land to the darker confines of the Kurhal. Neither one considered they'd appear in the main hall of the tower. Fortunately, their arrival was concealed by dusty pieces of armor. Anitta miniaturized as Jacob returned her to his pocket. With a deep breath, he came out from behind the gear and walked toward the crowd. People were arriving through the main entrance, but only a few guards were present.

"There's barely anyone here organizing the crowd," he whispered to Anitta.

"What do you mean?"

"No guards. No organization. No order. Just two guards by the entrance. All the guests are freely roaming..." Jacob paused. He observed the casualness of the guests. They all seemed to know the space very well, uninterested in its unique and startling appearance.

Jacob overheard a nearby conversation between three people.

"This is the most fun I've had in this building."

"It certainly won't be this entertaining when we return to work. He should do this more often."

"If only we could drink on the job."

Jacob understood the scenario. "Everyone here is employed by Brugōr. That's why there are no guards, they're off duty."

"How peculiar..." she replied.

"Now to find Brugōr," he whispered.

"Locate the party. I'd imagine we'll find him there." Jacob gazed upon the room and saw the guests entering the elevator. He followed them, blending in with the crowd.

36

"There is a sound barrier surrounding its cage," Brugōr exclaimed, as Promit continued to thrash. "We're unable to hear him and he's unable to hear us. His screeches and howls are uncomfortably high pitched. Besides, he doesn't need to hear us speaking about him," he sneered.

"What do you plan to do with him?" one of the guards asked.

"Learn everything there is to know about his race. Where they've been, how they've survived, what their customs are…" He paused, excited at the prospect. "Everything."

The room fell silent again as everyone watched his prisoner act out in rage. Brugōr stared too, but in concern. He assumed the creature would be angry, but the level of rage worried him. There was critical, precious knowledge to obtain from the quorian and Brugōr worried for his sanity. After answering a couple more questions, he decided it was enough and activated the quorian's concealment

"Alright," Brugōr interjected, "that's enough for today. I need to look out for the well-being of this creature." He nodded toward the guard to return it to his lair.

"I know this may concern you, seeing these creatures return. The Divinity King and his army risked their lives to ensure a safe future for our race, and somehow they survived so many years later." Worried whispers filled the room. "To everyone here and within The Barren Land, I promise to ensure the safety of you and your loved ones. Like the Divinity King, I'll sacrifice my life for the safety of our land." Everyone clapped, some stood up in honor. There were a few, however, who questioned his comparison to their king. They wondered if they were the only ones seeing through his speech of lies. "So tonight, let's drink!" Brugōr shouted, holding his glass up for a toast. "Let's drink to honor!"

"Honor!" the crowd shouted back.

"Let's drink to valor!"

"Valor!"

"Let's drink to redemption!" he shouted louder, gaining momentum within the banquet room.

"Redemption!" they howled back. Amongst the rowdy bunch was Vanilor, shouting proudly. Since the speech had ended, swarms of people surrounded him to ask questions and thank him. No longer did he limit himself to only higher ranking officials. Peculiarly, Mortimer, who remained silent and seated the entire time, remained alone. He preferred it, especially since it'd make for an easier escape when it was time to leave.

As the room settled down, Brugōr called one of the servers over.

"Can you ask the chefs to skip the next two courses and jump to the main entree? Also, have them come out and introduce themselves to us. We're yet to meet them," he said with a grin. "And, for Vin's sake, clear our fuckin' plates!"

As the elevator doors opened, Jacob jumped back from the sound coming out of the banquet hall, while the other passengers exited without hesitation.

"Redemption!"

Jacob crept out until the closing doors forced him to exit.

"What's with the yelling?" Jacob whispered to Anitta.

"Be careful. We're in uncharted territory."

"Right."

As Jacob approached the banquet hall, the volume subsided. Opposite of what he'd expected, but a pleasant surprise. As suggested, his outfit was perfect because none of the strangers he'd passed looked twice, though they were inebriated. He knew it'd be a high energy environment, but his anxiety was higher than he'd ever experienced.

"The quicker we get to Brugōr, the less likely we'll get involved," he whispered, trying to calm himself down. "Deep breaths."

"You can do this, Jacob. Giddeom and the Divinity King wouldn't have sent you if they expected you to fail." Anitta prepared to aid in Jacob's mission both physically and mentally. She'd helped enough guardians to know the first mission was always the toughest.

Walking into the banquet hall was an experience Jacob knew he'd never forget. Not only was the room massive, but the floor to ceiling windows provided a view he could've never imagined. The one room alone surpassed anything he'd seen in Sartica, including the Subterranean Domain. Standing in the entryway, he scanned the room for the leader who matched the description of Brugōr, whom he quickly identified. Jacob's hands became sweaty, and he wiped them on his pants. Quickly shaking his head, he reminded himself to focus on his words, not his hands.

To his right, Jacob noticed a large crowd praising a man. As he slowly walked toward Brugōr, he practiced what he'd say.

Hello, my name is Jacob, and I'm the Guardian of Emblems, here to warn you because...

Jacob shook his head.

Are you Brugōr? My name is Jacob Emmerson and I was sent here by Giddeom to warn you you're in danger.

Jacob chuckled. His target was vastly approaching. He noticed Brugōr speaking to a guard and momentarily stopped, allowing them to finish, buying himself more time.

Hello, my name is Jacob. Giddeom sent me. We need to leave right away. The artifact is in danger.

The guard scurried away toward a door in the back corner. Jacob hadn't noticed it before but thought it good to know in case he needed a second exit.

He guessed there were about fifteen steps left until he was face to face with the leader of The Barren Land. His heart was in his throat and a few droplets of sweat formed on his forehead. Memories of his journey fluttered through his mind as he continued his steps.

Fourteen...thirteen...

His first experience with Giddeom, when he didn't know who he was. The doorknob shaking from the other side.

Twelve...eleven...

The Subterranean Domain and Sir Kalvin. Being knocked unconscious to meet with Giddeom.

Ten...nine...

Visions of Giddeom's family appearing in his mind. His family. Their family.

Eight...seven...

His companion, Anitta, one of the ancient artifacts. Though many unanswered questions remained, she brought him much-needed reassurance.

Six...five...

His great grandmother, Edith. Jacob wished he'd met her. To understand her more as a woman, as a family member, and as a guardian.

Four...three...

His sister, Catherine, ready to deliver his niece. He hoped he wouldn't miss it. Balancing his time between family and being guardian had already proven to be a difficult task.

Two...one...

His mother's face, Anna Emmerson. Having her blessing allowed Jacob to accept his role as guardian and pursue a life that she wasn't capable of fulfilling.

"Hello," Jacob mustered. Suddenly, all his visions vanished as he stood in front of Brugōr. Being so close to a powerful man was more intimidating and frightening than he had imagined.

Instead of wasting words on him, Brugōr just expressed a curious look.

"Hello," he repeated, with confidence. "My name is Jacob Emmerson and I was—" Brugōr put his hand up and extended his index finger at Jacob.

"Why haven't we met before?" Brugōr's bold voice sent chills through him. "Anytime we take in a new degreant, I meet them personally...but you..." He paused. "You're new."

"As I've said, my name is—"

"I know what you've said, Jacob Emmerson. I'm more concerned with how the fuck you entered my valley, my region, without my knowledge." Brugōr stood up, forcibly knocking his chair backwards and shaking Shrenka's empty chair beside him. A few guests turned their heads, but quickly resumed their socializing.

"I-I-I'm—" Jacob stuttered in fear.

"Giddeom!" Anitta shouted. "Tell him about Giddeom!" Jacob was in too much shock to speak.

"You gunna answer me, boy?" Brugōr warned. After a moment of silence, Brugōr reached his hand out for Jacob's neck. About halfway through, Anitta released a short burst of energy, jolting Jacob back to action.

"Giddeom!" he shouted. Brugōr's fingers had nearly reached his neck when he stopped.

"What...did you just say?"

"Giddeom sent me here since I'm the new guardian and your artifact's in danger, so you need to make sure it's safe, otherwise it's going to be really bad and this is my—"

"Whaat!?" Brugōr shouted. This time, the entire banquet hall went quiet. Jacob, along with the brute leader, were the center of attention. He felt eyes on him from behind, but thought it best to not break eye contact.

"This way, *now*," Brugōr demanded in a much lower tone. "Everyone continue to drink up!" he shouted as he stormed off toward the back door. Jacob hastily followed. Unsettled by the view of the valley on his right, he looked left, momentarily making eye contact with a slender man drinking alone at a table. Jacob found it peculiar he'd been alone with everyone else socializing.

When he entered the room, he was surprised to see it was a large kitchen. Jacob noticed a few servers, a guard and two chefs working.

"Everyone out. Get out, *now*," Brugōr ordered. Everyone made their way to the exit including Osvita and Nigel. "Except you two." Brugōr put his hand out, making sure they remained inside the kitchen. They stood in silence, waiting for the room to clear out.

Nigel instinctively placed his hands on Osvita's shoulders, knowing this wasn't part of the plan. His fear made Osvita worry more, but Nigel intended to keep his promise to her, and Lazarus. She was his priority and would protect her by any means necessary. Both the chefs looked for the closest kitchen device as a means of self-defense.

"Don't even think about it," Brugōr said, aware of their wandering eyes. Once it was just the four of them, Brugōr gained control of the situation. "Alright, Jacob. You talk a big game, go. Speak."

Jacob had no idea who the two chefs were and why the leader wanted them to stay. As he tried to calm his nerves, he sensed the strangers were at the leader's mercy while Brugōr was clinging to what he had to say. Jacob questioned why he was sent to help a cruel leader, but remembered Giddeom's famous words.

Your focus isn't to pass judgement or question morality.

With a deep breath, Jacob found some courage.

"My name is Jacob Emmerson and I'm…" He paused, looking at the two strangers, then back at Brugōr.

"Piss on them for now. Continue," Brugōr replied.

"I'm here to let you know that your ancient artifact is at risk of being stolen or, worse, destroyed. Giddeom, whom I believe you know of, sent me here to inform you and…" Jacob paused, omitting the word 'assist' so as to not volunteer himself. "Well, to let you know about what's to come."

Shit, Nigel thought. *Who the hell is this guy? Who's Giddeom? How'd they blow our cover?*

"Giddeom…that's a name I haven't heard in a while. Who are you to him? To *them?*" Brugōr asked.

"I'm the newest Guardian of Emblems, here to help guide you to protect the ancient artifact in your region." Jacob wished it'd come out sounding better. He wanted a cool and catchy title and made a mental note to work on it.

"The Guardian of Emblems?" Osvita whispered.

"Shh," Nigel insisted.

Osvita struggled to hide the panic behind her eyes. *Whark, Rexhia, Grum…What if this was all a trap*? she thought. She trusted Nigel, but had no clue who Lazarus truly was, or if he could be trusted.

"Hmph. So someone's going to try and take the Vin damn tablets, eh?" Brugōr turned, gazing upon Nigel and Osvita. "You wouldn't happen to have any idea who that may be…would you?"

"We have no idea what you're talking about or who this man is. We're here to cook your—"

"Enough!" Brugōr shouted. "You think I'm clueless as to who your fucking husband is, deary?" He chuckled. Osvita would've collapsed had Nigel not stabilized her. The roles had flipped. While Jacob became lost in translation as personal histories unraveled, they knew why Brugōr had them stay in the kitchen.

"Shrenka hired you before anything happened with your poor excuse of a husband. You were the best fucking chef in the valley, so naturally we wanted your culinary skills. Unfortunately for your family, your husband meddled in affairs that didn't concern him. I had far worse plans for you, but Shrenka insisted otherwise." He paused. "Where is that woman?" Brugōr wondered, not having seen her since his arrival. "Doesn't matter. Point is, you've got balls, lady. If you're here, I assume that means you haven't seen your precious Whark yet, which means he's still out there for us to hunt." He grinned. "As is your daughter."

"Don't you even—"

"I'm not in the mind of killing children…but if you remain quiet, I'll have no choice," he said, sighing with pleasure.

Osvita lunged forward but Nigel stopped her. Staring at the monster, she noticed him excessively blink, straining his eyes, struggling to focus.

"Don't," he whispered in her ear. "It won't end well."

Hearing Brugōr express his disdain for her and Rexhia, Osvita knew he wasn't involved in their pardon. Shrenka's desire to have them cater the event confirmed she was behind the letter.

Jacob couldn't believe what he was hearing. Having Giddeom and the Divinity King defend power in the hands of a monster made him want to leave. Strangely enough, Jacob deeply worried and sympathized for the two strangers, whose names he didn't even know. He had gotten himself too involved without realizing it.

"So what—" Brugōr stopped as the floor underneath him violently vibrated. No one spoke or moved. Though they were all silent, they heard the excessive socializing in the banquet hall.

BOOM.

A deafening sound echoed through the tower and the entire valley. It was instant, short, and everyone but Brugōr ducked for protection. He walked toward the windows, but stopped halfway, shaking his head to focus. Looking outside, he saw nothing unusual as the night sky illuminated the sandy valley below.

Nigel grabbed Osvita's hand to get her attention. She looked up, still enraged at the leader threatening Rexhia, as he tried to communicate with her.

"This is it," he mouthed silently. "The plan. It's begun." Osvita's eyes widened as she understood.

Uncertain of what the sensation was and confused by no visual changes, Brugōr continued as if it hadn't happened. "Get up, it was nothi—"

Another boom echoed throughout room, causing the banquet hall to go quiet. Everyone looked around, wondering what had happened. Mortimer remained in his seat and shot the remainder of his drink back with a smile.

Here we go, he thought.

Vanilor was surrounded by a sea of silent fans and curious minds.

"Ahh, it was nothing," he said, hoping to regain the attention he'd lost. "Who else had a question?" Over the deafening silence, Vanilor was heard throughout the hall. Minor cracks suddenly formed in the marble floor. Everyone watched in utter disbelief, frozen.

Back in the kitchen, the floor began to form cracks too. Osvita and Nigel were shocked at the damage while Jacob fought the urge to flee for his life. Brugōr noticed the cracks and considered the threat serious. Causing such damage to the Kurhal required more planning than he knew the two chefs were capable of.

"Jacob," the leader yelled, grabbing his wrist. "Let's move!"

Jacob nearly stumbled as Brugōr's bulging hand refused to let go. As they headed for the door, another loud boom echoed and vibrated the tower. The massive leader struggled to remain upright as he stabilized himself against the quartzite countertop. Finding his unbalanced behavior peculiar, he turned and glared at Osvita. The two locked gazes. Though no words were exchanged, his eyes expressed doubt, while hers exuded confidence.

The two quickly exited the kitchen as another loud boom echoed. Storming through the banquet hall, Brugōr's weight left crumbled pieces of marble under each footstep. Seeing their leader flee caused an eerie panic. People calmly grabbed their belongings and headed for the door. Just then, a series of loud explosions and violent vibrations erupted, all of which swayed the Kurhal. Most of the guests dropped to the floor in fear of moving while some took the risk and began to flee.

BOOM.

Swinging open the kitchen door, Osvita and Nigel crawled on the floor into the main hall, immediately turning right to get away from the windows.

BOOM.

Screams sounded throughout the banquet hall. Plates, glasses and silverware all rattled and clanged to the floor.

BOOM.

One of the crystal chandeliers came loose, crashing onto the floor, pinning one of the guests. A loved one ran toward him, but he had already died. The shouting and yelling turned into loud screams of horror as everyone realized they were in a death trap.

BOOM!

The pressure of the vibrations was so overwhelming for the tower that every floor-to-ceiling window shattered. Shards of glass lunged at the guests like homing missiles, striking some of them down in searing pain. With Osvita and Nigel on the floor, they escaped serious injury. The two continued to crawl to reach behind the bar for safety.

With each movement they made, they heard more destruction around them. More chandeliers crashed down, people pummeled over one another. Osvita was terrified, uncertain she could continue, but the thought of Rexhia pushed her onward.

Even though Nigel knew the plan, he had expected they'd be out of the tower before the explosions started. He was furious and petrified, but maintained his composure for Osvita's sake.

As they cornered the room to regroup behind the bar, Osvita, who was in front of Nigel, abruptly stopped. Wondering what had happened, Nigel looked ahead and noticed a familiar face had already taken shelter.

Mortimer.

Surrounded by the sound of death, Jacob Emmerson was undergoing the most traumatic event he'd ever experienced. The comforts of his home in Sartica prevented him from imagining such heinous possibilities. It made him momentarily miss the mundane worries of his unemployment or the convoluted discussions with his father. His new path had thrown him directly into a lethal situation.

As the Kurhal continued to sway and crack, Jacob anticipated fleeing from the ground floor and running for his life. Unfortunately, their trip rerouted from the main level to a hidden elevator along the northern wall. Brugōr pressed the only button that was available inside the cab.

13ᵗʰ Floor – Brugōr's Lair

It wasn't until the doors opened into his personal space that Brugōr released his clutches on Jacob's arm. He let out a huge exhale, immediately rubbing his bicep. An imprint of his gargantuan hand was still visible from the pressure.

"I don't know what's going on," Brugōr said as he scurried toward the back corner of the room, "but if you're right, prepare yourself." Jacob remained still as he watched Brugōr closely examine the wall, touching it in certain spots.

"Uhh…what's going on?" Jacob said in a low voice.

"That's what we're about to find out," he replied. Brugōr lowered his hand and confidently walked into the wall. Within a second, the brute had vanished. Jacob widened his eyes. He couldn't fathom the world he'd entered and questioned reality.

Slowly approaching the corner wall, he hesitantly reached his hand out. Brugōr's walls were built of obsidian, like the exterior castle wall, but had hints of maroon throughout.

"Anitta, you there?" he whispered. "Think I could pass through this one too?"

"You've already seen it done," she replied.

Similar to how he penetrated the castle wall, Jacob began the same process of concentration. Envisioning his hand through the wall and freely opening his fist up, he closed his eyes and gave an even stronger punch than he had delivered before. As Anitta had expected, it was successful and Jacob slowly brought the rest of his body through it.

Before he could even fully pass through, Jacob heard the brute leader shout.

"What the fuck do you think you're doing!?"

Jacob hurried upstairs. Since his arrival, he'd questioned helping the nefarious leader. He was puzzled at Giddeom's instruction to do so, and why an ancient artifact was left in a monster's possession. Fighting against his anxiety and fear, Jacob pressed onward, up to the fourteenth floor.

"Don't move another step or I'll destroy it," a stranger warned. Jacob didn't recognize the gray-haired, statuesque man.

"And who the fuck are you to make such a demand?" Brugōr asked with a smirk.

"My name is Lazarus Docaras and I'm the leader of the Anti-Regime. Perhaps you've heard of us."

"You... " Brugōr said with disdain. Well aware of his gang, he never knew who was in charge. Brugōr always considered it cowardice to remain hidden. "You've got some fuckin' nerve, you know that?" He stepped forward.

Without hesitation, Lazarus pulled out a small firearm and pointed it directly at Brugōr.

37

Diveria had proven to be a startling world for the cleverly disguised quorians. Fravia and Smolar's journey was tumultuous, yet rewarding. They'd been able to reveal their true feelings, but their appearance was anything but familiar. Their excessive traveling had been exciting for them all, yet pleasantly boring as well. The sights were unusual and peculiar. Whether it was the unfamiliar animals scurrying around, the pungent plants deterring others from their paths, or the questionable, seemingly large serpent, floating high in the air to the north. Though Rhugor pointed it out in surprise, they continued on their path.

After an exhausting journey, following the guidance of Fravia's parents, the group identified the large, spherical dome in the distance. Having a clear and concise path to The Barren Land excited the group. They'd arrived at their destination.

Approaching The Lost Sphere was intimidating for everyone. Recent, unpleasant memories jolted Fravia's mind, reminding her how dangerous the world outside could be. She considered themselves lucky the first time, but knew there wouldn't always be a Sam to save them. Smolar glanced over, squeezed her hand, and smiled. He was confident in Lady Vixa's plan to bring down the seemingly impenetrable forcefield. The sight, though impressive, didn't worry him. He feared for Promit's condition, and that they may be too late.

As Smolar stepped toward The Lost Sphere, Fravia instinctually reached her arm out to grab him, but stopped. She knew what he had in his possession.

"Be careful," she instructed.

Approaching the barrier, he was surprised at the lack of sensation as the vicious sandstorm whipped around in a continuous circle. He heard the crackling wind from within, but felt nothing as he stood just feet away. He fought the urge to look up, aware of its terrifying size.

Smolar removed the Amulet of Eymus from around his neck and into his hands. Its crimson color began to glow, in anticipation for what was to come. Sensing its power and energy, he reminded himself of the agony and pain it took to transform it into a weapon.

"Come on…" he whispered. Without further hesitation, he squeezed the amulet tightly and, with all his strength, tossed it up into The Lost Sphere. Standing beside one another, the three of them locked their gaze on the amulet's position, frozen in place as the storm continued to spiral.

"What's happening?" Smolar asked. "Why isn't it moving?" They watched, waiting for a reaction. The Amulet of Eymus continuously illuminated between a deep crimson and ruby, casting a red shadow around its location. Unfortunately, nothing seemed to happen and, after a short while, the amulet was banished from the barrier.

"No!" Fravia shouted. Before she or Smolar could lunge forward, Rhugor's reflexes ensured its recovery.

"Got it," he exclaimed, muffled from catching the amulet with his mouth. He walked to Smolar and placed it in his hands. "Now what?"

"Maybe Lady Vixa can shed some light," Fravia suggested. With only one Pendant of Perception remaining, Smolar contacted their Quorian Ruler.

"Hello," she said. "Smolar? What's your status? Everyone okay?"

"Lady Vixa. Hello, we're all well. We've reached The Barren Land—"

"Technically, we've reached The Lost Sphere," Fravia corrected him.

"Right. Just outside The Barren Land, in front of The Lost Sphere. I just tossed your Amulet of Eymus into the spiraling storm…" Smolar stared at the jewel in his hand, curious of its capability.

"And?"

"Nothing. It remained suspended until it eventually shot back out at us. Now we're standing here with the amulet in our possession, unsure of what to do."

"I have an idea," Rhugor explained. He carefully took the amulet out of Smolar's hands with his mouth and ran in the opposite direction. Firmly planting his burly paws into the sand, he turned around to showcase his rich, golden eyes and took a charging stance. "Here goes nothing."

Rhugor lunged forward with all his might, hurling sand behind him. His eyes locked onto the target, maintaining a steady line. Fravia and Smolar braced for impact as he approached them but right before a worrisome collision, Rhugor changed course. With a heavy footing on his back legs, he thrust his body upwards, giving the illusion of flight. With his head cocked, he forcibly released the amulet, planting it significantly higher within The Lost Sphere until it vanished behind the debris of the storm.

Gravity pulled Rhugor back down, forcing him to maintain his balance as his four paws collided with the ground. He groaned, holding still for a moment, before relaxing his muscles. The landing was impressive, even with four legs.

"Holy!" Smolar shouted.

"Rhugor!" Fravia exclaimed. "That was magnificent!" They both rushed toward him.

"Thanks," Rhugor said, short of breath. He looked up at the never-ending barrier. "Let's just hope it works."

No one could physically see the amulet at such a height, but they knew there could only be two options. Either The Lost Sphere would crash down or the amulet would.

38

The upper level of Brugōr's lair had a cosmic appearance with black, purple and blue hues. With a seemingly endless ceiling and soundproof walls, the space still felt confined. Its musky smell of an abandoned library implied the room was old, rarely visited. Though dimly lit, a bright light shined down upon an altar holding the ancient artifact – the Transcending Tablets.

Brugōr was impressed at the guardian's reflexes and timing as he anticipated the bullet, gracefully moving the leader out of harm's way. Though Brugōr appreciated the assistance, he refused to praise him. With an unexpectedly hazy mind, he prepared to manage the situation himself.

"How'd you—"

"There's no way out for you, Lazarus," Brugōr interrupted him, drawing his large obsidian sword from his scabbard. The hilt was matte black and the double-sided, obsidian blade glistened with a single strip of white down the middle. Jacob's eyes widened as he stood against the wall, watching the two men face off. Brugōr, blocking the only exit, confidently wielded his sword in an offensive stance as Lazarus firmly gripped his handgun.

"Give up now," Brugōr exclaimed struggling to focus. "Your plan won't work. Leave, before you lose your life."

Lazarus chuckled. The two men stared at one another until Brugōr charged and swung his weighted blade. Though lethal, his obsidian sword moved slowly, allowing Lazarus to dodge. He tried a few more times to make contact with the thief, but started to become disoriented.

"Everything's going exactly as planned," Lazarus remarked. Aiming his gun at Brugōr once more, he closed one eye and fired another shot at his torso, confident he wouldn't miss. Having envisioned the scenario just moments before it occurred, Jacob hastily moved into position, his heart racing. Undetected by both men, he instantly appeared on the ground, in front of Brugōr, struggling to push his sword upwards.

"Anitta, help me," he whispered. Releasing a strong burst of energy, she jolted his strength, pushing the blade up in Brugōr's hand as the bullet approached its target. It collided with the weighted blade and Brugōr's strength ignited, firmly holding his weapon in position.

"You son of a bitch," Lazarus uttered, peering at Jacob. "You're the exception. We hadn't expected *you* here." Adjusting his aim, the silver-haired aggressor pointed the barrel at Jacob. Envisioning his evasion, Jacob confidently charged at Lazarus in a circular motion as he pulled the trigger. The bullet dug into the floor, and Jacob lunged at the shooter. Sensing the assault, Lazarus spun around and pistol-whipped him across the face.

"You may be quick, but I'm quicker." Lazarus stared down at him. Jacob learned a limitation of his ability as a crippling headache formed. "Who are you? Where'd you come from?"

"I'm here to help Brugōr protect the tablets," he gritted through the pain.

Jacob wasn't a fighter, nor a confrontational person. He started off confident with his ability, but faltered when it failed and he succumbed to pain. As he stumbled to his feet, heading toward the protection of the double-edged blade, Jacob realized he hadn't thought about his movements. Every step he made and effort he took was instinctual.

Lazarus planned to aim his gun at him again, but noticed Brugōr prepare for another swing. Cognizant of his opponent's slothful movements, Lazarus leapt toward the altar. By the time the obsidian sword collided with the ground, he'd obtained the Transcending Tablets.

"No!" Jacob shouted. He and Brugōr blocked the only exit. Lazarus, wielding his gun and the tablets, stood beside the altar.

"While your precious tower crumbles, the castle grounds are in ruins and your beautiful obsidian wall has been destroyed. We were able to infiltrate your inner circle, in your own home, and gain access to your precious ancient artifact. It's time for a shift in this region. You've destroyed enough lives and spilled enough blood for nothing." Lazarus scowled, then looked to Jacob. "You know you're on the wrong team, right? You know you're defending a monster."

"The name's Jacob Emmerson, and I'm the newest Guardian of the Emblems to defend that artifact."

"Jacob," Brugōr murmured, "shut the fuck up."

"How can this be…Emmerson…?" Lazarus wondered.

Choosing to ignore Brugōr's warning, Jacob responded to Lazarus's uncertainty.

"That's right. Jacob Emmerson, and you're not leaving with the Transcending Tablets in hand."

"Jacob! That's enough." Brugōr, fighting to keep his eyes open, hurled his massive obsidian sword in Jacob's direction, but he dodged it.

"See? You're on the wrong side," Lazarus said. "You can't even trust the person you're here to defend."

"I was summoned for a mission that I'm capable of accomplishing."

"Or Giddeom, and your precious Divinity King, are running out of options, and you were their last resort."

Though Jacob didn't trust him, Lazarus spoke with such conviction. It was challenging for him to not question his knowledge, especially considering his awareness of those residing in Diad. Jacob realized he was exhausted and fed up with coddling others when no one did it for him. He was drained.

"What…did you just say?" Jacob asked, but Lazarus just smiled.

"Don't listen to him." Brugōr said.

"When their initial plan didn't result in their anticipated outcome, your Divinity King took matters into his own hands. You, Jacob, were never supposed to be here," Lazarus proclaimed with a smirk, standing tall as he examined the Transcending Tablets. "This is better than I could've ever anticipated."

Nerves filled Jacob's body, hindering his concentration. He was too overwhelmed, uncertain who to defend and where his loyalty should lie. Brugōr had only expressed terror and agony, but Jacob knew he couldn't morally judge the man. He was given a job, and needed to complete it. Lazarus was clearly committing a wrongful act, but Jacob sensed he'd possibly support such a plan if he lived in the valley. Civilians can only withstand so much turmoil before seeking retribution. He also couldn't shake the words he was spewing. As much as he'd like to ignore them, he sensed some truth to them.

"You can't use the fucking tablets, you mindless fuck. Give up," Brugōr exclaimed. Uncertain why his grogginess worsened, he fought against it with all his strength. With one long stride, Brugōr swung his double-edged sword up from the floor and grazed Lazarus's arm.

He recoiled in pain, tightening his grip on the tablets, making sure not to drop them. "That's what you think," Lazarus said. Wiping the blood from his wounded arm, Lazarus opened the Transcending Tablets to a particular incantation.

"What do you think you're doing? It won't work. The artifact is bound to my bloodline," Brugōr pressed on.

Lazarus laughed. Heavily focused on the page, he outlined a large-shaped symbol with his blood. To Brugōr's surprise, the tablets began to glow, slowly illuminating his lair. Though he had no idea which incantation Lazarus chose, the leader of The Barren Land had to stop him.

Brugōr tossed his massive sword to the ground, causing a deafening echo, and prepared to charge his foe.

Riddled with anxiety and indecision, Jacob didn't notice the intruder quietly climbing the staircase behind them. As Brugōr built his forward momentum, he felt a surge of pain from his left ankle. Falling forward, he felt the same pain in his right ankle. Brugōr collapsed, bleeding out onto the floor, enraged when he turned around and identified his attacker.

"*You*," he hissed.

"Get over yourself, old man," Shrenka said with a grin, showcasing her obsidian dagger with pride. "You refuse to embrace the true capability of power. You think being the leader of this pathetic region is power? You're poorly mistaken."

With the damage done, Jacob ran toward Brugōr while Shrenka stood beside Lazarus.

"I should've never trusted such a bitch," Brugōr shouted, unable to stand.

"Hold still, I need to apply pressure and stop the bleeding," Jacob instructed. Looking down, he realized the tendon had been severed in both ankles.

"Fuck that," he rebutted. Brugōr tried to stand, but it was no use. He collapsed, stricken with severe pain. Shrenka laughed at how easy it had been to take him down while Lazarus smiled, continuing to smear his blood along the symbol.

"You done?" she asked.

"Almost…" Lazarus said, speeding up his hand.

Unable to get up, Brugōr shouted, "What're you two dimwits doing?" He glanced at Jacob, who was whispering to himself as he focused on his injury.

"What should've been done years ago," Shrenka replied. "Relinquishing your control and power over this region."

"And just how do you two assholes plan on doing that?"

"By destroying your Lost Sphere, of course."

"There's no way you have the ability to do that," Brugōr insisted. "What're you doing back there?" he asked Jacob. "Much fuckin' help you are."

"Just a few moments longer. Stay still," Jacob replied.

Brugōr was stunned by Shrenka's betrayal and deception. Her attack wasn't just personal – it involved his region and his control. Standing beside one another for years, he knew the perception of their relationship. Constantly judged and ridiculed with assumptions, he never focused on the whispers because he knew what they had.

Focused on his reign and power, he wasn't an affectionate man. Though his form of expression wasn't desirable, Brugōr loved Shrenka. Instead of praising her with flowers, compliments and chivalry, he provided her with wealth, power, and sex.

"What happened to you?" Brugōr asked, fighting the disorientation.

"Don't give me that bullshit, Brugōr. You're too much of a bitch to be the man I need. Sure, you were a good lay, but I need someone who wants more. Someone who isn't afraid to take a chance and see the potential in future endeavors." Shrenka grinned. "Once your protective barrier is down, the region will be free to roam. Any power you had will be ripped away, especially when we take the tablets with us."

"Shrenka," Lazarus said sharply. "I'm done. It's time. Let's move." As he walked away from his opponents with the Transcending Tablets pressed against his chest, Shrenka followed with her dagger in hand.

"Besides," she whispered to them, "Lazarus is far more of a man than you'll ever be, you old shit. He's got the body and the brains, something you're partially short of." Giggling as she descended the stairwell, Brugōr was seething, ready for murder.

"I thought you were here to fucking help! What good are you, you piece of shit? Get the—"

"Go," Jacob said.

"What?"

"Do you feel any pain?"

"How the fuck did you…?" Brugōr was stunned. Kneeling on the floor, his wobbling head turned to see his legs in a pile of blood, yet his armored boots were dry and fixed, as if no damage had been done. He placed his fingers inside and touched the exact spot she'd severed. "You…you—"

"Go!" Jacob shouted. "Get them. I'll be right behind you." Though aware the brute leader wasn't innocent, Jacob didn't trust Lazarus's sinister actions either, especially given his distressingly vast knowledge. His and Shrenka's motives seemed to be deeper than just revenge against the leader.

Just as Brugōr was about to stand and march onward, he noticed a glass orb beside Jacob with bubbling red fluid in the center. "The fuck's that?"

"It's my own ancient artifact," Jacob replied. "We'll talk later. We must go, they're getting away."

With a strong nod, Brugōr stumbled up and grabbed his double-edged sword.

"You feeling okay?" Jacob asked. "You seem…"

"I don't…" He paused. "Not important. I'll be better when I catch those fuckers." Brugōr stammered off down the staircase.

"I'm sorry I didn't come out to help," Anitta said. "Those two…they're no good. Had they seen me, I believe you'd be dead and I'd be off with them."

"It would've been great to have your help," Jacob said, "but I trust you. It wasn't worth the risk. You came through helping Brugōr's wounds. That's what counts, so thank you."

"Thank you, Jacob. Your words are appreciated." Anitta hadn't worked with a guardian who'd shown her compassion. Having always been seen as an object, she found herself growing fond of him.

"We should move. I can barely hear Brugōr's footsteps," Jacob said, placing Anitta back into his pocket.

39

"Osvita, you must calm down." Nigel tried his best to help her focus, but failed. As she confronted Mortimer, he'd never seen her so enraged. Empathetic for her sense of deception, it pained him to see her in such a state, unable to help.

"He facilitated that quorian's capture! I can't—"

"It's unforgivable," Mortimer replied, "but let me explain."

Osvita shook her head.

"We must put our differences aside if we plan to escape with our lives," Nigel reminded them. "We must go, *now*."

Osvita knew he was right, but it required every effort to maintain her sanity. Though the explosions had stopped, the turmoil throughout the tower and the ground below had only begun. A gust of cold air rushed through the banquet hall from the busted-out windows, reminding them of their fate if they overstayed their welcome.

"There's a stairwell in the entryway, near the elevators. We should use those to get down," Mortimer said.

"Let's go," Nigel replied, smiling at Osvita.

The three of them carefully walked toward the hall's exit, attempting to avoid the bludgeoned bodies, fallen beams and shattered chandeliers.

Nigel had never seen such a catastrophe and knew he'd never be able to escape it. Osvita, on the other hand, had a strong purpose to escape. Though saddened by the loss of life around them, she was driven by the safety of her daughter and the whereabouts of her husband.

She replayed Brugōr's threat against her family. Crouched in the kitchen with Nigel beside her during the explosions, she'd felt safe. She suddenly remembered the stranger with Brugōr.

"Say, Mortimer?" Osvita asked.

"Yes?" he replied, continuing to walk slowly down the hallway, making sure to not aid in any additional shift in the tower. Unlike Nigel and Osvita, the only emotion Mortimer felt was guilt.

"Have you ever heard of a man named Jacob, or a Guardian of Emblems?"

"That's right," Nigel added. "Brugōr was with that man when the explosions happened. He was trying to warn him." Mortimer turned around in confusion. "He said he was sent to protect the ancient artifacts throughout the region and that someone had planned to capture his tablets. Brugōr blamed us, thinking we had knowledge of attack."

"Hmm…ancient artifacts around Diveria? Can't say I know anything about that, or any guardian of some sort. But…" Mortimer paused. "I wonder if Lazarus planned to steal those tablets."

"You think he—"

"Helllppp…" a voice attempted to shout in the distance. Nigel immediately turned and followed the voice to a man who was pinned under a fallen beam near the elevator doors. "Please…help me…"

"Guys!" Nigel shouted. "Come here! Help me!" He tried to lift the beam off the man's leg, but it didn't budge. The man had endured multiple lacerations, but nothing life threatening. Osvita looked to her right, where the door to the staircase was and sighed. Turning left, she approached Nigel and the man.

"Alright, let's make this quick," she said. "Come on, Mortimer. The least you can do is help us help this poor man." To their surprise, the pinned man jerked his head in Mortimer's direction, who hadn't moved any closer to assist them.

"Guys…" Mortimer said.

"You plan to come here and help or just stand there?" Nigel gritted.

"The man your saving is Vanilor," he informed them. Osvita instantly shot up.

"What!? You mean…"

"Yes, my ex-partner from the quorian mission."

"Alright, no more wasting time. Let's go." Osvita stood up and began to walk away when Nigel shouted.

"Osvita! I know you wouldn't leave a defenseless man here to wither away and die."

"Please…I beg of you," Vanilor added.

"A defenseless man, no. A quorian killer, yes. Yes, I would," she venomously proclaimed.

Nigel knew their time was limited, so he took a risk that he felt confident would work. "Well I'm not leaving until this man is freed. Would you leave *me* here to die?" The words quivered from his mouth as he tested their love for one another.

She turned around in despair and defeat. Osvita knew she'd never leave him to die, as did Nigel. With a large exhale, she crawled back down to the floor and began to assist with the beam.

"Mortimer, get down here now. If I can suck it up, so can you. Let's free this degenerate and get out of here."

Following her orders, Mortimer joined the group and assisted in pushing the beam off of Vanilor's leg. With every attempt, he shrieked in pain. Eventually, the three of them were able to move the beam enough to pull his leg out from under it.

Vanilor gripped his limb and evaluated his condition. "Thank you," he said with a smile.

"Of course," Nigel replied. Osvita and Mortimer remained silent.

"What a shit show this turned out to be, eh, bud?" Vanilor motioned to Mortimer.

"Sure did, and I ain't your bud."

Vanilor made a hissing sound as he wrapped his tie around the wound to help the bleeding. "The fuck has gotten into you? It's like I don't even know you anymore."

"The Mortimer you once knew died," he remarked. "I deeply regret everything we accomplished, the entire mission, and all the pain I've caused."

"You sound like a pussy," Vanilor sneered. "What we did was miraculous. Astonishing. Our discovery will change the world."

"At what cost!?" Mortimer shouted. "Look around you, *buddy*, the world is crumbling and piling up with dead bodies. Only a monster would welcome this. That's why I donated everything to the Anti-Regime to help execute this plan."

Vanilor's jaw dropped. "What?"

While Nigel knew of a large financial supporter, he was clueless as to who it had been. Osvita, just as stunned as Vanilor, noticed the change Mortimer had spoken of earlier.

"You heard me."

"How fucking foolish can you be!?" Vanilor shouted.

"Hey, guys," Nigel tried to interject.

"Me!?" Mortimer said.

"Yes, you dumb fuck. Brugōr may be rough, but it's for the safety of The Barren Land. You just facilitated an attack on our own region that will probably lead to its destruction. You're a fucking terrorist!"

"Safety of The Barren Land!?"

"Guys!" Nigel yelled.

"We captured a poor, innocent quorian, caused Osvita's husband to be chased down by the entire castle regime, killed that assailant who followed us, facilitated the death of a guard, and then poor Michael…"

"Poor Michael!?" Vanilor was surprised to hear the stranger's name. "The guy we stole the car from!?"

"ENOUGH!" Osvita shouted. "Nigel and I are leaving, so either come with us or keep bickering like children."

"Right." Mortimer sighed. "We must hurry." He looked down at the injured Vanilor. In a wave of compassion, Mortimer extended his hand to help him up. Nigel and Osvita admired his attempt to move forward, but Vanilor rejected the help and pushed himself up off the ground. Mortimer didn't offer assistance a second time when Vanilor began hobbling with a heavy limp. He was able to stand, but couldn't bear much weight on the leg.

"This way," Nigel said, as he and Osvita headed to the stairwell.

"I…" Vanilor said after a few attempts of walking. "I'll take the elevator down."

"That's crazy, who knows if it's even working. With all the damage the tower endured, it's not safe." Nigel was the only one genuinely concerned for him.

"What's crazy is walking down the stairwell when I can barely walk two fucking steps."

"Let me help you," Nigel offered, walking toward him, but Vanilor stumbled backwards against the wall, pressing the button for the elevator. Immediately, a hum began as the cab ascended to their floor.

"Don't fucking touch me," Vanilor hissed. "The elevator is on its way, so you go your way and I'll go mine."

"Come on, don't—" Nigel tried once more. Vanilor grabbed a large, broken piece of wood and defended himself, ensuring distance between he and Nigel.

"I *will* kill you if you come closer. Don't fucking test me."

Nigel stopped, stunned at his actions. They'd just helped the man from a slow and painful death. He couldn't understand how someone could be so rude and heartless.

Ding.

The elevator doors opened, showcasing an untouched, damage-free interior. Vanilor hobbled in and pressed the button to the bottom floor.

"Good luck getting out of here, fuckers," Vanilor proclaimed as the doors closed and the cab began to descend.

"You tried," Osvita said, aware of Nigel's state of mind. She admired his attempt to help.

"The man is a greedy son of a bitch," Mortimer revealed. "His goal in life is to be a bigger and badder Brugōr. There's no reasoning with that kind of crazy."

Nigel shook his head. "What an asshole."

Surrounded by destruction, the remaining three made their way toward the stairwell. There were a few lifeless bodies beneath it all, leaving an awful stench that even the airflow from the shattered windows couldn't repel. Nigel opened the door to invite them all down when Osvita heard a shriek.

She turned and retraced her steps.

"Vita?" Nigel asked. Mortimer remained quiet, watching curiously.

"Eeee…" a voice billowed from beneath the rubble.

"Did you hear that?" she whispered.

"Hear wha—"

"Shhh." She looked at Nigel. "Not so loud."

"Ugh…" This time they all heard the grunt, which was slightly louder. Nigel and Mortimer walked toward her, shutting the door to the stairwell. With a few more moans and movements, the trio dug through the debris, moving what they could to follow the sound.

"It's getting louder," Osvita said with excitement.

Mortimer moved a larger, fragmented piece of metal that caused an echoing clang. Upon further inspection, he noticed it was caught between two metal bars. He froze, realizing what it was. *A metallic cage.*

"How can this be…?"

"What?" Osvita wondered, slightly behind him.

"It's the quorian, or at least it's the cage he was imprisoned in."

Osvita leaped forward to save him.

"No!" Mortimer shouted. Aware of the surroundings, he knew the cage was pinned down by numerous beams. Though it blocked them from moving the cage, it prevented the abundance of shrapnel, boulders, gravel and shards of glass from filling the quorian's prison. What was containing him was also saving his life. As Mortimer explained the situation, Nigel and Osvita wondered what they could do.

"What if we—" Osvita continuously suggested, but they were all risky. Her desperation to save the quorian hindered her ability to think clearly.

"There has to be a way to take him with us and sneak him out," Nigel said.

"That's it!" Mortimer shouted. "You clearly have a smart head attached to that handsome body of yours," he blurted out. They were all startled by his admission, including Mortimer. "I know how to free the quorian!" he shouted, hoping to change their conversation.

As Mortimer headed toward the banquet hall, they heard a deafening crash within the elevator shaft. They all turned, startled to see the doors partially destroyed and bent from the pressure within. The number, stuck on twelve, was proof Vanilor never reached the bottom. The three of them locked eyes, aware that he'd met his death.

Nigel, with his sympathetic heart, was the only one who felt bad for the man. Osvita didn't like to see anyone die, but she couldn't get past his unforgiving sense of pride for capturing a quorian, and the apparent wrong he'd strived for. Mortimer was a strong believer in justice. He knew Vanilor was filled with evil and greed, sensing it'd eventually catch up to him. The only sadness Mortimer felt was for his wife and children.

Still no words murmured by anyone, Mortimer fled to the banquet hall to retrieve what he thought could help free the quorian.

"Seems like you have an admirer," Osvita whispered with a grin, shifting their focus. Nigel blushed, raised his eyebrows and widened his eyes, remaining quiet.

He'd never experienced another man complimenting his appearance, though appreciated it.

"Well that…was unexpected."

"He isn't wrong," Osvita smirked.

Eagerly awaiting Mortimer's return, she heard the quorian grunting and approached the cage.

"Just hold on, friend. Help is on the way."

With the heavy gusts of wind from the shattered windows, Mortimer was uncertain if he'd find what he was seeking. Heading toward the back of the room, shuddering at the valley below, Mortimer carefully approached Brugōr's podium, monitoring each step. The pressure built up, until he felt his heartbeat in his throat.

One wrong move, and he dies.

Scanning every inch, Mortimer desperately tried to search for his saving grace. With a heavy heart, he succumbed to sadness, uncertain how he would change the course for those he'd wronged.

He wondered if he'd ever meet Michael again to explain the situation and explore his emotional turmoil.

He wondered if an innocent family would reunite once again in their fight to stay alive.

He wondered who the assailant outside the region was, and the guard Brugōr killed, knowing they had both died from his actions.

Finally, he wondered if he'd be able to save the captured quorian who had survived an infamous genocide.

Mortimer wiped a single tear from his cheek. After an unsuccessful inspection of the podium, he sighed in defeat. It wasn't until he noticed an unusual piece of wood that he took a double take. If he didn't know it's appearance, it would've gone unnoticed. Following his curiosity, Mortimer was pleasantly surprised to see the magical device.

With excitement, he carefully exited the banquet room and returned to the group.

"I got it!" he shouted.

"What do you plan to do with that?" Osvita wondered.

"This is the Novalis Rod. It's uh…it's what we used to capture the poor thing back in Tillerack," Mortimer admitted. "We could transfer him from the cage into this, and then release him again."

"Brilliant idea."

"We must be careful though," Nigel added. "This quorian is Brugōr's prized possession. Maybe we should transfer him into that apparatus, but wait until it's safe to release him."

"What? You can't be serious. The poor soul has been tormented enough," Osvita rebutted.

"The last thing I'd want to do is torture the poor being even more," Nigel replied, "but if we aren't careful, he could end up in the wrong hands again, or worse."

"He makes a good point," Mortimer admitted.

"I'm sure there are others looking for him," Nigel added.

"There was another quorian when we captured this one. Fortunately, he escaped."

Agitated by his words, Osvita tried her best to not scowl too hard at him. She had seen his change of heart, but couldn't yet excuse his sins.

Raising the Novalis Rod, Mortimer focused on the caged quorian beneath the rubble, inches away from being smothered to death. The device immediately activated, picking up on the presence of a quorian.

"How does that thing work?" Osvita asked, curiously observing the rod as its panels began to lower.

"When the device recognizes a strong quorian presence, it activates and captures the quorian, pretty simple. Vanilor used it during the mission, but it does

441

all the work, the wielder just holds it up." Mortimer turned his head toward Osvita, away from the illumination.

"Oh…" Osvita said, hesitant, her head lowered. She slowly began to walk backwards, away from the device. "Don't you think you should get closer to the quorian?" she suggested. "Just to ensure its aim?"

"This distance should be sufficient enough," he said as the rod began to vibrate in his hand.

"Too bright for you, Vita?" Nigel chuckled, as she continued to step away from the men.

The quorian moaned from the rubble.

"It's working."

As the Novalis Rod vibrated in Mortimer's hand, lighting up the entire floor of the Kurhal, Osvita's heart raced.

She wondered how the quorian must've felt the first time he was captured.

She wondered how such a device could be created.

She wondered if he'd feel any pain.

Finally, she wondered why she suddenly felt a tingling sensation throughout her entire body.

Mortimer felt the Novalis Rod pull in the opposite direction. He tried to maintain the rod's position over the caged quorian and yet…it wanted to move. Aware that the device ultimately had control, Mortimer relinquished his resistance. The rod pulled to the right and he rotated in place. Nigel ducked as it passed by him and continued to move. Facing the opposite direction, the Novalis Rod illuminated much brighter than before. The three of them all lowered their heads as the luminous rod activated on its target.

"You're facing the wrong direction!" Nigel shouted.

"I have no control over it!"

"What…is happening!?" Osvita yelled. Nigel couldn't entirely see her, but he noticed her feet levitating off the ground. He blindly ran and leaped toward her, but crashed down upon the marble floor. He looked around, but she was nowhere to be found. He was surrounded by a plume of small, blue granules heading toward the Novalis Rod. Still too bright to focus on its center, Nigel tried his best to look around and flail his arms in an attempt to grab Osvita.

Just seconds after Nigel noticed the blue grains vanish, the blinding radiance of the rod came to an end. Mortimer collapsed to the floor from sheer exhaustion while Nigel feverishly surveyed the perimeter.

"Where is she?" he yelled, stomping toward Mortimer. "What have you done with her!?"

"Back off!" Mortimer shouted. "*I* didn't do anything."

"I thought you said that weapon only captures quorians! Have you been playing us this whole time!?" Not only had Nigel worried for Osvita's safety, but he'd forced himself to maintain his composure for her sake. With her sudden disappearance, he felt no need to contain himself.

"Of course not!" he rebutted. "The Novalis Rod is only capable of capturing those with quorian blood."

"Well, there must be some fucking mistake!" Nigel's veins bulged from his neck and one in his forehead. His eyes enraged. "Get your ass up and bring her back, n*ow*."

"Uuuhg…" the quorian mumbled, reminding the men that they needed to free the caged quorian before it was too late.

Mortimer stood up, wielding the enclosed Novalis Rod once more. Swirling it a few times high in the air above his head, a golden hue began to form around the dull, brown appearance. He then heaved it forward, maintaining a tight grip, and the panels seemed to fly off the rod, revealing the blinding illumination once more. As Mortimer turned to protect his eyes, Nigel covered his own with his hand, looking down in search of her feet.

Blue grains appeared and eventually formed into the shape of legs. He watched until they solidified into a recognizable vision. Nigel lunged forward, colliding with Osvita. Before they hit the ground, he quickly rolled to ensure she'd fall atop him for protection.

The Novalis Rod returned to its calm state and the three of them were able to see their surroundings once more.

"Osvita!" Nigel shouted. "Are you okay!? What happened? What did he do to you!?"

Though she seemed disoriented, Osvita was unharmed. Her troubled mind began to panic as she accepted her imminent reality.

My cover is blown, she thought. *It's over.*

"Osvita, say something," Nigel urged.

"Are you alright?" Mortimer asked, walking over, still wielding the rod.

"I'm fine," she said, accepting Nigel's assistance to stand.

The caged quorian groaned again. While Nigel was completely confused, Mortimer felt confident in his comprehension. He and Osvita locked eyes and there was a mutual understanding, which he respectfully remained silent about.

"We still need to save the caged quorian. He's been tortured enough. I've been where he's been, and it's safe there." Osvita paused. "Morty, are you confident you can save him?"

"Yes."

"Okay then. I'm heading down the stairwell." She brushed herself off. "Activate the rod to rescue him, then we can release him once we're somewhere safe, preferably far, far away from this place."

"What's going on!?" Nigel yelled, but it went unheard. Mortimer prepared to use the rod while Osvita continued toward the stairs. "Vita, I'm coming with you, wait up." Nigel followed her and the two let the door close behind them as they began their descent.

"What is going on, Osvita? You seem awfully calm." Nigel placed a concerning hand on her shoulder. She knew he had the best intentions, but was terrified to have the discussion she'd sworn to never divulge.

"We can talk about it later, Nigel."

"We have a long way to go," he rebutted. "Seems like now is the perfect time."

"It's…a long story."

He froze in place, letting her scurry ahead until she stopped, realizing he was no longer moving.

"Wait…" Nigel's eyes wandered around the room. "A long story? That rod's only meant to capture quorians. Instead of taking the caged one, you somehow entered the device." For a moment, Nigel thought about the possibility of her death from the device. "I don't know what I'd…" He stopped himself. Osvita could hear the fear and sadness in his voice. "I expected you to be just as surprised as I am. Confused. Shocked. Yet, instead…you just say it's a long story."

SLAM!

"I got him!" Mortimer's voice echoed from the top of the stairwell.

"Perfect!" Osvita shouted back, staring at Nigel. "I'm shocked and confused too, but there's also a lot going on behind the scenes," she admitted, her tone defeated.

Whether it was her adrenaline, the mutual understanding between her and Mortimer, or being fed up living a secret life, Osvita decided it was time for a change. A time for retribution. No more would she cower to others, including the leader of her home.

"What do you mean?" Nigel asked. "Please, Vita, you know you can talk to me." They continued down the stairs. "Osvita!" He shouted, causing her to stop.

"What do you want me to say!?" she shot back at him.

"Just talk to me," he pleaded. "I've loved you for years, you have to know that by now. Especially after our kiss…" There was a moment of silence between the two. Though she knew his feelings, it wasn't something they'd ever spoken about. "I always want what's best for you, this mission included. I warned Lazarus that *you* were my priority. Not the Anti-Regime, not Brugōr, nothing else. Your safety's all I'm concerned with. If anything were to ever happen to you…I…"

Nigel paused, sickened by the thought of Osvita's death. "I'm just asking you to please be honest. Tell me what's going on."

"You can't handle what's going on right now," she proclaimed. Osvita had a love for Nigel that ran deep, but like most of her emotions, she suppressed those feelings. Not only was she already married to Whark, but her insecurity made her feel Nigel might flee if he learned the truth. It was a heartbreak she couldn't fathom experiencing, and yet she feared her protection had come to an end.

"How many times are you going to have me beg you to talk to me?" he pleaded. Nigel and Osvita remained still in the stairwell with Mortimer quietly hovering a few flights above. Terrified of the result, yet aware of their urgency to flee, she exhaled and blurted everything out without thinking.

"Years ago, Whark and I had to leave our quorian home, known as The Quo. We relocated to The Barren Land. It's a complicated story which I refuse to go into right now, but yes…my blood is that of the quorian race. He and I both are. Before we left, our appearances were permanently altered to fit into…the Outer World."

Osvita felt her knees buckle but her arms held onto the railing tightly. Uncertain if she should be happy, she was at least relieved. "I'm of the quorian race," she repeated, for herself. What once seemed like a terrifying sentence proved to be an empowering statement.

Osvita slowly began her descent. As the stress of her secret rolled off her body, the fear of Nigel's opinion crept in. Terrified at what he thought, she remained silent. At first, she only heard her footsteps moving on the stairs, but then she heard others in the distance – Mortimer's. She stopped and looked backwards. Nigel was looking down in utter disbelief. He placed one foot in front of the other and took his first step. Her enlightened attitude quickly changed to a heavy heart, fearing his love for her had vanished.

The three of them continued down, in silence, until they eventually reached the ground level, where more screaming and howling ensued.

40

As the Kurhal struggled through the explosions surrounding the castle grounds, a more unsettling scene was unraveling on the main floor.

Out of an unmarked door from the back, Osvita entered the heart of the chaos. The grand entryway that was once a showstopper had become a death trap. Elaborate metalwork had been destroyed, luxurious crystal chandeliers had shattered into dozens of pieces, and twenty-foot pillars had fallen, tarnishing everything around it. Curtains covered portions of the carnage, which aided in hiding the sadness. Underneath the rubble lay dozens of bodies sprawled out like flies splattered on a wall. The stench of death was strong due to the enclosed space.

Amidst the chaos and carnage, there were still a plethora of workers, family members and guests running around. Some fled for their lives, others searched for their loved ones, and a few helped those near death. Since the explosions had stopped, the space echoed the eerie moans and yells. It was the kind of horror nightmares were made from.

Osvita paused from the shock, allowing for Nigel to catch up. Though the tension was palpable, they witnessed the devastation that unfolded on the ground level.

"Come on," he whispered. "Let's get out of here."

Before they stepped forward, the door swung open behind them. Considering they'd only met twice, Mortimer was happy the three of them remained together. As they made their way across the grand entryway, it became obvious just how big the space was, but navigating through the debris and bodies was troublesome.

"Hey!" someone shouted, as the three of them maneuvered through. "Nigel! Over here!" All three looked up and followed the voice.

"Lazarus!? Is that you?" Nigel shouted as the two men hurried toward one another. Eventually they all met almost halfway through the space.

"Nigel! You're still here! I expected you to be long gone."

"Where'd you think we'd be!?" Nigel wanted to persecute Lazarus for letting the explosions happen so early, but he understood the answer wouldn't change their situation. He stared at the familiar woman beside Lazarus.

"Shrenka?" The three of them were speechless. Osvita looked around, expecting Brugōr to be nearby. It gave them all an unsettling feeling to see her with the leader of the Anti-Regime during the plan they helped execute.

"What's *she* doing here?" Mortimer asked. Concerned, he had no intention of trusting her.

"She's been involved with the plan this whole time," Lazarus exclaimed.

"Your pathetic excuse of a leader is thirteen floors up, slowly dying as we speak. The mission was a success." Shrenka spoke confidently, with a sense of pride. Eyeing what was in Mortimer's possession, she watched him step back and place it behind him.

They all doubted Lazarus as he confidently stood beside the vindictive woman. Nigel couldn't help but sympathize for Brugōr. He knew they'd planned to ruin his succession and power, but he didn't anticipate it leading to his death.

"You killed him?" Mortimer confirmed.

"Sure did, and with his own weapon no less." Shrenka smiled, showcasing the small obsidian dagger, once belonging to Brugōr.

"Lazarus…" Nigel looked at him with disappointment. "Wait…what is that you have? Why is it glowing?"

"I'll explain later, my friend." He turned to Osvita. "Take this my dear, keep it safe and run." After placing the Transcending Tablets into her hands, he and Shrenka ran. Instead of heading toward the exit, they retreated into the tower.

"What are—"

"Didn't you mention earlier about…?" Mortimer stalled, mesmerized by the tablets.

"Is that the ancient artifact Brugōr and the guardian referred to?" Nigel wondered. "They did use the word *tablets*."

"I think so," Osvita admitted. "There is certainly something…special about them. I can't ex—"

A loud slam reverberated throughout the entryway, startling the group.

"Let's get out of here," Nigel insisted.

Mortimer led the pack with the Novalis Rod in hand, refusing to let anyone steal it. Osvita scurried along behind him, clinging to the tablets, with Nigel trailing at the back.

Another loud boom vibrated the floor.

"Are explosions still going off?" Osvita asked.

"No…those aren't explosions," Mortimer replied.

"Well then what—"

A deafening sonic boom blasted off the walls, causing everyone inside to shriek and pause. Osvita nearly dropped the tablets, but she tightened her grip.

"What in the world was that?" Mortimer wondered. The three of them turned around and, to their surprise, an unexpected guest had arrived at the ground floor.

"Brugōr's alive…" Nigel said. "And he brought a friend."

"They said they killed him…" Mortimer murmured.

"That's the guy we saw earlier!" Osvita added. "The guardian."

As Brugōr surveyed the room for his attackers, he was startled to see his precious Transcending Tablets in the hands of a woman whom, not too long ago, he'd cornered in the banquet kitchen.

"You!" His deep, enraged voice vibrated along the floor.

"Oh shit." Mortimer panicked. With the responsibility of justice and the quorian in his possession, he wasted no time following his suggestion. "RUN!" he shouted and bolted for the exit. Nigel grabbed Osvita's wrist and ran.

While the group needed to maneuver through the rummage, Brugōr carved his own way with his strength. As Jacob watched the leader create a path of destruction to retrieve the Transcending Tablets, he worried for Brugōr's condition. Unbalanced and disoriented, he knew something was wrong, but he'd made his decision. His role as guardian was to protect the ancient artifact and secure ownership.

"Alright, I'm going in," Jacob whispered to Anitta, following the path Brugōr made. He had expected to help Brugōr offensively, but after their fight against the thieves, he decided to maintain a defensive stance.

Mortimer exited the tower, ran down the stairs, between the spiked rose garden, and out into the open. Similar to the inside of the tower, the castle grounds were a disaster. Much of the castle wall had been destroyed.

Mortimer was stunned, yet impressed at the amount of damage the Anti-Regime had caused. "Come on!" he shouted.

As they ran toward the exit and approached the steps, Nigel turned around to see Brugōr quickly approaching. His dazed and hollow eyes were fixated on Osvita and the tablets in her possession. He sensed the rage in him, and his unwillingness to retreat. Envisioning his worst fear, while ensuring the destruction wouldn't be in vain, Nigel needed to make a hasty decision. With no time to analyze the repercussions, he urged Osvita to hand over the tablets.

"There's no time. Just keep running," she insisted as they reached the stairs.

"No!" he shouted, startling her. "I have an idea. Trust me."

"Once we get further away," Osvita urged, struggling to breathe.

As they fled the staircase, running between the spiked rose garden, Brugōr approached the landing and halted, his eyes straining to focus on the valley, and those in front of him.

A precognitive vision struck Jacob, and he witnessed the tablets in the air, quickly plummeting toward the ground. Knowing he could prevent it from breaking into a dozen pieces, he raced past the brute leader and stormed down the stairs before his vision came true.

Not being athletic, he struggled to breathe and maintain his speed, but knew the mission was nearly over. Jacob wanted to make his great grandmother proud and for his time away from family to not be in vain. It was enough to push him onward until another vision entered his mind. Frustrated, he wondered why his initial premonition hadn't included the whole scenario.

Terrified at the thought, he wanted to look back at Brugōr to stop him, but as he turned his head, a large spike from the rose garden soared past him, just inches from his head. The world around him stood still. Making eye contact with the leader, who remained atop the staircase, he heard the grunting and moaning of the victim Brugōr had impaled, followed by a painful scream.

From a single act of terror, Osvita relinquished the ancient artifact from her possession, tossing it up into the air. No longer focused on the mission, she collapsed to the ground in heart-wrenching pain, struggling to accept her reality.

Remaining perfectly still and without turning around, Jacob looked up into the night sky and saw the Transcending Tablets effortlessly floating down as if a gift from the Gods. Awaiting the reward, he thought about the significance of his twenty-third birthday. He'd considered himself young and feeble-minded until he met Giddeom. Though he still had much to learn, his life was on a fulfilling path of growth and exploration.

Catching the tablets, Jacob returned to the terrifying world around him. He watched as Brugōr cradled his head with one hand, the other holding himself up against the Kurhal. Taking a few steps toward the leader, he hesitated to look at what Brugōr had done. Though his vision notified him of the action, it didn't identify the victim.

Jacob slowly turned around and recognized the two chefs he'd met in his first meeting with Brugōr. Remembering the terrified looks on their faces, he struggled to believe either one was heavily involved in the attack. Regardless, the woman had been in possession of the tablets moments ago, which implicated her to some degree. He watched as her body trembled, sobbing in terror over the man who'd been impaled by Brugōr's spike. Piercing through the middle of his chest, even Jacob, a man with no medical expertise, knew he wouldn't survive. As the man lay face down in the sand, he yearned to help him, but knew it wasn't his place. Turning back to Brugōr as he approached the staircase, Jacob was enraged.

"Why'd you kill that man!? He didn't do anything!"

"The fuck if I know," Brugōr struggled, frustrated. "It's as though someone fucking drugged me!" he shouted, loud enough for everyone to hear. "I can't fucking see straight. You got the tablets, right?"

Jacob approached the steps and nodded.

Releasing all of her inner emotions, Osvita's wail was years of pent-up pain and angst as she watched the forbidden love of her life, Nigel Hatherton, dying. She desperately examined his condition, but she couldn't deny his fate.

"Nigel," she whispered. "Nigel, please…talk to me."

"Vita…" He turned his head left, as a pool of blood formed beneath him.

"How'd this happen? We shouldn't have agreed to this." Tears poured down her face. As Osvita sat beside Nigel, ignoring her surroundings, she felt the heaviness in her chest and the pain in her heart. It was torturous for her to watch the life of the man she loved slowly fade away, but she refused to leave his side. Osvita considered the countless moments he'd sworn to protect her and ensure her happiness.

The memories of jovial laughter.

The tears of tumultuous fear.

The culinary creations concocted by love.

Deeply saddened that the end was near.

Knowing death was imminent, Nigel used his strength to gaze into her piercing blue eyes one final time. As he lay on his deathbed, he ignored the curiosities that lingered between the two, most recently her quorian history. Nigel focused on the woman he'd grown to love and wished to spend his life with. Admiring Osvita's beauty, he gestured his final smile, happy to have spent so much time with her in his final days. He felt fulfilled and justified in his death to have ensured her safety.

"Osvita…my sweet love," he mustered. "I'll always love you…for who you are." Nigel coughed up blood, accepting he wouldn't be able to speak again.

As she watched his heavy eyelids, Osvita knew his time was fleeting.

"I love you, Nigel. I always have, and always will. I was always my happiest and safest when I was with you." She choked up as she noticed herself referring to him in the past tense, but Nigel widened his eyes and smiled at her words.

"We have to go," Mortimer said, his tone urgent but kind, resting his hand on her shoulder.

As she gazed upon Nigel one final time, their synchronous minds connected. They envisioned what their lives would've been like together. Living in a deciduous region, open farmland, surrounded by animals and a couple children while managing their culinary business together. Different from the life she once had and ended up with, it had become an unattainable dream. Nigel's expression relaxed as he exhaled his final breath, peacefully passing on from his physical body.

"We must leave *now*."

Osvita knew if it hadn't been for Mortimer, she would've died on top of Nigel's body. He made her stand as the two ran in the opposite direction, escaping with the Novalis Rod, the quorian, and their lives.

After handing the tablets to their rightful owner, Jacob returned to Nigel and knelt down.

"We have a situation here. I'm going to bring you out and see if you can do anything." Jacob brought Anitta out from his pocket and placed her on the ground.

"What do you think you're doing?" Brugōr shouted, but he ignored him. His words caught the attention of Osvita who turned around, focused on Jacob.

Anitta grew in size and evaluated Nigel's condition.

"Sorry, Jacob, but I cannot bring someone back from the dead. Once they've passed, it's too late," she said, her voice sorrowful.

"Shit," he replied. His eyes locked with Osvita's and before she turned away, he left her with a silent message.

I'm sorry.

With heavy hearts across the castle grounds, everyone was surprised by the discoloration in the sky. The Lost Sphere, the region's protective barrier for years, had begun to crumble. The localized sandstorm slowed down as the highest portions of the wall slowly dissipated.

"I don't understand." Brugōr stopped himself, rubbing his temples. "How's that possible?"

"How is what possible?" Jacob asked, ascending the Kurhal's stairs.

"Shrenka," he hissed. "That shrew. She must've obtained my blood. There's no other explanation."

"Your bloodline," Jacob remembered. "When could she have done that?"

"We…enjoyed extreme sex. It's not uncommon,"—he fought the disorientation—"for blood to shed."

"Uhh…"

"Only those with the purest of blood and blessing of a leader can activate an incantation. It's considered one of the cardinal rules."

With the Transcending Tablets back in his possession, Brugōr contemplated his next course of action. Hours ago, he was the most powerful man in the valley with a woman by his side and a quorian captured. He couldn't believe it had all vanished so quickly, though he wasn't entirely sure where the quorian ended up, due to his rage and delirium.

As he returned to the confines of the ruined Kurhal, Jacob trailed behind him.

"I guess my job here is done. The ancient artifact is back in your possession to do with as you see fit." Jacob felt relieved knowing his official responsibility had concluded, but sensed Brugōr's unsettling uncertainty.

"Aid in the destruction, and flee in the reconstruction," Brugōr proclaimed.

"I'll join you to safely return the artifact to its resting place." Sympathetic and confused, Jacob followed him up to his lair. "Are you sure this is still the safest place? Your tower has taken quite a punch. It could fall at any minute."

Brugōr stopped and turned to Jacob. "You really are a novice. An artifact's home is forever secure, so the Kurhal isn't going anywhere."

Jacob widened his eyes. "That would've been nice for Giddeom to share with me."

Far away in the distance, Lazarus and Shrenka lurked behind a pile of rubble and dead bodies, carefully watching the actions of Brugōr and his companion.

"Though we've had some unexpected events, everything ended well," Lazarus whispered.

"I didn't expect her to run back to the sacrificed one," Shrenka admitted.

"Me neither. I knew he foolishly loved her, but I didn't know where she stood, especially as a married woman. Fortunately, we were depending on his love for her, not her love for him."

"Are you sure it's a good idea to have him keep the artifact? Why can't we just—"

"We've been over this," Lazarus interrupted. "If that dumbass didn't keep the ancient artifact, who knows what Divinity and Giddeom would've done. Brugōr can keep it, for now. Besides, it's not even one of the most powerful ones." He chuckled. "We'll let them continue thinking their actions are unnoticed until we're ready."

"What…is that!?" Shrenka interrupted, pointing at Jacob. "Look at what's in his hand!"

"Shhh," Lazarus reminded her to remain quiet. He grabbed a pair of binoculars and focused in on his possession. "My word…"

"Is that…?"

"That's *the* divine artifact. I haven't been able to find any evidence of it. I started to believe it was a myth." Lazarus lowered the binoculars, relieved to visualize it with his own eyes.

"Should we go after him?" Shrenka prepared to charge.

"No." He put his hand out, glancing at them. "The acquisition of knowledge prompts prestigious strength. We know more than anyone would expect. Hell…we may know more than that old hag Giddeom. I wonder if he had any idea the divine artifact was right under his nose."

"He apologized…" Osvita sobbed to Mortimer, as he continued to ensure a safe enough distance between them and destruction.

Mortimer felt an unexpected bond with Osvita Dimmerk. They captured a quorian, learned of her origin, observed Lazarus's objective, momentarily obtained an ancient artifact, escaped death and, finally, watched her agonize over Nigel's death. Though they hadn't discussed their mutual feelings, Mortimer sensed their love.

"I…I can—" Osvita collapsed on the ground, forcing Mortimer to stop.

"Osvita, we have to keep going. We've seen how devious he can be. His actions cannot be trusted, especially in his altered state." He looked back and noticed Brugōr and Jacob walking into the tower. For the first time in a while, he exhaled in relief as their enemy retreated.

"I…I just…I can't breathe."

"Okay…" Mortimer surveyed their surroundings. "Looks like we can rest for a minute. The monster went back inside and no longer seems interested in us."

Placing the Novalis Rod down beside Osvita, he wanted to let the quorian free, but knew he couldn't manage both him and her mental state, so he waited. "I'm so terribly sorry, Osvita. I can't imagine…" He paused. "Is there anything I can do?"

"No…" She tried to compose herself, taking a few slow, deep breaths. "I'm eternally grateful for the experience and time I shared with Nigel. He was a great person and a…a good friend."

"You were both fortunate to have loved one another," Mortimer strategically expressed. Osvita sensed he'd known of their guilty secret.

"Yes…" She paused. "Mortimer, can you please not mention any of this to—"

"Whark!" he exhaled dramatically.

"Y-yes," Osvita stuttered, confused and concerned by his flamboyant expression. "I'd like to keep this between us. There's no—"

"Whark!" Mortimer shouted again. "Look, it's him! He's here!"

Disoriented from her saddened, emotional state, Osvita turned around and saw a vehicle steadily approaching them. She didn't actually think her husband, who'd been missing during her entire struggle, would suddenly appear. That fateful day at Grum's house seemed like a lifetime ago, especially after what had just happened. It was in that moment she thought about Grum…and Rexhia. *Her daughter*.

"How do you know what my husband looks like?" she asked.

"Castle guards asked if we'd seen him and showed us pictures." He paused. "I vowed to never forget his face, and to help him if I were given the opportunity. That's him, isn't it?" Osvita looked directly at the driver, who was steadily approaching.

"Wh…Whark?" Though it sounded like a question, she instantly knew it was her husband. "It's really him."

Startled by her lack of enthusiasm to see her husband, Mortimer helped Osvita stand up. He didn't know if she was excited to see him or if the sadness and exhaustion wouldn't allow it. Regardless, he knew she should put on a performance since it'd been so long.

"Smile." He patted her on the back. "I got you," he said reassuringly.

Osvita appreciated having someone by her side who had experienced the same turmoil. She never expected the man who captured the quorian to become her closest confidant.

The vehicle came to a screeching halt and the passenger door was the first to open.

"Osvita, ho ho!" Grum exclaimed with a grin from ear to ear. Osvita tilted her head, shedding a tear of happiness to see her funny, quirky friend. Out from behind him, the back passenger door opened and an excited Rexhia jumped out of the car, running to her mother.

"Mom!" she joyfully yelled. Osvita let her emotions run rampant as the stream of tears steadily flowed down her face. And so she cried.

For the excruciating mission to be over.

For the excitement of seeing her daughter.

For having her family back together.

And for losing the love of her life that she neglected to accept until it was too late.

The two embraced for a long while until Osvita released her daughter, taking a good look at her.

"My sweetheart, how are you? Are you hurt?"

"No, Mom! I'm doing great. Grum and I have been together the whole time." Rexhia's exuberant voice couldn't be tamed. Just then, a familiar little dog hopped out of the car and ran toward Rexhia.

"Is that Chowder!?" Osvita smirked. Elated to see her, it was a heartbreaking reminder of Nigel's death and that her tail would never wag for him. She knelt down and gave Chowder a tight squeeze, holding onto his spirit.

Osvita turned to her husband, locked eyes, and began to weep fresh tears. Tears that were meant for him. Though she struggled with her interpersonal happiness and a secondary love, it didn't diminish the love she had for Whark. They'd been through struggles only they could understand. Osvita knew she missed her husband, but it wasn't until she saw his nurturing face, that she realized she *needed* to see him.

As she walked around the car, maintaining eye contact with Whark, Rexhia and Chowder stood beside Grum, who placed his arm around her. Mortimer approached them and quietly introduced himself.

Osvita and Whark slowly walked toward one another. As their distance narrowed, Whark was uncertain what he should say. There were numerous emotions he wanted to express, but in the moment, nothing seemed clear to him. Osvita, on the other hand, charged forward with a smile, still crying, well aware of what her first move was.

SLAP.

The group was stunned. Rexhia placed her hand over her mouth. Grum chuckled to himself, which Rexhia smacked his belly for with the back side of her hand.

"That's for unsuccessfully finding us this whole time," she muttered before embracing him tightly and sharing a long kiss with him. Rexhia covered her eyes in disgust. Genuinely happy for her husband's return, she morbidly considered how her lips had just left Nigel's dying body and now went to her husband. She could feel her tears for him wanting to be released, but she suppressed them, for now.

"I hate to break this beautiful moment," Mortimer interjected, "but we should get out of here."

"By here, you mean...?" Grum wondered.

"The Barren Land." Mortimer replied.

"He's right," Osvita interrupted. "Look around. The Lost Sphere has nearly vanished." She paused, looking back. "Who knows what'll happen when the region becomes open to anyone, and anything."

"I say we get into your car, head straight into the upper level and out of the region's perimeter. Brugōr could reactivate The Lost Sphere at any moment, and then we're all trapped."

Mortimer made a good point, which everyone agreed upon. Whark, Grum and Rexhia had no idea how or why the protective barrier fell, but trusted his judgement.

"We can just swing by home and—"

"No need," Whark said. "We already grabbed all our important belongings. Something told me we may not have been able to return home for a while."

"Did you grab the—" Osvita eyed him, hiding her mouth with her hand.

"Yup," he whispered and nodded.

"Morty, did you want to swing by your home before we leave? Grab a few things?" Osvita asked. After what they'd experienced together, she considered him a friend for life.

"You know…" Mortimer examined the crumbling region around him. Aware of his participation in the destruction, he wanted nothing more than to run and start fresh. He patted his pants pocket, remembering the final amount of jinugery he had remaining from his reward. He hoped to one day arrive in Tillerack, meet Michael again, and start anew. Even after all they had been through, he couldn't shake the connection he'd shared with the stranger. Seeing Osvita and Nigel navigate their struggle to an untimely demise pushed him to accomplish his dream.

He facilitated the reunion of the Dimmerks.

He was leaving The Barren Land with the Novalis Rod in hand, prepared to set free the quorian he'd helped capture.

He planned to return to Tillerack and make amends with Michael.

Though unable to repent for the assailant outside the region and the guard who'd died in the meeting with Brugōr, Mortimer was pleased with his attempted recovery thus far.

"I'm okay," he finally responded with a smile. "Everything I wish to bring with me is already here."

With that, the reunited group entered Whark's vehicle and sped off toward the upper level of the valley for one final drive through the region of The Barren Land.

41

In what seemed like an eternal silence, they studied the sphere, questioning any changes, no matter how futile.

Fravia carefully observed the speed of the winds while Smolar darted his eyes, looking for any color changes within the wall. Rhugor stared at where the amulet had penetrated, prepared to catch it.

"Hey! I think I see something." Fravia and Smolar ran toward Rhugor and looked up. Unlike the region of Azjura, they could all visualize the amulet's rejection, once again removed from The Lost Sphere. Rhugor tried to catch it, but this time, Fravia and Smolar had the height advantage.

"I got it!" Fravia shouted and jumped up to catch it. Her hands immediately collapsed by the gravitational pull of the amulet.

"No go. Failed attempt yet again…" Smolar said to Lady Vixa, uncertain of their next step. Gazing upon The Lost Sphere, Smolar described its appearance once more, hoping Lady Vixa could provide more insight or a new idea. Nearby, Rhugor overheard their conversation, igniting a revelation. Aware of the never-ending sandstorm above ground, he wondered what would happen if he traveled underneath. Standing relatively close to the barrier, he feverishly began to dig. Smolar noticed him, quickly understanding his idea. Though he didn't assist, he appreciated Rhugor's creativity.

Ever since the Amulet of Eymus fell into Fravia's hands, she hadn't been able to look away. It mesmerized and captivated her, having never held a majestic artifact. She didn't know the history of it, but like Smolar, she'd always seen Lady Vixa with it around her neck. It had always appeared the same glistening ruby red. From afar, it seemed like an ordinary piece of jewelry; however, in her possession, it was completely different. Once she touched the amulet, it changed. Unaware that her cohorts had walked away, Fravia stared into the heart of the jewel. It began to glow from a vibrant ruby to a glistening silver. Eventually, Fravia felt a vibration in her hand.

"Guys…" she said softly, but no one heard her. The vibration increased, as if holding a fistful of bumble bees. She looked off in the distance; Rhugor was tirelessly digging and Smolar was heavily concentrated on the sphere, talking to Lady Vixa. Suddenly, Fravia heard a strange chant. It was short lived, but she was certain. She froze, hoping for it to return. After nearly a minute of silence, it happened again.

Iunge interiorem fortitudinem tuam. Tu es electus.

Fravia jumped, fumbling the amulet in her palm, but regained control. She'd never experienced such a visceral reaction with an object. While she hadn't dealt with enchantments before, she imagined it was what it would feel like. She was simultaneously frightened and excited as her mind yearned for more. Fravia heard the chant again, but louder.

Iunge interiorem fortitudinem tuam. Tu es electus.

"Do you guys hear that?" she asked, her volume higher than before.

Rhugor stopped. Uncertain of what she'd said, he poked his head out from the hole. He glanced at Smolar who had his back to them, still chatting with Lady Vixa. Turning to Fravia, his eyes widened, fangs exposed.

"Fravia!" he shouted. His roar reverberated the ground, which Smolar felt. He turned around, stunned at what he witnessed. Fravia, focused on the amulet, sensed strong emotions. Pain, sadness, sorrow, loneliness. It was a pandora's box of Lady Vixa's troubled feelings, as she had explained to them earlier.

"Hold on," Smolar said, running toward Rhugor. "What's going on!?"

"I...I don't know. She said something, but I couldn't hear it. When I looked up to ask her, that's what I saw." Rhugor extended his right paw with one elongated claw.

Levitating in front of The Lost Sphere was their companion, Fravia Deallius, with the Amulet of Eymus in her hands. With her brown hair flowing up around her, gravity ceased to exist in her presence. Smolar and Rhugor stood mesmerized.

"Fravia?" Smolar asked. "Fravia? Can you hear me?" He heard Lady Vixa ask if everything was alright. "Fravia's elevated in front of the sphere. The amulet's in her hands."

"It can't be...it—" Lady Vixa wished she could've visualized it.

"Tell Lady Vixa I'm sorry," Fravia's tone echoed through them. Her face expressed deep sadness. "I'm sorry for all the pain she's gone through. No one should suffer so much."

"She said she's s—"

"I heard..." Lady Vixa replied in shock.

"It's time." Fravia's soft blue eyes turned white, refocusing on the sphere. "Iunge interiorem fortitudinem tuam. Tu es electus," she repeated.

"What's happening?" Rhugor asked.

"Lady Vixa, what's this about? What's your amulet doing!?"

Fravia closed her eyes and separated her hands, allowing the amulet to levitate on its own. "Go. Express your pain. Help us by helping yourself."

Fravia spoke to the weapon as if it could hear her.

As if it were alive.

The Amulet of Eymus began to float toward The Lost Sphere.

"It's glowing!" Rhugor shouted.

"Did she activate it somehow!?" Smolar wondered. "Lady Vixa, please. You must know something. This is your amulet!"

"I'm just as surprised as you are, Smolar. I thought you'd be the one to do this, not Fravia."

Silence hung in the air as they watched Fravia slowly return to their level. There was a crackle within The Lost Sphere. Moments later, a loud boom reverberated from within the storm. Once Fravia's feet were firmly planted on the ground, Smolar and Rhugor ran toward her.

"Are you okay!?" Smolar asked, wrapping his arms around her.

"Yes…I-I think so." She was exhausted.

"What happened?" Rhugor asked. She turned to Smolar with a heavy heart, uncertain of what to say.

"I'm not entirely sure…" she murmured, rubbing her head in disarray.

Another loud boom was heard and they all jumped back. The rapid storm surrounding The Barren Land slowed down as its highest portions started to vanish. The orange, brown and yellow hue faded, turning to a thick, dense fog. Once more, another loud boom echoed from within the sandy walls.

"Is it…?" Rhugor hesitated.

"The Lost Sphere's falling!" Smolar shouted. "Fravia, you did it!" The two embraced and Rhugor joined on his hind legs.

"I'm so proud of you all!" Lady Vixa said. "Smolar, if you don't mind, I'd like to speak with Fravia."

"Of course," he replied with a smile. Smolar handed his Pendant of Perception over.

"Hello?" she answered.

"Fravia, listen to me. You've done a wonderful job awakening the Amulet of Eymus, and for that I'm proud, but now, it's your time to avoid any altercations or danger."

"What do—"

"Once you safely return home, we will discuss the matter further," Lady Vixa interrupted. "It's not ideal to have this conversation from such a distance, but…it's imperative that you be told. This whole time I assumed Smolar would be my successor, but it appears you're the selected one. Destiny has chosen for you to be the next Quorian Ruler."

"What!? You must be kidding." Her reaction caught the attention of the others. She waved them off, downplaying their conversation.

"Only the chosen ruler is capable of activating my amulet, understanding it's true emotions."

"You mean *your* true emotions." Fravia walked away from her companions. "How's this even possible? I'm not fit to rule."

"You may not be now, but you're on your way there. You're more prepared than you think," Lady Vixa admitted.

"And what about Smolar? He mentioned an apparition visited you, proclaiming he was next to succeed."

"Technically, that's not what was said," Lady Vixa explained, correcting the events that happened on that night many years ago.

As they privately spoke, away from Smolar and Rhugor, the barrier continued to dissipate. The debris could no longer be seen as the dense fog had consumed it completely. Just as Smolar was about to step forward to touch the smokescreen, a loud, vibrant crackle of lightning rushed down from the sky and they protected their eyes from the brightness. When they returned their gaze to the fog, each one of them froze with uncertainty and terror.

The Lost Sphere had completely vanished, the barrier lifted. The land was vast and wide, as far as their eyes could see, impossible to distinguish where the barrier once resided. It was the cleanest destruction they'd ever witnessed.

Excited at the prospect of saving Promit, Smolar searched for Fravia, noticing her distance.

"Hey!" he shouted. "Fravia!"

"Just a second," she shouted back, waving her hand, as Lady Vixa finished her explanation.

"But look! The barrier is gone! We can enter The Barren Land and save Promit!" He glistened with happiness and excitement.

"Brilliant!" she exclaimed, spinning her head around.

"Put him on and I'll talk to him," Lady Vixa said in her ear.

"Are you sure? Now?"

"I know now isn't the best time, but he must know. It's important that the future ruler of The Quo is protected, at all costs."

"She'd like to speak with you." Fravia kissed Smolar on the cheek and smiled, handing the Pendant of Perception back to him.

"So we're good to head ins—"

"Smolar, we need to talk," Lady Vixa intervened. Her tone calmed his excitement. "I'm going to tell you the same thing I told Fravia." She paused, aware the discussion with him would be very different. "After what we've just witnessed…Smolar, I was wrong. You aren't going to be my successor as the next Quorian Ruler – Fravia is."

Smolar remained quiet, so she continued.

"Convinced you were the next ruler, I gifted you the Amulet of Eymus. Unfortunately, fate had an alternative plan because it was Fravia who synchronized with it. She was able to awaken its core and understand its pain. Only the true successor could handle such a majestic power." Lady Vixa paused again, hoping for a response.

"But…what about the apparition? I thought it identified me as the ruler-to-be?"

"It certainly seemed that way at the time. Destiny did, and still does, have an imperative role for you to play, it's just different than what you…what *we* expected."

"And what role would that be?"

"The eternal love and support for your future Quorian Ruler. Fravia's love for you is powerful enough to demoralize her if something were to happen. You are her strongest ally and her greatest weakness."

Smolar knew they loved one another, but having Lady Vixa explain how deep her love ran surprised him. He glanced toward her, standing beside Rhugor, as they looked upon The Barren Land. His heart fluttered with love and excitement. Fravia turned around with a reassuring smile.

"I really do love her," he whispered.

"I know you do."

"But wait…how do you know all of this now?"

"Hindsight. This evaluation of the situation makes perfect sense. Fravia is a well-educated quorian that comes from a background of medical explorers. She's spent her life learning Quorian and Diverian history, while grasping important insight from her parents. The acquisition of knowledge prompts prestigious strength. While she focused on education, you've been able to understand the methodologies of a Quorian Ruler. Whether you realize it or not, you've gained invaluable insight and experience living under my roof. You've been exposed to situations others couldn't imagine. Paired with the unconditional love you two share, it allows for an inspirational and unstoppable new reign within our city."

The two remained silent for a moment, reflecting on their lives.

"If I can be honest, I'm partially relieved to hear all of this," he said with a smile. Lady Vixa exhaled a huge sigh of relief.

"Really?"

"Yeah. Sure, it seemed great, but I couldn't imagine the pressure and stress. I think Fravia would flourish in the position. She's well-educated and well-connected throughout the community. I'm confident she has what it takes to help guide the quorians into the next phase of our race's journey."

"And I'm confident you have what it takes to assist her in accomplishing those goals," Lady Vixa reassured him.

"Thank you."

As he made his way back toward the group, Smolar felt lighter than he had moments ago. Uncertain if it was the dissipation of The Lost Sphere, the relief of not being the next Quorian Ruler, or his love for Fravia exponentially growing, he silently approached and embraced her from behind, kissing the side of her neck.

"I love you," he whispered in her ear. "I'm so proud of you, and I'm here every step of the way." She turned around and gazed into his eyes, fighting the urge to cry.

"Thank you." She grinned and tightly embraced him.

"Hey, guys, I hate to ruin your special moment, which we'll get to later, but it seems we have company," Rhugor said, walking ahead of the two lovebirds with their hands still intertwined.

Looking out on the horizon, the three well-disguised quorians watched as a stream of civilians and vehicles rushed in their direction. Too far to identify any details, Smolar began explaining the scene to Lady Vixa.

"Uh, what's going on!?" Fravia widened her eyes. Rhugor immediately ran onward to better visualize the situation with his heightened sight.

"I can't tell if they're running toward us or just in our direction," Smolar told Lady Vixa.

"Hey," Rhugor shouted, "you should both come take a look at this!" Fravia and Smolar ran toward Rhugor. "Look!" He pointed downward with an extended claw.

For the first time in their lives, three quorians gazed upon the entire region of The Barren Land from up above. Dangerously high, they maintained their distance from the edge. Time ceased to exist as each of them absorbed the animosity and chaos amidst the region below. They were stunned not only at the size of the land, but the amount of turmoil they were witnessing. More importantly, they were clueless as to how they'd find Promit, or if he was still okay.

"Where do we even begin looking?" Smolar wondered.

"How do we even know he's…." Rhugor hesitated to finish the sentence. Smolar sighed.

"Promit's alive," Fravia said. "I know he is. Maybe the turmoil is connected with his presence. If they put as much effort into his capture as they did into maintaining his survival, chances are he's still alive...somewhere."

"You think they want to keep him alive?" Smolar wondered optimistically.

"You don't capture a supposed extinct race for sport. Not yet anyway. They want information, knowledge."

"Information on what?" Rhugor asked.

"How our race survived the genocide from their infallible king."

42

Arriving on the upper level of The Barren Land, everyone in Whark's vehicle sensed their lives permanently changing as they drove away from a region they'd called home. For the majority of the group, no one had seen such a spectacular view of Diveria since they'd first arrived. Mortimer's last experience was the unforgettable evening when he and Vanilor returned with the Novalis Rod through the border. He felt vindicated, and found it poetic, to remove the rod from the valley without his partner. Though it saddened Mortimer for anyone to perish, he felt no shame or guilt in Vanilor's death. It gave him hope that justice prevailed.

The only person who experienced the new world for the first time was thirteen-year-old Rexhia. With Chowder on her lap, and her trusty slingshot Sohnora by her side, she was excited to see what was beyond The Lost Sphere. Looking back one last time at the only home she'd known, Rexhia wondered if they'd ever return one day. Not sad to say goodbye, she knew the memories she held onto were stronger than any tangible remnant of the region.

"I think we're outside where The Lost Sphere used to be," Whark hypothesized. Mortimer surveyed their surroundings and nodded.

"Slow down!" Osvita shouted. Whark slammed on his breaks. Too focused on his surroundings, he hadn't seen the innocent bystander he nearly ran over.

Everyone in the car took a moment to realize how many civilians had fled the region. Some wandering alone, others walking in larger groups, and a select few had their vehicles to take with them in search of a new life.

"Everybody okay?" Whark asked, initially checking on his daughter who was tightly holding Chowder. They all confirmed their safety, readjusting their belongings. "Sorry about that."

"You know," Mortimer said slyly, "since we're outside the valley, we should really consider,"—he glanced at Rexhia, choosing his words carefully—"setting it free."

"My word!" Osvita shouted, embarrassed it had slipped her mind after Nigel's death. "We need to handle that right now," she demanded, stepping out from the vehicle. Mortimer followed and opened the rear passenger door.

"Wait…isn't that…?" Whark shuddered, delayed in his realization. His last observation of the Novalis Rod changed the course of his family's life. He exited the vehicle and stood beside his wife.

"I say we release him here," she suggested.

"You sure?"

"Release him?" Whark questioned abruptly. He glanced at his daughter, then whispered to his wife, "You know what's in there, right?" His gaze piercing through Mortimer.

"Honey," Osvita whispered, turning to her husband, "we have much to catch up on about each other, but for now, let me just tell you this. Mortimer was one of the two men who captured the quorian."

"That's where I recognized you from!" Whark shouted.

"Shh, keep your voice down," Osvita reminded him. "We shouldn't waste any more time, but believe me, I know. It was a troublesome start, to say the least. After some admirable actions and honorable loyalty, Mortimer and I have a unique bond," she said, smiling at him. "He's dedicated his life to correcting the wrongs he committed, including the captured quorian."

"So he's in there now? The quorian?" Whark whispered.

"Yes," Mortimer confirmed.

"Well, Vita, if you trust him, then so do I." Whark smiled at Mortimer with a sense of arrogance, as if he should be lucky to have his trust.

"Okay. How should we do it? We're in the open, but there are others around us." Osvita looked for a solution.

"We brought him here to set him free. Why not just release him and let him roam?" Mortimer's suggestion was heard, but not responded to.

"How about we release him into the car?" Whark said. "We can evaluate his condition, see how we can help, and maybe know where he'd like to go?"

Though Osvita agreed, Mortimer sympathized for the quorian, going from one cage to another.

"Are you sure?"

"Yes. If we release him here, who knows how long he'd survive. We should see if he needs help first."

"Rexhia," Whark whispered, putting his hand out to stop his wife. "What are we going to tell her?"

"The truth," she said. "We'll keep it simple, but let her know the quorian race was thought to be extinct, bad people wanted to harm him, and we saved him." Whark typically preferred protecting his daughter, but knew this was the right course of action, especially given their lineage.

"Sounds great, but…" He paused, looking at Mortimer once again.

"Oh yes." Osvita smiled, leaning in toward her husband's ear. "Mortimer knows of our identity. Don't worry, he won't say a word." Whark darted him a look of surprise. Though he hadn't heard their discussion, Mortimer knew what Osvita had said. He nodded to show his loyalty and respect.

Grum and Rexhia exited the vehicle. As she spoke, focusing on her daughter's comprehension, Grum and Mortimer discussed the events that unfolded.

"How'd they all die?" Rexhia asked, looking down to see Chowder calmly sitting beside her.

"We can go into that another time, sweetie," Osvita said. "Just know that what you'll see inside is a quorian. Though it may look different, they're harmless and kind. They believe in love, honoring one another, and respecting their environment, understood?"

"Okay, Mom." Rexhia smiled.

With her hands on her daughter's shoulders, Osvita nodded to Mortimer to activate the Novalis Rod. The rear passenger door was open as he repeated a motion that had unfortunately become familiar to him. The group admired the Novalis Rod until it activated, and the bright light forced everyone to protect their eyes.

Further away from The Barren Land's perimeter, Fravia, Smolar and Rhugor prepared to descend into the region with uncertainty. The future Quorian Ruler trailed slightly behind the other two, implementing a new dynamic. With a main goal of rescuing Promit in mind, it was also imperative that Fravia safely return to The Quo, no matter the cost.

To their surprise, as they advanced on the approaching wanderers, no one seemed hostile or agitated. Everyone they encountered was too preoccupied or startled to even acknowledge their presence.

"At least no one is trying to attack us," Fravia whispered.

"Everyone's just leaving The Barren Land?" Smolar wondered.

"More like fleeing," Rhugor corrected.

As they continued, they were suddenly blinded by a luminous flash of light, forcing them to turn away. Smolar instantly recalled a similar flash when Promit was captured, illuminating his escape path. He strained his eyes to visualize beyond the brightness. All he identified was a group surrounding a car not too far away.

"Rhugor, can you see anything?" Smolar asked.

"Not a thing."

"Gahh…" Fravia moaned.

"Fravia! Are you okay?" Smolar turned to inquire.

"Yes, it's just too bright. I can't even try to look."

"Don't," he demanded. "Protect your vision. Anything yet, Rhugor?" Smolar asked.

With one final effort, Rhugor struggled for as long as he could until he felt his eyes burn and lowered to the ground.

"Rhugor?" Fravia and Smolar inquired.

"I'm okay…" He sighed. "I saw a man holding a stick. The end was too bright to look at. I couldn't—"

"Did you see what the man looked like?" Smolar jolted upwards.

"He was tall, skinny…" Rhugor described. "His face wasn't memorable."

Smolar knew who it was, wondering how such a coincidence was possible. He tossed his head up, widened his eyes and charged.

"Smolar!" Fravia and Rhugor shouted, but it was no use.

Smolar tried his best not to look directly into the glistening void, but he refused to lose track of it. His eyes burned as tears rolled out the corners of his eyes and down his face. He wanted so badly to yell and scream, but he didn't want to scare his target away. If Smolar was correct, then the same man wielding the same weapon was either about to capture Promit once again or release him. Either way, he didn't intend to let him leave a second time. Fravia and Rhugor wanted to follow, but they remained back to ensure her safety.

Eventually the blinding light dissipated and Smolar collapsed to the ground. When he raised his head, his eyes still burned and his vision was blurry, but he identified his target's distance.

When Mortimer successfully released the quorian from the Novalis Rod, he slumped against the car, exhausted. Osvita checked to make sure he was okay, which he confirmed. Relieved to not use the Novalis Rod again, he tossed it to the ground. Grum grabbed Rexhia, stepping back to examine the quorian inside the car.

Osvita was pleasantly surprised by his quiet and curious demeanor, which was starkly different from the rage in the banquet hall. It brought her much pride to see a fellow quorian outside of their city, no matter the dangers. Uncertain whether The Quo would aid in his recovery, Osvita missed her true identity.

Captivated by the quorian, Rexhia was unable to look away. When the two made eye contact, she suddenly had a vision. Rexhia saw the same quorian from the car, surrounded by many others of the same race, in a large, cavernous city. The bioluminescent surroundings were breathtaking. She heard running water echoing around her. She could smell the damp, fresh air.

"Rexhia,"—Grum patted her shoulder—"you okay?" Her eyes opened as she jolted back to reality outside The Barren Land.

"Yes," she replied, looking at the quorian who was facing Mortimer. "I'm okay."

Chowder curiously inched toward the car, her sniffer running wild. Uncertain of the quorian and the dog, Rexhia swooped her up and held her tightly against her chest.

"What's that man doing?" Whark asked, pointing toward an average looking man with rich, royal blue eyes, cream skin and blonde hair approaching them in a fury.

While everyone looked up, Mortimer focused on the quorian inside the vehicle.

"Come on," he carefully whispered, quietly opening the back seat driver's side door. "You're free, run."

Mortimer had done it – he'd successfully corrected one of his biggest regrets. Finding internal happiness and forgiveness for his poor choice, he watched as the quorian approached the door.

"What're you doing!?" Osvita's jaw dropped. In a short amount of time, she'd gone from hating Mortimer to entrusting him with her most vulnerable secret. In that moment, she acknowledged her fragile mental state.

"Be free!" Mortimer shouted, uncertain if the quorian even understood him. He flung the door wide open and stepped back. The quorian leaped, taking advantage of the opportunity.

"No!" Osvita said, fearing for his safety.

The group stood around the car, stunned as the freed quorian ran away in fright.

As Smolar rushed toward the location of the Novalis Rod, he noticed a figure run out of the car and head straight in his direction. *A quorian.* Smolar's heart raced as he veered away from the group and toward his friend. With Fravia and Rhugor's eyes now adjusted, they watched Smolar.

"A quorian!" Rhugor shouted. The two sprinted toward the target.

"Is it…?" Fravia asked, breathing heavily.

"Promit!" Smolar shouted.

Everyone fixated on the confusion in front of them as the two ran toward each other. Rexhia took it upon herself to bring out her trusted sidekick, Sohnora. Within seconds, she effortlessly directed a shot with perfect aim into the back of the escaping quorian's right leg.

"What just…?" Mortimer shouted.

"How did—" Osvita turned, realizing her daughter was holding her slingshot. "Why would you do that!?"

"I thought—"

"That poor quorian has been through enough turmoil and torture," Osvita yelled.

"Smolar!" cried a voice in the distance.

Osvita and Whark spun around ignoring everyone, including their own daughter.

"No!" Smolar shouted as his friend collapsed to the floor. "Promit! It's me,

Smolar! You're alive!" he said, approaching his fallen friend.

"Sm-Smolar? Is it you? But—" Promit questioned his appearance.

Smolar remembered his altered state and quickly explained in as few words as possible.

"You're alive!" he said when he was finished, embracing Promit while on the floor. "We've been looking for you."

"We?"

"Fravia and our new friend, Rhugor," Smolar explained, pointing back to their approaching companions. "The three of us…We can explain later. We should move."

"Thank you…for coming for—"

"Save your efforts, my friend. Are you hurt? Can you walk?"

"I'm…I'm okay. That shot hurt," he admitted, rubbing the back of his leg, "but I'll be okay."

"Good, let's run."

Osvita and Whark were speechless, the shock rendering them unable to move. The name yelled from across the open desert was an unusually familiar name. Smolar had been the name of her great grandfather, a quorian she'd been closer to than her real father. In honor of him, Osvita had bestowed the name on her firstborn son. Trying to focus on the strangers across the way, she was about to head in their direction when she heard a deathly howl. Osvita turned to see Mortimer collapsed to the floor with a startling figure behind him.

Vanilor.

Grum instinctively grabbed Rexhia and Chowder, placing them behind him as he backed away from the violence.

"No!" Osvita screamed, glancing at her daughter, ensuring her safety.

"You son of a bitch!" Whark shouted.

They all watched in horror as the shorter, more disheveled looking man, violently stabbed and sliced. Mortimer moaned and shouted in agony. Whark was about to lunge forward when Vanilor retracted his arm and retreated.

"Consider this a warning to you all. Don't fuck with Vanilor Dipythian and the work we've accomplished in The Barren Land." His eyes darted to the quorian escaping in the distance. "Your attempted destruction upon the valley will allow for a revitalized foundation that the region so desperately needed. Mark my words, we will come for you *all*."

"*Our* attempted destruction!?" Osvita rebutted, but Vanilor had already stormed off back towards The Barren Land. Though she knew the destruction was at the hands of Lazarus, the argument was futile. She focused her attention on Mortimer.

"What can we do!?" Grum asked.

"Morty, stay with me. You're going to be okay. We'll get you through this." Osvita fell to the floor beside him.

"No," Mortimer muttered before spewing blood across the sand. Osvita and Whark exchanged glances as she struggled to contain her rage from the abundance of death.

"What can we possibly do?" Whark asked, as the sand beneath Mortimer turned dark red, soaking up the blood. With the little strength he had left, Mortimer reached into his back pocket, pulled out a folded piece of paper and handed it to Osvita, trying to keep it clean.

"Take this. Keep it safe." His face winced in pain as he spoke. Osvita accepted it, placing it into her pocket.

"Morty…"

"If you ever meet Michael in Tillerack, tell him thank you." Mortimer surrendered and eased into his final resting place, aware of his fate.

"I can't thank you enough for all you've done," Osvita expressed with a heavy heart, her eyes misting over. "I'm incapable of shedding any more tears after what happened at the Kurhal, but know my heart is breaking. The compassion and determination you've shown has enlightened my life. Your death won't be in vain and your message will be delivered."

With his head pressed against the sun-kissed sand, Mortimer turned his eyes to meet Osvita's and smiled. He appreciated her kind words, and the validation that his efforts were successful, even if he wasn't given the chance to complete them all. Succumbing to his injuries, a depleted Mortimer gazed out to the horizon, surprised at what would be his final sight.

Though his vision was fuzzy, he noticed the familiar two quorians from the Tillerack forest in the distance. The consequential mission with catastrophic repercussions had finally ended with a beautiful reunion. The same two terrified quorians he encountered, in what seemed like a lifetime ago, embraced one another once again. With the stark realization of what he had accomplished, Mortimer closed his eyes.

"Be free," he muttered, before releasing his final breath.

Osvita had nothing left in her to release. Her tear ducts were empty, her head and muscles ached. Escaping the Kurhal wouldn't have been possible without Nigel and Mortimer. Owing her life to the two of them, it pained her to lose them both. The guilt consumed her.

"Oh, darling…" Whark expressed his condolences, placing his hands on his wife's shoulders. Though she appreciated him, Osvita secretly wished it had been Nigel standing above her, which added to her guilt. "You said you had no tears left to cry from the Kurhal. What happened?"

"We can talk about it later." Discussing Nigel's death was unfathomable to her in the moment.

"Please, tell me. What happened?" he said as she let out a long exhale.

"Nigel died." Osvita shrugged to move Whark's hands off her.

"Vit…" he empathized as she walked away.

"Say," Grum interrupted, overhearing their conversation and Osvita's demeanor, "what was the piece of paper he gave you?" Pulling it out from her pocket, she'd completely forgotten about it.

"Oh my word..." Her eye's widened and jaw dropped.

"What is it, Mom?" Rexhia asked.

"What's it say, hon?" Osvita flinched at Whark's term of endearment, remaining silent.

"What are we, week-old glimboberries over here?" Grum cracked a small grin, trying not to be inappropriate over a dead man's body.

"It's a check, made out to cash, for ten-million jinugery."

"What!?" Grum shouted. "*That* man had *that* kind of wealth!?"

"Mortimer and that murderous Vanilor were each handsomely rewarded by Brugōr for capturing the quorian. He was the main donor for the Anti-Regime's plan, but I never knew numbers."

After a brief discussion of their unexpected inheritance, everyone remained quiet with their thoughts.

Grum never imagined his life would've brought him back outside The Barren Land. With no course of action or destination, he wondered where he'd go next. Having been alone for so long, he hoped the Dimmerks wouldn't mind him tagging along.

Rexhia was surprised by her tranquil disposition. Surrounded by death and murder, she understood the mechanics of life and reality. It was the unexplainable events, like her peculiar vision with the quorian, that she struggled to understand.

Whark couldn't believe the events that had unfolded before his eyes. As disturbed as he was, he was appreciative and happy to have his family together again, Grum included. He was yet to hear their entire story and to tell his, but he knew the time would come, probably sooner than later. Looking at his wife, who was staring off in the distance, he knew exactly what was on her mind, because it was on his too.

Their son, Smolar.

His heart was heavy. It wasn't a topic they'd often discussed because of the heartache. Whark walked up behind Osvita and embraced her.

"He's alive," he whispered in her ear. Her posture stiffened and she sniffled.

"We need to find him," she whispered back.

"Osvita, you know—"

"I don't care what was said." She turned around, looking him in the eye. "I'm going to find my son," she whispered demandingly. "Hey, Grum, do you know what's in that direction?" She pointed where the quorians fled to.

Grum observed the sky, evaluating his surroundings. "The only thing east this side of the ocean is…" He paused, having not said the once familiar region in many years. "Sartica."

"Sartica?"

"What a strange name," Whark added. "How in the world do you know that?"

Grum hesitated to answer, but knew there was no point in lying. "It's my hometown."

As the elated quorians frantically made their way back toward the sand dunes of Sartica, Rhugor became the unofficial protector of them all. Though adrenaline was still coursing through his veins, Promit felt good, but he remained surrounded by the three of them for protection. Unlike Rhugor and Fravia, his true identity had been exposed. Upon inspection of Fravia's bag, the metamorphic potion reserved for Promit had shattered. It wasn't possible for him to hide behind a disguise.

Smolar, like Promit, had relinquished his disguise too, in solidarity. His risky decision frightened Fravia, but the change occurred before she could voice her opinion. She considered it foolish, but knew it was a kind-hearted gesture.

The discussion between them was frantic and sporadic. Promit asked questions about the reactions back home, what had gone on, and any recent changes. In turn, the group asked about his confinement, his condition, who he had met, and what he'd seen. After the inquisition, Promit felt the exhaustion overwhelm him. His movement slowed and his mind felt fuzzy. Voicing his concerns, everyone eased up on the questions and focused on returning home. There'd be plenty of time to discuss and unravel everything.

Making their way across the open desert, they hadn't come across too many degreants, and those they passed seemed disinterested in their quorian appearance. It brought them much relief to know it was one less obstacle to overcome.

Lady Vixa was included the entire time to enjoy the glory, success and excitement via the Pendant of Perception. On multiple occasions, she'd expressed shouts of glee and pride. Since Smolar held the pendant for most of the time, he was able to experience a side of their Quorian Ruler he'd never seen before. It was delightfully refreshing.

"Smolar, can I speak with Promit for just a moment?" she asked, aware of his exhaustion.

"Of course," he replied.

Promit accepted the pendant and Fravia showed him how to properly use it.

"Hello?" Lady Vixa asked. "Promit? Can you hear me?" His eyes teared up, a smile widening on his face.

Uncertain he'd ever hear her voice again, he answered. "Hel-LO," he said, his voice cracking. "Lady Vixa," he tried again, clearing his throat. "It's wonderful to hear your voice."

"You too." Promit hadn't often interacted with her, but found her mood more enjoyable than he'd assumed. "I won't keep you long, but I wanted to say we couldn't be more excited for your return. The three quorians with you risked their lives to ensure your safety. I'm sure you've been through more than you could express, but we're all here for you."

"Thank you, Lady Vixa."

"I met with your father and sister too – they're excited to have you back and have missed you very much," she added. Promit remained silent. Though he appreciated the gesture, he knew his father wouldn't react that way. "Safe travels and see you all soon."

"Thank you again, Lady Vixa." Promit handed the pendant back to Smolar.

The quorian gang increased their pace as nightfall arrived across Diveria, successfully approaching the outskirts of Sartica before it got too dark.

"You don't think the swirling sands will return, do you?" Fravia wondered.

"I hope not." Rhugor sniffed around. "I don't think Sam would magically appear to save the day again."

"Who?" Promit asked.

Smolar smiled. "We'll tell ya about it later, friend."

43

As the Guardian of Emblems, Jacob Emmerson found himself internally battling with the notion of what was right and wrong. When Giddeom first informed him of the brute leader, he assumed Brugōr was a ravenous monster, incapable of rational thought. While that was his first impression, he saw another side of him. A side he understood, even if his actions were extreme.

The struggle continued during their altercation with Lazarus and Shrenka, but he displayed his loyalty for the leader, respecting his guardian duty. He wondered what would've happened if he'd taken an offensive approach, but pushed the notion out of his mind. Jacob reminded himself the mission was ultimately a success.

Finally, watching Brugōr chase the tablets and murder a seemingly innocent man forced him to question his judgement again. He struggled to find the justification in the man's death, unless it was simply due to the leader's disorientation. The powerful brute did what he knew to do – fight. Though it saddened Jacob to hear the wailing pain from the merciless death, he once again showed his loyalty to Brugōr. With the support of his great grandmother and his entire lineage, he sensed there had to be good in the role.

As Brugōr arrived at his chamber on the thirteenth floor with the Transcending

Tablets, he headed upstairs to securely return the artifact to its sacred podium. Jacob followed to confirm the job had been completed.

"Back home, where it belongs," Brugōr said.

"So what now?" Jacob asked.

"You leave, I suppose," Brugōr admitted. Though the brute leader didn't need him to stay, Jacob couldn't help but feel his presence was desired.

"What about The Barren Land? What do you plan to do?"

"Who the hell knows."

"You're not going to reactivate The Lost Sphere?"

"Why would I? It's clear everyone wanted out of the region. The fuckers are leaving by the clusters," he said, defeated. "I hoped The Barren Land would be a home for those who didn't fucking have one. A place for the rejected to be accepted. The Lost Sphere was put up as a protective barrier for those who were trying to escape a shitty life. Clearly others didn't see it that way."

Understanding Brugōr's methodologies confirmed he'd made the right choice. Jacob sensed the leader wasn't a bad man, he just didn't express himself well.

"Seems like you may have been misunderstood. You could use this opportunity to start fresh."

"We'll see...I just can't believe that bitch Shrenka. She played me..." Brugōr headed back toward the staircase. Jacob took one last glimpse at the Transcending Tablets before following him downstairs. Having seen two of the ancient artifacts, he wondered what the others looked like or were capable of.

"Why would she betray you?"

"That grimalkin is greedy. It seems she and Lazarus are after something much larger, more powerful. Well beyond what this region was capable of."

"What do you mean?"

"When I ordered for the quorian to be captured—"

"You captured a quorian? I thought—"

"Shit! The quorian...The fucker probably died with everything that happened."

He sighed. "Shit fucking hell. Well…you and the rest of Diveria assumed the fuckers were extinct, but nope. The bastards have been secretly crawling around for years. How'd an entire race, presumed to be extinct, survive without a trace under our damn noses? That takes organization, control and unfathomable competency. In my opinion, the quorian race secretly surviving a genocide is *real* power. I wanted to gain their trust, obtain their knowledge and ultimately lead them into a new era of freedom. Shrenka, however, felt differently. She considered the Transcending Tablets and other ancient artifacts throughout Diveria to be the true source of power."

"Do you think that's what she and Lazarus are planning to do? Hunt them down?"

"If that were the fuckin' case, why leave the tablets? They could've stormed off with the artifact if they wanted to. I don't know what they're up to, but that Lazarus character is no good."

"Do you know where they went?"

"Not a clue. Last I saw them was with you, and then somehow that shitty chef ended up with them outside the Kurhal. They're around…who the fuck knows where. Just make sure when you go back, tell them about the existence of the quorian race and to be on the lookout for Shrenka and Lazarus."

"You know, Lazarus mentioned Giddeom and the Divinity King. How does he know about them?"

"The fuck if I know. Your guess is as good as mine. Maybe they'll have an answer for you." Brugōr walked toward the elevator, calling the cab for Jacob to enter.

"But—"

"Say, how'd you heal my ankles up there?" he asked.

"Oh…well, I have my own ancient artifact."

"Of course you do." He smiled. It was the first time Jacob had seen a pleasant expression on the leader's face. "Before you go," he said, stomping toward a chest near the front of the room and quickly returning, "take this." Brugōr placed a short, wavy obsidian dagger with a silver hilt in the shape of a beast. "It's an obsidian dagger I had made years ago, but something tells me you'll need this shit more than I do. Ancient artifacts can be helpful, but you came to a showdown without a fucking weapon."

Jacob was touched, and smiled. It was the first weapon he'd ever wielded.

"Thank you, I'll keep it on me at all times."

"Yeah, yeah, you fucking better if you plan to be around for a while." The leader stood back as the doors opened. "You should get going. I have plenty to do here and I'm sure they're eagerly waiting for your ass." Brugōr pushed Jacob into the cab and pressed a button, shutting the doors on him.

"Hopefully I see you around soon. If you need—"

"See ya round, fucker," the brute leader exclaimed, forcibly ending their conversation.

Admiring his new weapon as the cab descended, Jacob tested its sharpness against his finger. Replaying the conversation with Brugōr, he thought about what Shrenka and Lazarus had planned. He assumed they wanted the artifacts, like he suggested, but it was strange to not keep the Transcending Tablets. Jacob remembered he used his own artifact a few times in their presence and wondered if they noticed. He made sure to be more careful when bringing Anitta into sight.

Jacob thought about the quorian race and how they'd existed throughout history, without a trace. Remembering his own history, he knew King Klai and his followers viciously attacked the Divinity King and their men. With their rivalry, he wondered how the news of their continued existence would be received.

"Did you know quorians still existed, Anitta?" Since she'd been around, he wondered what her knowledge was.

"No…I'd imagine not many know, yet. News like that could reshape all of Diveria."

"Yeah."

"Jacob, you must grasp the severity of the information. The ramifications of what it means. You're not only the protector of the ancient artifacts, but you're also the communicator between realms. The fact that the quorian race has been spotted changes everything. You're the guardian, so it's up to you what you reveal and how you do it."

"What I reveal?" Jacob repeated with uncertainty. "This entire time, I've struggled with where my loyalty lies, and I've decided to go with Brugōr, Giddeom and the Divinity King. I need to tell Giddeom so they can handle the situation. It would be a betrayal to withhold this information."

"There is certainly a divide. Divinity, Giddeom and Brugōr versus Lazarus and Shrenka, but there's another split. Brugōr expressed his curiosity with the quorian race and what his plans were. You must know that Giddeom and Divinity would...feel differently."

"So you're suggesting I hide this information from them?" Jacob whispered.

"I'm not suggesting any particular course of action. I'm just making you aware of the choices available. If Giddeom and the Divinity King learn of their existence, there would be a drastic shift in their agenda and your role as guardian. Divinity already attempted genocide once."

"For the protection of his own people."

"Stories are fragmented, like light through a prism."

"Choices are never easy."

"And they'll only get harder," Anitta admitted.

Jacob sighed. "I guess it's time to make the long journey back to the portal."

"I can help with that."

"What do you mean?"

"I can transport us there."

Jacob was stunned. "Why couldn't you just bring me here then?"

"A well-traveled journey aids in the arrival of your destination," she replied.

"Plus, I can only return us to the portal."

"You're always full of surprises," he said with a smirk. "Then let's go."

As he held Anitta in his hands, she used her energy, causing her crimson center to bubble until they vanished, leaving nothing but a small plume of translucent smoke. Reaching ground level, the elevator doors opened for a new passenger to use. Pressing the thirteenth floor, he waited for the doors to close before speaking.

"I can't wait to see what Brugōr will think about Mortimer's death and the fleeing quorian," Vanilor whispered to himself with a grin.

Once Jacob and Anitta arrived back at their starting point, he passed through the portal he used to enter The Barren Land. With the same gelatinous sensation, he quickly returned to the portal room. It wasn't until he saw his own clothes that a surge of exhaustion hit him. Jacob would've curled up on the cavern floor if he were able to.

"Hello?" a muffled voice said, following a couple knocks.

"Giddeom," Anitta said.

"Right," Jacob whispered. He walked toward the cabinet and removed his *armor* for The Barren Land to place his street clothes back on.

"Have you made a decision on what, or what not, to tell him?" Anitta asked.

"I'll decide after speaking with him," he whispered to ensure they weren't heard.

"Hello? Jacob? I received notice you've returned." Jacob realized he hadn't answered him yet.

"Hi, Giddeom, yes I'm here. Sorry, just exhausted. I'm just changing and I'll be out in a minute."

After no response, Jacob casually walked over to the door and exhaled. Dreading the conversation, he also knew the sooner it began, the sooner he could return home and sleep. Placing his hand on the doorknob, he heard an internal latch unlock.

Slowly opening the door, he saw an expressionless Giddeom standing in the doorway.

"I see you've returned in one piece, well done. How'd it go?" he asked. "Were you successful? Did you ensure the artifact remained safe in the leader's possession?"

When Jacob had first met Giddeom, he was intimidated by his stature and knowledge. Having had numerous interactions, a multitude of discussions and completing his first successful mission in a foreign region, Jacob no longer felt the same way. Instead of considering himself less than or beneath Giddeom, he saw themselves as equals. Somewhere along the journey, he'd found his sense of worth within the wild world he was still navigating.

"Yes, it was a success," Jacob informed him as he confidently, yet politely, walked past him. He halted, surprised to not have had a euphoric shift in his mental state. With a calm frame of mind, he already felt no stress or anxiety, so there wasn't a drastic shift. Jacob assumed his demeanor had changed, not the manor. "But I think we should have a chat."

"Yes, we should." Giddeom's response was more than what Jacob expected.

What could he want to talk to me about? he wondered.

The two walked in stride, passing through the double doors and standing outside Jacob's inner sanctum, a space only he, the guardian, had access to. Both men were friendly, but exuded confidence.

"What seems to be on your mind?" Giddeom asked.

"First, I should start with the mission. It was a success. Though close a few times, we ensured the safety of the Transcending Tablets."

"Brilliant."

"I did, however, learn something that would've been helpful. Brugōr said any structure that houses an ancient artifact is protected." Jacob squinted his eyes in frustration.

"That's mostly true. It can change form, but won't crumble or allow anything causing harm to the artifact. There was so much to discuss with your first mission, it must've slipped my mind."

"It would've been reassuring to know, being a mile high in the Kurhal Tower during several explosions," Jacob revealed.

"Explosions, eh? Wow." Giddeom's tone exuded a false interest, aggravating Jacob.

"When you're on the brink of death and your future's uncertain, it can be a bit more jarring than that."

"It's been so long I suppose I forget what that feels like." The two looked at each other, the silence deafening. "Was there something else you wanted to discuss?"

"Yes, actually. I'd like for you to clear something up. Lazarus, the man who tried to steal the artifact, cast a spell and—"

"Incantation," Giddeom corrected. "They're called incantations, not spells."

"Okay," Jacob said, annoyed his story was interrupted for a grammatical error. "He cast an incantation. Brugōr mentioned that he shouldn't have been able to use the artifact because it required the leader's pure blood. Is that true?"

"Yes."

"Once again, it would've been nice to know this."

"It's not typical or standard for the guardian to activate and use Divinity's artifacts."

"Regardless of whether I did or not, it's helpful to know this information, especially when it's my responsibility to protect them." He paused for a moment, remembering a quote he once heard. "The acquisition of knowledge prompts prestigious strength, after all." Giddeom smirked from Jacob's witty quote.

"You're right, I'll give it to you. I'll do better to explain the circumstances next time."

"I appreciate it," Jacob said, pleased. He hadn't expected Giddeom to utter those words. "Regardless of that," he continued, "Lazarus's incantation seemed to work."

"How do you mean?"

"He deactivated the entire perimeter of The Barren Land. What was it called, the...?"

"The Lost Sphere..." Giddeom finished. "This man...Lazarus. *He* deactivated The Lost Sphere?"

"Yes, I saw it with my own eyes."

"That's impossible. Something else must've happened."

"No," Jacob said abruptly. His certainty cast doubt for Giddeom.

"Are you sure there wasn't anything else going on? An outside force? Another side to the story? Someone or something else that could have lowered the sphere?" Giddeom carefully watched Jacob respond.

His inquisition made Jacob evaluate whether he should mention the quorians' existence. He knew they'd eventually find out, but wasn't sure if he wanted to be the catalyst for such change. He considered what Anitta had said.

There would be a drastic shift in their agenda and your role as guardian.

Since Jacob was the communicator between Diad and the other regions, he knew Giddeom didn't speak to the leaders directly, Brugōr included. That meant no proof he'd been told about the quorians. He decided it was best to hold off for now, but that he would meet with Giddeom again soon to discuss.

"There was nothing else going on, though there was an unexpected guest. Shrenka, Brugōr's partner, stood beside Lazarus in an act of betrayal."

"Oh? Why'd that happen?"

"According to him, they had different definitions of power." Jacob kept it short, knowing the split involved the quorian.

"Let me guess...she wanted more power than Brugōr had?" Giddeom rolled his eyes. "They always want more power. Unfortunately, most don't have enough knowledge and end up facing death sooner than anticipated."

"That's the peculiar part, Lazarus *was* aware of a lot. He knew of you and the

Divinity King."

"What?" Giddeom's eyes widened.

"Lazarus said you and Divinity were running out of options and I was your last resort. He said I shouldn't have been there." Jacob examined Giddeom's face as he raised his eyebrows, widening his eyes even more. The news startled him more than he'd expected. Giddeom looked around the room, deep in thought. "What did he mean that *I shouldn't have been there*?"

"He…" Giddeom hesitated. "You…"

"What is it?" Jacob asked. Giddeom exhaled, adjusted his posture and turned to respond.

"I'm sure Lazarus just didn't expect you to be there. He thought he'd be able to effortlessly steal the tablets, but fortunately you were there to save the day." Giddeom partially smiled.

Once again, Jacob questioned his loyalty. He sensed Giddeom knew more than he was revealing, especially given his uncomfortable flattery.

"I'm shocked he knew of us being here, in Diad. How does an outsider like Lazarus gain such knowledge? Did he say anything else?"

"No…" Jacob looked at him with a peculiar gaze. "He didn't."

"So what happened to them? Lazarus and Shrenka."

"I don't know. We never saw them again."

"They weren't killed?"

"No."

"So they could be waiting in the shadows to steal it again?"

"I don't think so. If they wanted the tablets so badly, they would've taken them. It was as though they gave up or became uninterested in them."

"That doesn't make sense. Why risk everything to give up the artifact in the end?"

"I was hoping you'd know."

Giddeom nodded with uncertainty. "Thank you for the information and your assistance in the mission. Sounds like working with Brugōr went well?"

"Not to say there weren't struggles, but I came to understand, and even sympathize with him."

"That's reassuring to hear," Giddeom remarked. "Your relationships with the leaders will either help or hinder the situations you find yourself in," he explained, looking off into the distance.

"Everything okay?" Jacob asked.

"Certainly. Just processing all you've revealed." Giddeom reverted his attention back to Jacob, unnervingly well. "You, however, should head home."

"It's been a while, yes," Jacob agreed.

"I've been informed of a structural shift within your family dynamic." Giddeom's tone was stern, assertive.

"The baby!" Jacob shouted with much excitement. "My sister must've given birth! Yes, I have to…" He turned around, looking for his inner sanctum.

"Over there," Giddeom pointed toward the door. "Good luck and take care of yourself, Jacob."

Jacob feverishly entered his inner sanctum and pulled the orb out of his pocket. "I hate to rush, but I must get home. My sister has given birth and—"

"Not a problem, Jacob," Anitta interrupted. "Let's go."

Jacob opened his palms and watched the glowing inscriptions swirling around. Mesmerized by its appearance, he waited as a white ball of energy appeared and eventually burst, exploding a bright beam of light, forcing Jacob to shut his eyes. With the excitement of meeting his niece, he envisioned what she may look like and if she had a full head of hair.

In an instant, the sensation was gone and Jacob felt his feet firmly planted on the floor. When he opened his eyes, a wave of peace and serenity settled over him. He was back. He was home.

Turning around to head downstairs, he noticed someone blocking the door. Jacob was uncertain who it would be, but the style of clothing gave him an inkling.

"Jacob," the man said, "I'm glad you finally returned from Giddeom and your mission." The tall, well-dressed man turned around, confirming Jacob's hunch.

"Sir Kalvin!? What in the world are you doing here?"

"We should talk," he said, motioning for Jacob to take a seat.

44

Astounded by the information Jacob had revealed, Giddeom wasted no time in meeting with the Divinity King. Through the hallway of eternal darkness, into the false throne room and down the secret passageway into the Imbroglio, Giddeom wished the journey to Him was quicker.

Recalling his conversation with Jacob, he knew the Divinity King would be happy the artifact safely resided in The Barren Land, but there were still concerns. Giddeom was shocked to hear Brugōr's partner had joined the rebellion leader in his poor attempt to steal the tablets. Uncertain of their whereabouts or intentions, he knew they'd need to be prepared.

The most startling revelation involved Lazarus's knowledge. Not only was he aware of Divinity's existence, but he sensed Jacob shouldn't have been there.

How in the world could Lazarus know Jacob was our last resort? he thought.

As he neared the end of the convoluted maze of the Imbroglio, Giddeom grew concerned for how his conversation with the Divinity King would go, fearful of his reaction. Opening the exquisite marble door into His sanctum, he gazed up at the monumental throne where his five-pronged, purple sorcerer crown resided.

"I hope you're here to tell me good news," the ambiguous voice echoed from above. Giddeom strained his neck upwards, watching as the crown levitated and rested upon the head of the Divinity King. "I'd sense if one of my artifacts were destroyed, so I know it's still intact," he said, without moving his serrated, silver facial features.

"Yes, Your Majesty," Giddeom responded. "It seems our new guardian has successfully completed the task. The Transcending Tables have been restored back into the hands of its leader, Brugōr."

"Excellent." The Divinity King raised his left arm and made a fist. Unlike his right hand, which resembled a human's with skin and fingernails, his left was mechanical with razor sharp claws. It was surrounded by a majestic, purple haze of energy. "It seems as though my attempt to revert history was a success."

There was a pause between the two. Giddeom hadn't the nerve to interrupt his excitement, but the tension could be cut with a knife.

"Hm, you are hesitant. What is it?" Though he was in a weakened state, he could always read Giddeom, sense his emotions.

"The reversal appears successful, but there were a few setbacks."

"I have risked too much to deal with issues. What is it?"

"As anticipated, Lazarus Docaras arrived to obtain the artifact, but he wasn't alone. He brought along an associate named Shrenka Malhazan."

"Interesting. So they both escaped with their lives?" Divinity gripped the arm of his throne with his human hand.

"Yes. Though they didn't flee with the artifact, they still escaped."

"So the mission was *not* a complete success. Seems like we must remain vigilant." Divinity sensed there was more for Giddeom to reveal. "Spit it out, tell me the rest."

"Jacob informed me of a conversation he had with Lazarus, which proved quite interesting."

"How so?"

"Lazarus wasn't only aware of our existence, but he told Jacob we ran out of options, that he was our last resort and he shouldn't have been there." Giddeom instinctually stopped breathing, nervous of the king's reaction.

Divinity remained still. Silence lingered for longer than Giddeom expected until he jumped in fright at something he'd never seen before. Sitting atop his monumental throne, the Divinity King turned and lowered his head.

"Are you telling me he is aware of the reversal?"

Intimidated by his gaze, Giddeom stalled to respond with the unpopular answer. "It sounds like it."

"How is that possible?"

"Though I have no information to support this claim, I had a thought. When this mission initially failed, Lazarus was one of two people who died. It was shortly after their deaths you harnessed your power to reverse time, to save the artifact and preserve your legacy."

"Our guardian for the first mission died before Lazarus, and yet she retained no memory. You confirmed that, did you not?"

"Yes, I carefully met with Catherine Emmerson shortly after the reversal and her failed mission was wiped from her memory. Lazarus, however, was a different scenario. He was in possession of the Transcending Tablets when he died. Is it possible his memory remained in conjunction with your power from the artifact?"

"I would be surprised if that was the case, but I suppose it could be possible." Divinity raised his head, tapping his mechanical index finger against the throne in thought. "Did Jacob inquire? Is he aware of his sister being originally chosen as guardian?"

"He asked about Lazarus's comments, but I downplayed them. Jacob remains unaware of the time reversal and his replacement for his sister's failed attempt."

"Good." Divinity relaxed his hand. "If your assumption is right, and his memory remained intact, then we must heavily protect the artifacts. I do not have the means to reverse time again."

"I understand, Your Majesty," Giddeom replied. "I'm still uncertain of Lazarus and Shrenka's objective. According to Jacob, he felt as though they'd given up on the tablets. All they did was deactivate The Lost Sphere."

"They deactivated it?"

"Apparently Lazarus did it himself."

"How is that possible?"

"I assumed Shrenka was involved in accessing Brugōr's pure blood."

"Possibly…" Giddeom was about to wrap up the discussion when the king continued. "The Lost Sphere is gone. Tell me, Giddeom…were there any outside forces involved? Did Jacob mention anything…*else* to you?"

"Nothing else. Should there have been?"

"Either one of you are lying or this is a big coincidence."

"I don't und—"

The Divinity King put his human hand out to silence Giddeom while his other one, surrounded in a purple haze, pointed to his crown. He motioned to remove something from one of the five prongs. A plume of smoke flowed from his fingertips as he pointed upwards. When the smoke slowly dispersed, a figure revealed itself, levitating motionless. Giddeom's eyes widened as his mouth hung open in shock.

"Is that a…?"

"Quorian," Divinity answered. "You bet it is. Now please, explain something to me." He paused. "How the fuck did I catch a quorian within Diveria!?"

"I-I…How is that…?" Giddeom was speechless. The last time he'd ever seen a quorian was on that unfathomable night eons ago. The ten men were confident they'd exterminated the race, as awful as it made Giddeom feel. "But we killed them all."

"Clearly you did not. If I found one, who knows how many others there are, or what they are doing." Giddeom stood there, amazed by what was in front of him. "Turns out this is one of the original quorians who escaped on that fateful night."

"How can you tell?" Giddeom asked.

"After some failed torture, it was all she revealed. Something tells me that

Lazarus did not successfully cast an incantation and their race had something to do with The Lost Sphere crumbling."

"But how? Why? What would they want with The Barren Land?"

"I have no idea. My limited energy is not expendable, but I sensed this pure blood with direct lineage to a fallen king. Similar to what we have discussed in other regions."

"You mean with Tillerack, Mariana and Azjura?" Giddeom asked, aware of their ties to fallen kings.

"Precisely. I have always sensed their presence, which we will discuss momentarily." He extended one elongated claw. "These creatures are back in numbers and with vengeance. I will be damned if they think they can take me and the world I created down."

Giddeom listened to Divinity's words while considering his lineage, particularly Jacob. Previous guardians were always loyal and honest, but the quorian revelation made him question Jacob's loyalty to Diad.

Did he know about them and not tell me?

A discussion was needed, but aware of current events in Jacob's life, Giddeom knew he'd need some time before being pressed for answers.

"What do you intend to do?" Giddeom asked.

"Between what you disclosed and what I found, we have our hands full, as does the guardian. Summon Jacob and inform him he must travel to Mount Marlock immediately."

"Mount Marlock..." Giddeom repeated, puzzled. "You want to send our final chance for a guardian on a suicide mission?"

"It is the only guaranteed way to wipe those wretched quorians from this planet for good. With no knowledge of their existence, location or agenda, we are far behind. They have had eons to rebuild while I presumed their extinction."

"Even *if* Jacob survived such a disastrous region, what would he even be going there for?"

"The Telepathy Stone," the Divinity King revealed. "Protected by the furious elements within Mount Marlock, the Telepathy Stone was forged shortly after King Klai's murder. It contains an inordinate amount of pure quorian blood, from Klai himself, which can be used to identify and locate any quorians across Diveria. We'd be able to locate their hideout and exterminate them."

"I understand." Giddeom bowed. "But Jacob will need some time. If we send him into the blazing depths now, he may never return." Divinity remained silent, evaluating the words. "If you allow, I think it'd be best if we wait—"

"Alright." The purple haze from his mechanical hand dissipated. "In addition to Mount Marlock, there has been heightened activity in Tillerack I want Jacob to investigate. Considering the environment is more welcoming than Mount Marlock, he can begin there if he would like. The choice is his, but he must get moving soon."

"If we allow—"

"Our conversation is over." Divinity raised his mechanical hand as the purple haze reappeared. "Time must not be wasted, and ignorance must not be overlooked."

Just as Giddeom was about to respond, the haze exploded, momentarily blinding him. When his vision returned, all that was left was the empty monumental throne.

Though Divinity was gone, Giddeom bowed his head as he walked backwards toward the door, reentered the Imbroglio and gazed out amongst the maze.

With an uncertain future, Giddeom found himself in unfamiliar territory. His life in Diad had often been predictable and within his control. Managing his family lineage of guardians brought him fulfillment in a region he couldn't leave – it was his connection to reality. Doubting Jacob, the unexpected guardian, saddened him, but he hoped he was unaware of the quorian revelation.

For the first time in a long time, Giddeom found himself in uncharted territory. The Divinity King's legacy, which he'd spent countless lifetimes protecting, was at risk, causing him to question his own loyalty. Though he understood the purpose, the primary plan for Jacob seemed like a death sentence. He knew it'd require much work to ensure his survival, but hoped he'd visit Tillerack before tackling the treacherous Mount Marlock.

Aware of the hardship in Jacob's imminent life, Giddeom made the decision to temporarily relieve him from a world he wasn't meant to experience.

45

Jacob couldn't fathom why the leader of Sartica would be at his home, specifically in his bedroom. Due to the events that had gone on, he felt their one and only meeting seemed like a lifetime ago. It was all surreal. Jacob recalled how anxious he had been in the Subterranean Domain, concerned with what Sir Kalvin's opinion would be of him.

This time, he felt more confident, whether from having a better understanding of his role, or from the turmoil he'd already experienced. Regardless, his awareness of such absence only pushed his confidence further.

"We should talk," Kalvin said softly.

"I'm certain whatever it is can wait. I've been away for a while and I wanted to—"

"It can't," Kalvin interrupted.

"The last time we interacted, you knocked me unconscious. I don't know what else I—"

"I apologize for that, but I think it proved to be helpful, no? Seems like you've been busy since we last met."

"You have no idea…"

"Before you head downstairs and lose yourself in your family, I think it's important we discuss what you've been through, what you've seen and where you've been."

That was when Jacob noticed the sound coming from outside.

Rain.

It rarely rained in Sartica. He always wanted to experience it when he could. Looking out the window, he noticed the driveway filled with cars. *Everyone's home.* Looking past the driveway, he realized the perimeter of the house was lined with flowers and plants. He was surprised and impressed by the celebratory gifts from within the community. Jacob was aware his parents knew many within Sartica from their business, but didn't expect such love and excitement.

"It seems as though the entire community, and the heavens above, are cheering for the birth of the new child," Jacob said with a smile, welcoming the rain.

"Praise Divinity," Sir Kalvin said coldly. The words struck Jacob harshly. "But, Jacob, we should—"

"Sorry, Sir Kalvin," Jacob said, pressing forward, "but we can talk afterwards. I've already returned later than I should have." Jacob exited his bedroom and just as he turned the corner, Kalvin sighed.

"Yes, you unfortunately did."

Jacob headed downstairs, expecting to see the family gathered in excitement and jubilation. No one was around. It was silent, desolate. He glanced around the house, looking for signs of life, but there were none.

"Hello?"

"Jacob!?" Ben popped up from one of the chairs in the living room.

"Oh, hey, Dad. How's it—" Before, he could let out another word, Ben rushed towards Jacob and embraced him.

"Oh, son, you're here." Jacob sensed his sigh of relief. "We had no idea where you…" Ben pulled away, looking at him. Jacob noticed how glossy his father's eyes were. "Doesn't matter, you're here now."

"I told you all I had to leave for work," Jacob said in his defense, "but I'm sorry for being away so long."

"After three days without word, we grew concerned. After five days, we reached out to Sir Kalvin. After seven days, today, he arrived, waiting for you," Ben informed him. Though annoyed and confused they had reached out to the leader of Sartica, Jacob was more startled by the time lapse.

"Seven days!?" His eyebrows curled. "I've been gone for a day, maybe two. How do you—"

"Seven." Ben pointed to the calendar on the wall across the room. Jacob walked over to observe it, noticing the various crosses for each day that had passed. He read "Jacob's First Day" on a Monday, Tuesday was blackened out, and the five subsequent days were crossed out.

"You're telling me it's the following Monday already?" Jacob didn't understand how that was possible. He remembered telling his family he had to leave, and though a lot had happened, it felt like everything was crammed into a quick twenty-four hours.

"Son, are you sure this job isn't too much for you? Are you sure it's a good choice?" Ben asked, concerned about his mental health.

"Yes…no," Jacob stuttered, still in shock. "No, it's not too much. It was all just a whirlwind. I suppose I was so busy time just flew by."

"Six days?" Ben wondered.

"Doesn't matter," Jacob said, brushing the conversation off, "it's time for me to meet my new niece," he said with a smile, glancing around the house. "Where is everyone? Where are the balloons and music? Excited chatter?"

"Let's talk, son."

"What? Why does everyone wish to talk? Let's talk af—"

"Sit your ass down, now," Ben demanded. It was very unlike him to be assertive, especially towards his children. Jacob respectfully followed his demand. "Sorry, but I…I need your attention for a moment. There's something you have to know."

"What could possibly be so important?" Jacob looked around, wondering where the rest of his family was. "Where is everyone? Where's the baby? Is she okay?"

"The child is perfectly healthy. She's an absolute delight, you'll be happy to finally meet her," Ben reassured him. Before he could utter the next words, his eyes began to weep.

Jacob knew his father tended to exaggerate and dramatize events, but he wasn't one to cry for no reason. "Dad, what is it?"

Ben tried his best to maintain his composure while he uttered the words no father should ever have to voice. "Catherine died last week. Tuesday."

Jacob mentally blacked out, though he maintained his posture. Everything that had happened over the last twenty-four hours – or week – vanished. He transcended into numerous flashbacks from their childhood.

The family gatherings where they were the only two children and entertained one another.

When Catherine tried to force him to consume alcohol, though she was still a minor herself.

Their completely opposite opinion on what constituted good music.

Consumed by his memories, Jacob expressed an awkward chuckle from one of his favorite memories they often laughed about. When they were younger, Catherine was instructed to pick her brother up from a friend's house. Once she arrived there, Jacob was nowhere to be found. She tirelessly roamed the streets in her car, asking groups of kids if they knew of her brother, Jacob. Though many knew him, they hadn't seen him. After an hour of searching, she returned home to see her brother sitting at the kitchen table. Stunned and upset for wasting her time, the two had a heated discussion, in which Jacob insinuated his sister was wrong. Catherine slapped him across the face, instigating Jacob to stand and shove her against the tiled wall like a rag doll, collapsing to the floor. Though concerning at the time, it had become a favorite comical memory within the family. Catherine always said it was the moment she knew she could no longer pick on her little brother anymore.

With his head slumped over, Jacob felt an immense sadness overwhelm him as he realized he'd no longer be able to relive those moments with her again. He'd lost his family partner – the only other individual who experienced the same upbringing as him. Suddenly, the sadness turned into a crushing pain in his heart. Jacob's mind wandered down a dark and depressing hole, but he was interrupted before going deeper.

"Jacob?" his father said, trying to get his son's attention. Jacob shook his head and looked up. "There you are. How are you?" Ben asked with tears in his eyes.

"I'm fine...I just...I just can't believe it."

"The baby was too big to have a natural birth, so they began the c-section surgery, but they...they found her uterus ravaged with cancer."

"What? Did she know? Did Andrew know?" Jacob was stunned. He knew Catherine took care of herself and visited doctors regularly if needed.

"It didn't sound like anyone had any idea..." The two stood silent for a moment. "Anyway, after they safely removed the baby, there was excessive bleeding and with the cancer everywhere, they said it couldn't be stopped." Ben paused to catch his breath. "They tried everything..."

"Is that why she had no idea of her pregnancy?"

"Apparently her pregnancy and condition were unrelated."

Though he still had an abundance of questions, he knew interrogating his father wasn't fair. Noticing an uncorked bottle of wine on the table, Jacob grabbed the neck and took a swig.

"Where's Andrew? The baby? Mom?" Jacob wondered, diverting his focus elsewhere.

"Everyone's out back, except your mother. She's upstairs in the bedroom."

"Let me greet the baby, see Andrew and the group...then I'll go upstairs to see her." Jacob expressed a poorly attempted smile for his father. For the first time in a while, he sensed a closeness with him. The two stood up and embraced, acknowledging each other's pain.

Ben trailed behind Jacob as he made his way toward the kitchen. He took a second, longer swig of wine, placed it on the dining table and walked out the backdoor.

"It's Jacob!" a familiar voice shouted before he even noticed. It was his aunt, Cynthia. Beside her, there was Andrew, the newborn baby, his parents and siblings, and a couple of their close friends. It was a large group considering how quiet the house was.

The gathering was huddled under a canopy to protect everyone from the rain. He suddenly thought about the flowers and gifts left outside their house, realizing everything was in celebration and condolences for their precious birth and tragic loss.

There were whispers amongst the group about Jacob's arrival. Some questioned where he'd been while others wondered how he was holding up from the news, or if he even knew. Ben nodded behind him, confirming the news had been delivered. Cynthia rushed up and embraced him.

"Hi—"

"Oh, I can't believe this." She burst into tears. "This is awful, how are you holding up?" she asked, separating to look at his face.

"Just in shock, I suppose," Jacob replied. He was never one to express emotions often, especially in public. He knew how others sometimes perceived his cold demeanor during a time of pain and sorrow, but he considered it his strength. Like Anna, he was a private person.

"Come," Cynthia said, escorting him towards Andrew, "come meet your new baby niece," she said with tears in her eyes, trying her best to express happiness for the child.

The two men looked at each other, neither one shedding a tear, though sadness could be seen on both their faces. Jacob's heart broke for him. Not only had he lost his wife, but there was concern for how he'd mentally manage with the newborn. He hoped Andrew's grief and sorrow wouldn't overshadow the happiness and patience needed for the child.

"Hi, Jacob," Andrew mustered. "I'd like you to meet your niece, Valentina." He expressed a minimal smile when saying her name.

"Valentina…" Jacob repeated, smiling. "What a beautiful name."

Andrew motioned an offer for Jacob to hold her, which he accepted. He felt something happen when he held Valentina. There was a sense of relief as he felt his sister with him, as if *she* were in his arms. It was a bittersweet moment that caused him to smile as a tear fell from his eye, directly onto Valentina's forehead. She shuddered and blinked from the drop. As gentle as he could, Jacob gave her a comfortable squeeze filled with love before handing her back to her father's arms.

"She's perfect in every way. What a beautiful gift for my sister to give you, and us all." The words just rolled from Jacob's mouth. A few onlookers sobbed.

"I'm forever grateful to her," Andrew said, looking down at his child, "and all of you," he finished, looking out toward family and friends. Some of them responded with sweet words while others just nodded.

"Isn't she just a bundle of joy?" Cynthia asked Jacob from behind. "Especially considering how unexpectedly fast she arrived," she added in a whisper. Though everyone knew of the birthing surprise, it wasn't mentioned by anyone else. Jacob wondered if it was out of fear for insinuating it caused her death.

"Absolutely." He smiled before embracing his aunt once more.

Jacob lingered for a short while longer, politely speaking with everyone at least once. Ben was kind to the guests, but he wasn't a social butterfly. With Anna absent from the gathering, Jacob stepped in, helping his aunt, Cynthia, as host. He thanked friends and family for visiting, checked to see if anyone needed a drink or wanted more food, which was catered. There were a couple of pasta dishes, buttermilk fried chicken, flat iron steaks, garlic mashed potatoes, and a couple of vegetable medleys. While its appearance was tempting and the smell captivating, he didn't have much of an appetite. Few did, but food was still necessary. The Emmersons always believed in having food around, regardless of the event.

While perusing through the crowd, a few guests asked about Jacob's disappearance. The questions were mostly being asked to make small talk, and without judgement. His answers were short, explaining he was away on work and couldn't be contacted during that time. When the follow-up question arrived, *what do you do for work*, Jacob made sure to be honest, yet simple.

"Unfortunately, it's classified." He knew the answer would only generate more curiosity, but he found it to be his best option in the moment. Jacob recalled Sir Kalvin's somber demeanor during their conversation and wondered if he was still waiting upstairs. He quickly followed up the answer with a question for them.

"Can I get you anything, Cynthia?" Jacob asked, finally approaching his aunt.

"No, honey. I'm good. How about you?"

"If everyone's okay here, I'm going to check on my mother."

"I'm not sure that's the best idea. No one here could possibly imagine the pain she and your father are going through."

"I know, but if for nothing else, I need to just let her know I'm home."

"Sure...but if she's asleep, don't wake her. It's best to get as much rest as possible."

"I won't," Jacob replied, walking back inside.

As he made his way toward the staircase, Jacob replayed the last conversation he had with his mother. It was on that same evening he saw any of his family. He'd revealed to Anna that her grandmother, Edith, said hello and then vanished without an opportunity to ask questions or react. He felt guilty to have dropped a bomb like that on his mother, but he knew a bigger bomb had fallen since.

Ascending the stairs, he envisioned his mother's condition. It had been nearly a week since Catherine passed, and Jacob had no knowledge on whether she'd been eating, showering, or had even left the bedroom. Just then, he realized he hadn't seen Chicken since he returned either. He hoped their dog was on Anna's bed, staying by her side for unconditional love and comfort. With his father going through the same pain, it could be difficult to rely on one another for support. Jacob tried to imagine what she was going through, but knew it was unfathomable. He didn't have children, but he understood the balance and order of life.

As painful as certain events were, he knew there was a typical process one goes through during their life cycle. The initial years as a child, the struggling adolescent years, navigating life as a young adult, and so on. Experiencing the death of a parent was tough, but inevitable. Even the death of a sibling or spouse, as terrible as it was, wasn't unfathomable. There was something hauntingly disgusting and atrocious about losing a child. It's an unnatural order of life.

"Sir Kalvin," Jacob said softly as he gazed out his bedroom window, "I'm going to check on my mother, then come back to wrap up our chat." The Sartician leader nodded.

As he approached his mother's bedroom, he placed an ear to the door. There was a slight hum from the television, but nothing recognizable. He rested his curled index finger to the door, prepared to knock, then he remembered Chicken may've been on the bed. He carefully turned the doorknob, squinting as he tried to view the contents of the room.

The curtains were shut and the lights were off. There was a slight glimmer from the television being on the incorrect input. Hearing the whispers from the group outside, Jacob knew if his mother was awake, she could hear the entire conversation below.

"Ma?" Jacob whispered. Though barely audible, Chicken curiously propped her head up. Even through the darkness, she knew it was someone familiar and safe. Her tail wagged as she slowly crawled to the corner of the bed. After a few gentle pets, she curled back up into a ball beside Anna, with her back to them. She remained still, with her head on the pillow, as if she were fast asleep.

"Ma?" Jacob whispered once more, disobeying the agreement he made with his aunt. He didn't really want to disturb her, but thought it was worth one more try.

"Jacob?" She turned her head slightly. Her voice raspy, as if she hadn't spoken in weeks. "You're home," she said in a peaceful tone. "I'm glad one…" She stopped herself, turning her head back around. "I'm glad you're home."

"Of course," he replied. "Mom, I'm so sorry…for everything. For what happened, for not being here, for—" He began to tear up.

"It's fine. You were doing what you needed to. You're here now." Her tone was stoic and firm, emotionless. "As long as *you're* safe, that's all I care about."

"Can I get you anything? Water. Wine. Food."

"No."

There was so much he wished he could say.

He wanted to discuss her emotions, help her in any way possible.

He wanted to talk about Valentina, and how beautiful she was.

He wanted to tell her about the unwavering support downstairs, and within the entire community.

But Jacob knew his mother was in too fragile of a state to maintain a conversation, even with him. The best thing he could do was let her know he was there for her.

"I'll let you go back to sleep, Mom. Let me know if there's anything you need. I'm here for you. I love you," Jacob said with a smile, regardless of her back being to him.

"A mother never sleeps; she only ever rests her eyes."

When Jacob exited his mother's bedroom, he wanted to go downstairs to rejoin the group. He felt guilty considering how long he'd been away, especially during their tragedy. There was, however, one other person he needed to speak with. Jacob sighed and walked toward his bedroom.

"Hello, Sir Kalvin," he said in a defeated tone.

"Jacob." He bowed his head with sorrowful eyes. "Please accept my deepest condolences from myself and the entire Troveria family. It's an absolute tragedy for this to have happened."

"Thank you. It really is a terrible situation." Jacob admired the candle that had once belonged to his great grandmother with a new perspective and appreciation. He decided he'd bring it to his inner sanctuary.

"I'm sure it isn't easy to go through, especially since you were away for it all." While Sir Kalvin's words seemed genuine and kind, his tone was open to interpretation, which Jacob noticed.

"Don't feed into it."

Anitta, Jacob thought. He'd forgotten about her. As Jacob and Sir Kalvin stared at each other, he wanted to ask what she meant, but he couldn't do it without him noticing. There was an awkward silence for a moment.

"Why's that?" Jacob said. Though the question was meant for his sidekick, Sir Kalvin assumed it was for him, and he cocked his head.

"Because you couldn't be here. You weren't able to spend these moments—" Kalvin responded, but Jacob stopped listening once Anitta replied.

"You don't genuinely know what his intentions are," she said.

Jacob nodded. "Yes, you're right." Once again, his response was delivered to both Anitta and Sir Kalvin. Jacob returned his attention to the Sartician leader. "It isn't easy, but sometimes duty calls, unexpectedly."

"Just know I'm always here if you ever need assistance or my services."

"Your…services?" Jacob asked.

"I know about everything in The Barren Land, the destruction that ensued." Silence fell between the two men.

"How does he know?" Anitta asked, seemingly reading Jacob's mind. It was difficult for him to believe a brute like Brugōr would've communicated with the prestigious Troveria family.

"I know you tried your best, and while you did save the Transcending Tablets, the region has become a nightmare. I'm sure it'll resolve itself though, it's not your responsibility after all, right?" Kalvin smirked. Once again, Jacob found his tone off-putting.

"I'm not sure what you're referring to."

"I don't trust him," Anitta said.

"Of course not, my guardian," Kalvin said, smirking. "Just know I can always assist you with the Transcending Tablets." He paused, looking around the room. "Or any other artifacts you may've come across."

"Other artifacts?" Jacob said aloud. *Was he talking about Anitta?*

"You know where to find me, and again, sorry for your loss," he said, passing by Jacob to exit his bedroom. Once he secured his privacy, Jacob removed Anitta from his pocket to discuss.

"How does he know about everything?" he wondered.

"It's not clear."

"He knew about Brugōr, what happened, the Transcending Tablets…and even insinuated he knew about you."

"Me?"

"I don't know what other ancient artifact he could be referring to," Jacob answered. "I won't let anything happen to you though." He knew it sounded silly, but Anitta appreciated the sentiment.

As Jacob stood there perplexed with Anitta, he heard the Sartician leader exit the home, saying goodbye to his family. It was clear to him that the seemingly fearless and resilient leader was playing a balancing act. Sir Kalvin was solidifying himself within the Emmerson family, though his reasoning was yet to be revealed.

Jacob's home life had forever changed from what it once was. Ever since the day after his twenty-third birthday, a shift had occurred. What he thought was a fortuitous vision in a dream turned out to be an intentional message from another realm. Standing in the middle of his bedroom, Jacob looked around, contemplating his choices.

He was tempted to return to Diad. Surprisingly, the events he'd experienced in The Barren Land seemed less stressful than Sartica. His role as guardian came with a heavy responsibility, yet offered him a distinct personal distance. Instead of handling ethically gray areas, there was a stark understanding for what needed to be done.

Jacob's mental health was strained from his constant fear and anxiety. Experiencing the manor without the emotion allowed him to identify the burden in his daily life. Forced into strenuous situations as guardian helped his confidence, but Jacob instinctually eased his discomfort the only way he knew how – with his analytical mind and wine.

Though he was confident in his method, he learned of the fallacy when Catherine died. Jacob knew if he had a better grip on his anxiety, he wouldn't have ran for the bottle to self-medicate. Living with it for years, identifying his mental state proved challenging. He acknowledged the difference between acceptance and resolution. Refusing to berate himself, he made sure to keep an open mind as his journey toward finding peace had only begun.

Jacob was aware of the impact Catherine's death not only had on him, but his entire family. Though he expected to grieve, he also knew it was imperative to be the support system for them.

Cynthia was a kind soul who Jacob had always gotten along with. He felt the need to help and support her through the process. Even though it wasn't her daughter, she had been close to Catherine over the years. The two had shared a strong bond over family values. Jacob also knew that his mother couldn't help anyone else, so Cynthia would be without a niece and, for the time being, without a sister.

Jacob felt his father was trying his best to stay strong, even though he sensed a part of him had also died. He knew it was going to be difficult to continue on from the loss of his child, especially given how close they were. His intuition consoled him though, sensing Ben would eventually heal with the support of family.

Unfortunately, his same instinct wasn't prevalent for his mother. Jacob was gravely concerned for her well-being the most. Not only did he feel that losing a child was against the cycle of life, he feared as a mother, Anna would feel a sense of regret he didn't think was warranted. It was no secret that Anna was a little tougher on Catherine in their upbringing, though he never understood why. Love was never in question, as they both cherished one another. It was simply a different relationship than he'd experienced, and he wondered if she'd go so deep as to question her parenting. Jacob hoped he was overanalyzing.

The only other individual he felt a need to watch over and be with was his beautiful, newborn niece, Valentina. She was their reason for joy and happiness during such a dark time. There was no doubt in Andrew's ability to be a father, but Jacob wanted to offer help whenever possible. There's a special bond between siblings, no matter their relationships. He would forever know who his sister was – her values, her traits, her strengths, her battles. As Valentina got older, Jacob wanted to be there along the way, providing invaluable insight about her mother.

And finally, there was himself.

Once an ordinary young man with a comfortable life in Sartica, Jacob had found his purpose, working toward a healthier, fulfilling path. His life had been a whirlwind ever since he turned twenty-three, but he was eager for the next step of the journey.

The death of Catherine would leave a scar on his heart, and the hearts of his family. Having spent his effort on the struggles in The Barren Land and Diad, Jacob knew he needed to remain home, ignoring any summons from Giddeom, focusing on the challenges that faced him and his loved ones in Sartica.

46

Flabbergasted by a ghost from her past, Osvita tried to calm her nerves. Too much had gone on for her to process at once. She smiled at Grum, appreciating his presence, which she knew was imperative for Rexhia's sanity and safety. They shared a genuine bond that she was envious of, but was relieved her daughter could depend on it through all the turmoil they'd endured.

Osvita considered the heavy conversation she and Rexhia needed to have. Not only had they all been in the presence of a quorian, but she and Whark felt confident they'd encountered their first-born son, Smolar. The revelation introduced a more pressing matter – their origin. They weren't certain how Rexhia would feel about not only having a brother, but being a part of the quorian race. With their journey leading toward their quorian past, Osvita knew the conversation needed to be had sooner rather than later.

Admiring her husband, her heart fluttered. Though battling with the crippling loss of her recently acknowledged forbidden love, Osvita still loved Whark.

She'd always sensed the love he had for her. With his effortless, timely arrival, her knight in shining armor had gathered a vehicle, packed it with their belongings, and gathered the family up to escape The Barren Land. It seemed nearly impossible in such a chaotic environment. It was admirable.

Regardless of what she knew, Osvita couldn't help but compare what Nigel would've done if given the chance. She knew he'd never abandoned them at a friend's home, no matter the circumstances, but pushed the judgement from her mind.

With a heavy sigh, Osvita realized she had no knowledge of Whark's journey, how he arrived when he did, and how he even survived.

"Let's get back in the car," Whark said. "Sounds like we've decided upon our next destination."

Osvita walked over to her daughter and Chowder, embracing them each with a kiss. Whark got into the driver's seat, with Grum, Rexhia and her furry friend entering the back. Osvita lingered beside her door, glancing at the fresh mound of sand where she, Grum and Whark had buried Mortimer, in honor of his sacrifice. She felt he'd tried his best to make amends for his wrongdoings. With a thankful nod at his final resting place, Osvita turned to see the tattered region she'd called home for many years one more time before entering the vehicle.

When everyone was safely buckled up, Whark started the engine, slowly putting distancing between them and their previous home. As they sat in silence, Grum wondered if he should reveal some information about Sartica. He didn't care to go into detail about his past, but knew it would be best to have some information about the region. Just as he was about to speak up, someone beat him to it.

"You know," Osvita said, breaking the silence, "after everything that has happened, I'm the only one who wasn't a part of what had gone on. I have no idea what happened to you all and how you ended up arriving here at the perfect time," she said, looking at them. "It'd be a wonderful distraction from…" She winced in emotional pain.

"Dad just found us at Nigel's home!" Rexhia shouted. "Isn't that right, Chowder?"

Grum chuckled.

"When we left Nigel's, I felt bad leaving the little baby alone in the house. Now with…what happened," Rexhia said with sadness in her eyes, alluding to Nigel's death, "I'm glad I took him. He would've been home all alone." She squeezed the dog as he panted with excitement. Osvita knew having a dog in their situation was less than ideal; however, she also saw the joy it brought her daughter. Sensing Nigel's presence with the dog, she knew Chowder would be helpful for more than just Rexhia. Osvita and Whark glanced at one another with a smile, happy to see their daughter was okay.

"Well then, let's hear it. What exactly happened after you fled Grum's house?"

"After Grum suggested I slip out the back door," Whark started, implying it wasn't his choice to leave, "I tried to quietly sneak away, but my movement attracted the attention of a guard. Fortunately, he didn't shout or cause a scene. I don't think he was certain it was me and didn't want to cause a commotion for nothing. Regardless, he couldn't find me as I swerved through blocks and alleyways."

"I remembered noticing one of the guards disappeared for a while, too," Grum confirmed. "Bonkers! Didn't we leave a guard tied up at my house? What was his name…?"

"Vincent," Rexhia recalled.

"Yes…wow. I wonder what happened to him."

"I would've never remembered had you not said that. So much has happened since then. I'm sure he escaped, probably returned to the castle by now," Osvita mentioned.

"Grum updated me on what happened after I left…" Whark paused for a moment. "I'm so sorry, Vita. I'd have never left if I knew…"

"It's okay. We made it out of there, didn't we, Rexhia?"

"We sure did!" she confirmed, almost too excited over the murder that had taken place.

"So you lost the guard in the depths of the Bazaar?" Osvita confirmed.

"Yes, I was completely lost and ended up who knows where. After what seemed like forever wandering around, I met this kind woman named Kimber."

"Kimber!?" Osvita jolted. "Tall, blonde, muscular?"

"That's her!" Whark responded. "You know her?"

"She manned the door at the Anti-Regime meeting I attended with…"

"Nigel?" Whark confirmed.

"Yes. She was very kind, at least to me."

"She was nice to me too. Kimber welcomed me into her home for some time to rest and rejuvenate. Eventually, I disclosed the entire situation to her, minus the quorian finding. Kimber was shocked and wanted to help, but felt it was beyond her capability. She said she knew a man who'd have the answers, so obviously I was interested and agreed to meet him."

Whark paused, focusing on the direction he was driving, making sure he was still heading east with The Barren Land behind him. His eyes met with Rexhia's and the two shared a smile. Whark's heart warmed to see his daughter smile, back in his company once again.

"So I went with Kimber to a place not too far away, and met with a man named Lazarus," Whark continued.

"I knew you were going to say his name," Osvita said. "He's the founder of the Anti-Regime."

"I assume you met him too?"

"Yes, we drove him with us to the castle grounds at the beginning of their plan. Seemed nice, at first, but…"

"Yeah…not so much," Whark revealed. "At first he was understanding, showed genuine interest and concern. Once Kimber left us, he mentioned how it'd be best to keep me hidden. We instantly trusted one another. He knew I wasn't going to leave out of fear and I knew he'd keep me secluded from the world. Seemed like the perfect plan. That was…until time went by. Day after day, being stored in different rooms and confined spaces. I went without food for what seemed like days, though I completely lost track of time. I didn't know when it was day or night."

"Are you kidding me?" Osvita had her doubts about the man, but didn't expect such cruel treatment.

"Aw, Daddy," Rexhia said with sadness, hugging Chowder in comfort. He rolled his eyes toward Osvita, not wanting to discuss such matters in front of her.

"Daddy's fine, honey," he replied.

"Yes, Rexhia. Just like our tough times, Daddy's had his too. Sometimes these things happen in our lives, but we must remember we become stronger when those scary moments are over." Osvita's words comforted her daughter, as well as Whark.

"Until one day, *your friend* Nigel had a meeting with Lazarus in a back room." Osvita nearly jumped out of her seat. It was the most visceral reaction Whark had seen from her, including their reunion. She wanted to ask what was discussed, but didn't want to seem too eager. Osvita wondered if Nigel confessed anything to Lazarus.

"He had me hidden under a desk. Their meeting lasted for quite some time, but it was in that discussion I learned about the entire plan. They mentioned having you and Nigel go to the castle grounds to sneak him in. You'd both provide the dinner, as anticipated, then leave. There was mention of the explosions going off to destroy the Kurhal and the surrounding land. There was talk of an artifact or something? I don't really remember. He also mentioned The Lost Sphere deactivating, opening the region to the rest of Diveria. By the time their conversation ended, I was just focused on how I would escape Lazarus's confinement to find you."

"That's very sweet, dear," she replied, yearning to hear more about Nigel.

"I'd do anything for you, darling," he reaffirmed. "You know that, right?"

"Of course." While her words were perfect, her tone seemed distant, uncertain if it was due to her emotions or her recent stress.

"When the meeting ended…" Whark hesitated. He vividly remembered the conversation he had with Lazarus.

Do you think he's fucking my wife? Lazarus wasn't too shocked by the question, which only concerned Whark more. Eventually, the two discussed the meeting further, which is where Whark picked up from. "Lazarus said that you were only going there to sneak him in, complete a job and leave. All the turmoil and chaos was planned for after the dinner had finished. Lazarus confirmed that your safety was of the utmost importance and Nigel was there to ensure that." Whark carefully watched Osvita's reaction.

"Oh," she replied. "Lazarus and Nigel made it clear my safety was their priority, so while there were scary moments, I always felt secure." Osvita wanted to let Whark know she felt safe and not worried, but was afraid her wording may have made it seem more questionable. "I never felt completely safe though, until you all arrived," she added with a smile, looking at Whark, then Rexhia and finally Grum, who saw right through her lie, but remained silent, smiling back.

"Well, I'm glad they did everything in their power to keep you safe," Whark said with determination and a sense of pride, considering Nigel had died.

"So, how did you escape?" Osvita asked, changing the subject.

"It was surprisingly easy. I think Lazarus was preoccupied with the plan's execution. Nor did he anticipate me wanting to flee. When he least expected it, I found an exit route, darted out and never looked back. Spending days wandering the alleys of the Bazaar, I eventually heard a very familiar phrase and tone." Whark looked at his friend with a smile.

"Ho ho!" Grum shouted. "Who would've known!?"

"You heard Grum?"

"I sure did. I followed the voice until I was able to reach him and Rexhia. It was a wonderful reunion." Whark smiled.

"I was so happy to see you, Daddy."

"It was a delight to see you, my friend," Grum added.

"Meeting up with you both gave me the confidence I needed. We nearly had our group back together again. It was in that moment we decided it was time for a change, time to leave The Barren Land behind. Taking Chowder with us, we devised a plan to go to our home, find you, and get out of there."

"Seems to have worked?"

"We're getting out of here now, aren't we?" He smiled. "Everything seemed to click once the three of us got together. Unfortunately, we couldn't take the chance to return to Grum's home, so he grabbed a few things from Nigel's." Remaining quiet, Osvita widened her eyes and made eye contact with Grum, curious what he obtained. "When we arrived at our house, there were three guards around the perimeter. We assumed they were awaiting our return. Fortunately, that was exactly when the explosions occurred. It shuddered the entire valley. Though it didn't cause destruction in our area, the quakes were felt. All the guards fled to the epicenter of the commotion. Rexhia and I went inside, grabbing the essentials and important belongings, while Grum kept watch. We were able to return to the car with everything without being caught. From there, we headed toward the castle grounds."

"Wow…"

"It took some time to arrive at the castle because of crowds, guards all over, destruction…it was a mess. I'm sure nothing like you experienced, but it certainly affected the entire valley," Whark said.

Osvita was deeply touched by the story of his bravery and determination. It was a side of her husband she hadn't often seen.

"Thank you," she said, placing her hand in his. "Thank you all. For all you did."

They all reciprocated the appreciation.

As Whark continued to drive, the crowds eased up and the land opened. Osvita desperately looked out onto the horizon, hoping to see the quorians returning home.

"We'll find them," Whark reassured her. "We'll find him."

"Who?" Rexhia asked. "Who are you looking for?"

Osvita and Whark glanced at one another, realizing it was time for more honesty. With no view of Sartica on the horizon and The Barren Land barely visible behind them, Whark stopped the car.

"Rexhia, sweetheart," Osvita said nervously, "I think it's time we have a conversation."

"Okay?"

"I'm going to step out, give your family some privacy," Grum kindly insisted. Osvita and Whark hadn't expected the gesture, but appreciated it. "Hand me Chow—"

"No!" Rexhia yelled. "Please stay?" Her parents agreed and the four of them prepared themselves for a life-changing discussion.

"Of course, but it would probably be more comfortable outside the car," Osvita suggested and the four of them got out. Rexhia sat on the hood with Chowder beside her, her parents in front and Grum beside them.

"Rexhia," Whark started off, "as you know, you were born and raised in The Barren Land. Your mother and I came here…went there," he corrected himself, "a little over thirteen years ago."

"Mmhm."

"Have you ever wondered where we were originally from?" Osvita asked.

"Not really. Somewhere else, I guess. Sartica? Where we're going?"

"Not quite." Whark chuckled. Osvita slapped his leg for laughing.

"Honey…" Osvita paused, unsure how to reveal their true identities. "Remember the quorian that was in our car not too long ago? The one Mortimer released from captivity?" She stopped herself, looking at Whark and Grum. "Did either one of you pick up the Novalis Rod?" They both shook their heads.

"I was too surprised by it all, I didn't even think of it," Grum replied.

"Me neither. There was so much going on," Whark said. With disappointment,

Osvita knew the rod was lost. The endless sand made it impossible to retrace their steps. She turned to her daughter and repeated the question.

"Yes, he had kind eyes. He was sad, scared."

"Yes," Osvita remarked, happy to hear her daughter speak of a quorian positively. "He was terrified to be outside of his home, away from his race." There was a short silence until she continued. "Well you see…Daddy and I…we…"

"Your mom and I were both born of the quorian race," Whark announced. "The way he looked is how we used to look…for most of our lives."

Grum maintained a stoic demeanor, focusing his efforts on Rexhia.

"What!? What do you mean? You look like that? But how? I thought—"

"I know it's a lot to take in, but what your dad said is true. We were born as quorians, in the city named The Quo. It's a place far, *far* away from here."

"Then why don't you look like them now?"

"It's a long story…" Osvita replied with a sad tone, not wanting to get into it. "We don't need to—"

"No," Whark interrupted, "she deserves to know." He paused, sitting beside his daughter to explain what had happened. "When Mommy and Daddy first met, we fell in love and got married in that city, The Quo. After some time, Mommy and I…we…had a baby boy."

"You…had a baby? Before me?" Rexhia asked. "That means I have a brother somewhere?"

Grum's jaw dropped.

"Yes, honey." Osvita exhaled, knowing she couldn't remain quiet. "We named him after my grandfather, Smolar. It isn't a very common name."

"But…why did you leave? Do you plan to leave me?" Both her parents lunged forward and embraced their daughter, adamantly rejecting the notion, easing her worry. "Then what happened?"

"Similar to the leader in The Barren Land, there was one particular quorian who ruled the city. Unlike Brugōr, she was quiet. She didn't get involved in too much, but would step in when needed. Anyway," Whark said, stumbling over how to explain the situation. "Uhh…" he looked at his wife for help as Rexhia smiled in excitement to hear of a female in charge.

"We were asked to explore the world outside of our city. Lady Vixa, the gentle Quorian Ruler, informed us that Smolar was to be the next ruler and it was our responsibility, as his parents, to seek out information to aid in his reign." Whark darted a look at his wife's false story. "Isn't that right, honey?"

"Y-yes, absolutely," Whark replied, seeing Rexhia's eyes widen, shocked and fascinated by the story.

"So when we released this quorian from the car and he ran towards his friends, we heard his name called when the quorians reunited. It's safe to assume the quorian in our car knows our son and your brother," Osvita admitted.

"I thought I heard it too!"

"Now that he's out of the city, we think it's time for us to go back."

"Wait, but if you left home for just a while, why haven't we gone back yet? And why haven't you told me this before?" While Rexhia was filled with questions, the thought of having a sibling excited her.

"We were told we'd be notified when it was ready, but it's been so long. Since we've seen him outside the city, we think it may be our time to return home." Osvita smiled with reassurance, uncertain how to answer the second question.

"We didn't want to tell you until the time was right," Whark took over. "Remember what we mentioned about the quorian history and their race?"

"Yes, you said they were all hunted. Why? Who wanted to harm them? How did they…you…we, all survive?" Whark and Osvita saw their daughter spiraling with questions and doubting her identity.

"Rexhia," Osvita pleaded, "we should keep moving and let everything settle. You've had a long day. There's been a lot of excitement, sadness and shock. I think the questions for now should wait and we can continue another time. Just know that this is something you *must* keep secret, just between us four."

She looked at Grum who immediately smiled and nodded.

Thank you, she mouthed to him.

As the conversation settled, everyone returned to the vehicle.

Click. Click. Click.

The sound echoed throughout the car, though no knew what it was.

"Oh, boy," Whark revealed. "Seems we've got an issue."

"What's going on?" Osvita asked.

"I think the battery's dead."

"You *think*?"

"I know," he confirmed. Whark tried it once more, and the same sound reverberated in the car.

Click. Click. Click.

"Sounds like it's dead to me, ho ho!"

"No time for *ho ho!*" Whark darted him a look.

"Whark…" Osvita said in a calming tone.

"How's your battery dead?" Whark shouted.

"It's an old piece of junk, but it always worked for the valley. Out here, in the open world and hot sun…it's probably too much for the ol' girl," Grum admitted.

After a few more frustrated attempts, the group accepted they'd be walking the rest of the way. It wasn't going to be easy reaching Sartica, especially with their baggage. As they removed everything from the back of the car, they itemized their belongings and kept only what was necessary for their journey.

Grum never imagined he'd return to his hometown. He kept his connection to the region and the reason he'd left a secret. His priority and focus had been on Rexhia, the unexpected and unofficial daughter he never had. Confident she felt the same, it warmed his heart, reassuring him he was on the correct path in life. Giving up his life in The Barren Land was worth the experience. Though he never found the love of a woman, he captivated the soul of a child.

"Doing okay, nibling?" he quietly asked.

"Mmhmm." Rexhia smiled as her parents were just far enough away from them to not overhear. "I feel *right*. I just can't believe I have a brother."

Relinquishing her feeble-minded objects, Rexhia maintained Sohnora by her side, though she'd made room for Grum and Chowder. Blind-sided by their friendships, she wasn't sure she'd have been able to get through it all without them, especially Grum. As a soon-to-be fourteen-year-old girl, she considered herself wiser than her years. She knew her life had been different than most, and recent events proved her theory. Witnessing the death of countless individuals, one by her hand, forces a child to grow. The adventurous and intimidating situations she was put in taught her lessons she'd otherwise never experience. Through everything she'd seen, there was nothing she felt ruined her upbringing. She was a realist and appreciated experiencing life for what it truly was.

Learning about her familial identity startled her, though not as much as finding out she had a brother. Changing an identity, though surprising, didn't seem unnatural or strange – it excited her. There were so many questions she had, but Rexhia recognized the pain and exhaustion on her parents' faces. Though unaware of their exact strife and turmoil, she identified a disturbance between them, yet still sensed their unconditional love for one another. She knew there'd be plenty to discuss and unravel on their long journey, but Rexhia was excited to do what was necessary to meet her long-lost brother, Smolar.

Osvita's mind remained a whirlwind of shock from all the destruction, yet somehow, beyond all of her worst nightmares, she experienced great hope in hearing her son's name. Not only did it lead to revealing their true identity to her daughter, but it allowed them to go in search of their long-lost child. Her life had turned out to reveal exactly what she fought so hard to keep secret.

As the reunited and enlightened family of four-and-a-half pressed on toward Sartica, Osvita welcomed and accepted a lesson she'd fought hard to ignore.

Veracity wasn't meant to be concealed, nor could history ever be erased.

47

Fortunately for Promit and his rescue team, their return home proved easier than their departure.

There were no dangerous sand dunes to overcome or attackers to defend themselves against. With a clear understanding of their path, the group managed to travel down into their secluded caves, reaching the Enchanted Gate that protected their sacred city of The Quo.

Fravia consumed her metamorphic potion, embracing the comforts of her quorian appearance. Having already given up his appearance during Promit's rescue, Smolar immediately embraced her, finally expressing his love in their natural form. Though they'd kissed as humans, it didn't compare to their first kiss as quorians.

Standing on four legs, sensing the pressure from everyone, Rhugor didn't want to return to his original appearance. Though he was comfortable with his mighty quorian physique, he'd unexpectedly found a deep connection in his new skin. It had nothing to do with his identity, as he still considered himself a quorian. Rhugor found a sense of fulfillment and acceptance within himself he hadn't known was possible.

Proudly standing in front of the group, he nervously revealed he had no intention of drinking the metamorphic potion. Fravia and Smolar verbalized their concerns for how he'd be perceived, but after further explanation of his reasoning, they supported and understood his decision. Remaining quiet, Promit smiled in support.

As Fravia, Smolar and Rhugor were excited to return home, Promit recalled the last time he'd seen the Enchanted Gate, and the terrifying experience he and Smolar had in the forest.

"You alright, buddy?" Smolar patted his shoulder.

"Yeah," he said, shaking his head. "Just surreal to be back. There were many moments I doubted ever seeing this gate again." Fravia embraced him as his words saddened the group.

"We had the same worries," Smolar admitted.

"But we're so happy to have you back home. Us quorians must stick together," the future Quorian Ruler said.

"You guys ready?" Rhugor hesitated, remembering how sick he felt the last time he passed through the Enchanted Gate. Fravia and Smolar laughed.

"What's so funny?" Promit asked.

"When we transported through the gate before to find you…" Fravia paused, glancing at Rhugor. "Let's just say Rhugor didn't have a pleasant experience."

"Ugh." He grunted from the memory. "I was so sick."

"Oh boy…" Promit smiled.

"Well there's no time like the present. Let's go!" Smolar shouted. Filled with excitement for Promit's return, he grabbed the key from the bag to place into the gate, but halted.

"What's wrong?" Fravia asked.

"It's probably best for the future Quorian Ruler to get used to it." With a supportive smile, he handed the key over, which she graciously accepted.

Future Quorian Ruler, Promit wondered, but before he could vocalize his question, the transportation had begun.

Moments later, they all appeared within the city walls, noticing the Preservation Ensorcellation was still activated. Though it seemed larger than when they'd left, its purple hue was the same, distorting the view of the other side.

"Lady Vixa?" Smolar called into his Pendant of Perception. "You there?"

"Sm...olar? ...you? I...rly h...r you." Her voice was muffled through the static.

"We're here!" Smolar shouted. "We've returned to the city!"

"Wh...e t...d I pr...d?" she replied.

Smolar removed the pendant and spoke to his comrades. "I think the Ensorcellation is interfering with the pendant. I'm not sure how we can—"

"Smolar," Fravia interrupted, "mind if I give something a try?"

"Be my guest, my lady." He bowed sarcastically; aware he'd one day be respectfully bowing out of honor.

"So am I misunderstanding, or is Fravia the next Quorian Ruler?" Promit wondered.

"No, you're correct," Rhugor confirmed. "It's a long story, one I'm yet to understand, but with the use of Lady Vixa's amulet, she deactivated The Lost Sphere that surrounded The Barren Land." Promit had only ever seen the sphere once through the windows of the banquet room.

"Wow..." Promit raised his eyebrows as Fravia handled the Pendant of Perception.

At first, she placed it on her ear, trying to communicate with Lady Vixa, but as Smolar experienced, the transmission was too jumbled. Fravia removed it and admired its glistening silver through the convoluted light of the Ensorcellation. Closing her eyes, she held the pendant in her hands, pressing it against her chest. She whispered a few inaudible words before startling everyone around her.

"No!" Smolar shouted.

"Fravia!" Rhugor yelled.

In an instant, she tossed the final enchanted object they were given from Lady

Vixa into the forcefield. Similar to when they tossed the moonstones in, it grew in size. They all stepped back, uncertain and afraid of what Fravia had done.

"We're running out of room back here," Rhugor said, crawling backwards.

"What's happening!?" Promit feared he'd finally made it home only to perish.

"Fravia, what'd you—"

"Wait for it!" she affirmed. Sensing the energy from the Preservation Ensorcellation, they were terrified of being disintegrated after surviving their tumultuous adventure. Fravia stretched her arms out as wide as possible to protect the quorians behind her. With the forcefield barely grazing the tip of her nose, it suddenly vanished, imploding into itself, leaving no evidence of having ever existed.

The group exhaled as Fravia collapsed into Smolar's arms from exhaustion.

"What was that about?" Smolar looked around, mesmerized.

"How'd you know it would work?" Rhugor wondered.

"I didn't. I just had a hunch."

"You have some good luck."

"Or maybe your powers are growing, in anticipation of what's to come," Smolar suggested. She laughed it off, but the idea resonated with her.

"I guess Lady Vixa's going to need another stalagmite from inside the Enchanted Reservoir to fabricate another Ensorcellation," Rhugor informed them.

"Hm?" Smolar wondered.

"Remember, she said she wanted to keep the barrier up to protect the gate once she makes her announcement at the Blue Diamond Jubilee," Rhugor reminded him.

"Which looks nearly ready to celebrate," Fravia added, pointing up toward the Belvase.

They all admired the view. Even from the fifth floor, they could partially see the twenty-seventh floor prepared with decorations and lighting for the event. Though exhausted, all four of them were excited to see what it looked like, with it being such a rare occurrence.

"That looks exciting!" Rhugor exclaimed, bouncing a few times on all four legs.

"Calm down," Fravia chuckled. "Remember your appearance. We should see what Lady Vixa has to say about it."

"Speaking of which, we should probably head up there. She'll be concerned about the broken communication," Smolar suggested, which everyone agreed to.

Promit's mind spun as they made their way toward Lady Vixa's home. Once he realized his life wasn't over from being held captive, he learned fate had an alternate plan for him. After everything he'd gone through, he accepted his second chance at life to see his family again, and he was going to take advantage of it to the best of his ability.

When the elevator cab door opened, an excited group was huddled outside Lady Vixa's home, eagerly awaiting their arrival.

"They're here!" Lucemia shouted, forcing everyone to turn in their direction and shout their names.

Smolar!

Fravia!

Rhugor!

"PROMIT!" they yelled even louder.

Fravia immediately ran toward her mother and father, both of whom ran to her. The family of three embraced one another in unison.

"You're home!" Reagor shouted.

"It's wonderful to see you, honey." Lucemia shed a tear of joy, elated to have her daughter home safe.

"Promit!" a young, jubilant voice yelled. Promit frantically headed toward the familiar sound until he came across her, crying in excitement.

"Bindetta!" Promit hugged his little sister, struggling to release her. "I'm so happy to see you again! I was scared I'd…" He stopped himself, not wanting to scare his little sister. "I'm just so happy to see you." After holding each other for a moment longer, Promit asked, "Is Dad—"

"Hello, son," a male voice said from behind Promit. He released his sister and turned toward his father.

"Hi, Dad," Promit replied.

"It's nice to have you home, son," his father admitted.

"It's great to be home." It was an uncomfortable, yet sweet, reunion. Though they hadn't been close since Promit's mother died, his father expressed his happiness the best way he knew how.

Admiring everyone outside her home, Lady Vixa was relieved to see the two males embrace and the Deallius family welcome Smolar. Remaining in her entryway, the Quorian Ruler noticed an elongated, golden figure hidden in the shadows with piercing blue eyes. Startled but not frightened, she approached him.

"Rhugor? Is that you?"

"Yes, Lady Vixa." He bowed his head, lowering his two front legs.

"It is *I* who should bow down to you and your comrades," she insisted. "Why haven't you used the metamorphic potion? Did you lose it on your travels? I could—"

"Lady Vixa," he interrupted, "my apologies, but I'd prefer to remain this way, if you'd allow it. I feel more comfortable in this skin than I thought possible. My senses are heightened, and I feel I could be of better assistance with four legs than two." Rhugor looked out amongst the group, watching everyone embrace their family and loved ones. Lady Vixa noticed the sadness in his eyes having no one to greet him.

"That's a bold decision," she said with a smile, impressed by the confidence in his choice. "Are you sure?"

"I feel more connected, more grounded, this way. It has nothing to do with my identity as a quorian," he reassured her. "I'm a proud quorian and will always be.

We are an incredible race with endless possibilities. Who says we can't look a little different?"

"I can't say you're wrong there," she reassured. "With such a unique and beautiful appearance though, I fear it may startle many in the city. It may be more overwhelming than you imagine." Rhugor knew she was right, but still didn't want to relinquish it. "How about this: I'll conjure you up a particular enhancement that, when consumed, will permanently allow you to switch between your quorian and alternative form, at your own discretion. You will have the freedom to go between them as you wish."

"I'd be eternally grateful. Thank you so much, Lady Vixa." Rhugor bowed once more.

"Rhugor!" Fravia shouted. His ears perked up. "Get over here!" His tail instantly swayed in excitement.

"My word," Lucemia said, reacting to his appearance.

"Whoa," Reagor exclaimed, stepping back.

"What is that thing?" Promit's father shouted.

"No," Fravia insisted. "This is Rhugor Horwick, still in his metamorphic state as a golden lynx. He proved to be an invaluable asset. None of us would've survived had he not embraced his alternative form." Rhugor stood proudly at the words of his good friend.

Lady Vixa looked at the pair, surprised to see how much they'd grown on their expedition.

"To Rhugor!" Reagor shouted.

"To Rhugor!" Everyone else chimed in afterwards, showing their acceptance of his appearance. Rhugor's tail swayed as his piercing blue eyes glanced around the room.

"Thank you," Lucemia said to him. "For everything you've done to protect yourself and one another."

As they admired Rhugor's new look, Smolar approached Promit and his family. "I'm so sorry any of this had to happen."

"It's okay," Promit's father excused. "Lady Vixa spoke with us a while back and told us everything. She ensured his safe return, I trusted her, and I'm glad to see she upheld her word."

Smolar looked at his friend, sensing his father's icy tone.

"It's water under the bridge." Promit forcibly smiled, before dragging his father and sister over to meet Rhugor.

"Can you believe we made it?" Fravia whispered in Smolar's ear.

"I can't believe it's over."

"Oh...I wouldn't say it's over. Something tells me our new lives have only just begun," she said, giving him a flirtatious smile.

"Well if that's the case, I suppose we should have our Proclamation soon."

"What!?" Fravia's jaw dropped.

"Oh, nothing." He chuckled.

"Don't *oh nothing* me," she fought back. "Proclamation? Do you really see that happening?" Smolar knew he couldn't avoid the question, so he decided to be honest with his emotions.

"Of course," he said jovially. "Fravia, I love you more than I can put into words. We've spent many years together, yet apart from one another. I don't want another day to go by without you and the whole city knowing how much you mean to me. I would love nothing more than to be your husband if you'd be willing to be my wife."

Fravia's eyes swelled with happiness and excitement. It was what she'd been wanting to hear for years, but never thought would happen. She thought back to the days, not too long ago, where they were just friends and Smolar was oblivious to her love. She remembered all the conversations she'd had in her mind, questioning her sanity, wondering if her dreams weren't meant to be. Now the love of her life stood in front of her, confessing his love, wanting to solidify their lives together for all eternity. Her heart wanted nothing more than to scream *yes* and embrace him for the city to view, but her mind knew it wasn't the best option.

"Smolar…"

"Well, that's never good," he said, shrugging.

"No, no!" She stopped him from turning away. "Listen to me," she said, forcing him to make eye contact. "You know how much I love you. You and I both know my love for you has run deeper and much longer than yours for me," she guilted him. "And it's okay! I understand that. What's important is that we are here now, together."

"Then what?"

"Life is a lot different than what it was before we left. You had a slight inclination you were set to be the next Quorian Ruler and I was a blissfully unaware book nerd. We weren't aware of our purpose, if I may be so bold as to say. Now, after risking our lives in a world outside of our own and confessing our love for one another, we learn I'm prophesied to be the next Quorian Ruler with you alongside me." Smolar absorbed her words, nodding. "You have to understand that maybe we need a bit of rest and time to process before adding that to our agenda."

"I suppose when you put it that way…"

"Hm?" She smirked.

"Yes, okay…fine. I think I see why you're the next Quorian Ruler."

"Why's that?"

"It's easier to persuade others with the beauty you possess." Fravia blushed and hugged him tightly.

"I promise to make you the happiest husband," she whispered.

"And I promise to make you the happiest wife." Smolar suddenly had a pivotal realization. "Fravia," he paused, gazing into her eyes. "You know my family history has been…complicated, to put it lightly." The two shared a smile, aware of the unfortunate circumstances in his past. "Regardless of what's to come, it shouldn't affect what I'd like to attain in the future. And what I'd like to do is start a family, with you." Fravia's eyes widened.

"Really!?" she said with excitement.

"Yes. I'd like to eventually find my parents, but it shouldn't hinder me from my own goals. They shouldn't define the possibilities or limitations in my life."

"Smolar…I don't know what to say." She fought back the tears. "I'm just so proud of you and the quorian you've become. I know if your parents were here to see you now, they'd be proud." The two embraced, tighter than ever, excited for their future.

After watching their embrace, Lady Vixa summoned Fravia over for a discussion. The two went inside the comfort of her home for privacy.

"Thank you for joining me, Fravia. I know emotions are high, but I'd like to take a moment to briefly discuss a few things."

"Of course, I understand." The two sat in her living room.

"As discussed via the Pendant of Perception…" Lady Vixa started, then paused as her memory resurfaced. "By the way, what happened to them? There were three."

"Yes, well you see…they were unfortunately lost in the journey. We only lost the final one once we reentered the city," Fravia revealed.

"What do you mean?"

"The Preservation Ensorcellation. It was still activated, and without communication, we had to take matters into our own hands." She paused, realizing her mistake. "*I* took matters into my own hands. Though it managed to deactivate the barrier, allowing us to enter the city, it seemed to have destroyed it."

"I see…"

"But you can find another stalagmite in the Enchanted Reservoir and create another, right?" Fravia wondered.

"Let's hope so…" She pondered for a moment. "So both the Ensorcellation and three pendants have been destroyed?"

"Unfortunately so…"

"Okay. That just means a little more work for me. Nonetheless, we still need to have a discussion. First, I'd like to congratulate and apologize to you for being selected as the next Quorian Ruler. I believe it was a little different for me, as I never had any interest in lying with a male quorian and bore no children. I'd always assumed Smolar would be next, but your actions have proven otherwise.

"I congratulate you because it's a prestigious honor, but I apologize for the agony and pain you may endure from being given the role. It's consuming, exhausting and challenging, especially since there's no expiration date. It's a role you take on until the end of your life. Every waking day will be spent trying to aid those you can, while worrying and questioning if your efforts are justified. Your mind will consistently provide you with validation and doubt. It may be unbearable at first, but in time, you'll find your own way to manage it all."

"I'd imagine it'll be particularly difficult in the beginning," Fravia agreed. "Fortunately, I have Smolar and my family by my side to help keep me grounded. To ensure I'm not acting out of sorts and am within my limitations."

"That's true. You do have a strong advantage I didn't. In addition to that, my father didn't prepare me nearly enough for what the position entailed. He hoped, and ultimately expected, for me to hand over the role to the quorian male I chose to spend my life with. I refuse to let history repeat itself. If we don't learn from our past, how are we to improve the future?" Lady Vixa chuckled, hoping Fravia agreed. "I plan to instill any and all knowledge I have to help you along the way."

"Thank you, Lady Vixa. I couldn't be more appreciative and grateful for your compassion and understanding. I won't lie, it's terrifying and intimidating to know one day, I'll be in your shoes. There's no way I'll ever be able to live up to your legacy, but I'll use that as my driving force to persevere. Doing everything in my power to make you, and King Klai, proud. Us females have to stick together. I mean…what are the chances The Quo gets blessed with two female rulers in a row?" They both chuckled as they felt the bond between them grow. There was no one else to experience their chemistry and interaction. It was a moment meant only for the two Quorian Rulers.

"Now that we've got that out of the way, there are a few other topics I'd like to mention. At the Blue Diamond Jubilee, I'll be announcing you as my successor. It'll be the first time it's officially mentioned, so prepare yourself. Quorians will perceive you differently. You'll see others change their mannerisms and actions when you're around. It'll be a strange shift, but I plan to spend some time with you after the Jubilee and onward to assist."

"Okay." Overwhelmed by the reality, Fravia didn't have much to say. She wanted to absorb as much information as possible.

"Now that I've probably scared you entirely, I must admit there are some perks as well." Lady Vixa smiled. "As you've already seen, the Quorian Ruler maintains control of the Klai Chronicles. It holds the record of our entire race, going back to the Age of Kings, with records of King Klai himself. Being the avid reader you are, I'm sure it'll be a delight for you to dive into. In addition to the history, the Chronicles also house the necessary enchantments to maintain a safe and stable environment for the city. Not only are there particular seals which need continuous binding, but there are abilities you'll need to understand to ensure order in The Quo. There are an abundance of other enchantments that I'm confident you'll become more familiar with than I ever could."

"Well that's certainly a bit more uplifting." Fravia chucked. The current ruler and the ruler-to-be embraced, appreciating one another's understanding and patience. "Thank you, Lady Vixa, for taking the time to work with me. I know this must be an awkward and challenging process."

"Actually, my dear, I've been long awaiting this day. I'm just happy I'm standing here with you, surpassing all of my expectations," Lady Vixa announced. Fravia wasn't sure if it was a comment against Smolar or a compliment towards her, but she appreciated her kind words.

Knock, knock.

"Sorry to interrupt, but Promit and his family are heading out. Rhugor is about to leave as well," Smolar said, peering through.

"Don't let anybody leave yet," Lady Vixa insisted. "We'll be right out, and I'd like to say a few words before we part ways."

The two royal quorians rejoined the others, the ruler-to-be walking down to stand between Smolar and Rhugor. *Her family.* Standing above the group in her entryway, Lady Vixa was touched to be in her current position. She hadn't ever thought her reign in The Quo would amount to anything, but somehow, though near the end of her time, she had managed to create a new family of quorians. They were all eternally bonded through their shared experience. As she looked down at the smiling faces of those she deeply respected and loved, Lady Vixa realized they all felt the same way toward her. It was unfamiliar, yet identifiable. She was used to stoic, cold looks – quorians forcing their respect and professionalism. The feeling Lady Vixa sensed now was warm, comforting and inviting, but most importantly, it was genuine. There was nothing forced by any quorian, and for that, she'd always remember the moment.

"We've all been through a whirlwind of emotions as there was nothing simple or easy about the task. Sometimes we experience circumstances that are beyond our control, and no matter how difficult they may seem, they always serve a purpose. Though unintentional, unexpected and unsolicited, we bonded, working through necessary challenges, and for that, I'm eternally thankful. There aren't enough words to accurately express my gratitude for each and every one of you."

As Lady Vixa continued to praise and thank them all for their resilient bravery, strength and efforts, everyone found themselves holding hands with those beside them, or wrapping their arms around one another. Promit's head rested against his father's shoulder while Smolar's hands clasped with Fravia and Reagor. A few quorians had tears in their eyes, sensing the lighter air around them. Everyone gleamed as they focused on Lady Vixa and her speech. It solidified the mystical bond that the quorians would forever share.

48

"It's because of you, collectively, we stand here together unified and stronger than ever. We are on the precipice of a new era. The dawn of a new day."

Lady Vixa stood on the Belvase, addressing the entire quorian community. Surrounding them was a plethora of decorations, an abundance of food from every eatery within Restaurant Alley, jovial music and every quorian out in support of the Blue Diamond Jubilee!

She was dressed in her honorable white robe with her long white hair flowing down her back. The robe she wore belonged to her mother many years ago. Lady Vixa never felt worthy of wearing it until that day. She finally found pride in the role she had accepted one-hundred years ago.

Most noticeably, however, was what was missing from around her neck – her Amulet of Eymus. As she continued her speech, Lady Vixa noticed they were all looking at her the same way the group had outside her home. She sensed her community genuinely respected her, but knew there was still one more wrong that needed correcting.

Neetri.

Lady Vixa didn't want to tarnish the excitement and jubilation during the private meeting. Not everyone was privy to their mission. Having consistently checked Neetri's status via the Klai Chronicles, she knew it would be their immediate order of business with Fravia by her side.

Then she did something she'd never done in public. Lady Vixa, the Quorian Ruler, wept. There was a unified *aw* that echoed throughout the city. Though she just wanted to cry more as her heart fluttered from the outpouring of love, Lady Vixa knew she had a job to do. She stiffened her upper lip and continued her speech.

"I know many quorians out there have had their opinions of my leadership, or lack thereof. I've been quietly standing aside when I should've been more involved. That's why I'm taking the time today, during this magical time of the Blue Diamond Jubilee, to announce my previous method of leadership ends now."

There was roaring applause. As Lady Vixa gazed upon the city, smiling at everyone, her eyes met two familiar faces. *Lucemia and Reagor*. They stood together in a sea of quorians and for a moment, the room silenced. Locking eyes with them both, the Quorian Ruler nodded, which they reciprocated.

Having had their disagreements with Lady Vixa in the past, Lucemia and Reagor were excited to see her take action. Not only did they feel she had found herself, but they felt she'd regained the strength in their race. While their daily work, in conjunction with recent events, had told them to expect the unexpected, they were excited for the future. Being the two main medical specialists in the city, Reagor and Lucemia made their wealth of knowledge available to others and began teaching the lessons they'd learned. This would allow other quorians to provide the same medical benefits as they had, so the responsibility wouldn't be on them alone. Additionally, they dedicated their remaining time toward exploration and adventure. With Lady Vixa aware of their work, and wanting to know more of it, they began organizing their information in a way for others to comprehend.

"I'd be lying if I said this revelation was self-inspired," Lady Vixa continued. "I know there have been whispers and rumors, but I'm going to set the record straight." There was anticipation in the air, awaiting what she was going to say next. "There was a recent incident that forced a handful of our own to leave the city and enter the Outer World...Diveria." It was the first time the land was officially mentioned by name.

There was a universal gasp among the crowd and whispers between some quorians.

"Please, please, let me finish," she said, and the crowd eased. "The situation was delicately handled and properly managed. Safety was our top priority, not only for those who departed, but for everyone here and the city itself. What's important was the wealth of knowledge we learned and not the details of the mission, which will remain classified. There is an entire world out there, outside of our own city, eager and waiting for the quorian race to return, reclaiming what was once ours."

Just then, Lady Vixa made eye contact with yet another familiar face – *Rhugor*. He had his same rugged appearance as when she first recruited him, but there was a noticeable difference. When he smirked at her, his eyes flickered gold, showcasing the golden lynx that resided within him. She smiled in return, happy to see him more fulfilled and satisfied than when they had first met.

Rhugor was elated to have been summoned for a death-defying adventure, and he knew it wouldn't be his last. His unexpected journey helped him realize he didn't need to find love in another person to be happy – it had to come from within. Though he knew it would take time for other quorians to identify and accept, Rhugor was happy to have found fulfillment in his life.

"And that is exactly what I intend to propose. I'd like for us, the quorian race, to begin exploration outside of our city walls." The crowd gasped again. "I know this is a controversial topic, and we'll have time to discuss the matter further, but it's important to realize that limiting ourselves from a world with vast knowledge and materials doesn't aid in our growth, it inhibits it.

"We all know the history of our precious King Klai's murder at the hands of

Divinity. We know of the original quorian race that was nearly expunged. It was an unforgivable, catastrophic event that should've never taken place. Ever since, we've remained hidden and secluded in our city. As magnificent and comforting as it's been, we're still trapped, locked within beautiful confinement." Lady Vixa paused, allowing the crowd to process the abundance of information she had tossed at them.

Whether it was fate or a simple coincidence, Lady Vixa spotted Promit and his family out amongst the crowd. While his father's face was stoic and stern, she noticed him wearing the Enchanted Ring she gifted him as he scratched his chin. Promit and Bindetta were smiling with glee and pride. Considering how young Bindetta was, Lady Vixa wasn't surprised by her reaction. What shocked her was how jovial Promit looked. Considering everything he'd been through – the torture, turmoil and fear for his life – she expected him to be terrified at the idea. She was proud of him, and their whole race, to see how resilient they were when they came together.

Promit felt his sister squeeze his hand the moment Lady Vixa looked down at them. She was elated to see their Quorian Ruler spot them out of the entire crowd. Though she didn't say anything, Promit suspected she'd want to be more involved in exploration, though he'd try his best to persuade her not to.

He never anticipated his life to have taken him so far away from home, to see so much pain. Considering the heinous acts he'd seen and endured, Promit felt he was managing it well. Once the shock began to dissipate, he found it helpful to write his experiences and emotions down, to organize his thoughts. Unable to honestly speak to his family, and not wanting to unload his burden and guilt on Smolar further, Promit was pleased to have found an outlet.

He knew Lady Vixa planned to continue explorations in a cohesive, safe manner, but he wasn't sure he was ready to leave The Quo, or if he ever would be. Though he was in the process of healing, Promit felt his experiences had left a scar on his soul that would permanently disable him from participating in certain events – leaving The Quo being one of them.

"Now I know an overzealous mission such as safe exploration outside The Quo is going to take time," Lady Vixa continued. "It's not going to be something that'll happen overnight. It'll take meetings, discussions and the assistance of others within our community. I'm not going to stand here and begin appointing individuals, but there's one role I feel is crucial to mention at this point in time." Lady Vixa scanned the floor, looking for a particular quorian. "Hmmm," she said aloud, shocked it hadn't crossed her mind to have organized their placement for this section of the meeting. She scanned the room long enough that other quorians began looking around, wondering what or who she was looking for.

Eventually, she identified the quorian, cocked her head and smiled. *As expected*, she thought.

Fravia and Smolar were standing in the middle of the crowd, surprisingly far away from her parents. They'd been spending their own time together, without anyone around to disturb them.

"As we all know," Lady Vixa addressed the Belvase, "I've been the Quorian Ruler for one-hundred years now." She paused as the crowd applauded. "I mean, obviously…" She chuckled. "We're here celebrating the Blue Diamond Jubilee."

Once the cheering subsided, she continued. "With that in mind, it's inconceivable to think I'll be around to actually see this exploration mission executed to its fullest potential. As I said, it's going to take time, effort…and resources." Lady Vixa looked back at Smolar and Fravia with a loving smile, one he hadn't ever seen expressed toward him. "So without further ado, I'd like to introduce you to your next Quorian Ruler…"

Silence spread as the crowd momentarily stopped breathing, awaiting the announcement. No one had anticipated such news.

"Fravia Deallius!" Lady Vixa shouted, extending her arm out to her. The crowd gasped as they stepped back from around the couple, giving them their space. There was just a moment of silence, and then the crowd roared, louder than they'd ever cheered for Lady Vixa. The entire city howled with jubilation as they watched their future ruler walk up to the podium.

Smolar released her hand to let her walk, but she held on.

"You're coming with me," she demanded.

"No, this is your—"

"Also," Lady Vixa shouted over the crowd, "allow me to introduce you to Lady Fravia's future husband, Smolar Dimmerk!"

"They're in love!?" a quorian shouted.

"Young love!" another remarked.

"They're perfect for one another!"

"They look so happy!"

"See?" she yelled at Smolar. "You're coming up with me."

With a grin on her face, Fravia pulled him toward her and the two graciously stood beside Lady Vixa. As Fravia and Smolar waved, watching the entire community roar for her new role and their young love, they couldn't help but smile. They glanced at Lady Vixa, who momentarily stepped away from the spotlight, clapping joyfully.

Having introduced her successor, Lady Vixa was beside herself with emotion, stunned for such change to be implemented on her one-hundredth anniversary. While she was filled with excitement, anticipation and happiness, a sadness lingered within. She thought about the little girl she once was with her father, Lord Erko.

As a young quorian, Lady Vixa made it her mission to make him proud. After his death, she lost herself. She was unprepared, nervous and shy. A novice, she was tossed into a position her father hadn't prepared her for. It not only affected her personal life, but it trickled down and manifested into how she governed. She felt an abundance of guilt and shame for her wasted time, but accepted she couldn't change that now. Her best option was to do better going forward and to encourage the next Quorian Ruler to not make the same mistakes.

As the two lovers stood in front of the entire quorian race, Fravia and Smolar waved, their free arms intertwined with one another.

Fravia shook with excitement and fear. Looking out amongst the crowd, she noticed an abundance of familiar faces and began to personally wave at each of them. Extended family, friends and acquaintances who had known her through the years.

Subconsciously, she felt as though she was preparing for an important, mysterious role her whole life. Though she knew being the Quorian Ruler would cause her moments of extreme highs and challenging lows, she was prepared to tackle what came her way. Not only was she beside the love of her life, with both her parents supporting her endeavor, Fravia appreciated the willingness of Lady Vixa to help guide her. She was the only other quorian who could truly understand the unique position she was in.

Being chosen to enter the role made her sympathize with the ruler. Fravia couldn't imagine how lonely she must've been to not have had the appropriate guidance, nor the support of the entire community. She knew, in time, the two of them would form an impenetrable bond, forcing Fravia to make her proud by her actions as Quorian Ruler.

Unlike Lady Vixa's experience, Fravia Deallius was immediately welcomed. The entire community was rooting for her, as well as her relationship with Smolar. The unwavering love and adoration they were given at the Blue Diamond Jubilee solidified the choices she had made in her life. It was the reaction she needed to boost her confidence for the path of exploration Lady Vixa had planned to initiate.

As the crowd's roar began to subside, a confident and exhilarated Smolar turned to look at Fravia. He couldn't believe after all their years of friendship, he had overlooked so many signs of their love for one another. In that moment, it was clear to him their love was deeper than he expected.

Smolar was intimidated having the entire city cheer for their success, but he told himself the majority of it was for her. Fravia had immediately become the curiosity and obsession of everyone within the crowd. As he looked at all the smiles, he was reminded of how he and Lady Vixa thought the role of Quorian Ruler was reserved for him. Though he was momentarily disappointed in the change of leadership, it was instantly followed by relief. He hadn't realized how constricted he felt until the pressure was removed. Experiencing the stress allowed him to understand Fravia's emotions. He knew his role was to be her unconditional support system through everything, which was something he signed up for before they ever learned what destiny had prepared.

Ready to move forward in his new life with Fravia, Smolar couldn't help but acknowledge the guilt that he still felt. He knew of its origin and why it followed him, but he hoped to one day resolve it, as he knew it wasn't a burden he should continue to carry. The guilt came from the harm Promit had experienced outside of the city. Smolar eagerly awaited the opportunity to speak with him, to reveal their true feelings and thoughts. He hoped for it to be cathartic for them both.

As their journey of exploration officially began under Lady Vixa's reign, Smolar anticipated leaving The Quo on numerous missions. Though uncertain of his limitations as the future husband of the future Quorian Ruler, he'd always had a yearning for more. Knowing his parents were banished from The Quo, he knew he needed to make every effort to find them. He wanted to learn who his parents were, to help shape him into the father he'd one day become.

Though he had no resentment or anger toward Lady Vixa's actions, he knew a conversation needed to be had with her and his future wife, asking for assistance in the matter. He knew it would be a dilemma, but he was confident they'd help however possible, especially now that the new Quorian Ruler was chosen.

When the crowd fell silent once more, Lady Vixa stepped up to the podium to finish her speech.

"We've done it!" she shouted. "This officially concludes the excitement for our Blue Diamond Jubilee! I'd like to wish you all a safe celebration! And to the little ones in the crowd..." She looked out, gazing upon the young quorians. "Work hard, educate your mind and never falter. Remember this moment, because one-hundred years from now, you may be at Lady Fravia's Blue Diamond Jubilee!"

"To Lady Fravia!" she shouted.

"To Lady Fravia!" the crowd rejoiced.

UNTIL WE MEET AGAIN...

ARCHAIC DECEPTION

Sign-up to our realm for:

Exclusive Short Stories

Free Content

Merchandise Giveaways

Discussions with Characters

Updates on Future Releases

WWW.ArchaicDeception.com

Share a photo reading this novel with the following

hashtags to be showcased:

#ArchaicDeception   #GuardianofEmblems

OUR STORYTELLER

BORN AND RAISED IN NEW YORK, JOE DAYVIE SPENT TEN YEARS IN NEVADA BEFORE MOVING TO CALIFORNIA, WHERE HE CURRENTLY LIVES. HAVING WORKED AS A RADIATION THERAPIST FOR OVER TEN YEARS, HE SUPPRESSED HIS LIFELONG PASSION FOR WRITING UNTIL HIS MOTHER REIGNITED HIS CREATIVITY SHORTLY BEFORE HER PASSING.

JOE PROUDLY CONTINUES TO EXPLORE HIS IMAGINATION WITHIN THE REALM OF ARCHAIC DECEPTION AND BEYOND. WITH A CAREFREE, FUN WRITING STYLE, HIS MESSAGES AND SYMBOLS ARE AN ENIGMA FOR READERS TO INTERPRET AND DISCOVER.

HTTPS://WWW.INSTAGRAM.COM/JOEDAYVIE

HTTPS://WWW.TWITTER.COM/JOEDAYVIE

HTTPS://WWW.GOODREADS.COM/JOEDAYVIE

CPSIA information can be obtained
at www.ICGtesting.com
Printed in the USA
LVHW050926210622
721759LV00002B/86